CN
CARTOON NETWORK

ADVENTURE TIME

MARCELINE

kaboom!

Designers **Chelsea Roberts & Scott Newman**
Assistant Editor **Michael Moccio**
Editor **Matthew Levine**

With Special Thanks to Marisa Marionakis, Janet No, Austin Page, Conrad Montgomery, Kelly Crews, Scott Malchus, Adam Muto and the wonderful folks at Cartoon Network.

Ross Richie CEO & Founder
Joy Huffman CFO
Matt Gagnon Editor-in-Chief
Filip Sablik President, Publishing & Marketing
Stephen Christy President, Development
Lance Kreiter Vice President, Licensing & Merchandising
Arune Singh Vice President, Marketing
Bryce Carlson Vice President, Editorial & Creative Strategy
Scott Newman Manager, Production Design
Kate Henning Manager, Operations
Spencer Simpson Manager, Sales
Sierra Hahn Executive Editor
Jeanine Schaefer Executive Editor
Dafna Pleban Senior Editor
Shannon Watters Senior Editor
Eric Harburn Senior Editor
Chris Rosa Editor
Matthew Levine Editor
Sophie Philips-Roberts Associate Editor
Gavin Gronenthal Assistant Editor
Michael Moccio Assistant Editor

Gwen Waller Assistant Editor
Amanda LaFranco Executive Assistant
Jillian Crab Design Coordinator
Michelle Ankley Design Coordinator
Kara Leopard Production Designer
Marie Krupina Production Designer
Grace Park Production Designer
Chelsea Roberts Production Design Assistant
Samantha Knapp Production Design Assistant
Paola Capalla Senior Accountant
José Meza Live Events Lead
Stephanie Hocutt Digital Marketing Lead
Esther Kim Marketing Coordinator
Cat O'Grady Digital Marketing Coordinator
Amanda Lawson Marketing Assistant
Holly Aitchison Digital Sales Coordinator
Morgan Perry Retail Sales Coordinator
Megan Christopher Operations Coordinator
Rodrigo Hernandez Mailroom Assistant
Zipporah Smith Operations Assistant
Breanna Sarpy Executive Assistant

kaboom!™   **CN** CARTOON NETWORK.   FREDERATOR

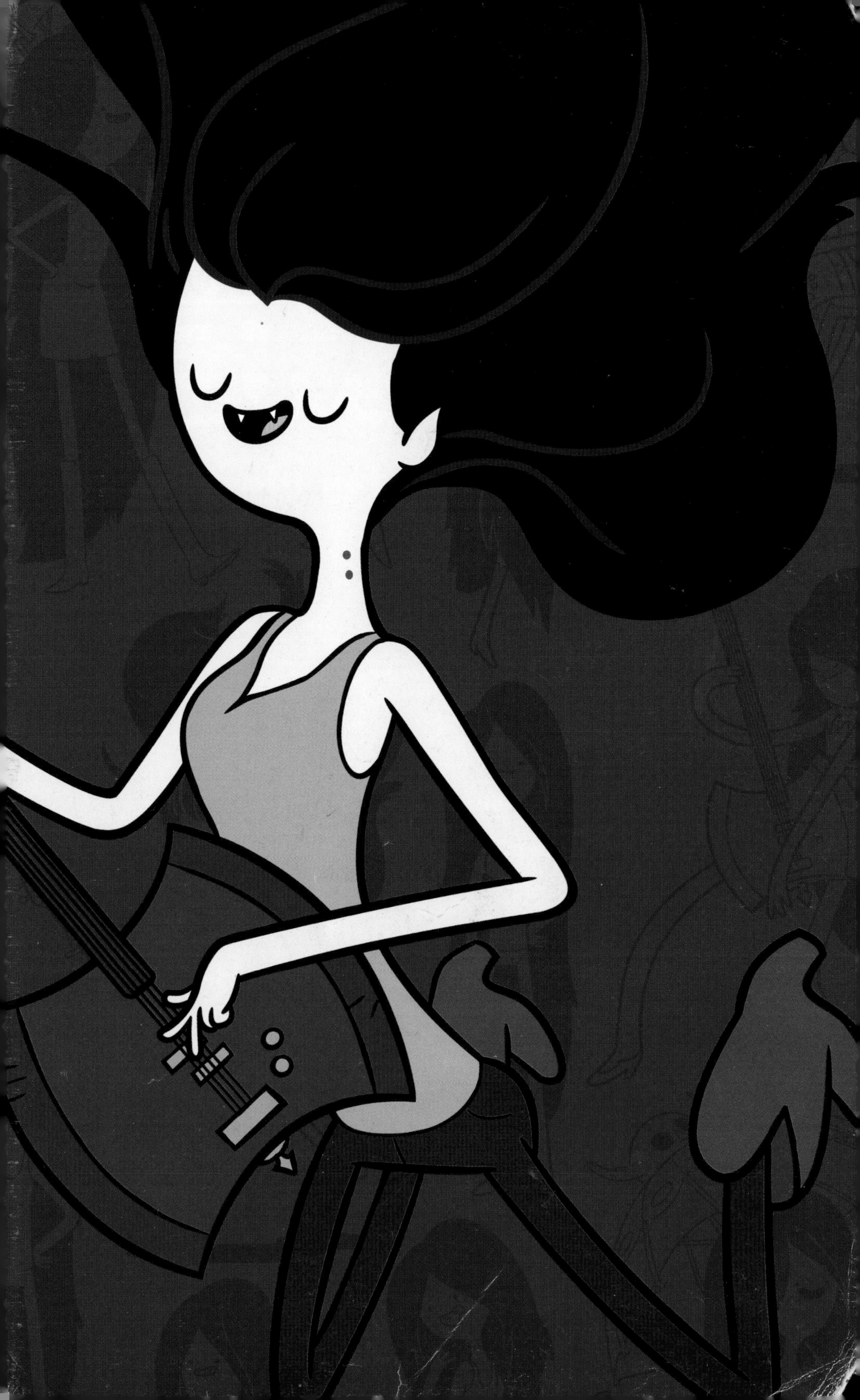

CN CARTOON NETWORK
ADVENTURE TIME

Created by **Pendleton Ward**

"Laundromarceline"
Written and Illustrated by **Lucy Knisley**

"Resurrection Song"
Written and Illustrated by **Jen Wang**

"Grumpy Butt"
Written and Illustrated by **Faith Erin Hicks**
With Story by **Tim Larade**
Colors by **Mirka Andolfo**

"Bad Girl Gone Good"
Written by **Kevin Church**
Illustrated by **Jen Vaughn**

"The Moon - ECLIPSE"
Written and Illustrated by **Hanna K**

"Adventure Time: Marceline and the Scream Queens"
Written and Illustrated by **Meredith Gran**
Colors by **Lisa Moore**
Letters by **Steve Wands**

"Echoes"
Written and Illustrated by **S. M. Vidaurri**

"Moon Beam"
Written and Illustrated by **Aatmaja Pandya**

"Broken"
Written and Illustrated by **Bethany Sellers**
Colors by **Joana Lafuente**
Letters by **Jim Campbell**

"Visions of Paternity"
Written by **Ryan Cady**
Illustrated by **Jorge Monlongo**

"Marceline the Derby Queen"
Written by **Chelsea Van Weerdhuizen**
Illustrated by **Reimena Yee**

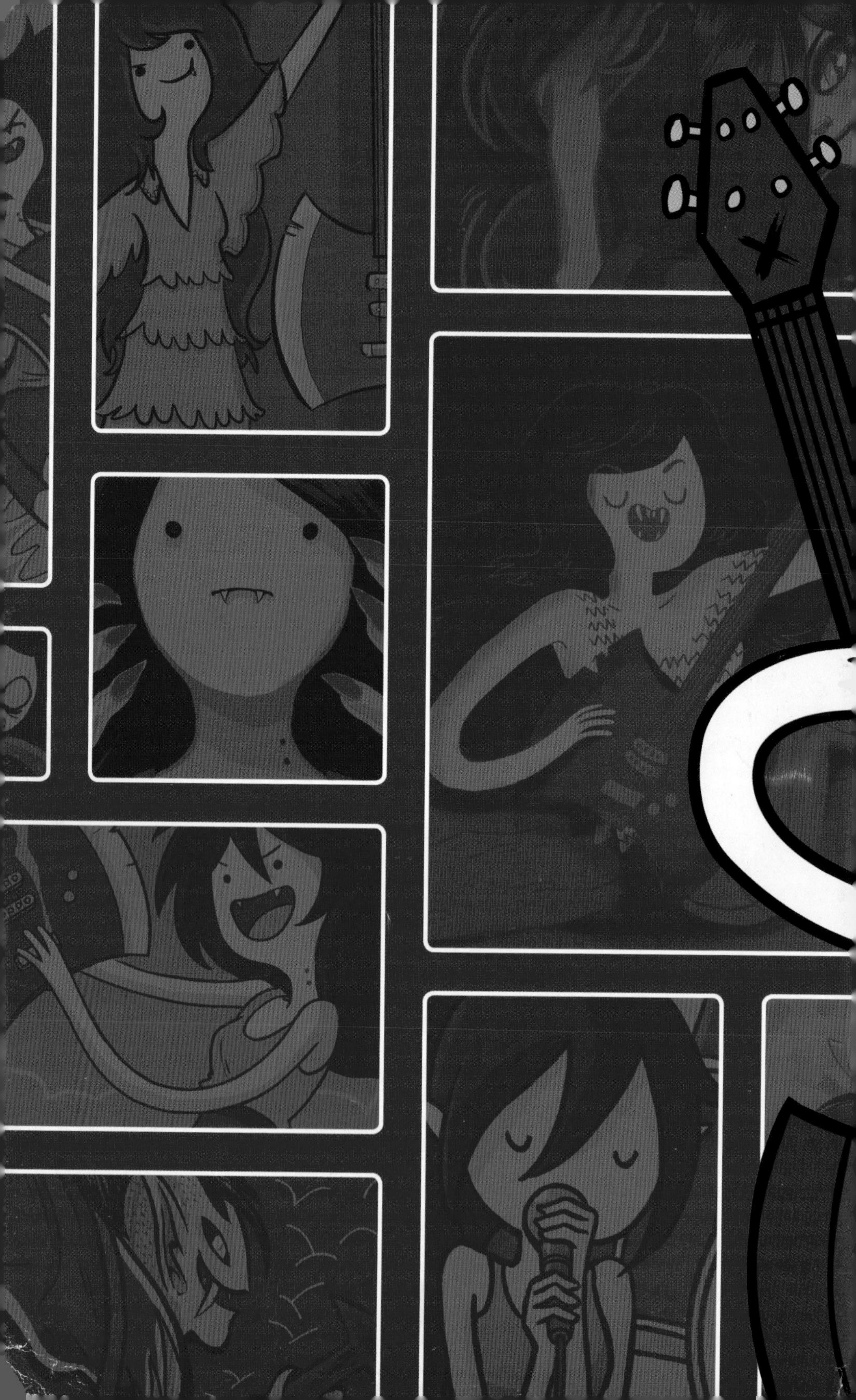

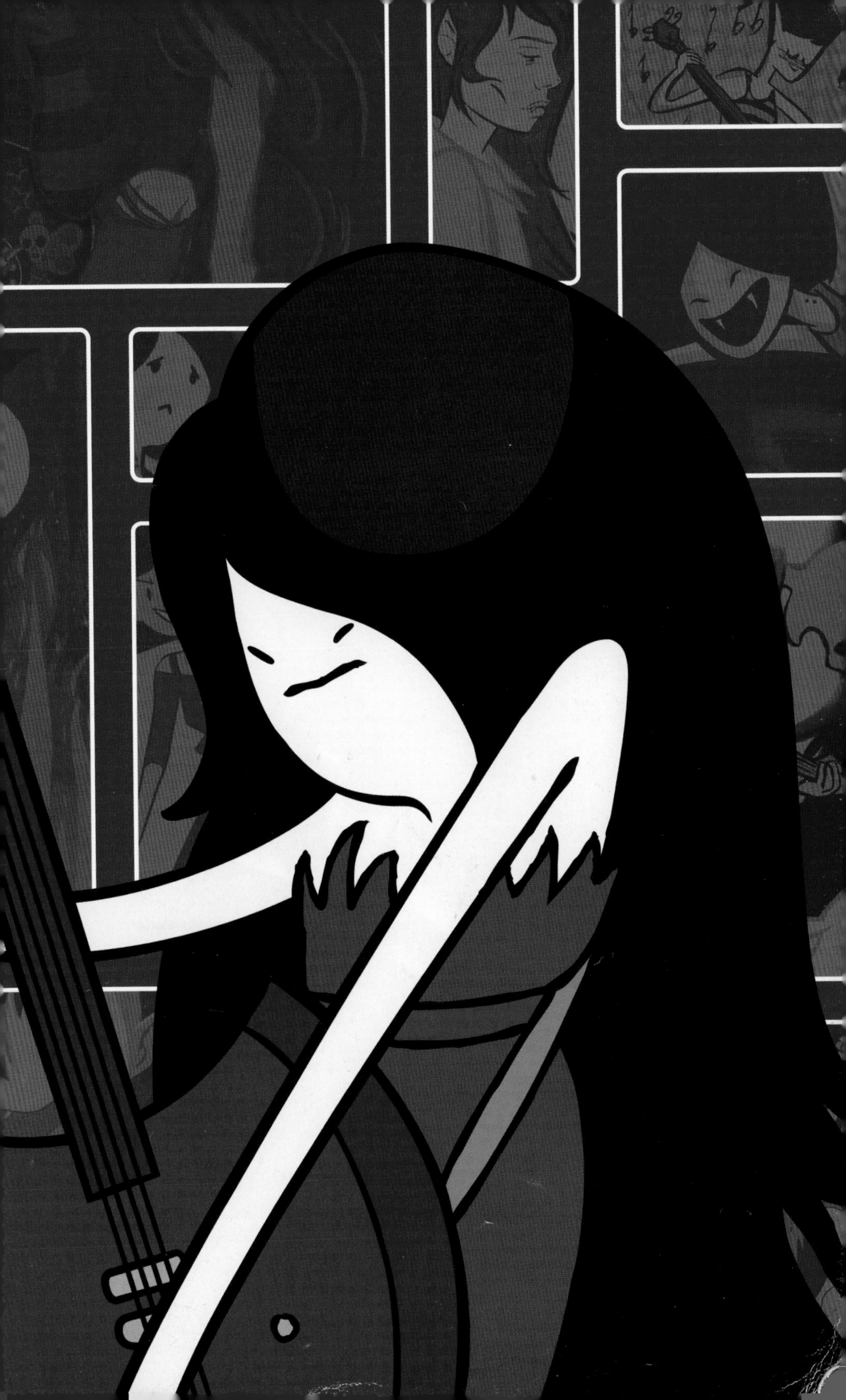

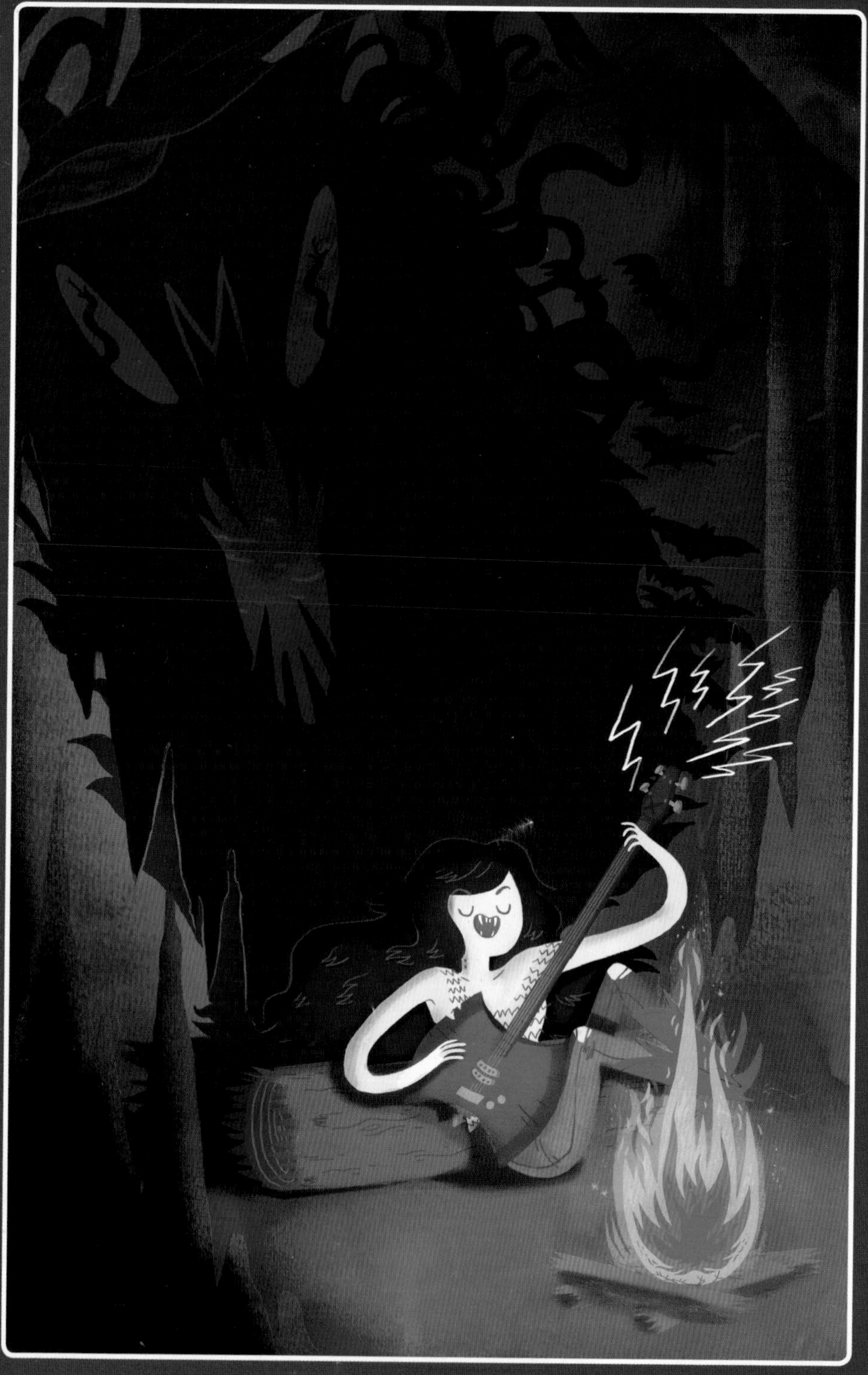

Adventure Time #2 Cover C by **Emily Carroll**

"Laundromarceline"

Written and Illustrated by **Lucy Knisley**

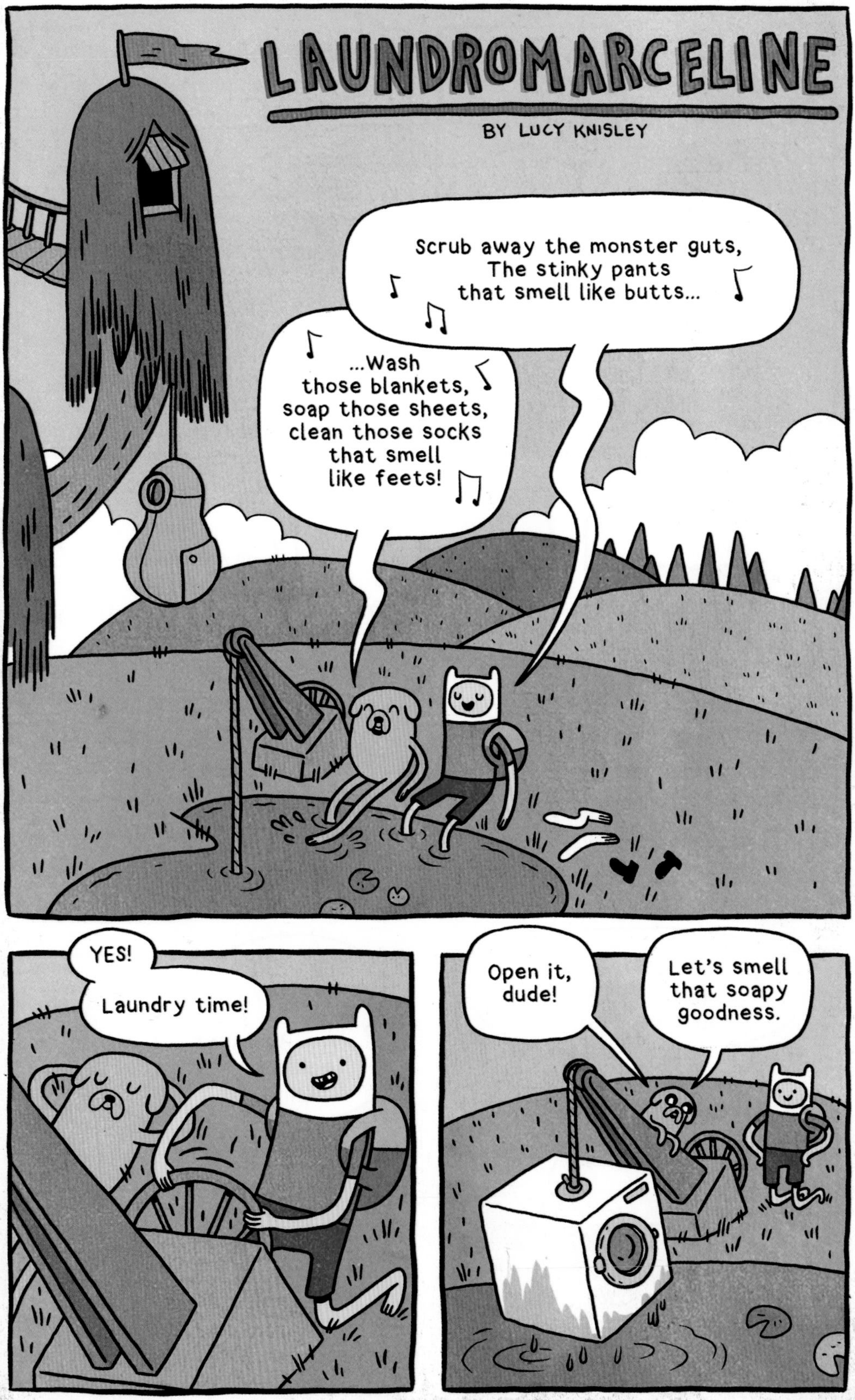
LAUNDROMARCELINE
BY LUCY KNISLEY
Scrub away the monster guts, The stinky pants that smell like butts...
...Wash those blankets, soap those sheets, clean those socks that smell like feets!
YES!
Laundry time!
Open it, dude!
Let's smell that soapy goodness.

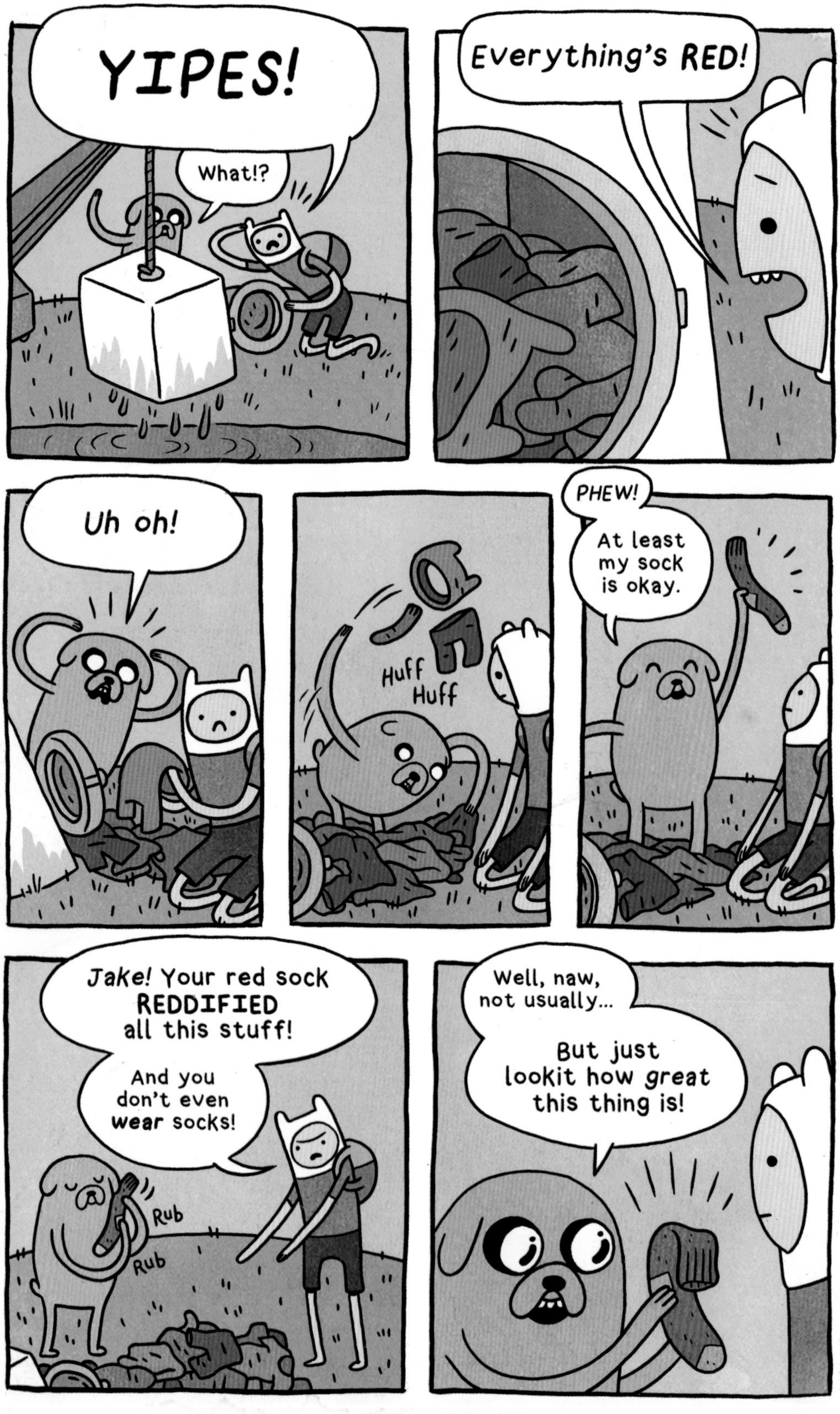
YIPES!
What!?
Everything's RED!
Uh oh!
Huff Huff
PHEW!
At least my sock is okay.
Jake! Your red sock REDDIFIED all this stuff!
And you don't even wear socks!
Rub
Rub
Well, naw, not usually...
But just lookit how great this thing is!

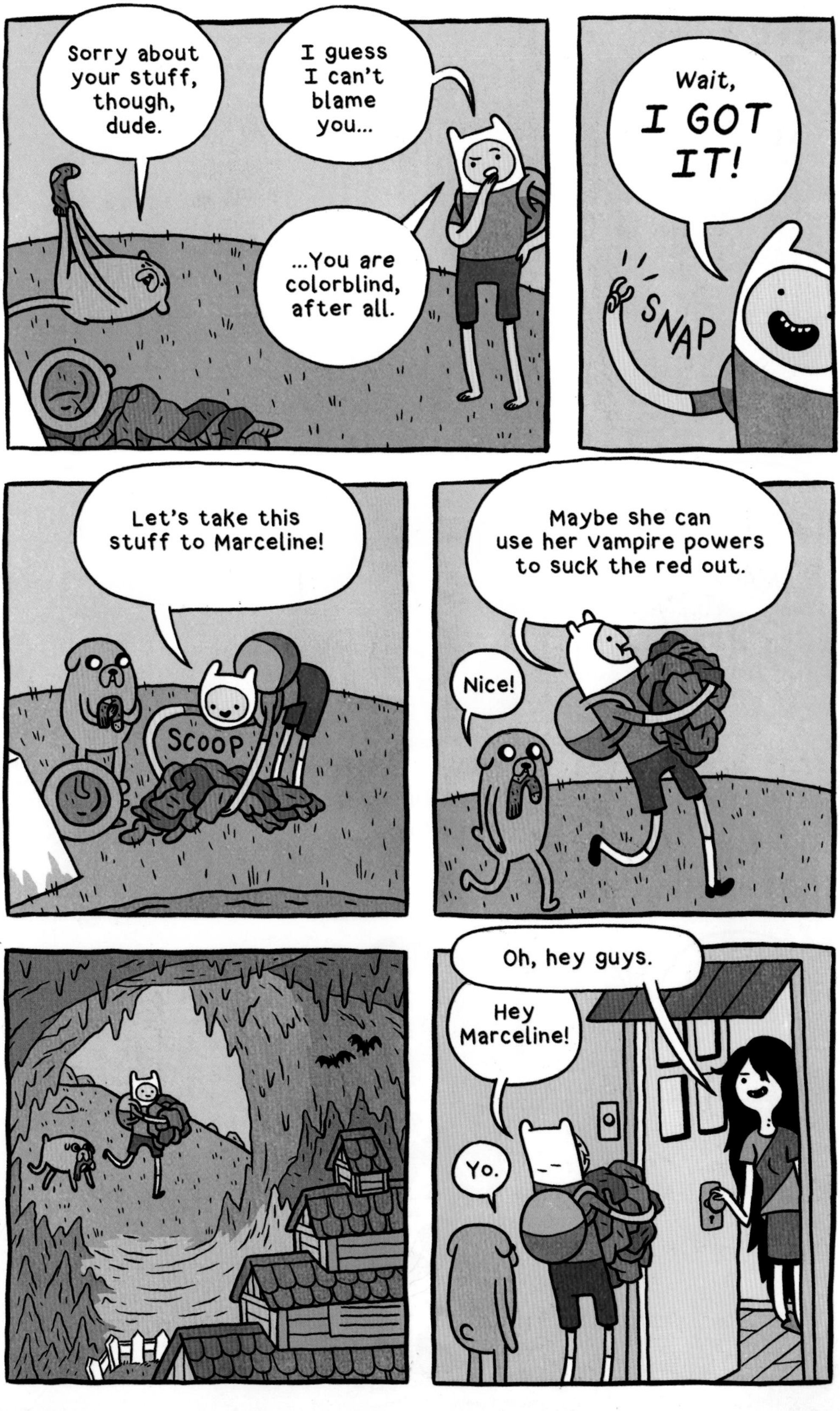
Sorry about your stuff, though, dude.
I guess I can't blame you...
...You are colorblind, after all.
Wait, I GOT IT!
SNAP
Let's take this stuff to Marceline!
SCOOP
Maybe she can use her vampire powers to suck the red out.
Nice!
Oh, hey guys.
Hey Marceline!
Yo.

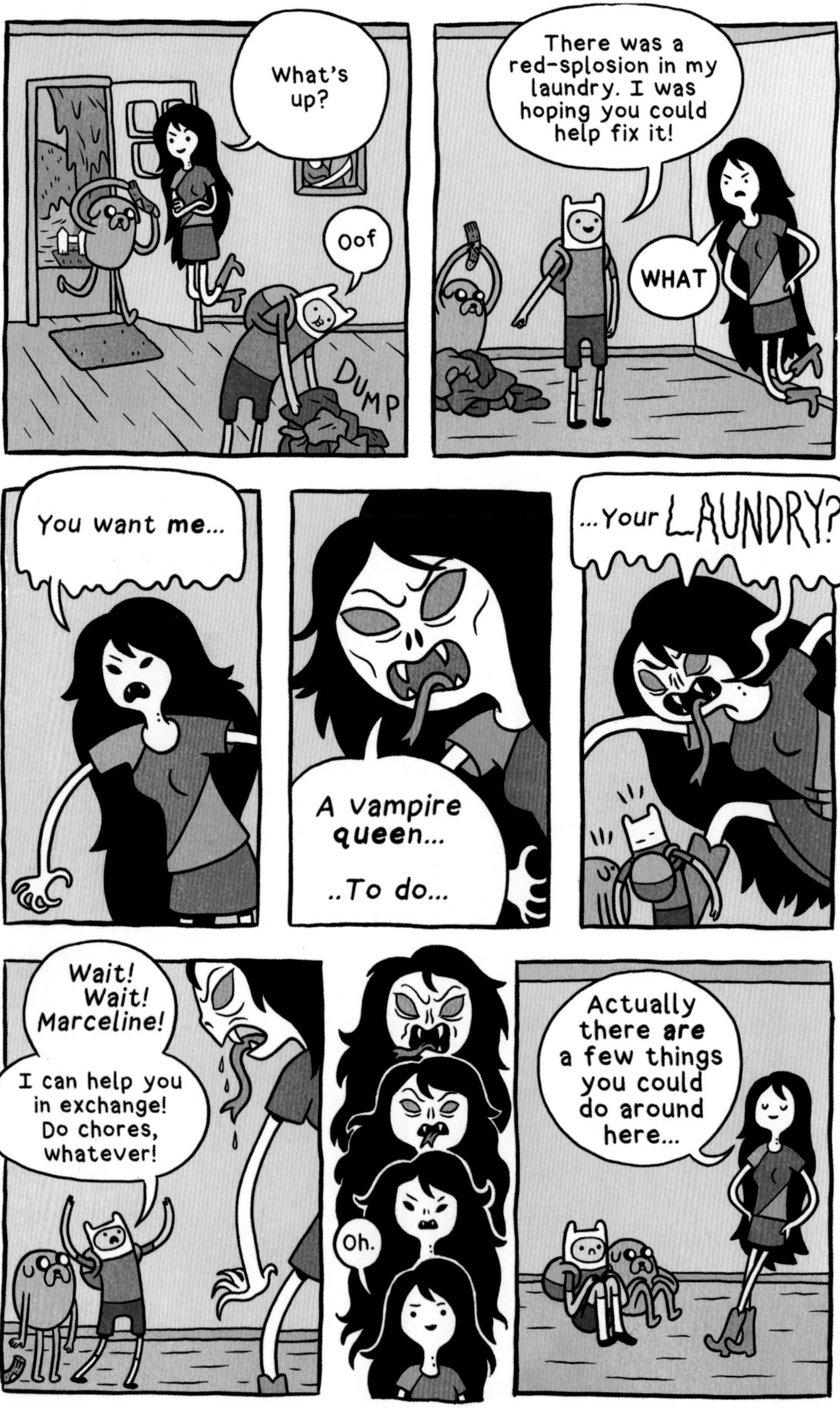
What's up?
Oof
DUMP
There was a red-splosion in my laundry. I was hoping you could help fix it!
WHAT
You want me...
A vampire queen...
..To do...
...Your LAUNDRY?
Wait! Wait! Marceline!
I can help you in exchange! Do chores, whatever!
Oh.
Actually there are a few things you could do around here...

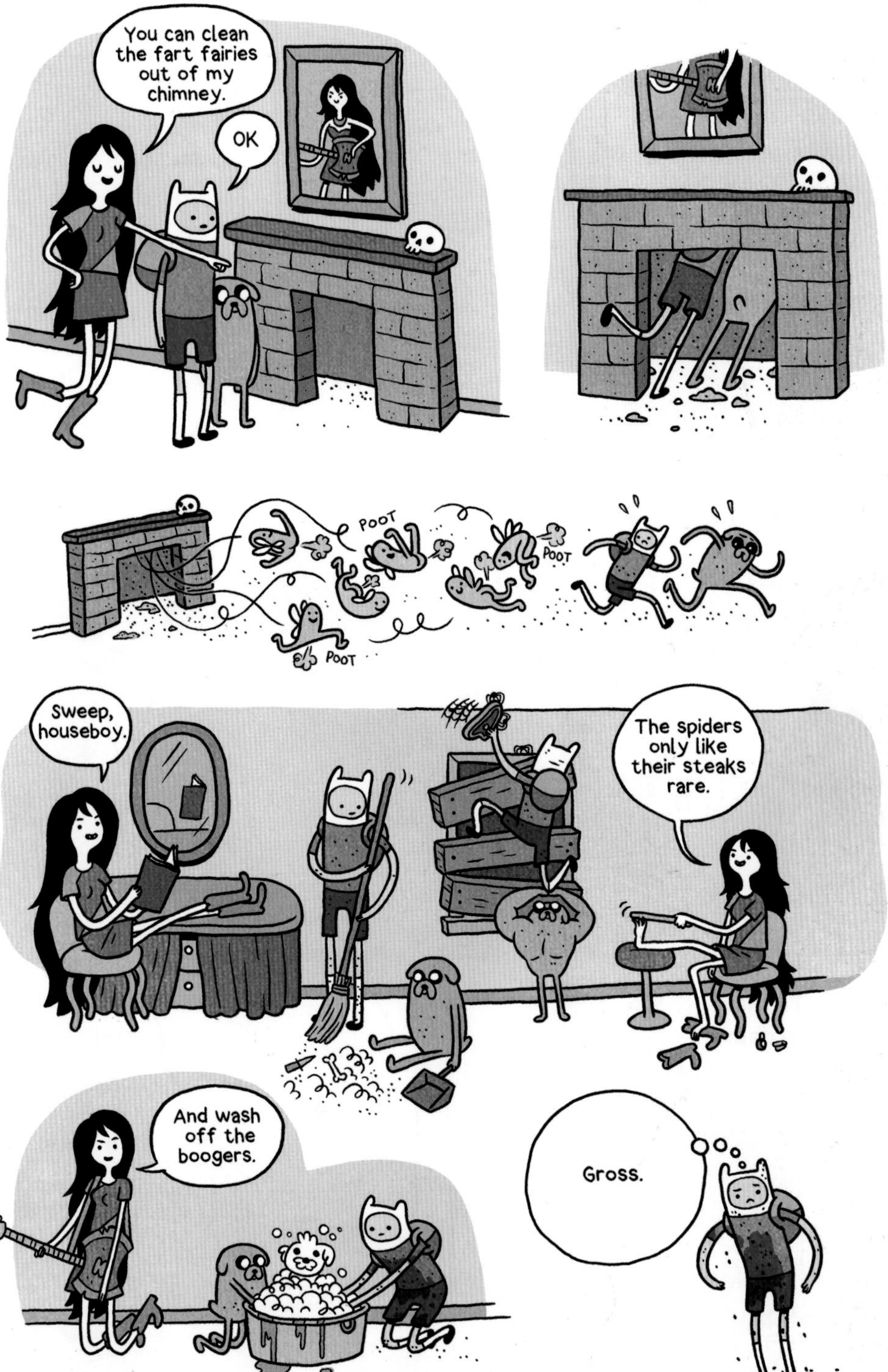
You can clean the fart fairies out of my chimney.
OK
POOT
POOT
POOT
Sweep, houseboy.
The spiders only like their steaks rare.
And wash off the boogers.
Gross.

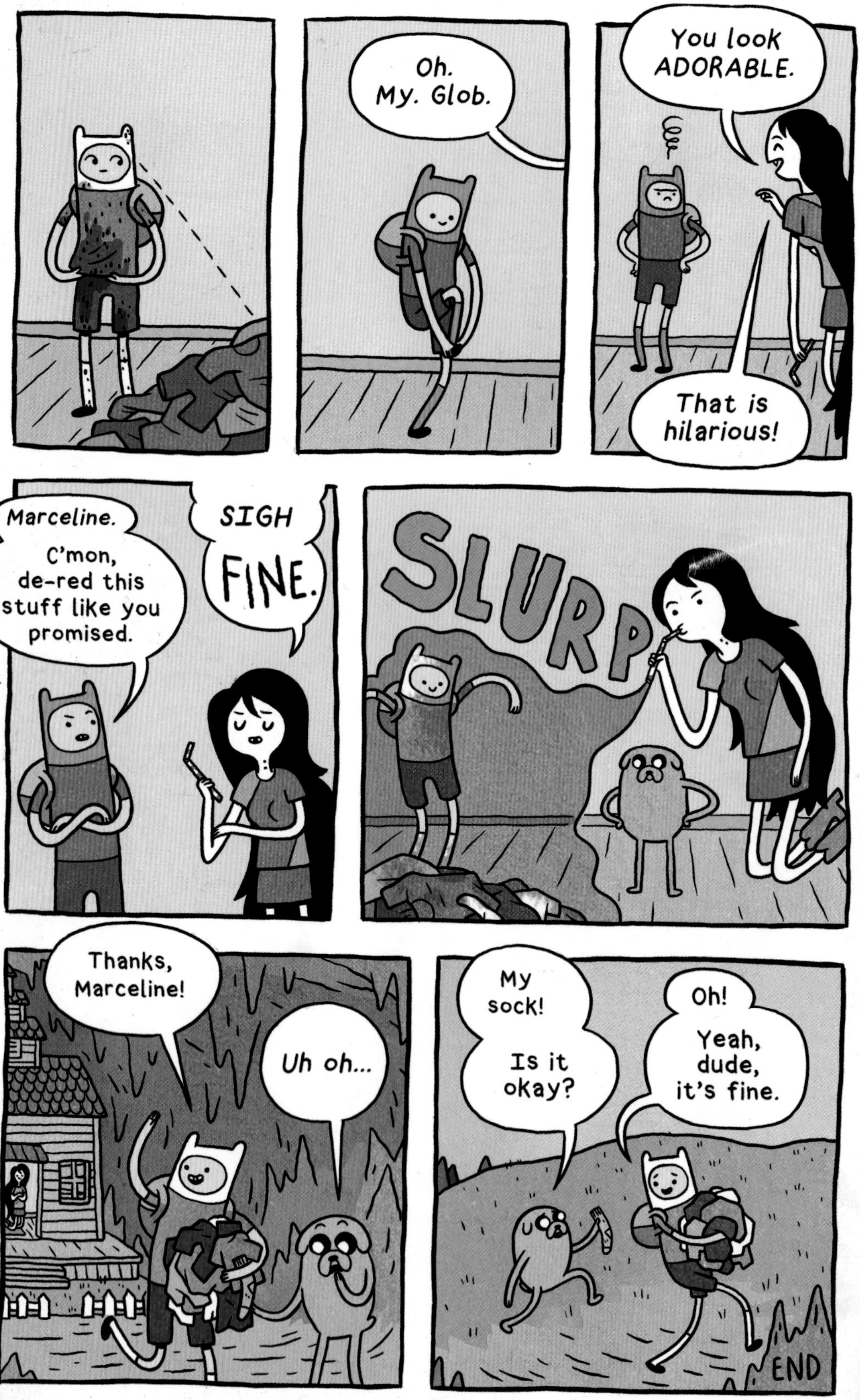
Oh.
My. Glob.
You look ADORABLE.
That is hilarious!
Marceline.
C'mon, de-red this stuff like you promised.
SIGH
FINE.
SLURP
Thanks, Marceline!
Uh oh...
My sock!
Is it okay?
Oh!
Yeah, dude, it's fine.
END

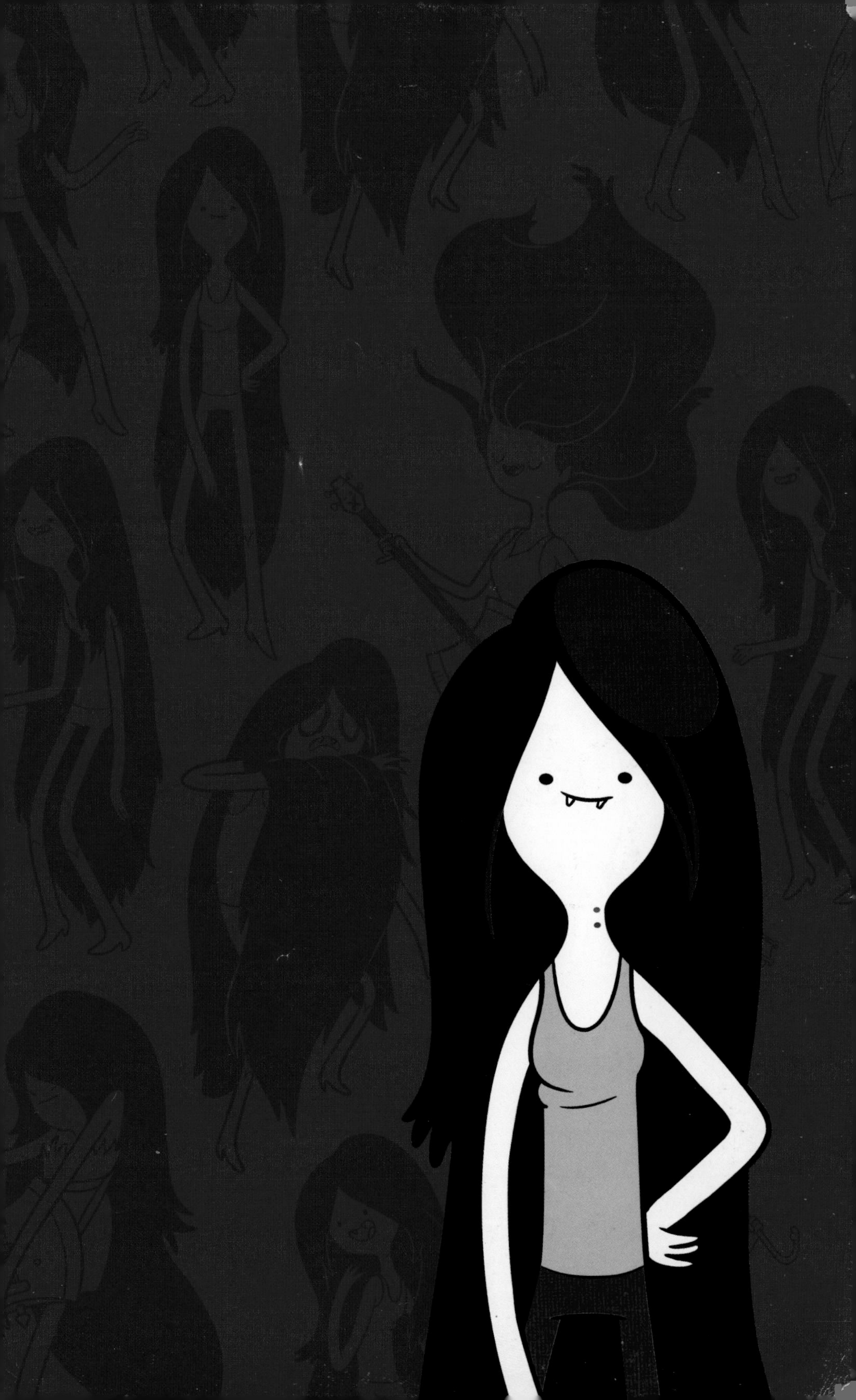

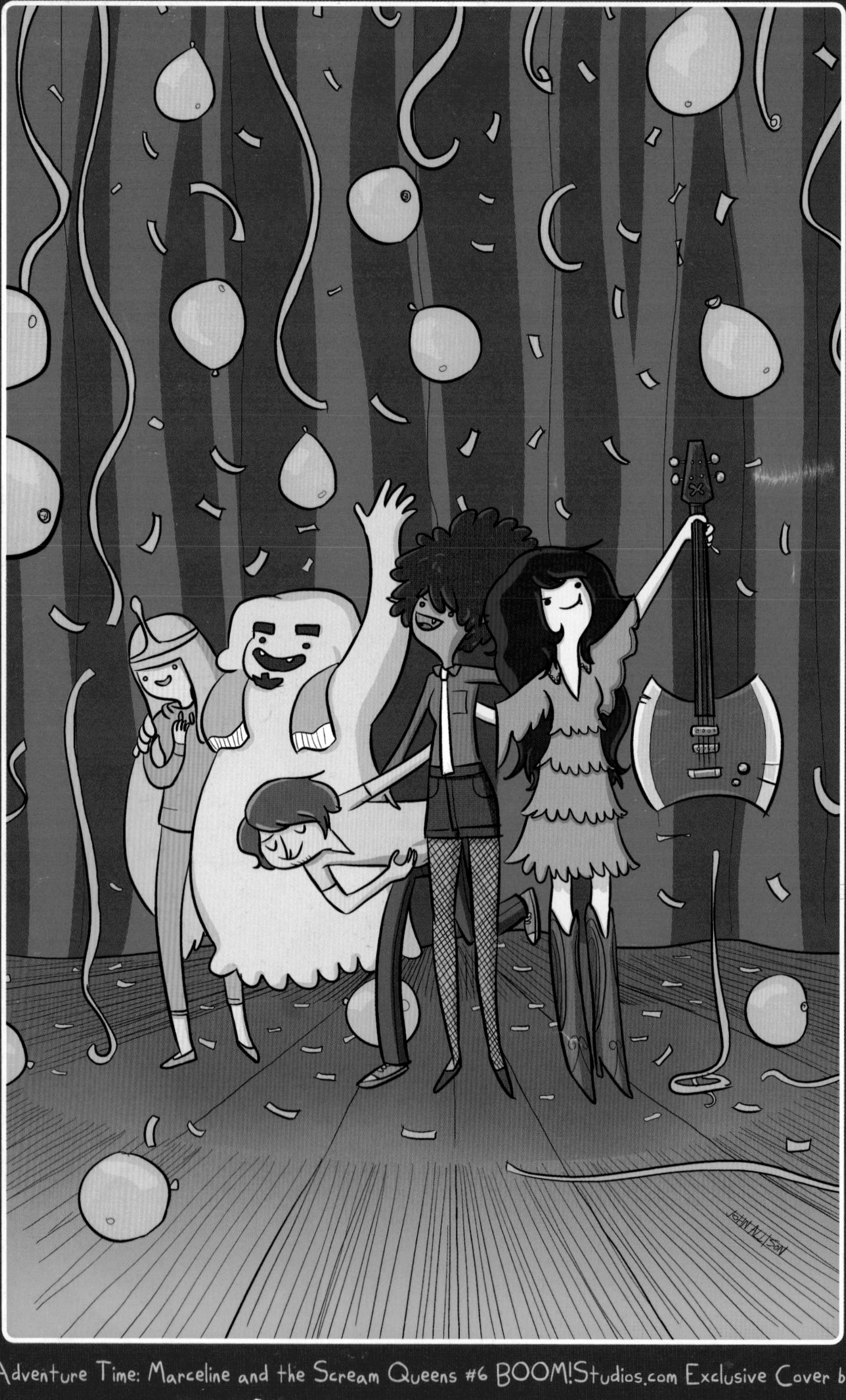
JOHN ALLISON

Adventure Time: Marceline and the Scream Queens #6 BOOM!Studios.com Exclusive Cover by

John Allison With Colors by **Steve Wands**

"Resurrection Song"

Written and Illustrated by **Jen Wang**

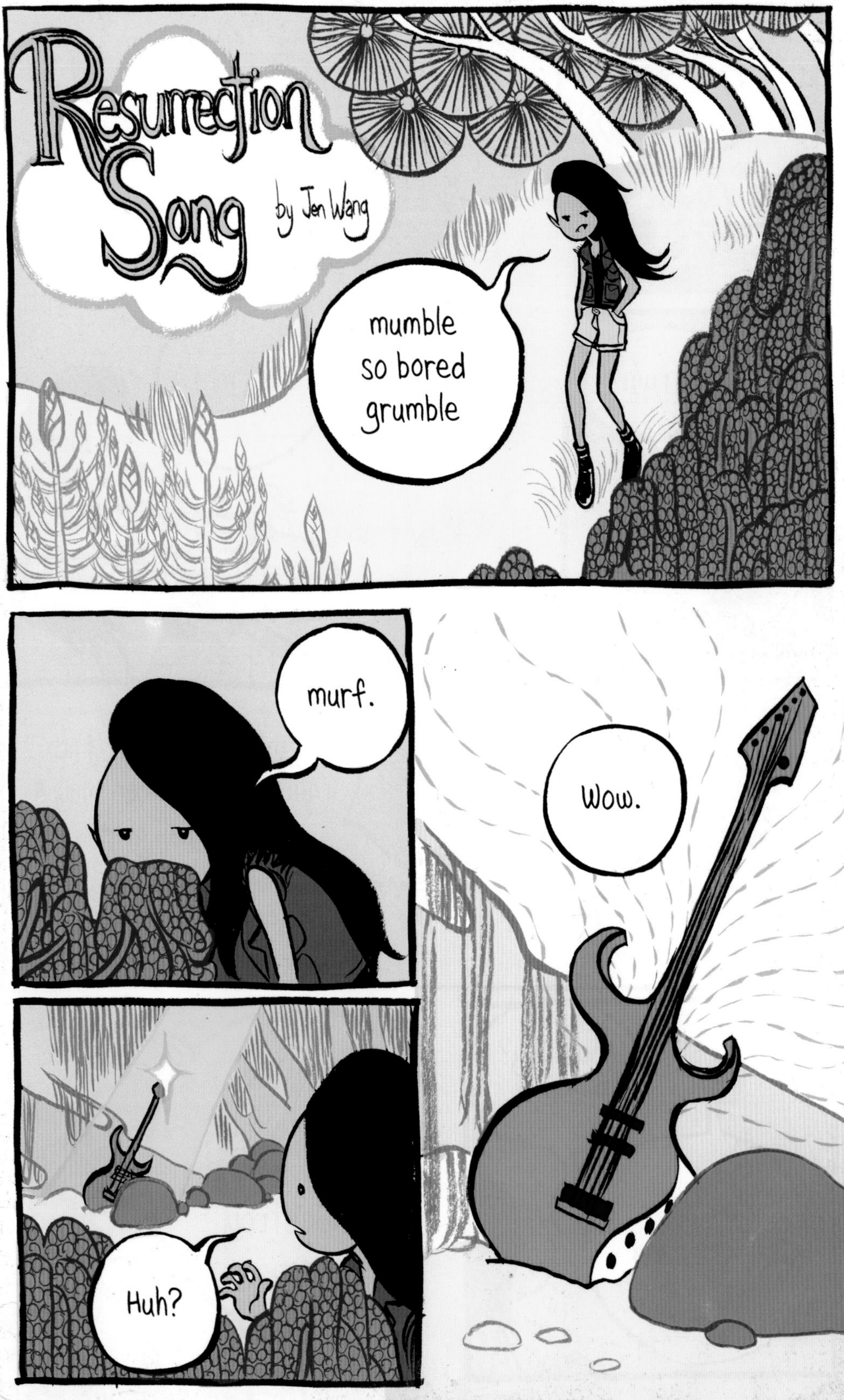
Resurrection Song
by Jen Wang
mumble so bored grumble
murf.
Huh?
Wow.

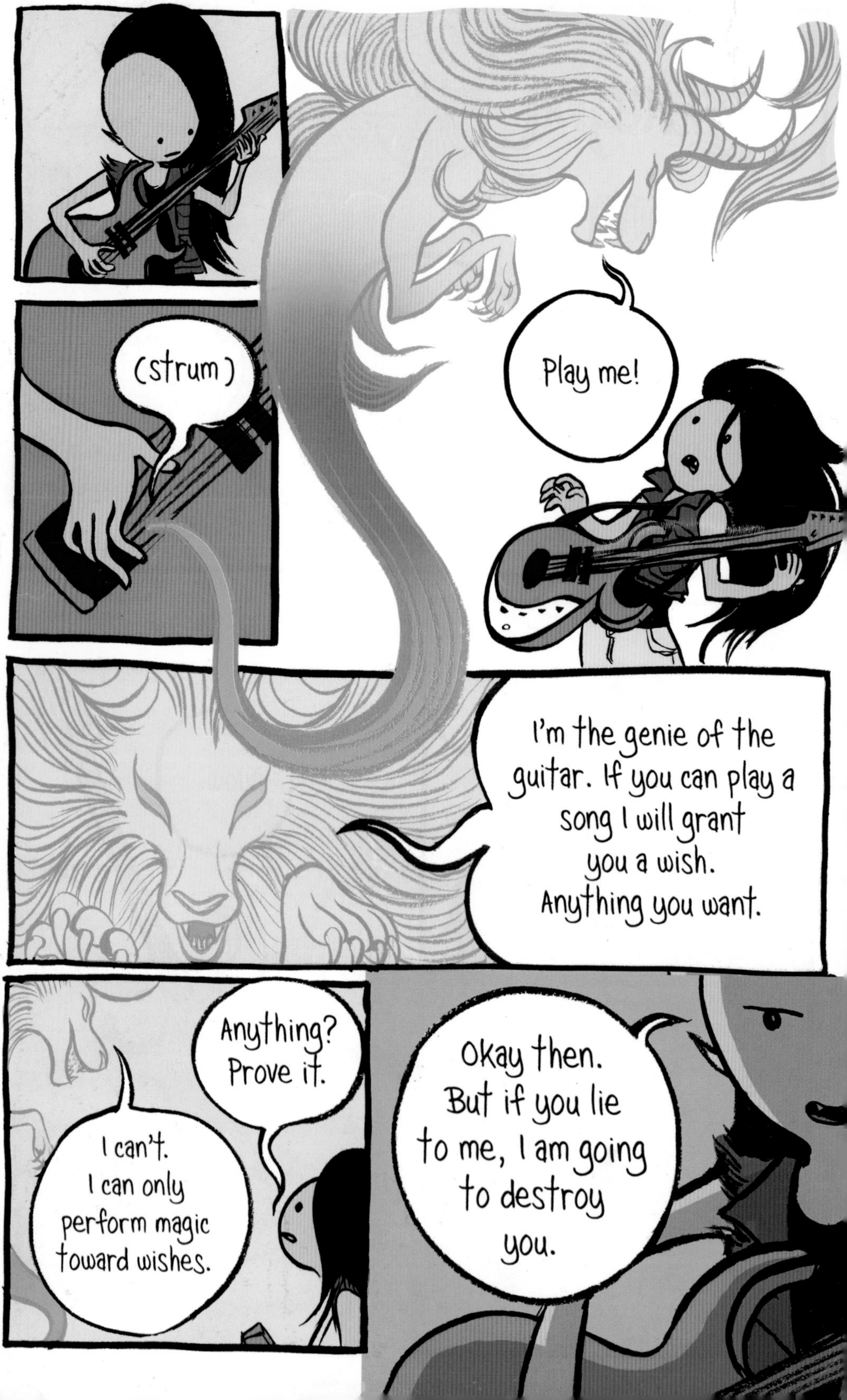
(strum)
Play me!
I'm the genie of the guitar. If you can play a song I will grant you a wish. Anything you want.
Anything? Prove it.
I can't. I can only perform magic toward wishes.
Okay then. But if you lie to me, I am going to destroy you.

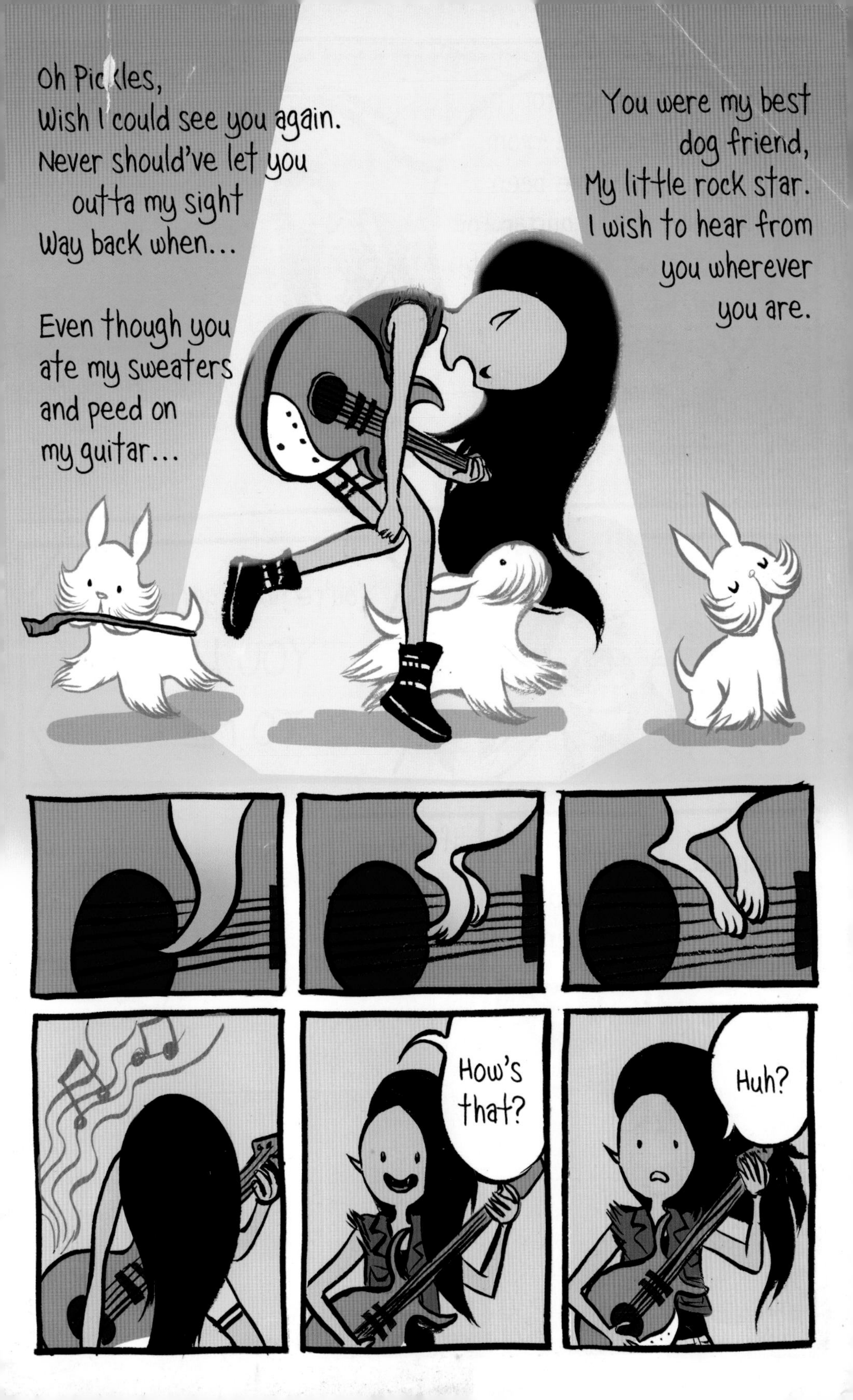
Oh Pickles,
Wish I could see you again.
Never should've let you outta my sight
Way back when...
Even though you ate my sweaters and peed on my guitar...
You were my best dog friend,
My little rock star.
I wish to hear from you wherever you are.
How's that?
Huh?

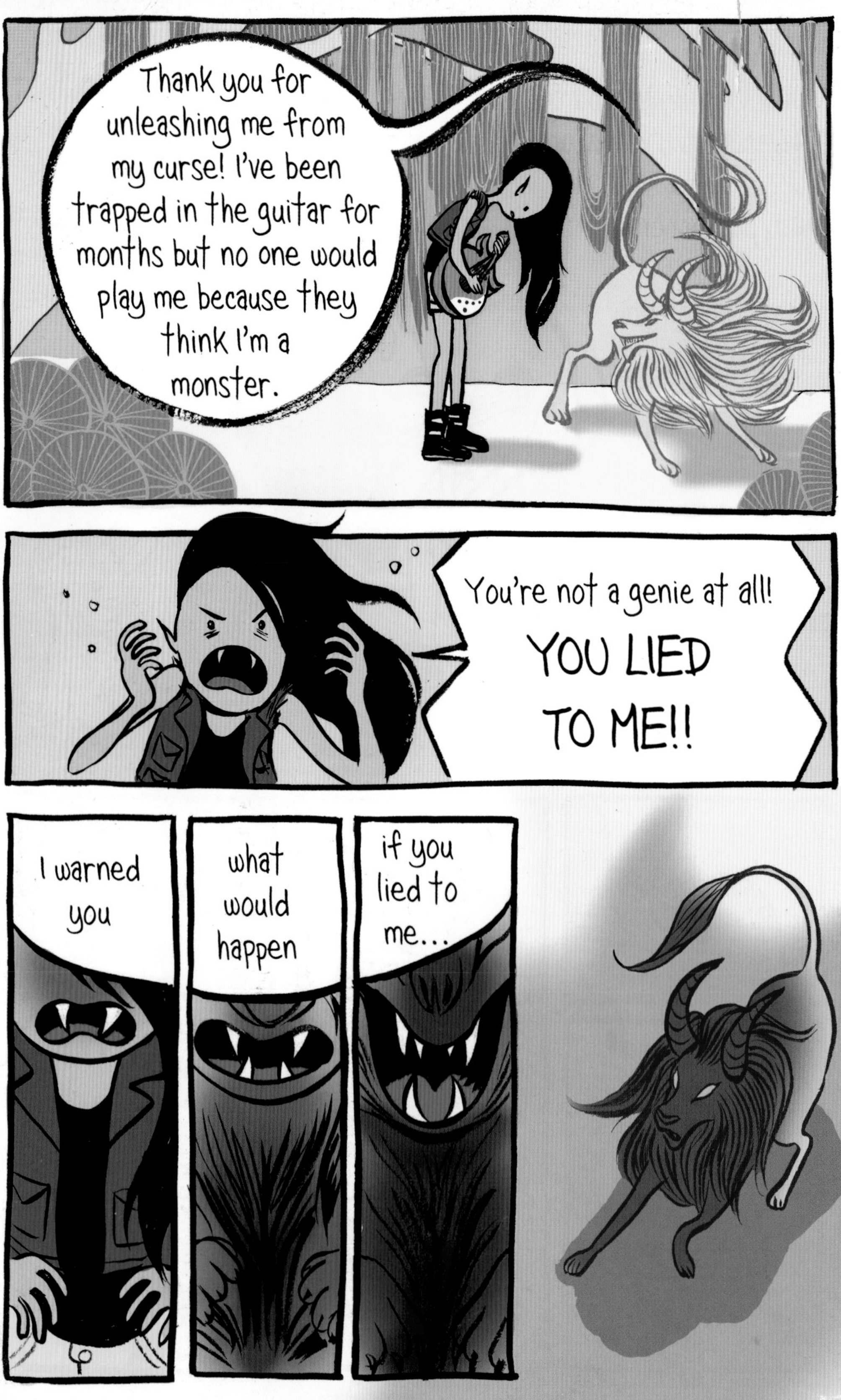

Thank you for unleashing me from my curse! I've been trapped in the guitar for months but no one would play me because they think I'm a monster.
You're not a genie at all!
YOU LIED TO ME!!
I warned you
what would happen
if you lied to me...

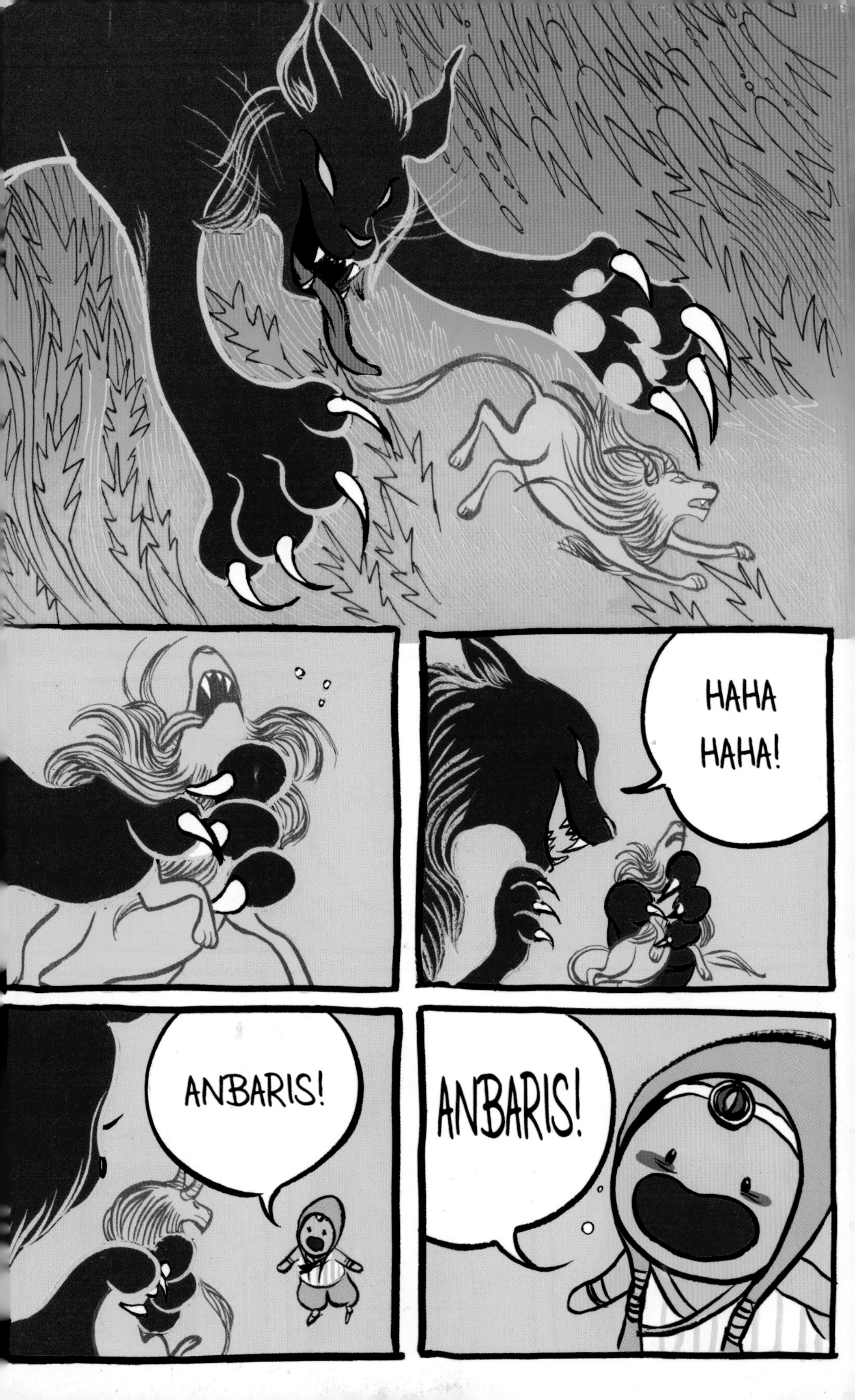
HAHA HAHA!
ANBARIS!
ANBARIS!

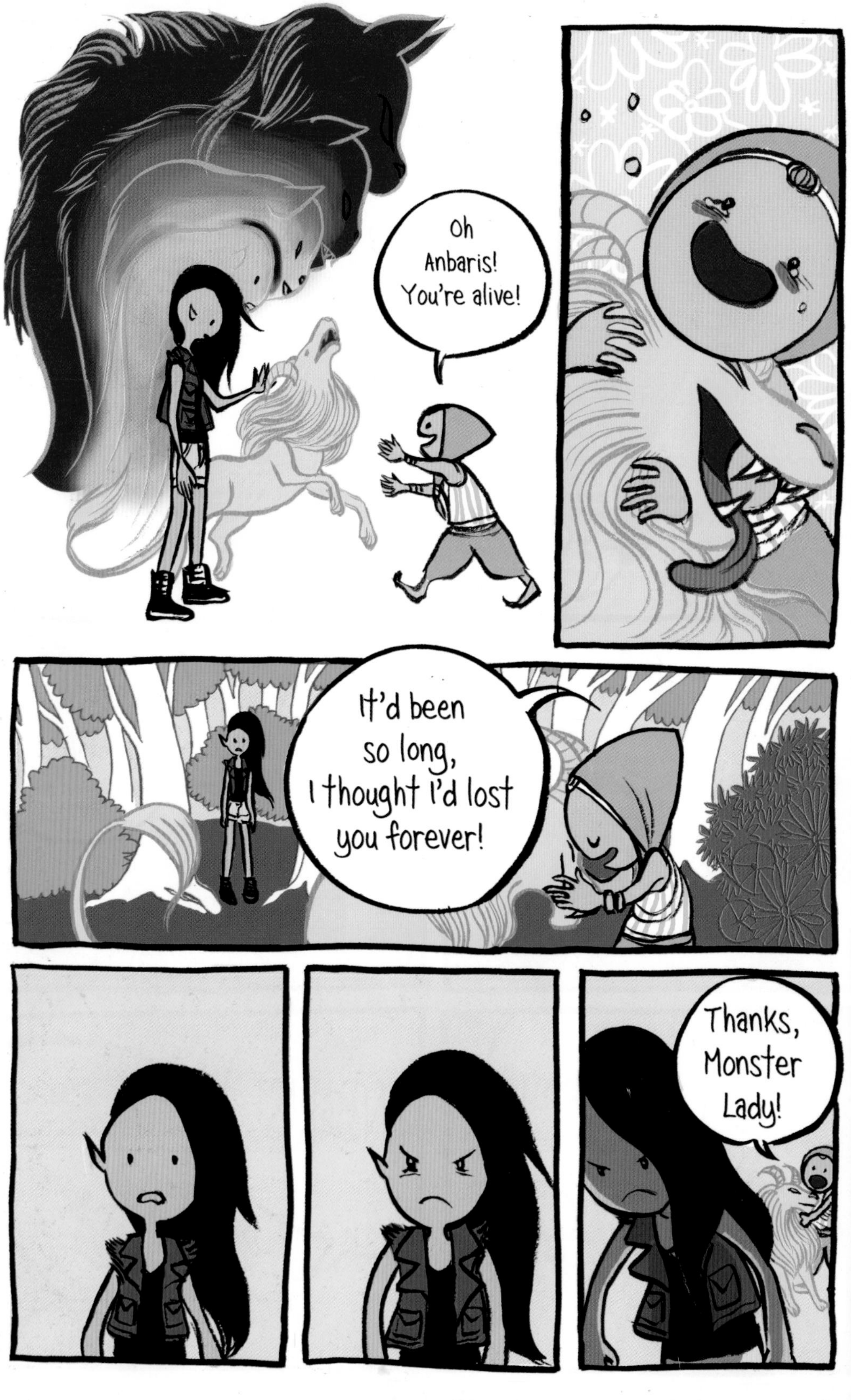
Oh Anbaris! You're alive!
It'd been so long, I thought I'd lost you forever!
Thanks, Monster Lady!

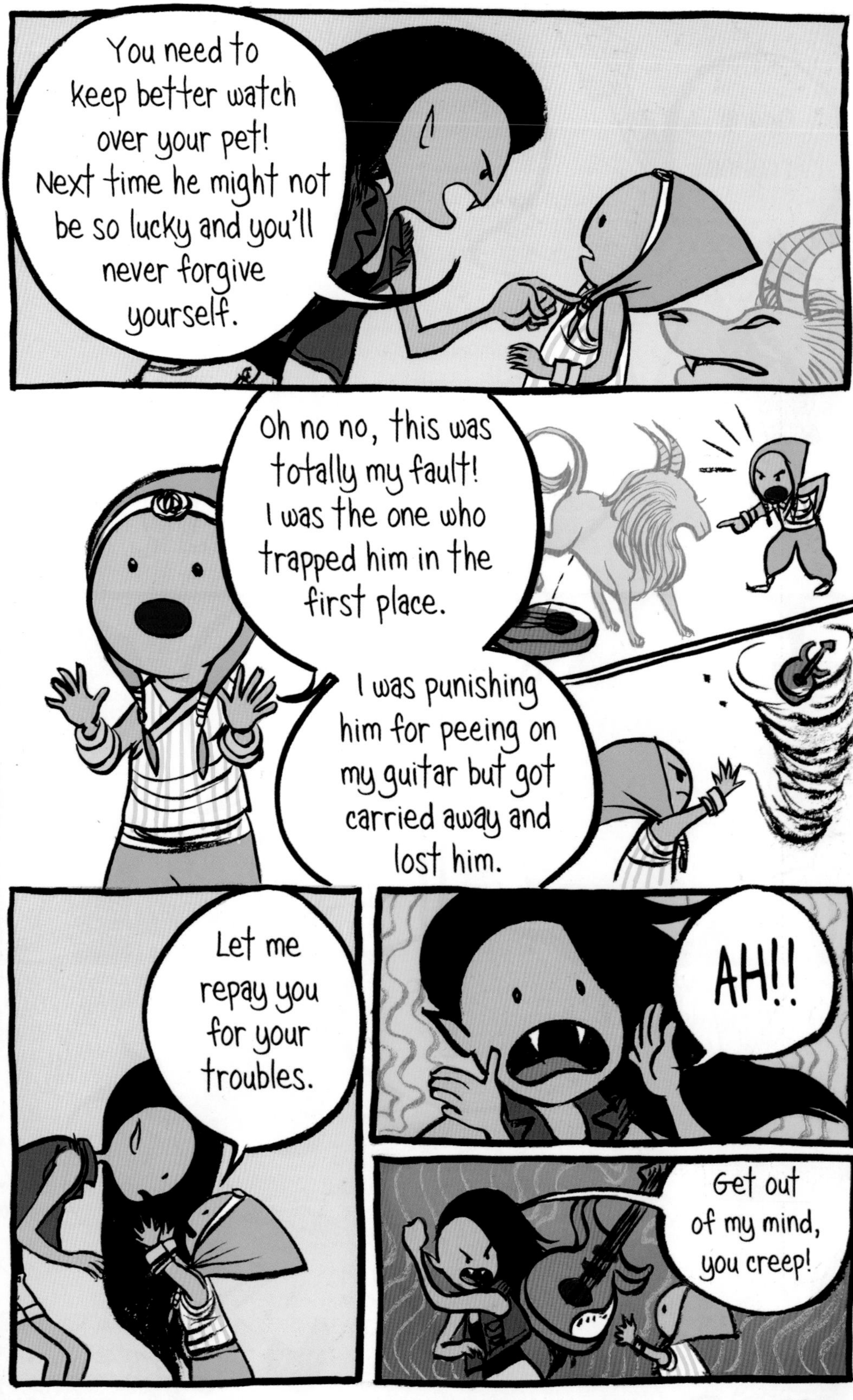
You need to keep better watch over your pet! Next time he might not be so lucky and you'll never forgive yourself.
Oh no no, this was totally my fault! I was the one who trapped him in the first place.
I was punishing him for peeing on my guitar but got carried away and lost him.
Let me repay you for your troubles.
AH!!
Get out of my mind, you creep!

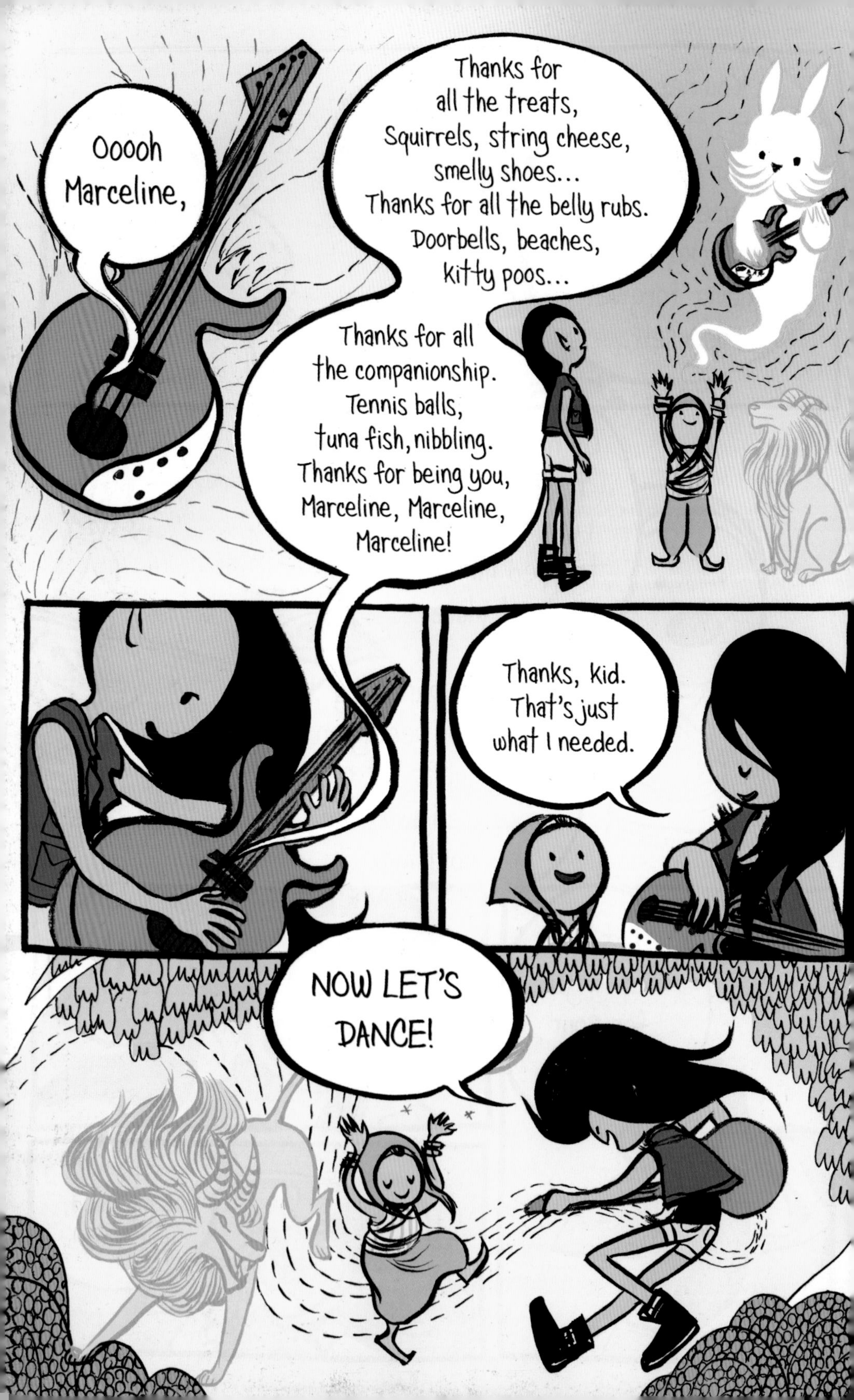
Ooooh Marceline,
Thanks for all the treats, Squirrels, string cheese, smelly shoes... Thanks for all the belly rubs. Doorbells, beaches, kitty poos...
Thanks for all the companionship. Tennis balls, tuna fish, nibbling. Thanks for being you, Marceline, Marceline, Marceline!
Thanks, Kid. That's just what I needed.
NOW LET'S DANCE!

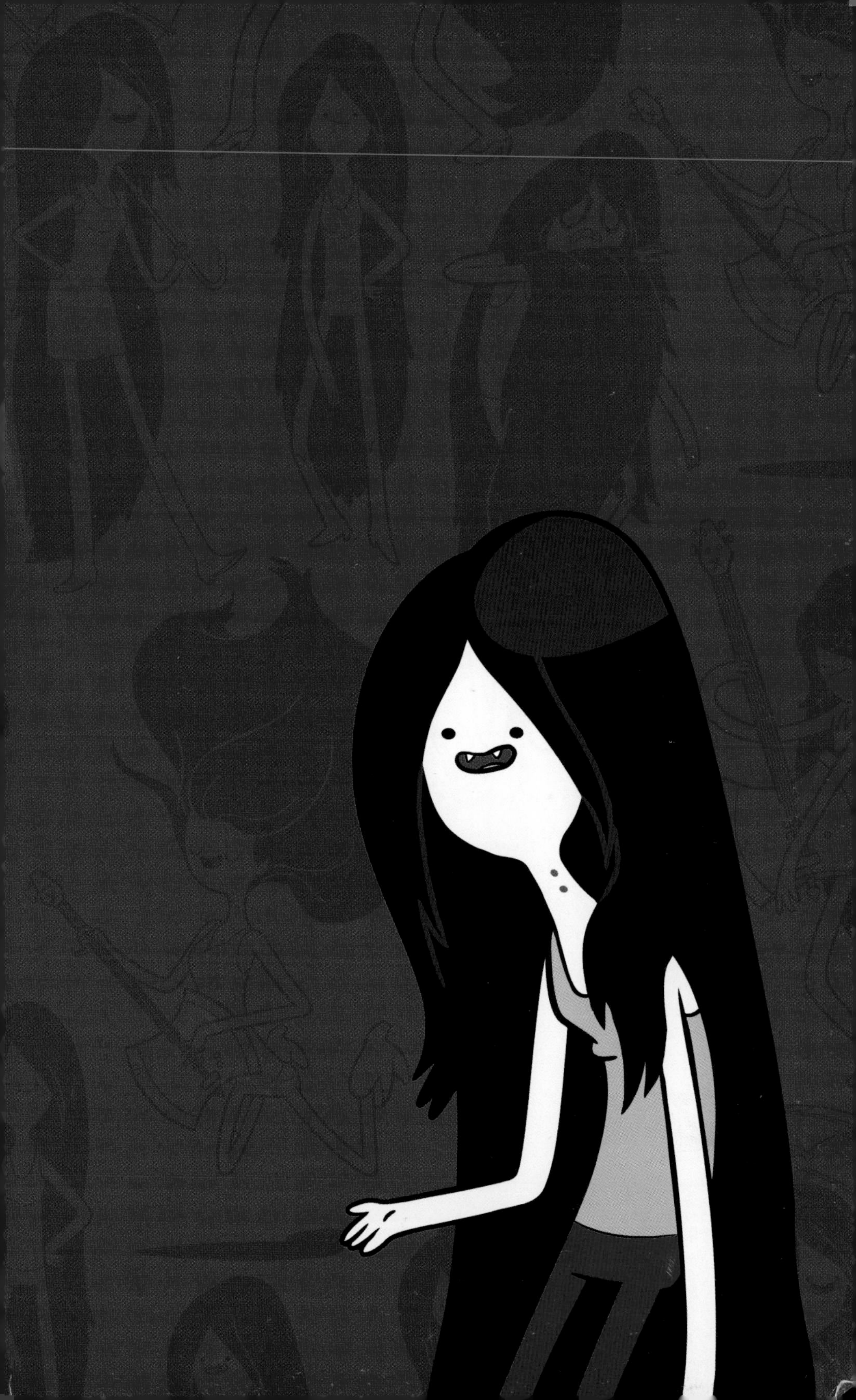

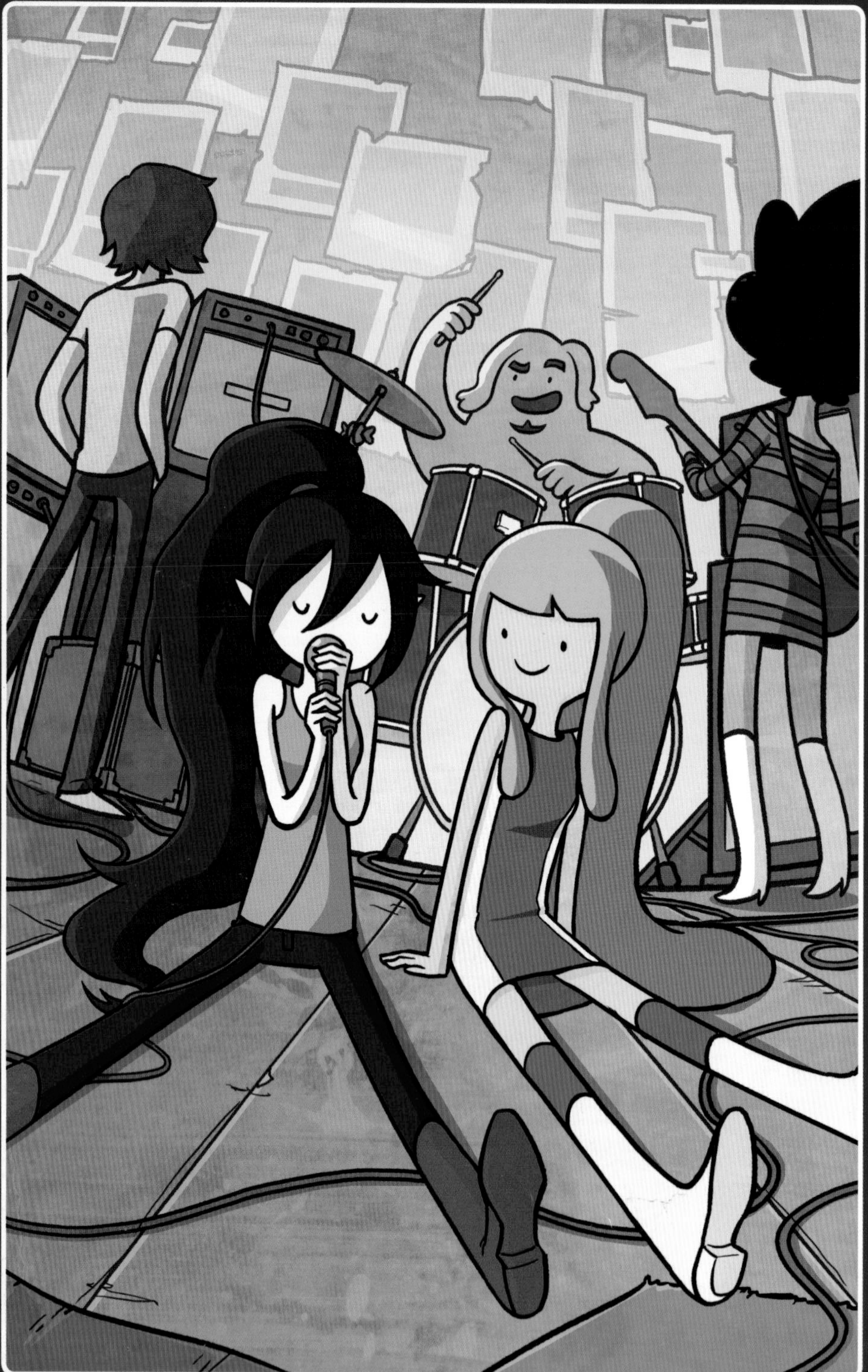

Adventure Time: Marceline and the Scream Queens #4 Cover A by **Jab** With Colors by **Lisa Moore**

"Grumpy Butt"

Written and Illustrated by **Faith Erin Hicks** With Story by **Tim Larade**

Colors by **Mirka Andolfo**

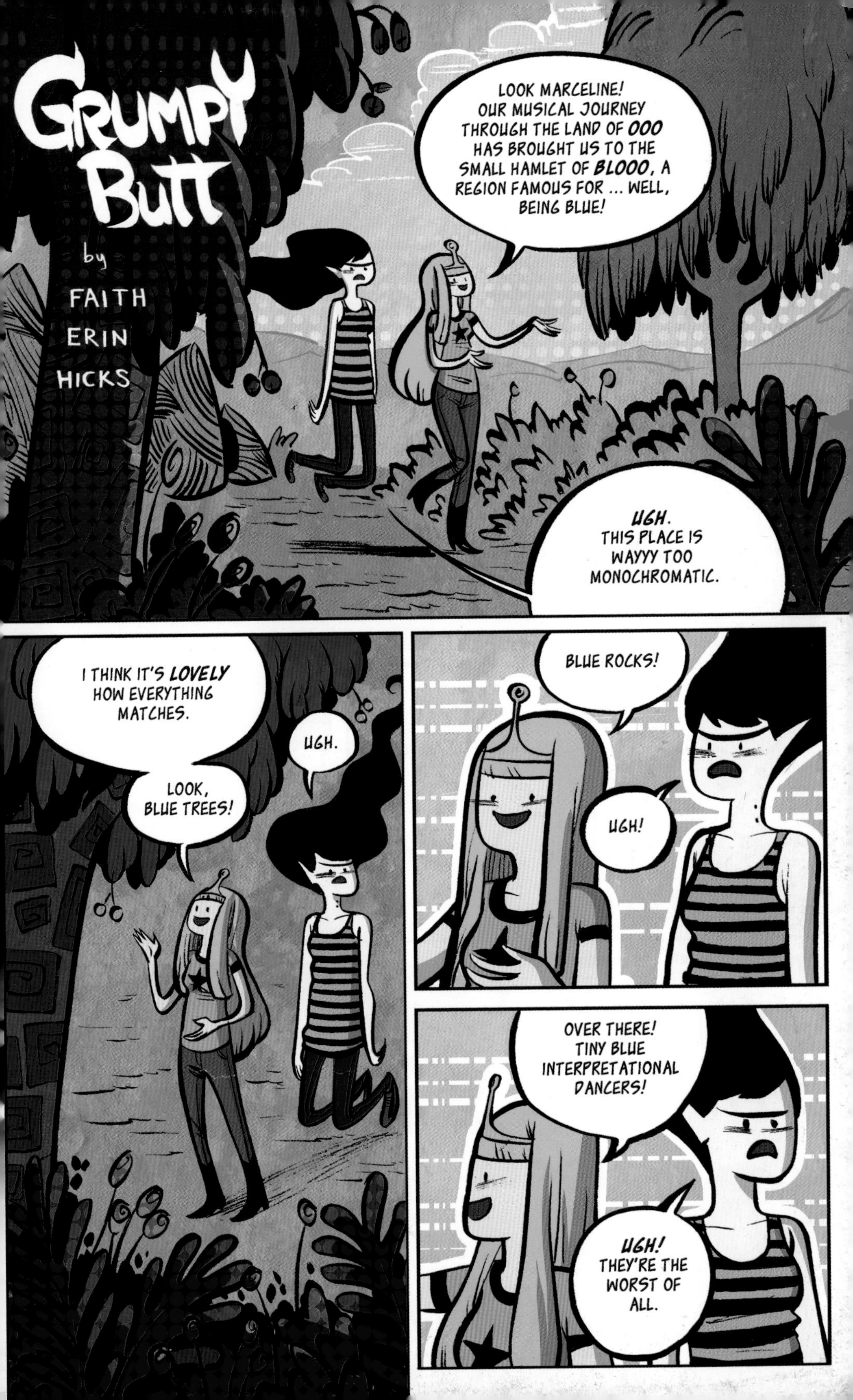
GRUMPY BUTT
by FAITH ERIN HICKS
LOOK MARCELINE! OUR MUSICAL JOURNEY THROUGH THE LAND OF OOO HAS BROUGHT US TO THE SMALL HAMLET OF BLOOO, A REGION FAMOUS FOR ... WELL, BEING BLUE!
UGH. THIS PLACE IS WAYYY TOO MONOCHROMATIC.
I THINK IT'S LOVELY HOW EVERYTHING MATCHES.
UGH.
LOOK, BLUE TREES!
BLUE ROCKS!
UGH!
OVER THERE! TINY BLUE INTERPRETATIONAL DANCERS!
UGH! THEY'RE THE WORST OF ALL.

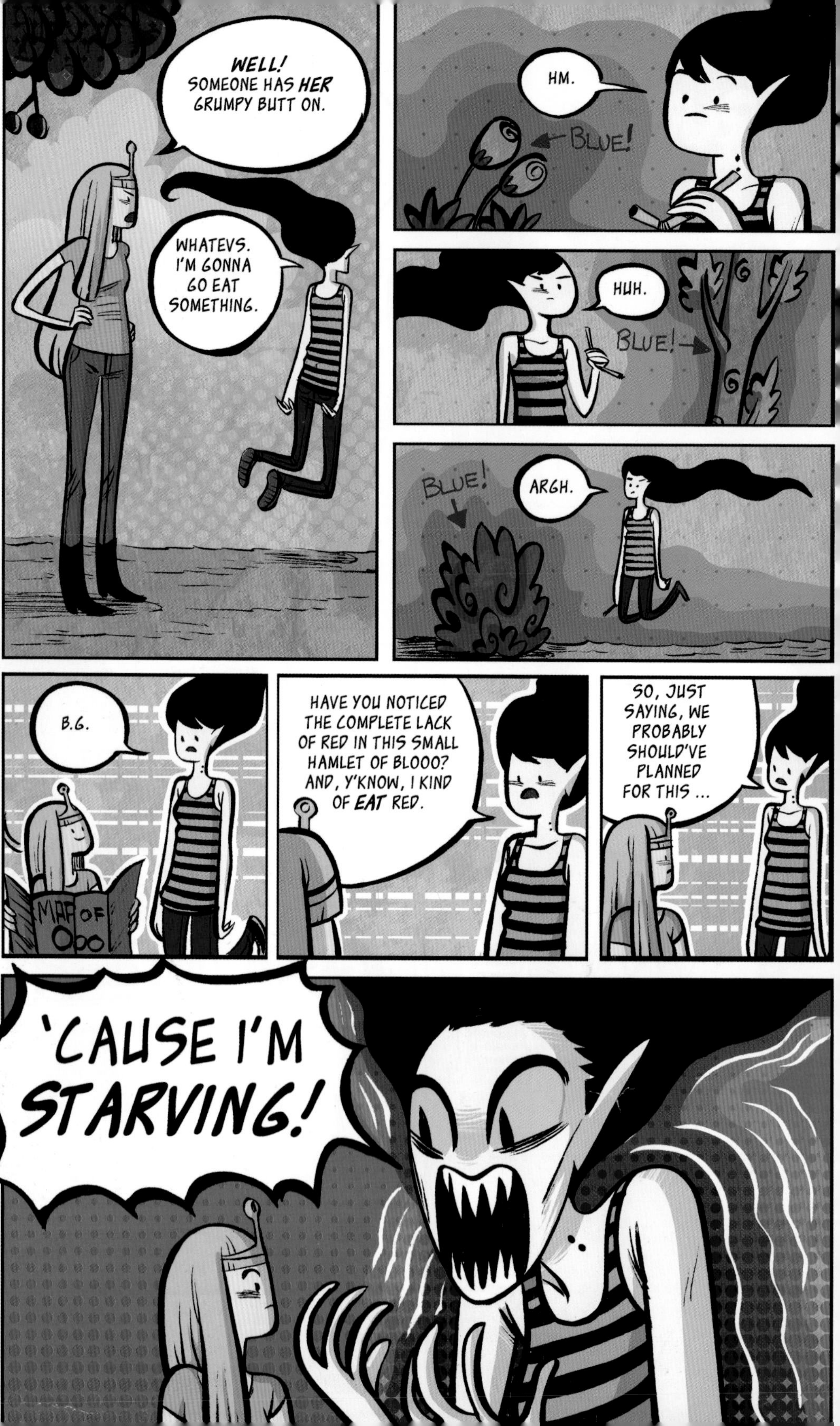
WELL! SOMEONE HAS HER GRUMPY BUTT ON.
WHATEVS. I'M GONNA GO EAT SOMETHING.
HM.
BLUE!
HUH.
BLUE!
ARGH.
BLUE!
B.G.
MAP OF OOO
HAVE YOU NOTICED THE COMPLETE LACK OF RED IN THIS SMALL HAMLET OF BLOOO? AND, Y'KNOW, I KIND OF EAT RED.
SO, JUST SAYING, WE PROBABLY SHOULD'VE PLANNED FOR THIS ...
'CAUSE I'M STARVING!

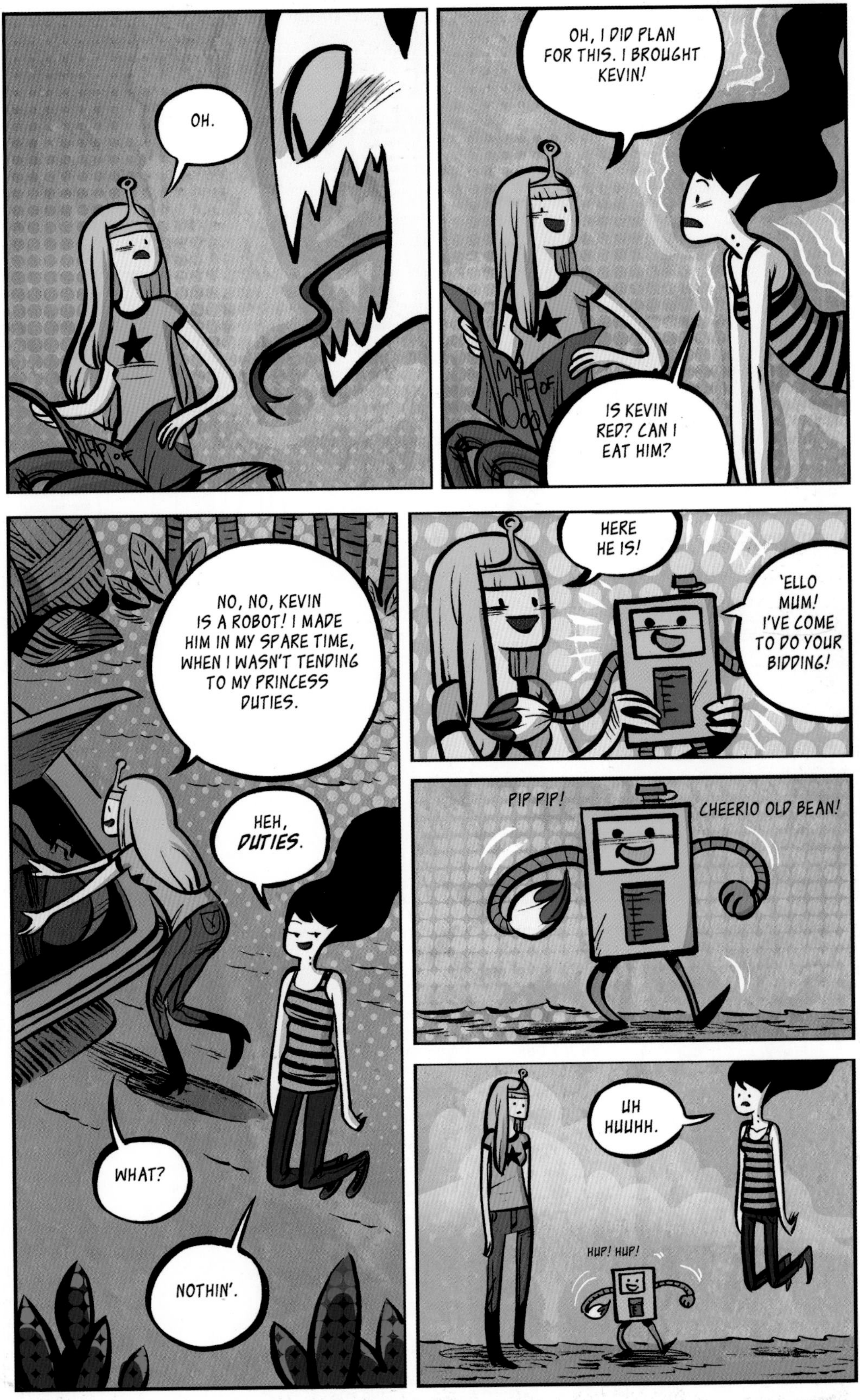
OH.
OH, I DID PLAN FOR THIS. I BROUGHT KEVIN!
IS KEVIN RED? CAN I EAT HIM?
NO, NO, KEVIN IS A ROBOT! I MADE HIM IN MY SPARE TIME, WHEN I WASN'T TENDING TO MY PRINCESS DUTIES.
HEH, DUTIES.
WHAT?
NOTHIN'.
HERE HE IS!
'ELLO MUM! I'VE COME TO DO YOUR BIDDING!
PIP PIP!
CHEERIO OLD BEAN!
UH HUUHH.
HUP! HUP!

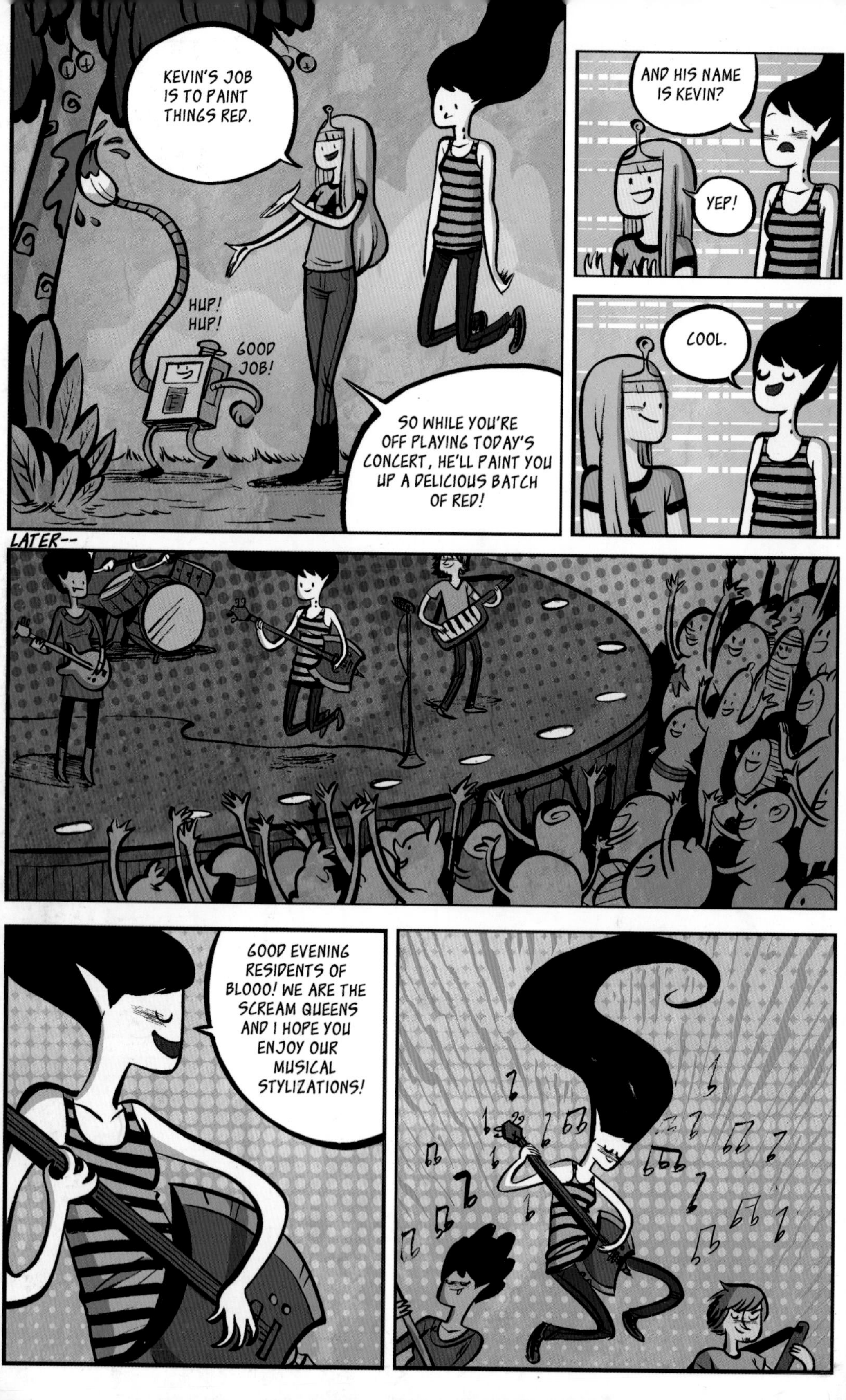
KEVIN'S JOB IS TO PAINT THINGS RED.
HUP! HUP!
GOOD JOB!
SO WHILE YOU'RE OFF PLAYING TODAY'S CONCERT, HE'LL PAINT YOU UP A DELICIOUS BATCH OF RED!
AND HIS NAME IS KEVIN?
YEP!
COOL.
LATER--
GOOD EVENING RESIDENTS OF BLOOO! WE ARE THE SCREAM QUEENS AND I HOPE YOU ENJOY OUR MUSICAL STYLIZATIONS!

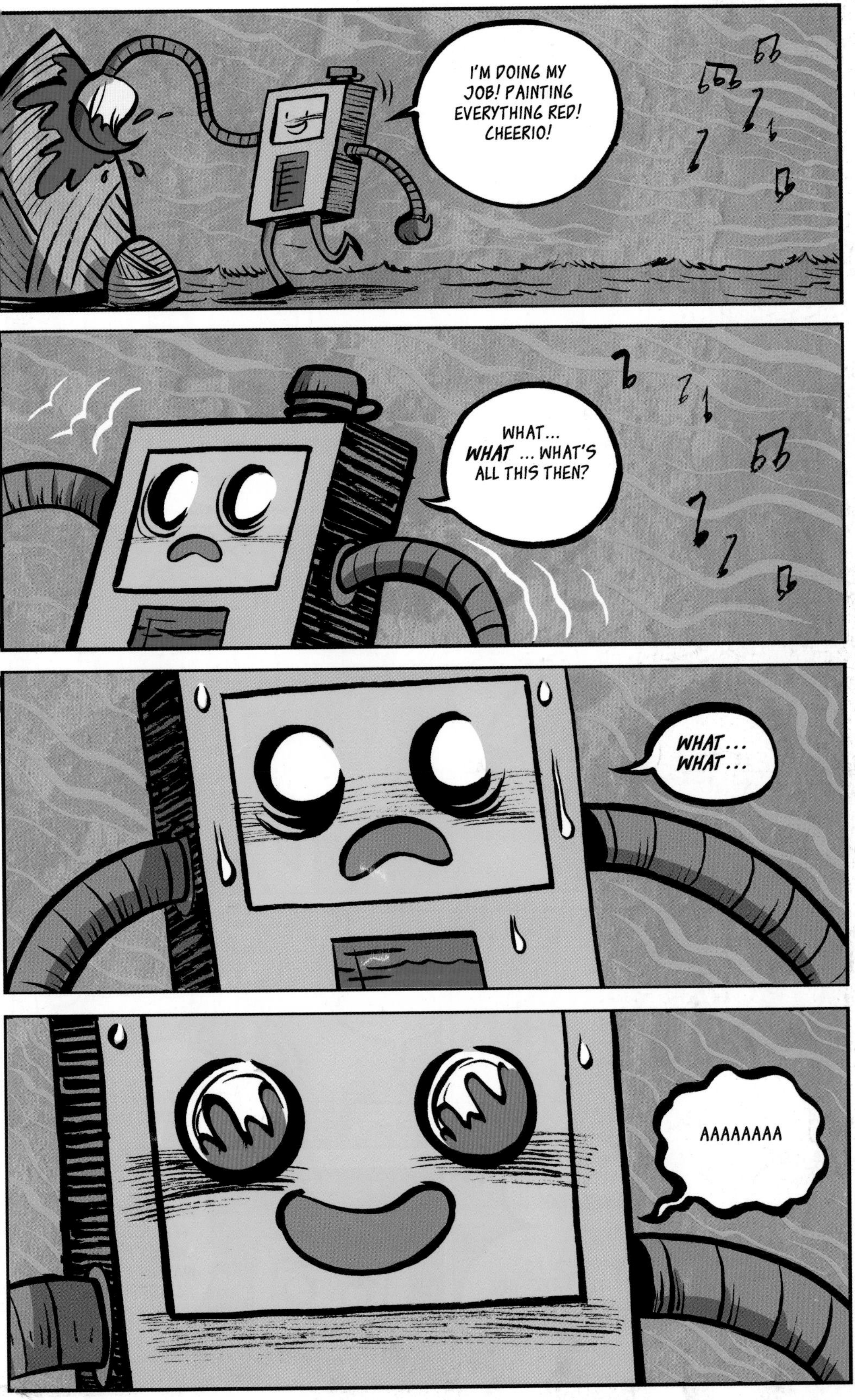
I'M DOING MY JOB! PAINTING EVERYTHING RED! CHEERIO!
WHAT... WHAT ... WHAT'S ALL THIS THEN?
WHAT... WHAT...
AAAAAAAA

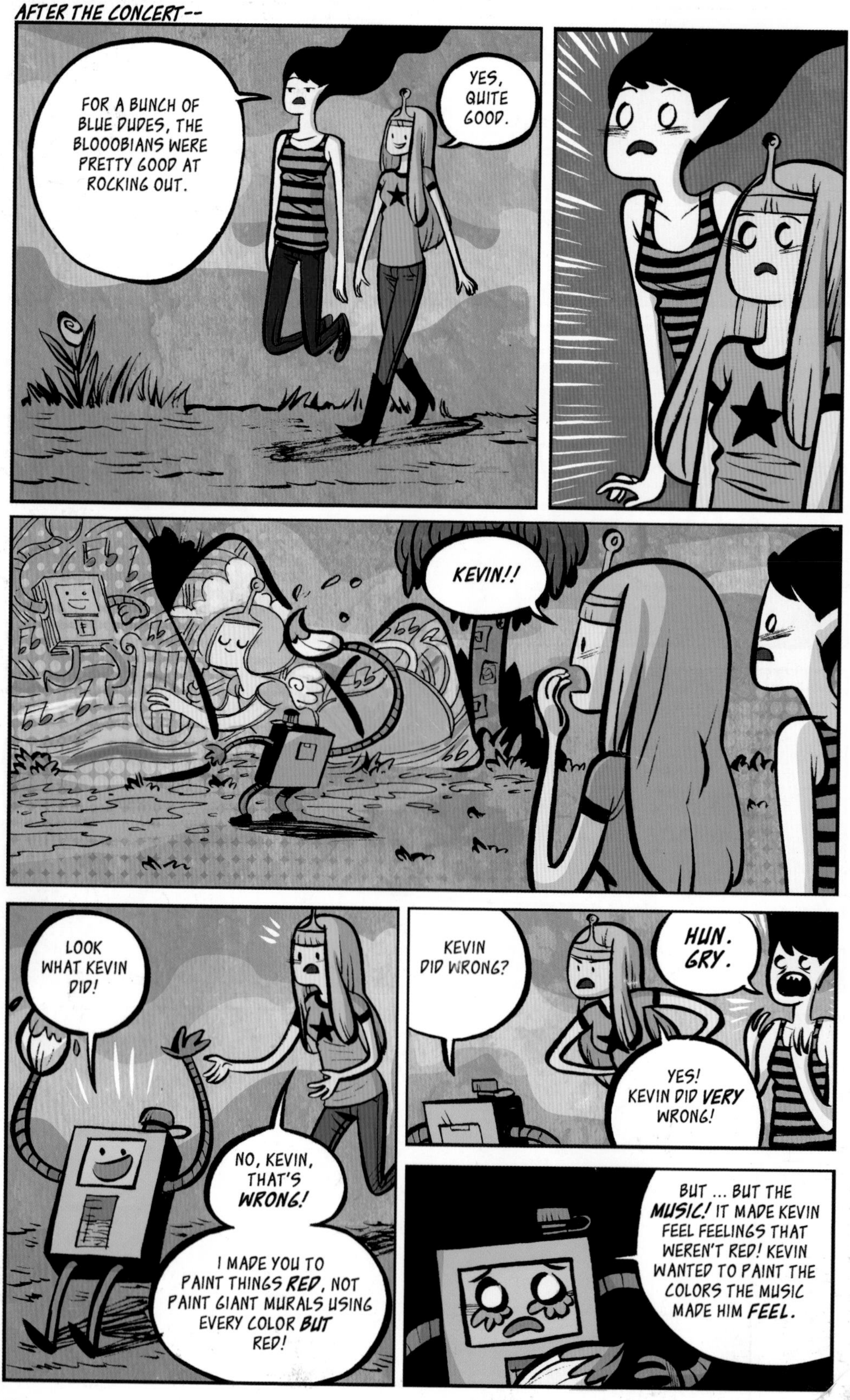

AFTER THE CONCERT--
FOR A BUNCH OF BLUE DUDES, THE BLOOOBIANS WERE PRETTY GOOD AT ROCKING OUT.
YES, QUITE GOOD.
KEVIN!!
LOOK WHAT KEVIN DID!
NO, KEVIN, THAT'S WRONG!
I MADE YOU TO PAINT THINGS RED, NOT PAINT GIANT MURALS USING EVERY COLOR BUT RED!
KEVIN DID WRONG?
HUN. GRY.
YES! KEVIN DID VERY WRONG!
BUT ... BUT THE MUSIC! IT MADE KEVIN FEEL FEELINGS THAT WEREN'T RED! KEVIN WANTED TO PAINT THE COLORS THE MUSIC MADE HIM FEEL.

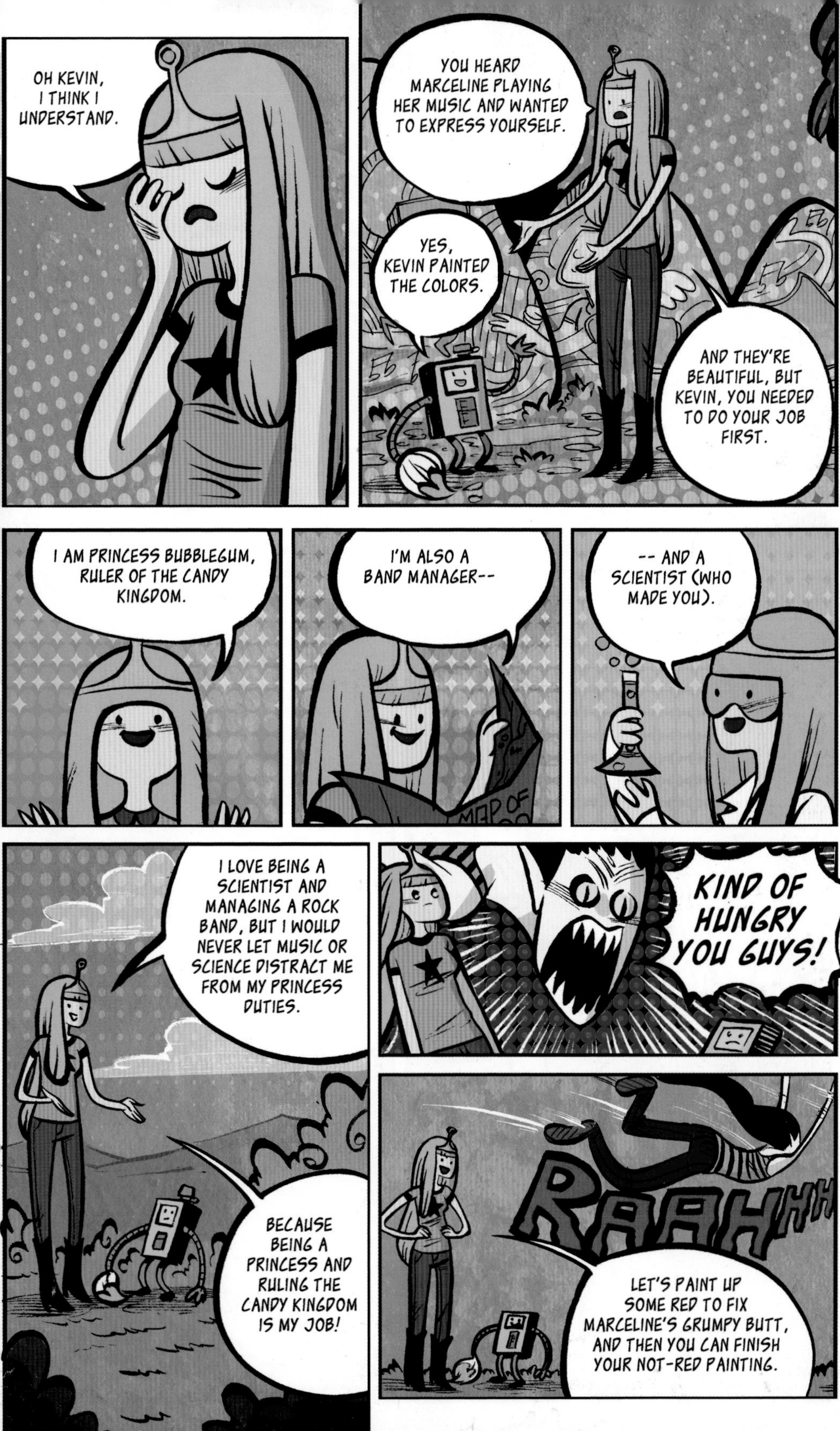
OH KEVIN, I THINK I UNDERSTAND.
YOU HEARD MARCELINE PLAYING HER MUSIC AND WANTED TO EXPRESS YOURSELF.
YES, KEVIN PAINTED THE COLORS.
AND THEY'RE BEAUTIFUL, BUT KEVIN, YOU NEEDED TO DO YOUR JOB FIRST.
I AM PRINCESS BUBBLEGUM, RULER OF THE CANDY KINGDOM.
I'M ALSO A BAND MANAGER--
-- AND A SCIENTIST (WHO MADE YOU).
I LOVE BEING A SCIENTIST AND MANAGING A ROCK BAND, BUT I WOULD NEVER LET MUSIC OR SCIENCE DISTRACT ME FROM MY PRINCESS DUTIES.
BECAUSE BEING A PRINCESS AND RULING THE CANDY KINGDOM IS MY JOB!
KIND OF HUNGRY YOU GUYS!
RAAHHH
LET'S PAINT UP SOME RED TO FIX MARCELINE'S GRUMPY BUTT, AND THEN YOU CAN FINISH YOUR NOT-RED PAINTING.

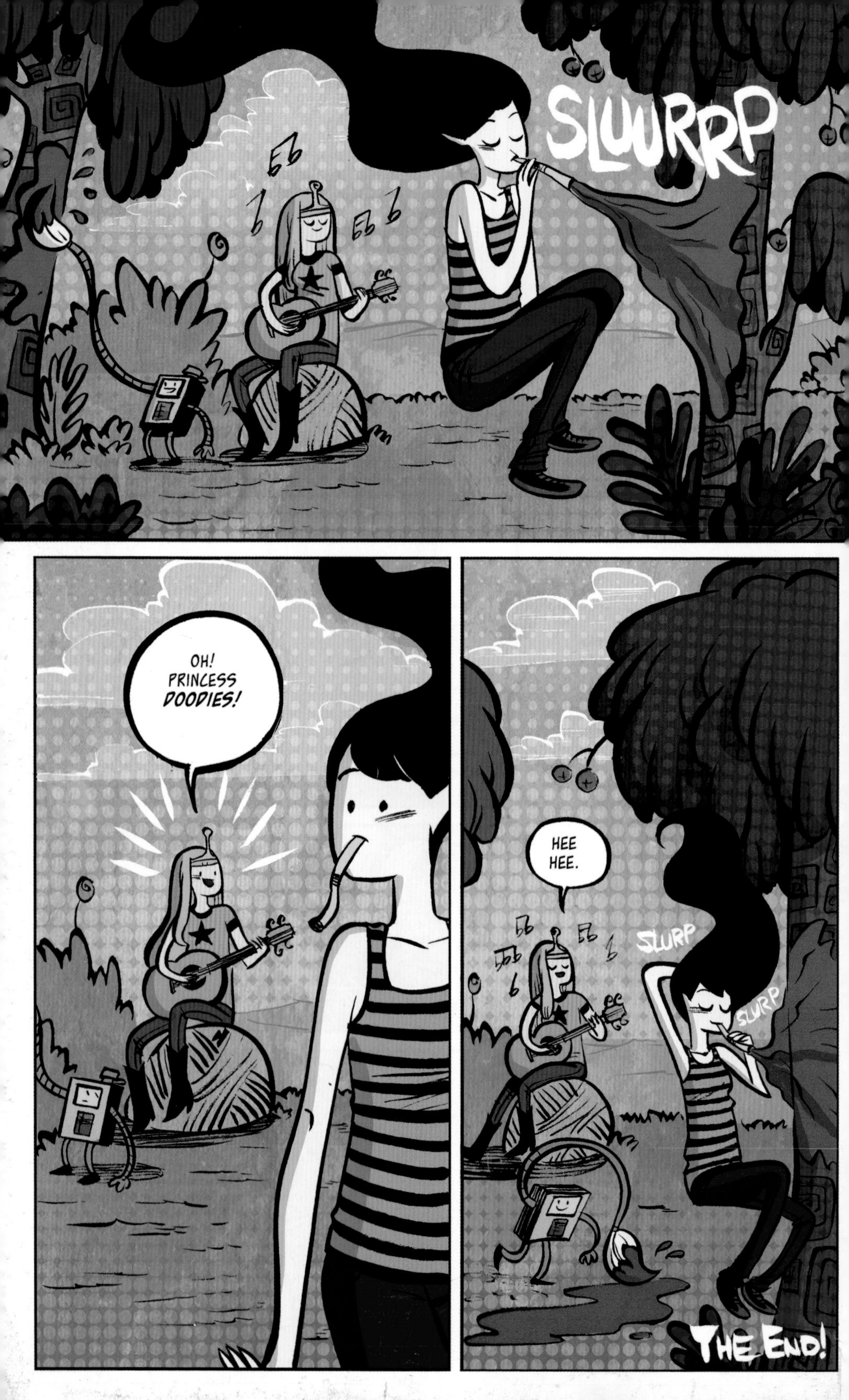
SLUURRP
OH! PRINCESS DOODIES!
HEE HEE.
SLURP
SLURP
THE END!

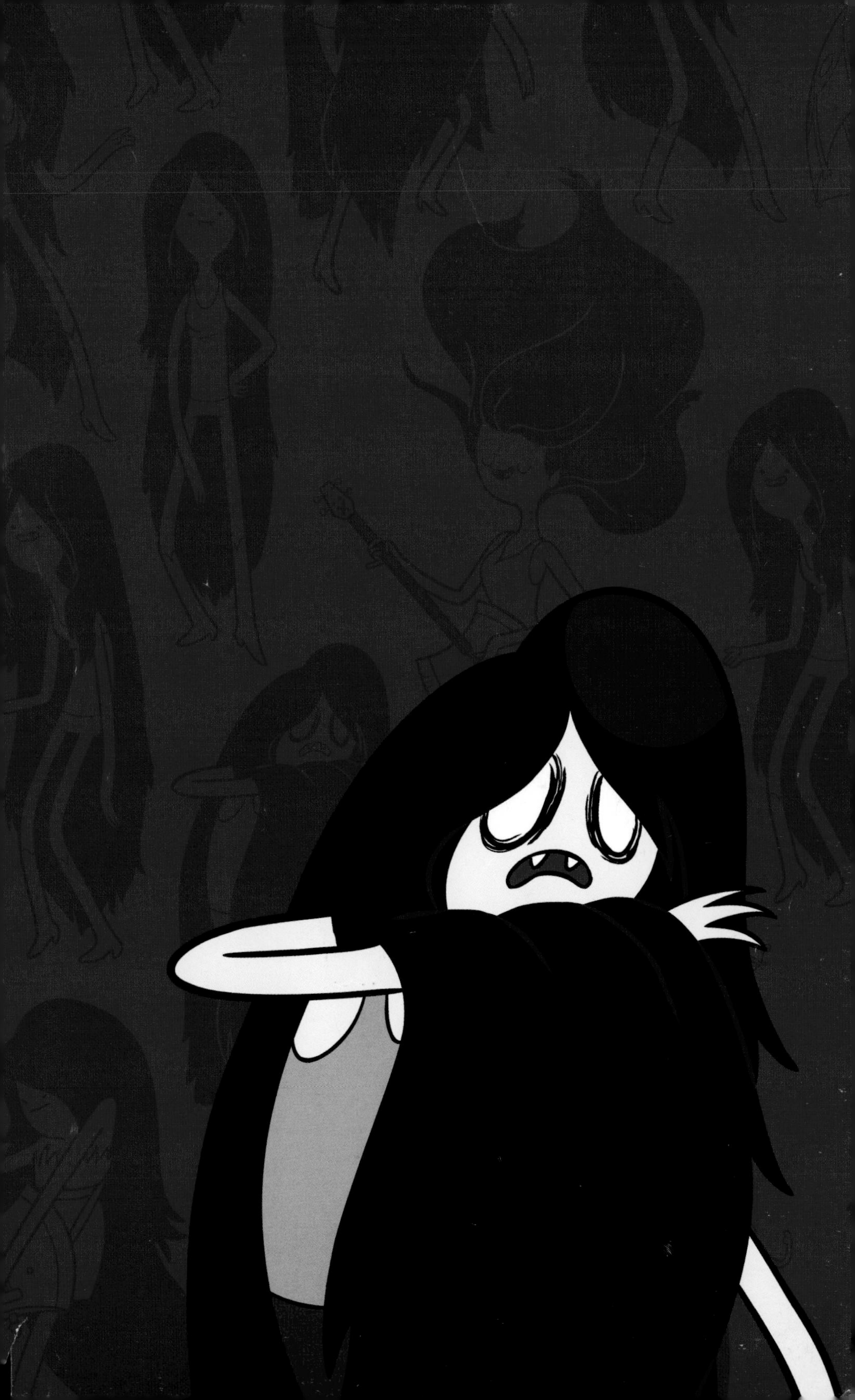

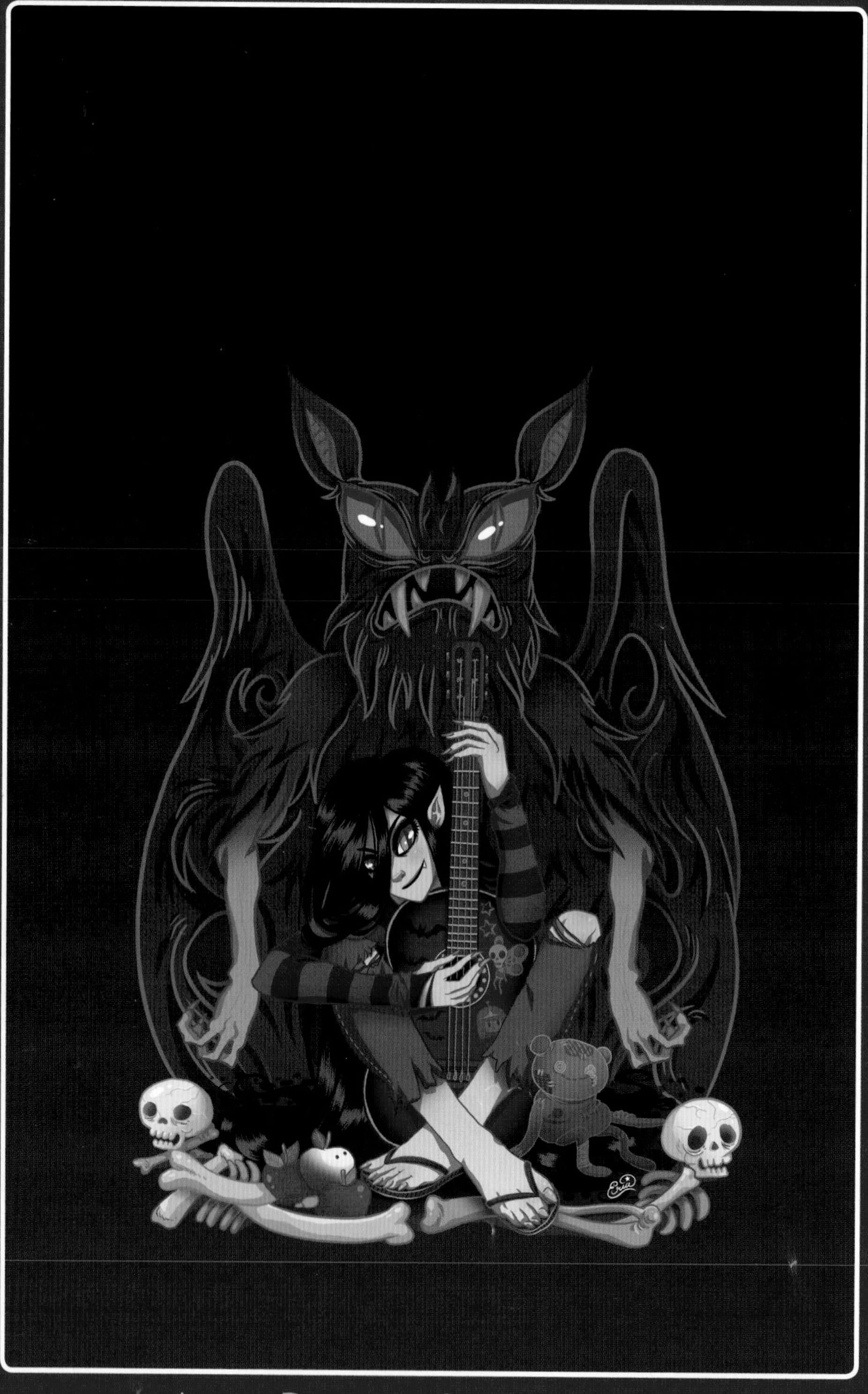

Adventure Time #24 Cover D by **Eva Cabrera**

"Bad Girl Gone Good"

Written by **Kevin Church**

Illustrated by **Jen Vaughn**

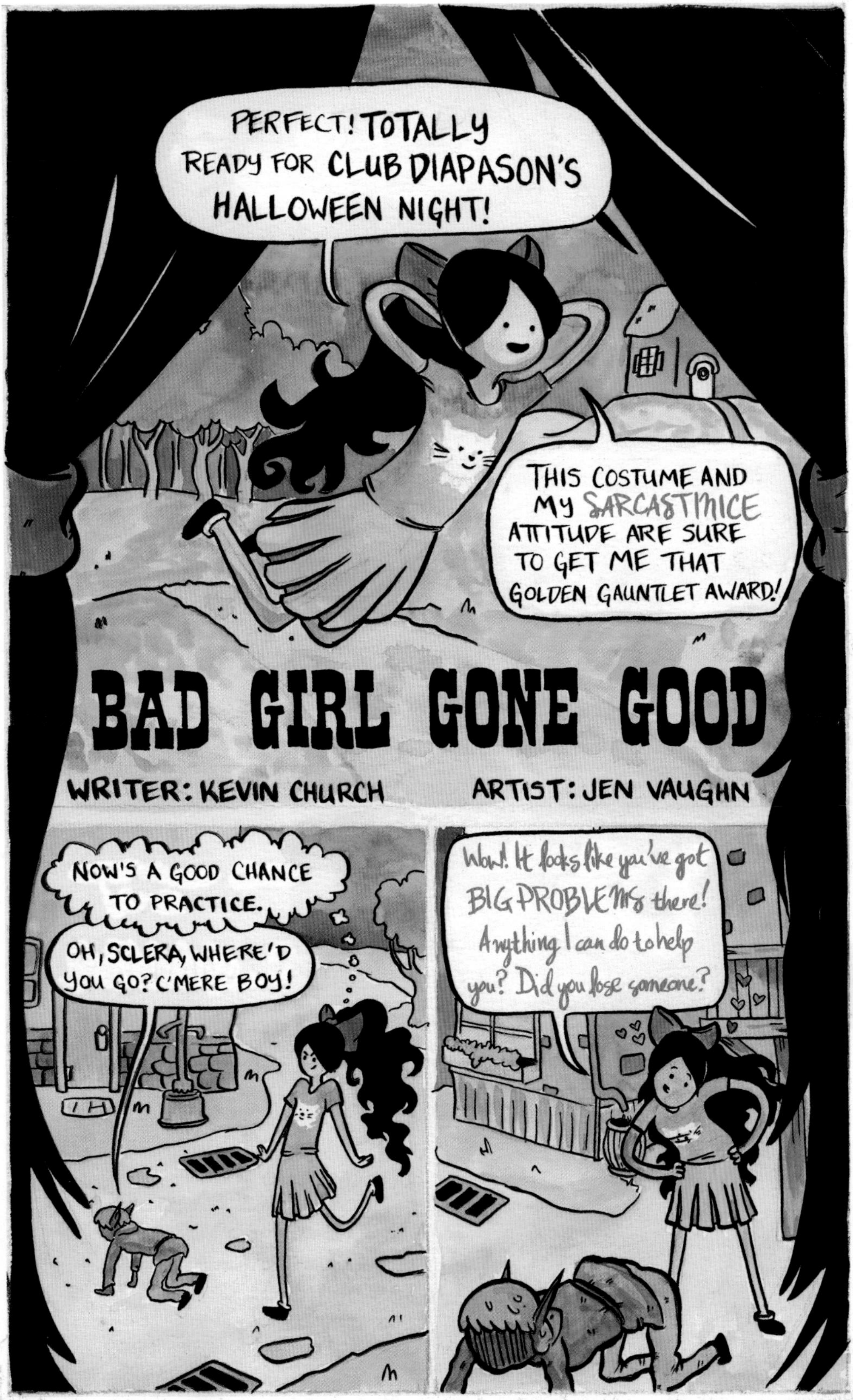
PERFECT! TOTALLY READY FOR CLUB DIAPASON'S HALLOWEEN NIGHT!
THIS COSTUME AND MY SARCASTIMICE ATTITUDE ARE SURE TO GET ME THAT GOLDEN GAUNTLET AWARD!
BAD GIRL GONE GOOD
WRITER: KEVIN CHURCH
ARTIST: JEN VAUGHN
NOW'S A GOOD CHANCE TO PRACTICE.
OH, SCLERA, WHERE'D YOU GO? C'MERE BOY!
Wow! It looks like you've got BIG PROBLEMS there! Anything I can do to help you? Did you lose someone?

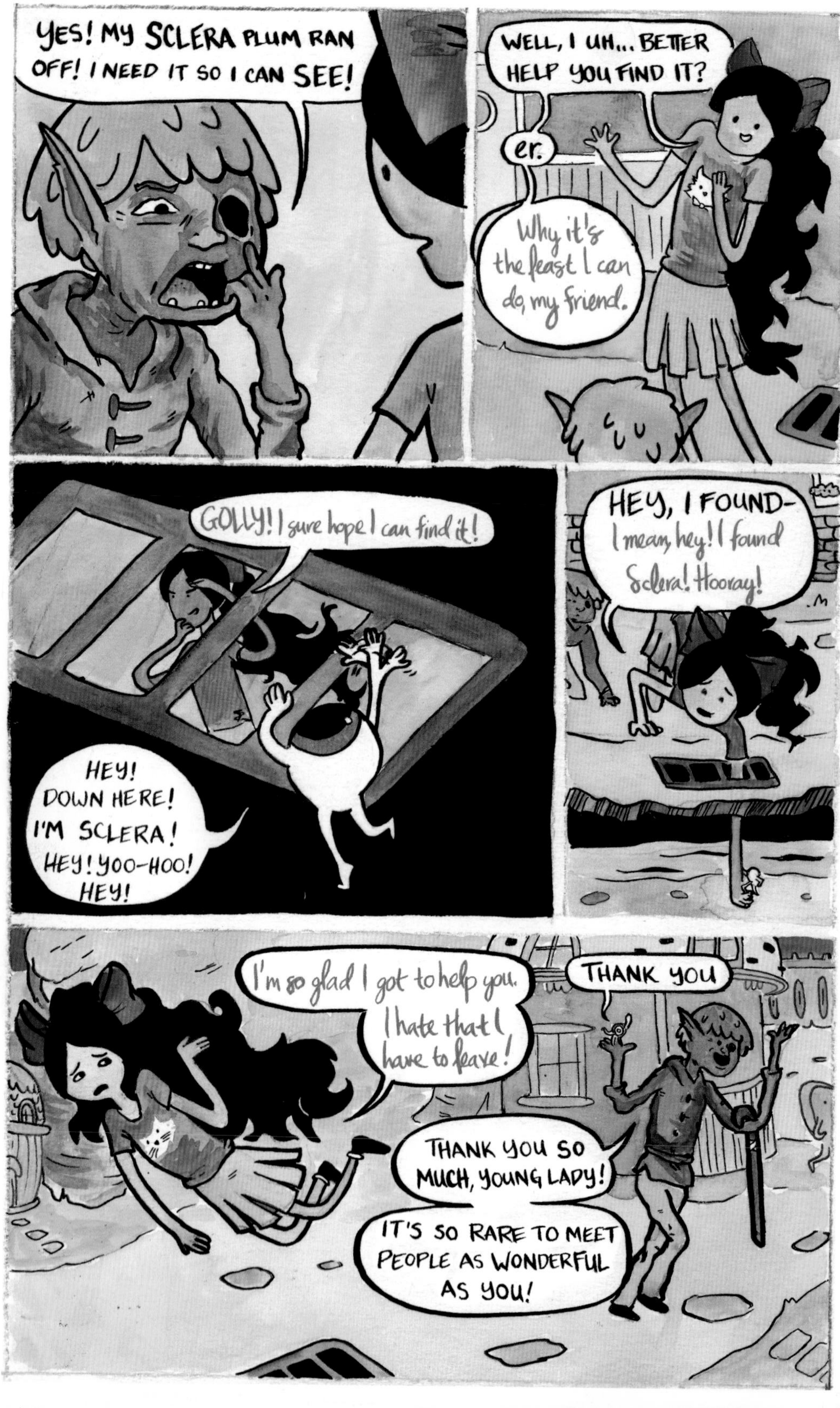
YES! MY SCLERA PLUM RAN OFF! I NEED IT SO I CAN SEE!
WELL, I UH... BETTER HELP YOU FIND IT?
er.
Why it's the least I can do, my friend.
GOLLY! I sure hope I can find it!
HEY! DOWN HERE! I'M SCLERA! HEY! YOO-HOO! HEY!
HEY, I FOUND- I mean, hey! I found Sclera! Hooray!
I'm so glad I got to help you. I hate that I have to leave!
THANK YOU
THANK YOU SO MUCH, YOUNG LADY!
IT'S SO RARE TO MEET PEOPLE AS WONDERFUL AS YOU!

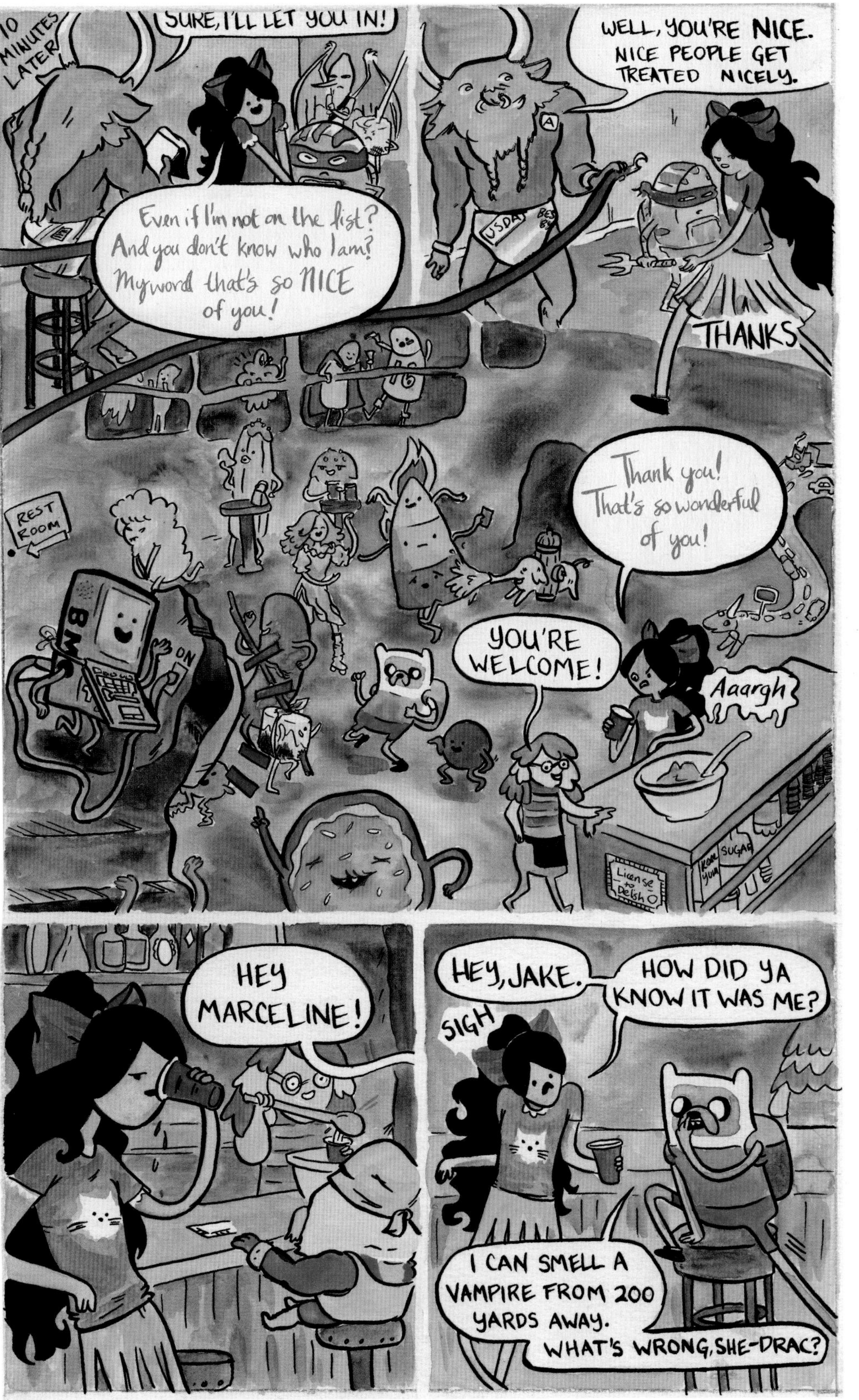

10 MINUTES LATER
SURE, I'LL LET YOU IN!
Even if I'm not on the list? And you don't know who I am? My word that's so NICE of you!
WELL, YOU'RE NICE. NICE PEOPLE GET TREATED NICELY.
USDA
THANKS
REST ROOM
BMO
ON
Thank you! That's so wonderful of you!
YOU'RE WELCOME!
Aaargh
License to Delsh
KOOL YUM
SUGAR
HEY MARCELINE!
HEY, JAKE.
HOW DID YA KNOW IT WAS ME?
SIGH
I CAN SMELL A VAMPIRE FROM 200 YARDS AWAY.
WHAT'S WRONG, SHE-DRAC?

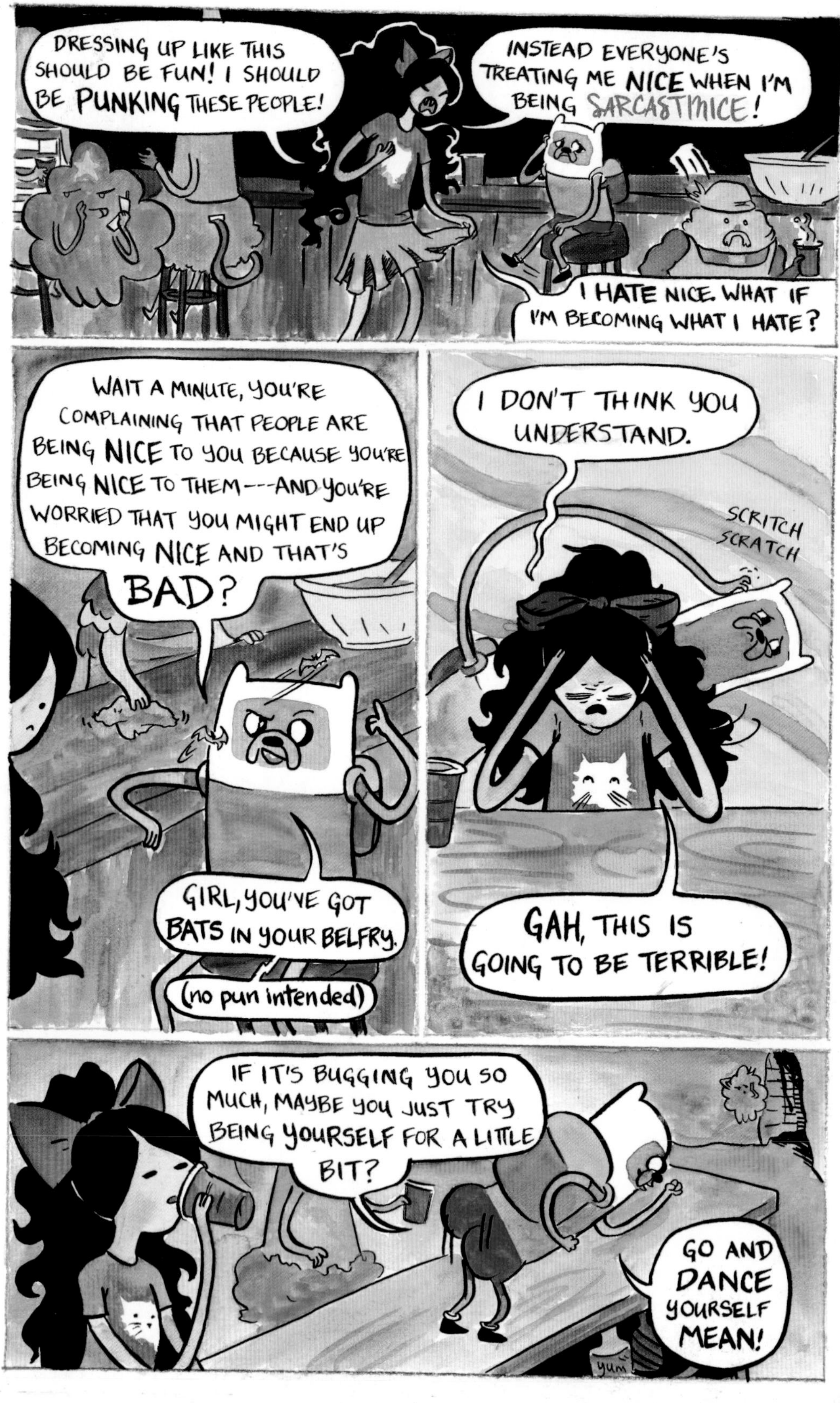
DRESSING UP LIKE THIS SHOULD BE FUN! I SHOULD BE PUNKING THESE PEOPLE!
INSTEAD EVERYONE'S TREATING ME NICE WHEN I'M BEING SARCASTMICE!
I HATE NICE. WHAT IF I'M BECOMING WHAT I HATE?
WAIT A MINUTE, YOU'RE COMPLAINING THAT PEOPLE ARE BEING NICE TO YOU BECAUSE YOU'RE BEING NICE TO THEM---AND YOU'RE WORRIED THAT YOU MIGHT END UP BECOMING NICE AND THAT'S BAD?
GIRL, YOU'VE GOT BATS IN YOUR BELFRY.
(no pun intended)
I DON'T THINK YOU UNDERSTAND.
SCRITCH SCRATCH
GAH, THIS IS GOING TO BE TERRIBLE!
IF IT'S BUGGING YOU SO MUCH, MAYBE YOU JUST TRY BEING YOURSELF FOR A LITTLE BIT?
GO AND DANCE YOURSELF MEAN!
yum

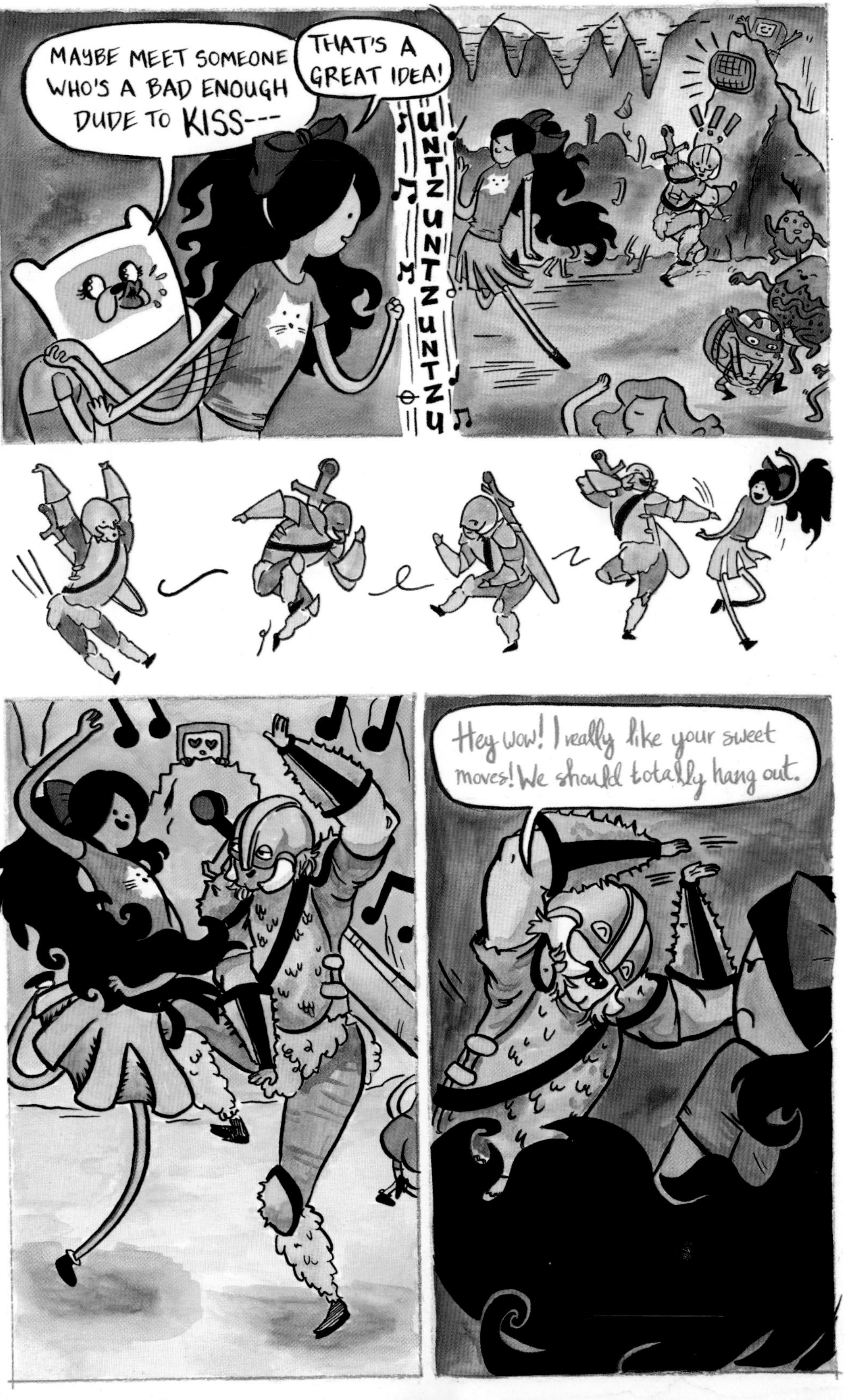
MAYBE MEET SOMEONE WHO'S A BAD ENOUGH DUDE TO KISS---
THAT'S A GREAT IDEA!
UNTZ UNTZ UNTZ UNTZ U
Hey wow! I really like your sweet moves! We should totally hang out.

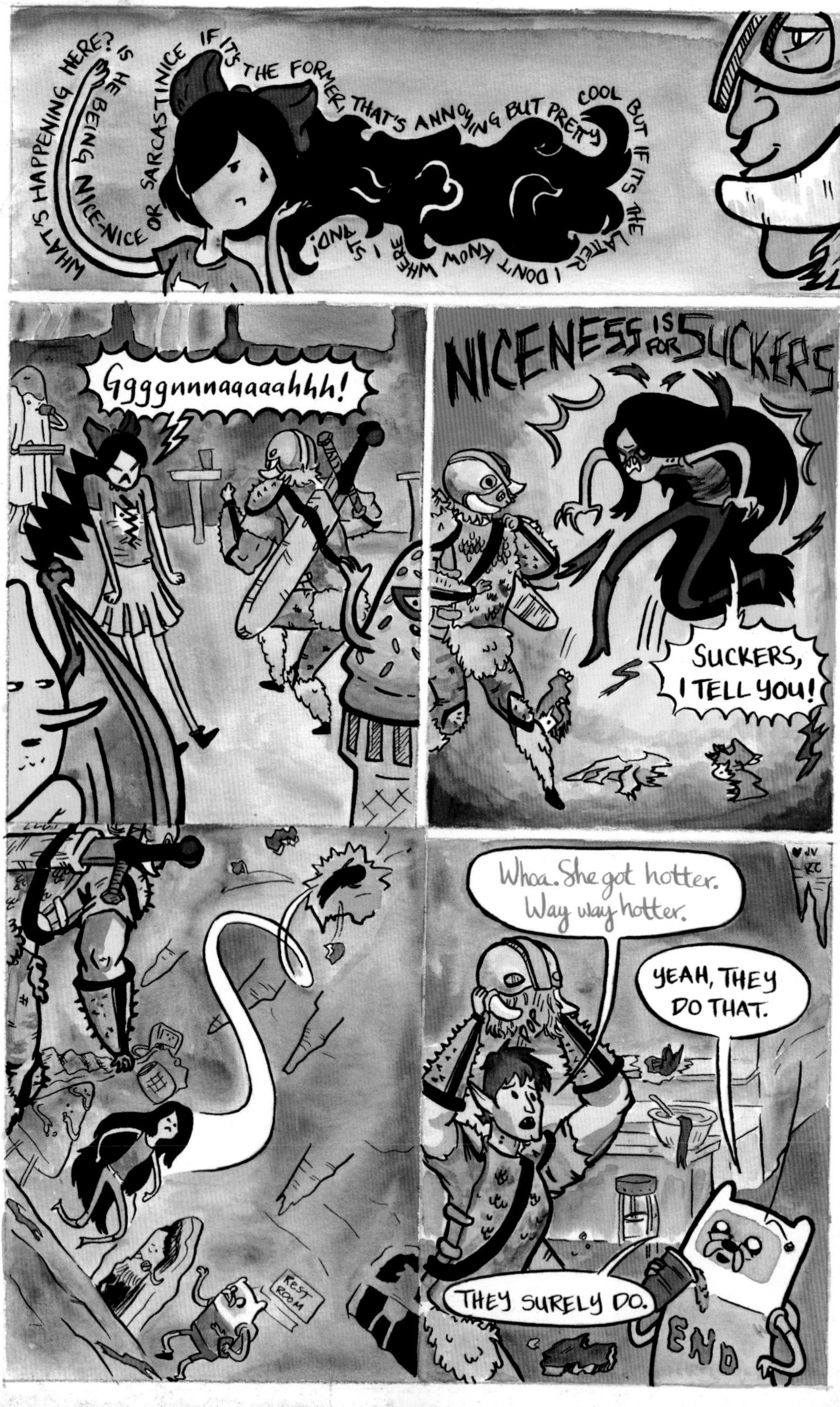
WHAT'S HAPPENING HERE? IS HE BEING NICE-NICE OR SARCASTINICE IF IT'S THE FORMER, THAT'S ANNOYING BUT PRETTY COOL BUT IF ITS THE LATTER I DON'T KNOW WHERE I STAND!
Ggggnnnaaaaahhh!
NICENESS IS FOR SUCKERS
SUCKERS, I TELL YOU!
REST ROOM
Whoa. She got hotter. Way way hotter.
YEAH, THEY DO THAT.
THEY SURELY DO.
END

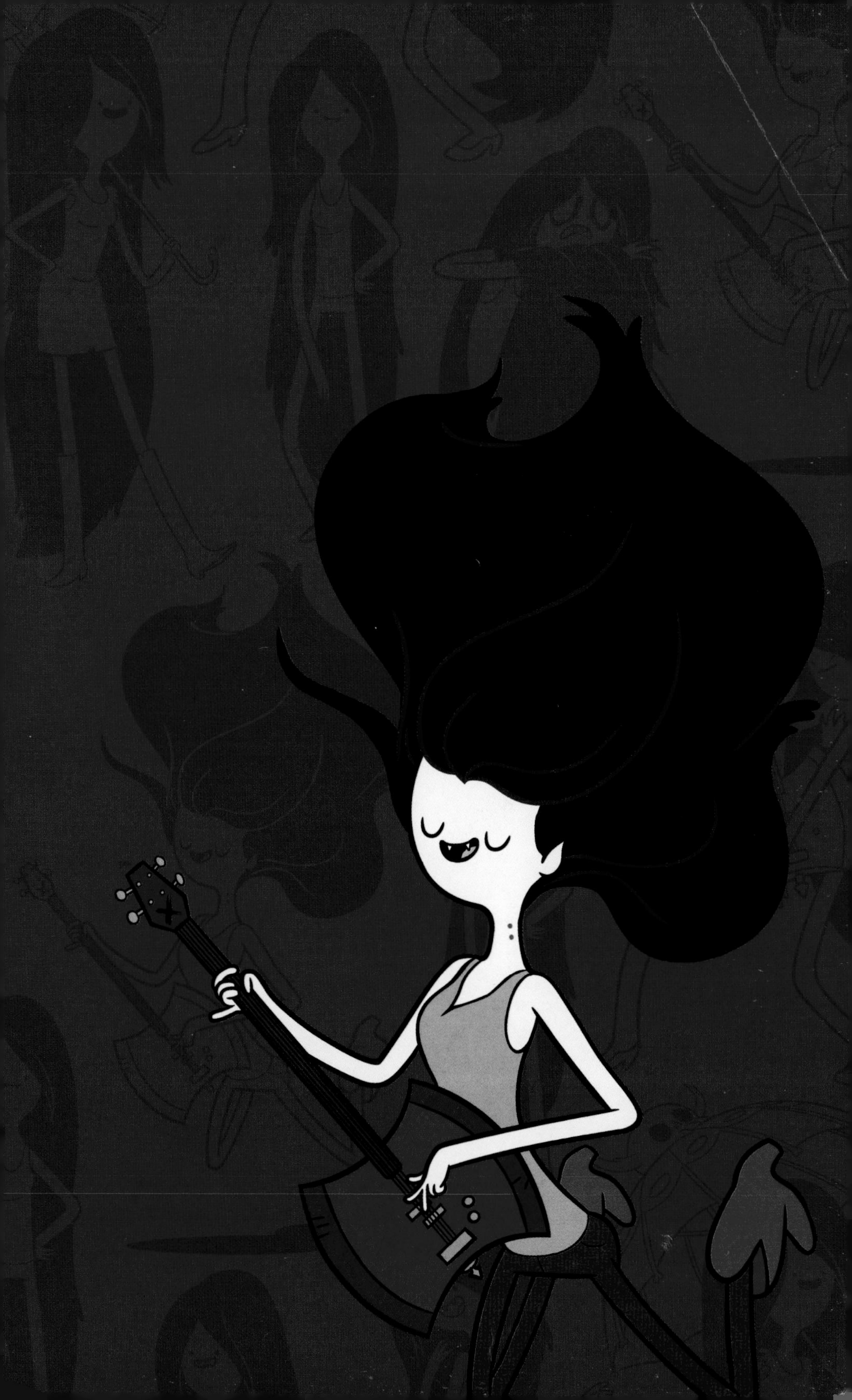

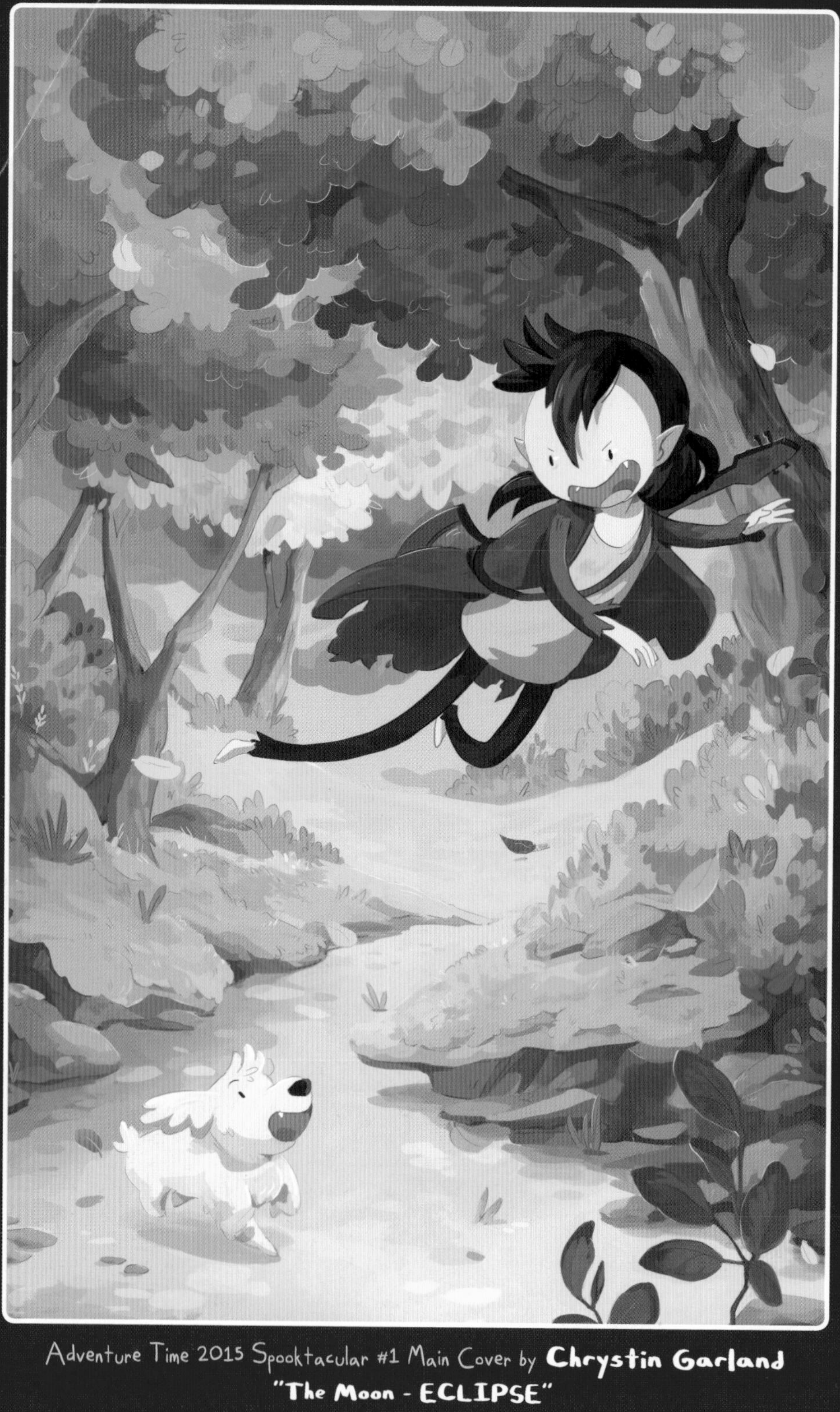

Adventure Time 2015 Spooktacular #1 Main Cover by **Chrystin Garland**

"The Moon - ECLIPSE"

Written & Illustrated by **Hanna K**

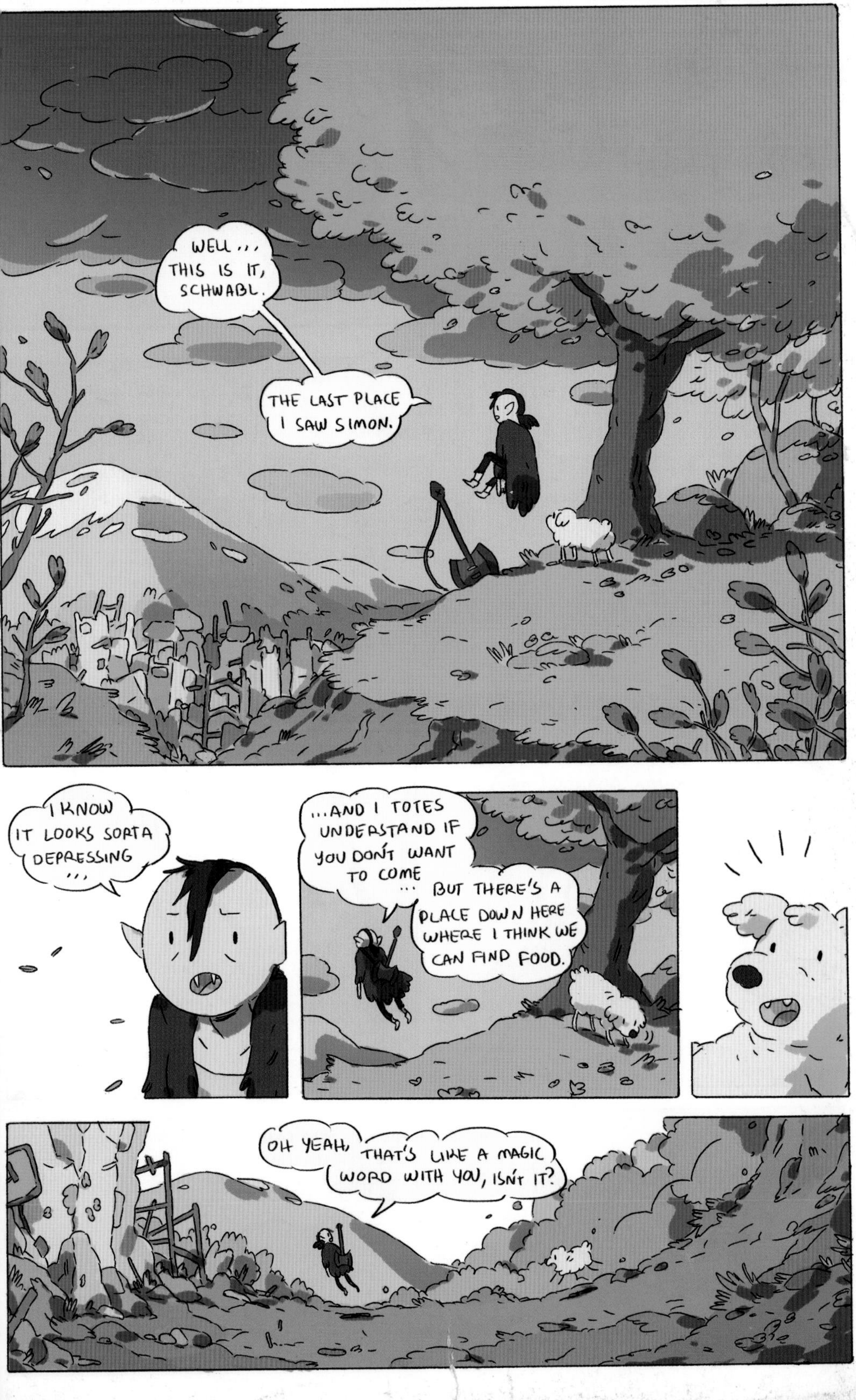
WELL... THIS IS IT, SCHWABL.
THE LAST PLACE I SAW SIMON.
I KNOW IT LOOKS SORTA DEPRESSING ...
...AND I TOTES UNDERSTAND IF YOU DON'T WANT TO COME ...
BUT THERE'S A PLACE DOWN HERE WHERE I THINK WE CAN FIND FOOD.
OH YEAH, THAT'S LIKE A MAGIC WORD WITH YOU, ISN'T IT?

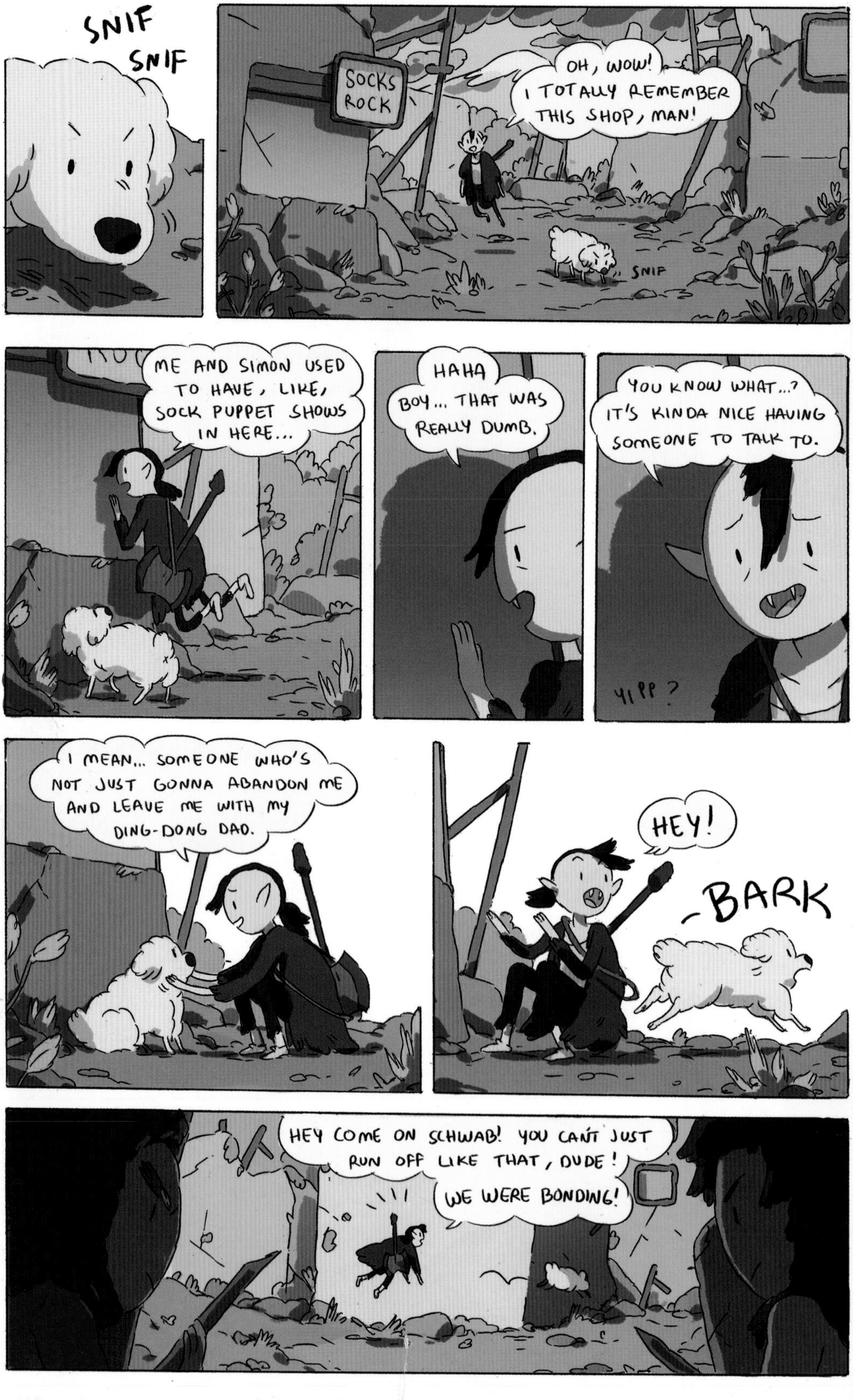
SNIF
SNIF
SOCKS ROCK
OH, WOW! I TOTALLY REMEMBER THIS SHOP, MAN!
SNIF
ME AND SIMON USED TO HAVE, LIKE, SOCK PUPPET SHOWS IN HERE...
HAHA BOY... THAT WAS REALLY DUMB.
YOU KNOW WHAT...? IT'S KINDA NICE HAVING SOMEONE TO TALK TO.
YIPP?
I MEAN... SOMEONE WHO'S NOT JUST GONNA ABANDON ME AND LEAVE ME WITH MY DING-DONG DAD.
HEY!
BARK
HEY COME ON SCHWAB! YOU CAN'T JUST RUN OFF LIKE THAT, DUDE!
WE WERE BONDING!

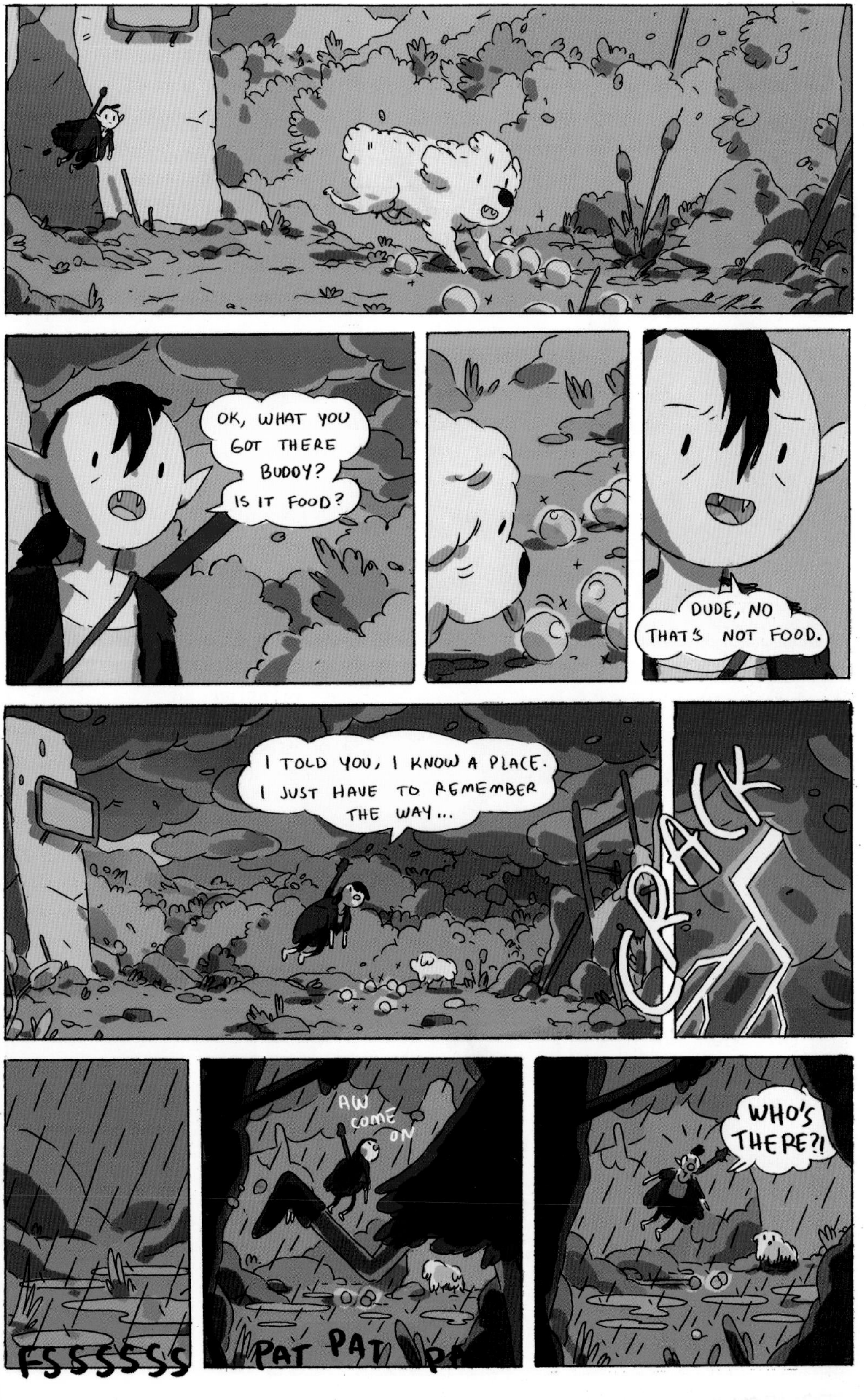
OK, WHAT YOU GOT THERE BUDDY? IS IT FOOD?
DUDE, NO THAT'S NOT FOOD.
I TOLD YOU, I KNOW A PLACE. I JUST HAVE TO REMEMBER THE WAY...
CRACK
FSSSSSS
AW COME ON
PAT PAT PA
WHO'S THERE?!

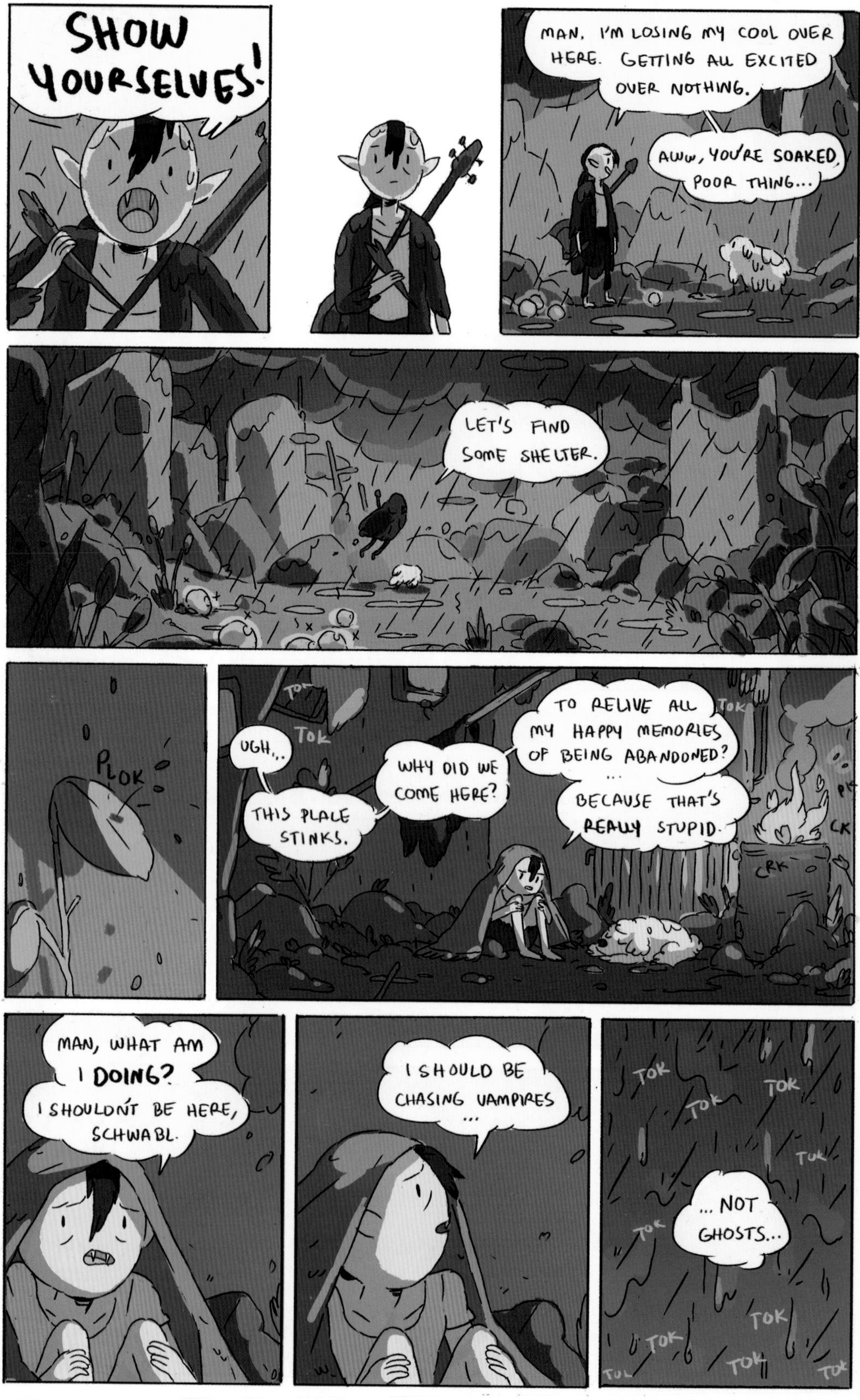
SHOW YOURSELVES!
MAN. I'M LOSING MY COOL OVER HERE. GETTING ALL EXCITED OVER NOTHING.
AWW, YOU'RE SOAKED, POOR THING...
LET'S FIND SOME SHELTER.
PLOK
TOK
TOK
UGH...
THIS PLACE STINKS.
WHY DID WE COME HERE?
TO RELIVE ALL MY HAPPY MEMORIES OF BEING ABANDONED? ...
BECAUSE THAT'S REALLY STUPID.
TOK
CRK
MAN, WHAT AM I DOING?
I SHOULDN'T BE HERE, SCHWABL.
I SHOULD BE CHASING VAMPIRES ...
TOK
TOK
TOK
TOK
... NOT GHOSTS...
TOK
TOK
TOK
TOK

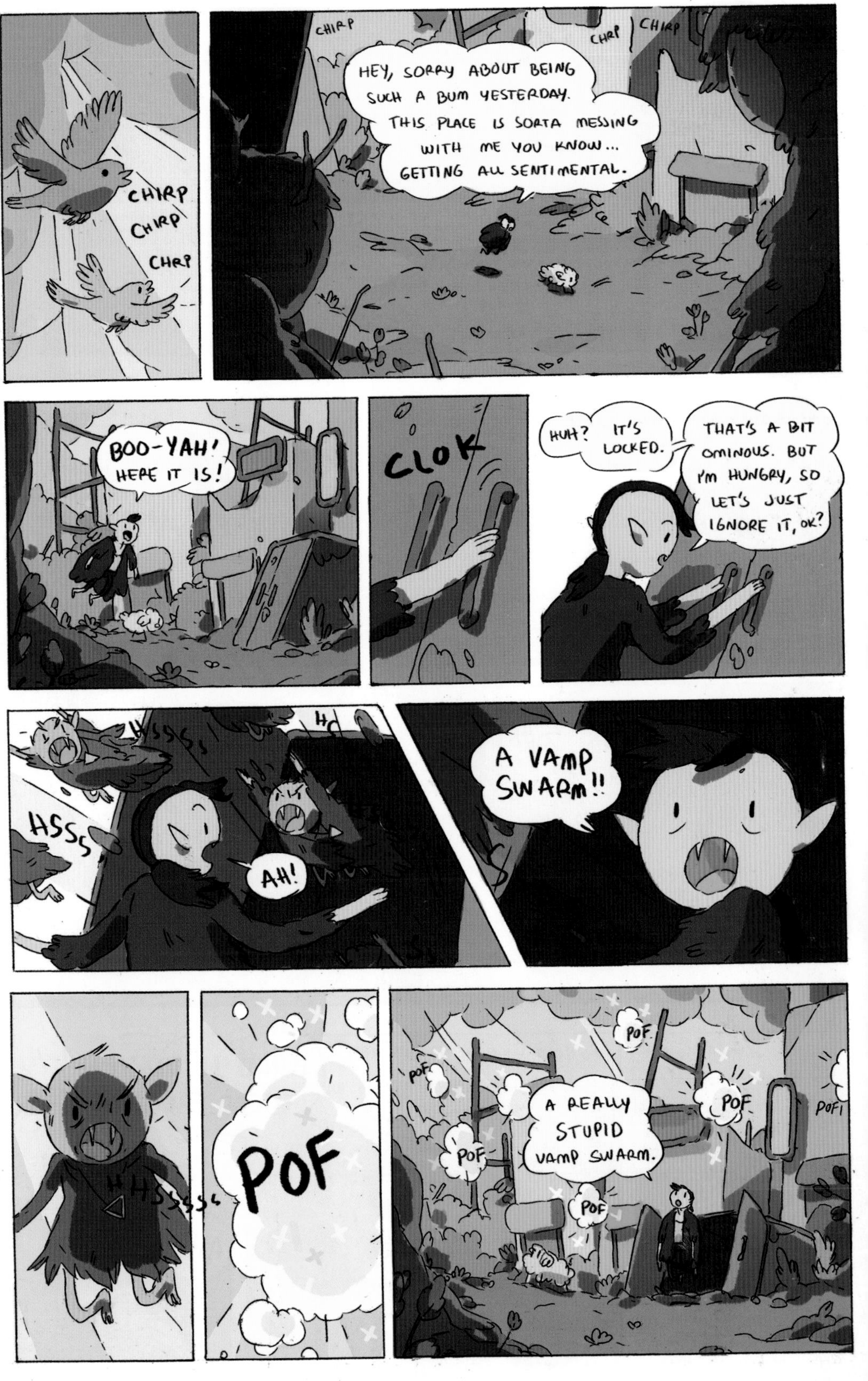

CHIRP
CHIRP
CHRP
CHIRP
CHRP
CHIRP
HEY, SORRY ABOUT BEING SUCH A BUM YESTERDAY. THIS PLACE IS SORTA MESSING WITH ME YOU KNOW... GETTING ALL SENTIMENTAL.
BOO-YAH! HERE IT IS!
CLOK
HUH? IT'S LOCKED.
THAT'S A BIT OMINOUS. BUT I'M HUNGRY, SO LET'S JUST IGNORE IT, OK?
HSSSS
HSSS
AH!
A VAMP SWARM!!
HHSSSSS
POF
POF
POF
POF
POF
POF
POF!
A REALLY STUPID VAMP SWARM.

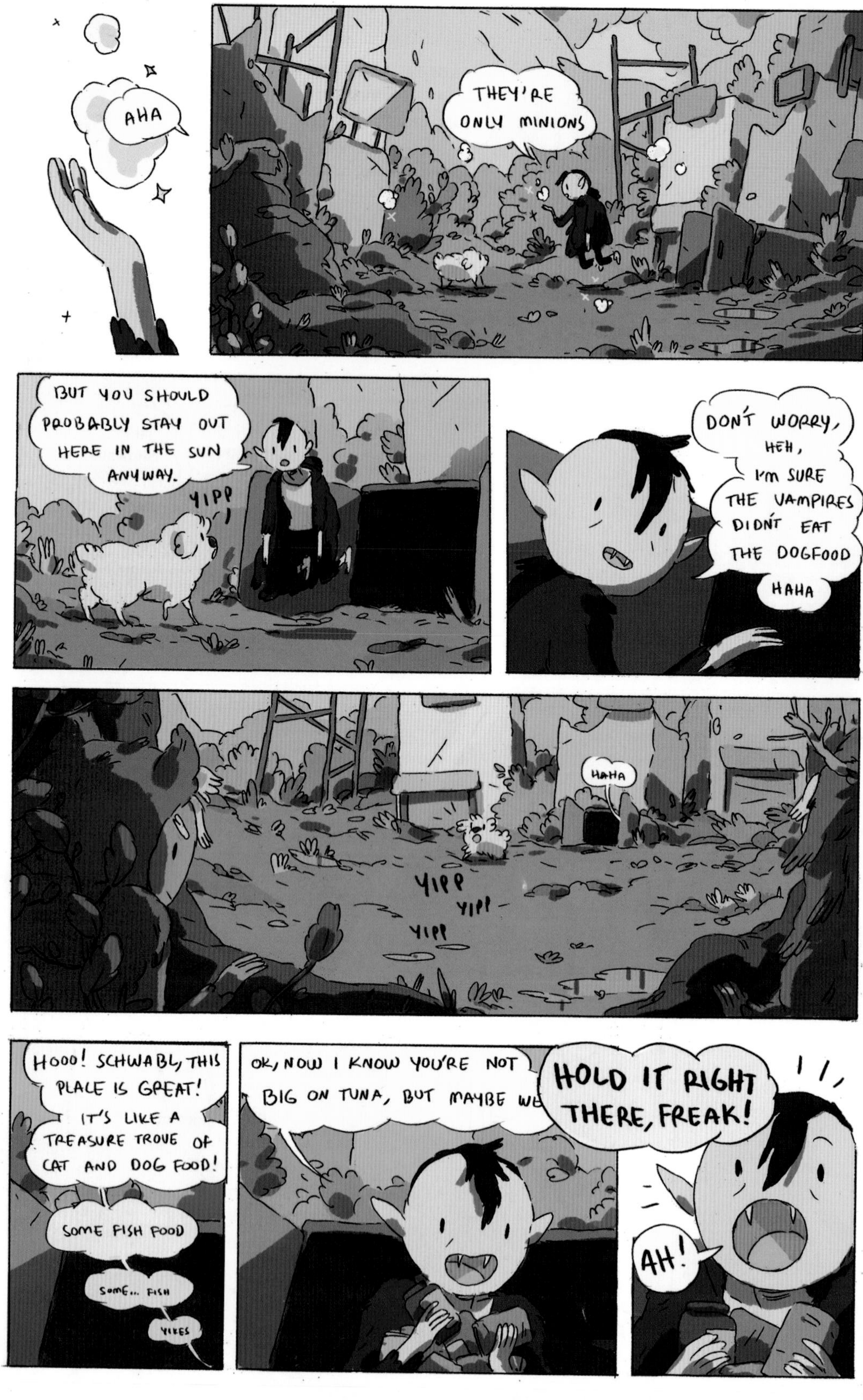
AHA
THEY'RE ONLY MINIONS
BUT YOU SHOULD PROBABLY STAY OUT HERE IN THE SUN ANYWAY.
YIPP
DON'T WORRY, HEH, I'M SURE THE VAMPIRES DIDN'T EAT THE DOGFOOD
HAHA
HAHA
YIPP
YIPP
YIPP
HOOO! SCHWABL, THIS PLACE IS GREAT!
IT'S LIKE A TREASURE TROVE OF CAT AND DOG FOOD!
SOME FISH FOOD
SOME... FISH
YIKES
OK, NOW I KNOW YOU'RE NOT BIG ON TUNA, BUT MAYBE WE
HOLD IT RIGHT THERE, FREAK!
AH!

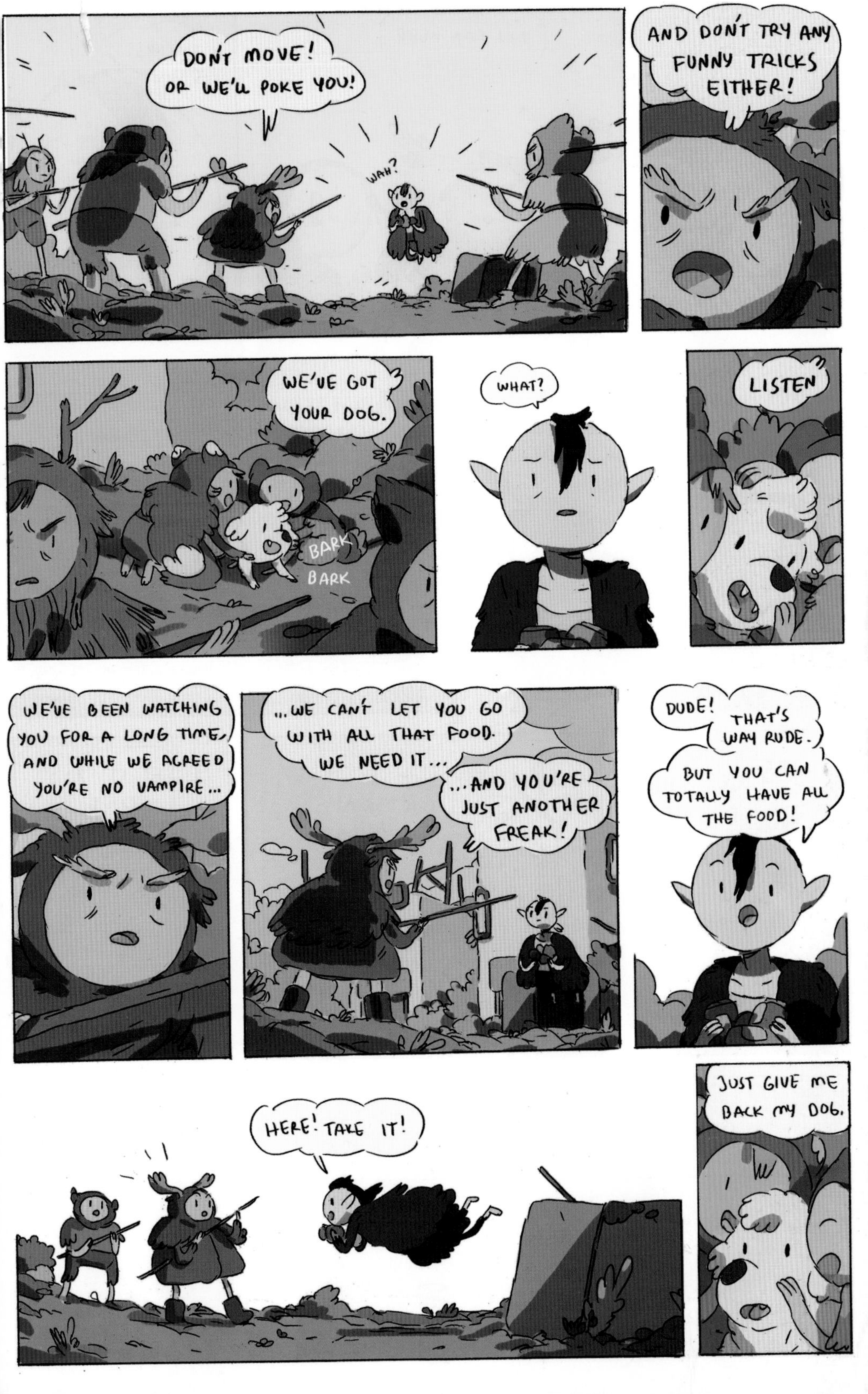
DON'T MOVE! OR WE'LL POKE YOU!
WAH?
AND DON'T TRY ANY FUNNY TRICKS EITHER!
WE'VE GOT YOUR DOG.
BARK
BARK
WHAT?
LISTEN
WE'VE BEEN WATCHING YOU FOR A LONG TIME, AND WHILE WE AGREED YOU'RE NO VAMPIRE...
...WE CAN'T LET YOU GO WITH ALL THAT FOOD. WE NEED IT...
...AND YOU'RE JUST ANOTHER FREAK!
DUDE!
THAT'S WAY RUDE.
BUT YOU CAN TOTALLY HAVE ALL THE FOOD!
HERE! TAKE IT!
JUST GIVE ME BACK MY DOG.

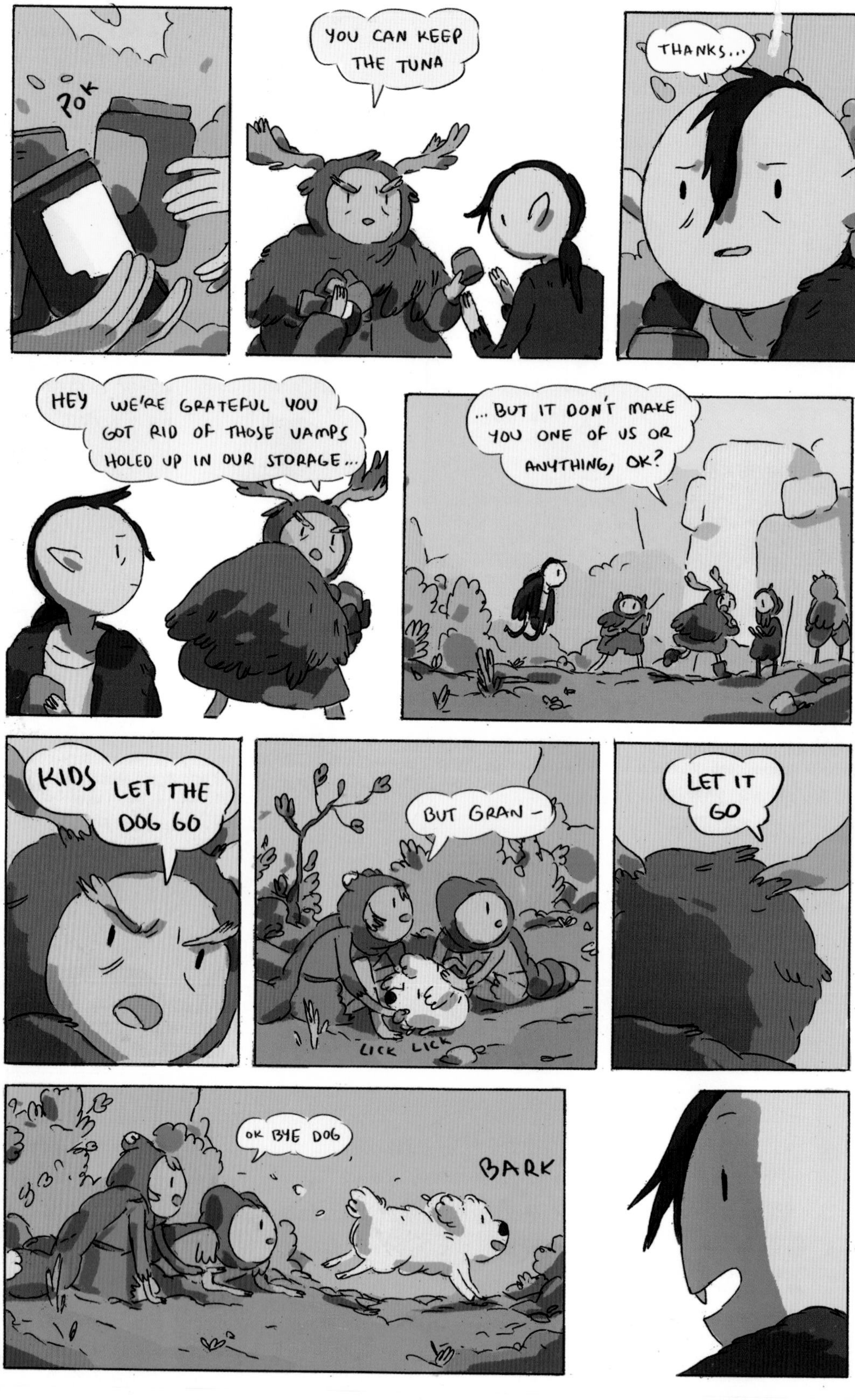
POK
YOU CAN KEEP THE TUNA
THANKS...
HEY WE'RE GRATEFUL YOU GOT RID OF THOSE VAMPS HOLED UP IN OUR STORAGE...
...BUT IT DON'T MAKE YOU ONE OF US OR ANYTHING, OK?
KIDS LET THE DOG GO
BUT GRAN -
LICK LICK
LET IT GO
OK BYE DOG
BARK

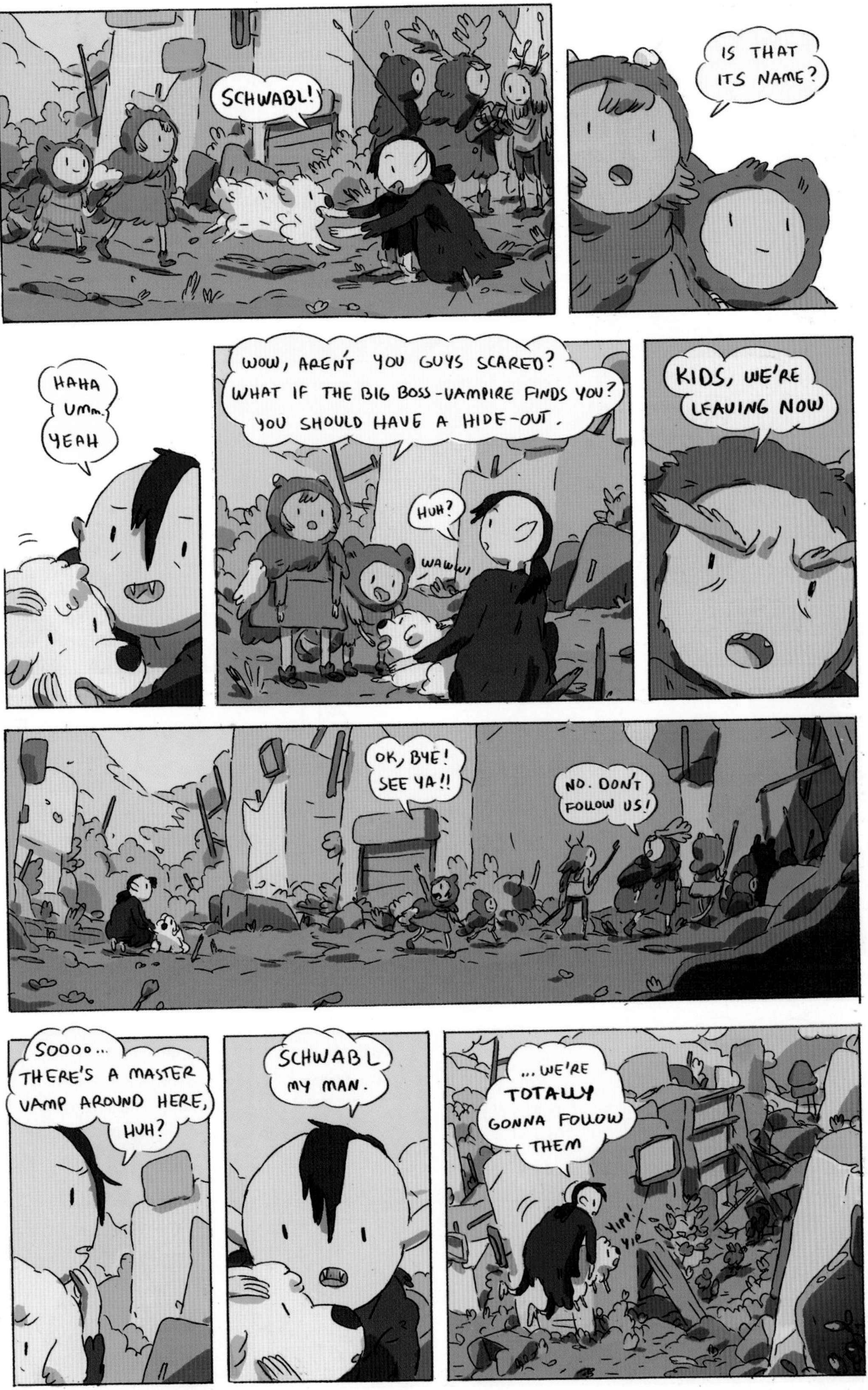
SCHWABL!
IS THAT ITS NAME?
HAHA UMM.. YEAH
WOW, AREN'T YOU GUYS SCARED? WHAT IF THE BIG BOSS-VAMPIRE FINDS YOU? YOU SHOULD HAVE A HIDE-OUT.
HUH?
WAWW!
KIDS, WE'RE LEAVING NOW
OK, BYE! SEE YA!!
NO. DON'T FOLLOW US!
SOOOO... THERE'S A MASTER VAMP AROUND HERE, HUH?
SCHWABL MY MAN.
...WE'RE TOTALLY GONNA FOLLOW THEM
YIPP! YIP

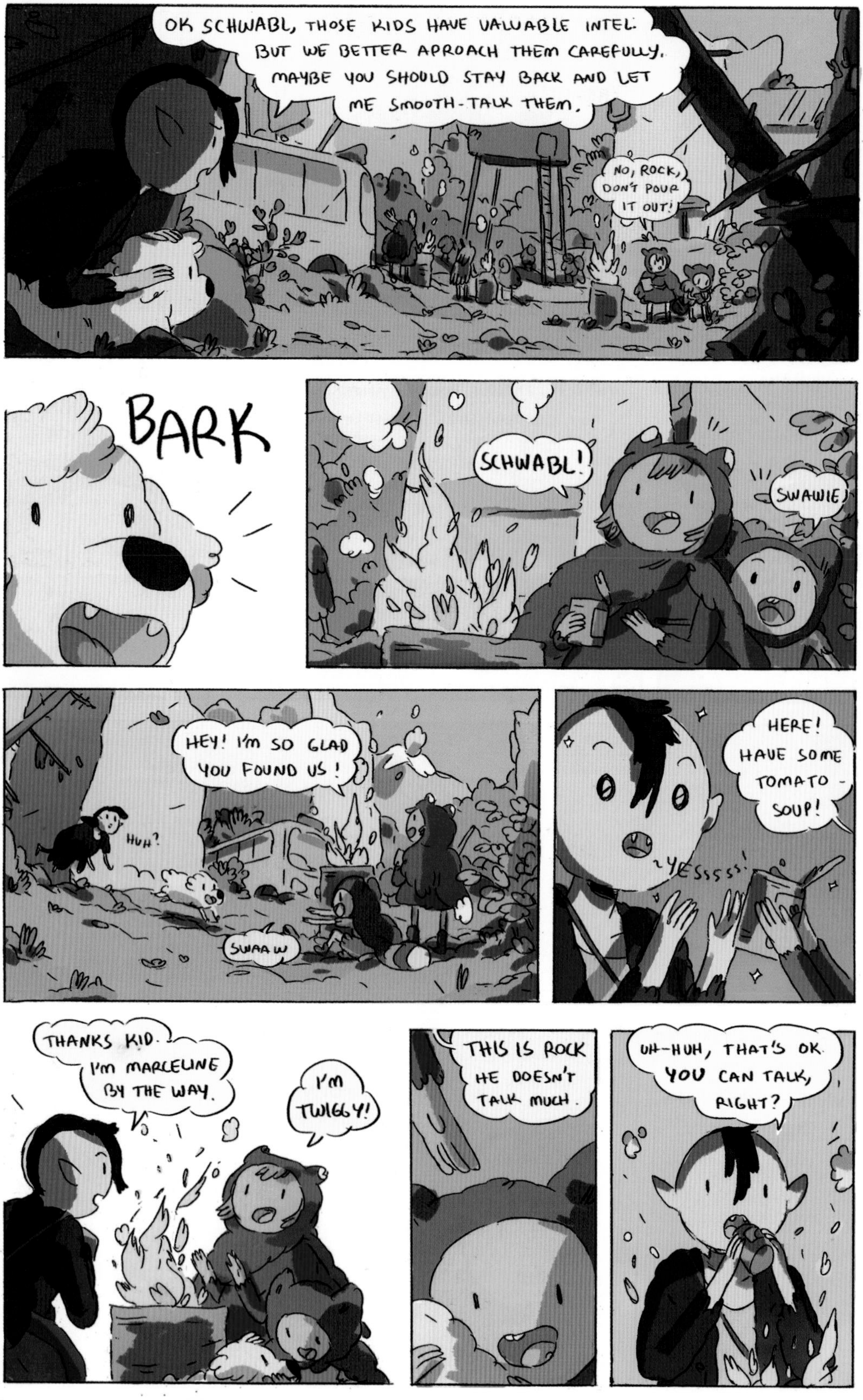
OK SCHWABL, THOSE KIDS HAVE VALUABLE INTEL. BUT WE BETTER APROACH THEM CAREFULLY. MAYBE YOU SHOULD STAY BACK AND LET ME SMOOTH-TALK THEM.
NO, ROCK, DON'T POUR IT OUT!
BARK
SCHWABL!
SWAWIE
HEY! I'M SO GLAD YOU FOUND US!
HUH?
SWAAW
HERE! HAVE SOME TOMATO-SOUP!
YESSSSS!
THANKS KID. I'M MARCELINE BY THE WAY.
I'M TWIGGY!
THIS IS ROCK HE DOESN'T TALK MUCH.
UH-HUH, THAT'S OK. YOU CAN TALK, RIGHT?

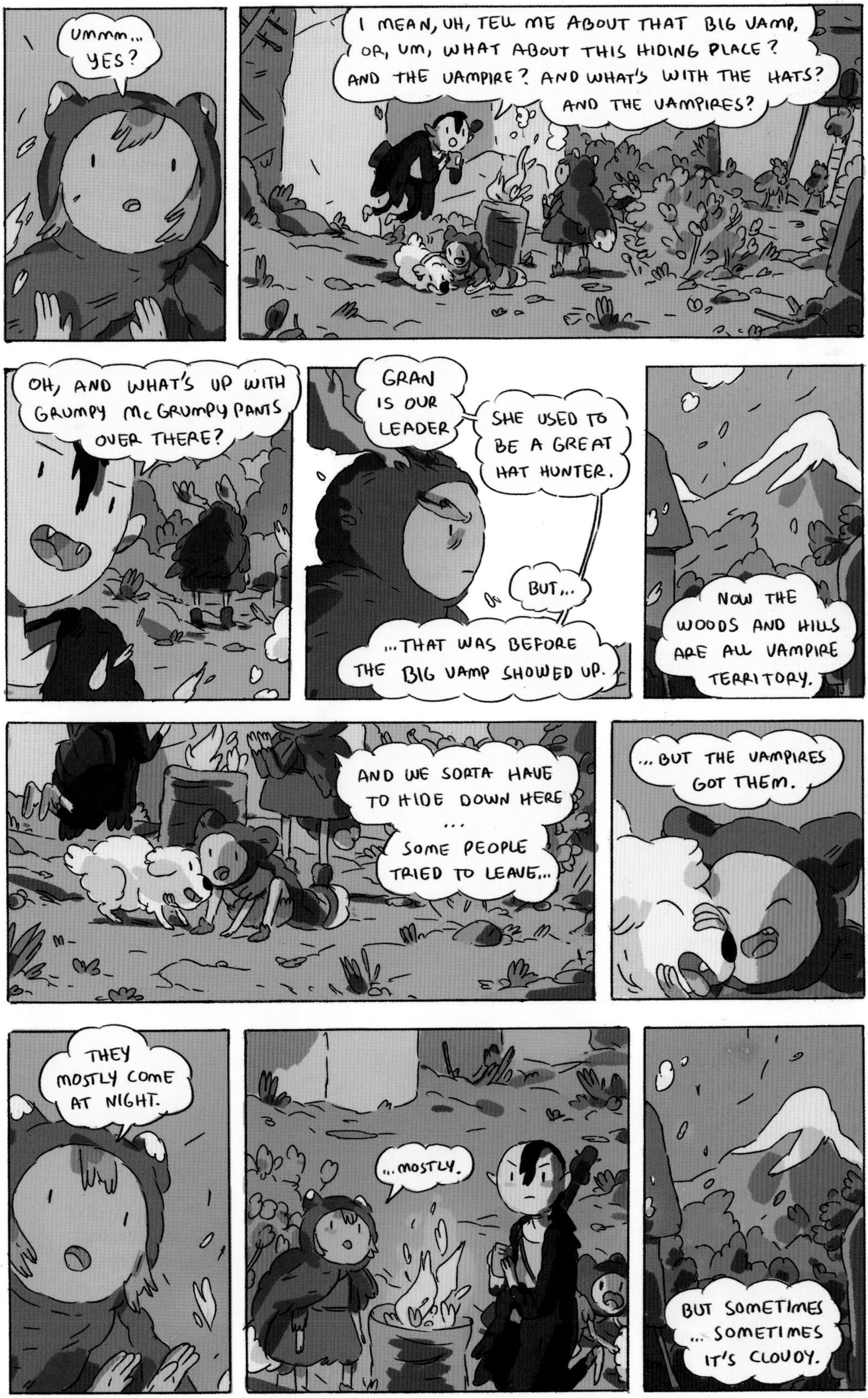
UMMM... YES?
I MEAN, UH, TELL ME ABOUT THAT BIG VAMP, OR, UM, WHAT ABOUT THIS HIDING PLACE? AND THE VAMPIRE? AND WHAT'S WITH THE HATS?
AND THE VAMPIRES?
OH, AND WHAT'S UP WITH GRUMPY McGRUMPYPANTS OVER THERE?
GRAN IS OUR LEADER
SHE USED TO BE A GREAT HAT HUNTER.
BUT...
...THAT WAS BEFORE THE BIG VAMP SHOWED UP.
NOW THE WOODS AND HILLS ARE ALL VAMPIRE TERRITORY.
AND WE SORTA HAVE TO HIDE DOWN HERE ... SOME PEOPLE TRIED TO LEAVE...
...BUT THE VAMPIRES GOT THEM.
THEY MOSTLY COME AT NIGHT.
...MOSTLY.
BUT SOMETIMES ... SOMETIMES IT'S CLOUDY.

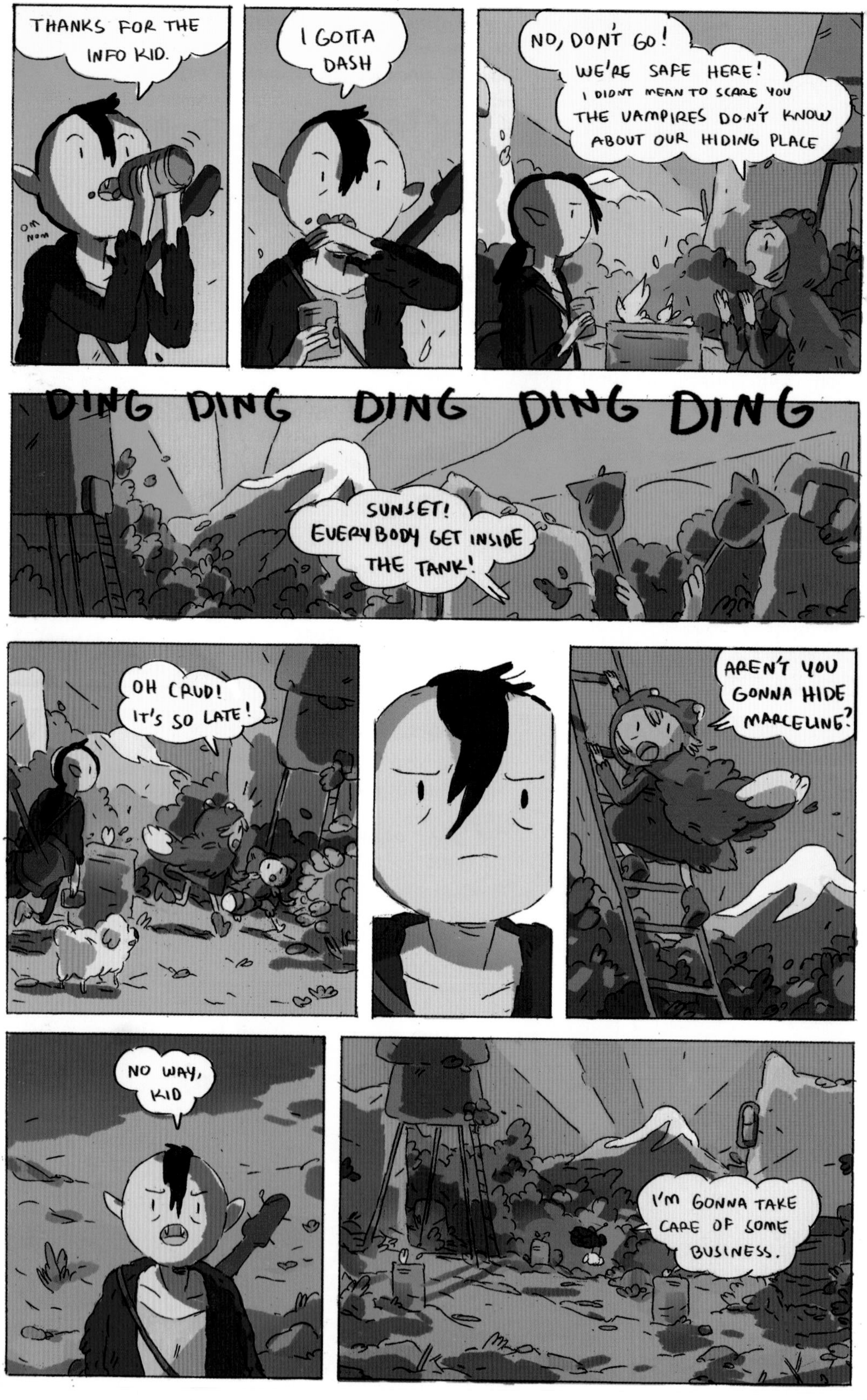
THANKS FOR THE INFO KID.
OM NOM
I GOTTA DASH
NO, DON'T GO!
WE'RE SAFE HERE!
I DIDN'T MEAN TO SCARE YOU
THE VAMPIRES DON'T KNOW ABOUT OUR HIDING PLACE
DING DING DING DING DING
SUNSET! EVERYBODY GET INSIDE THE TANK!
OH CRUD! IT'S SO LATE!
AREN'T YOU GONNA HIDE MARCELINE?
NO WAY, KID
I'M GONNA TAKE CARE OF SOME BUSINESS.

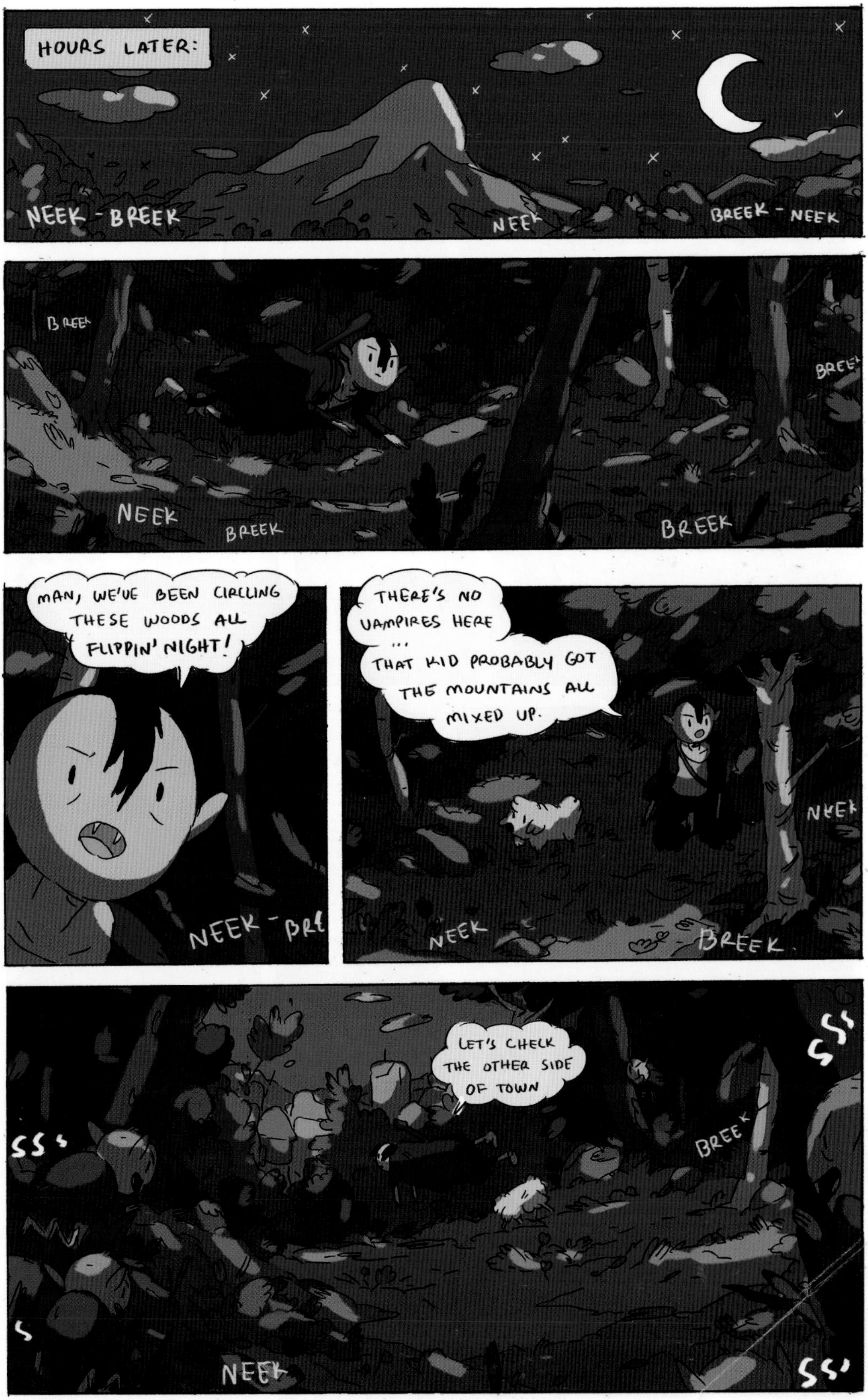
HOURS LATER:
NEEK - BREEK
NEEK
BREEK - NEEK
BREEK
BREEK
NEEK
BREEK
BREEK
MAN, WE'VE BEEN CIRCLING THESE WOODS ALL FLIPPIN' NIGHT!
NEEK - BRE
THERE'S NO VAMPIRES HERE ... THAT KID PROBABLY GOT THE MOUNTAINS ALL MIXED UP.
NEEK
NEEK
BREEK.
LET'S CHECK THE OTHER SIDE OF TOWN
BREEK
NEEK

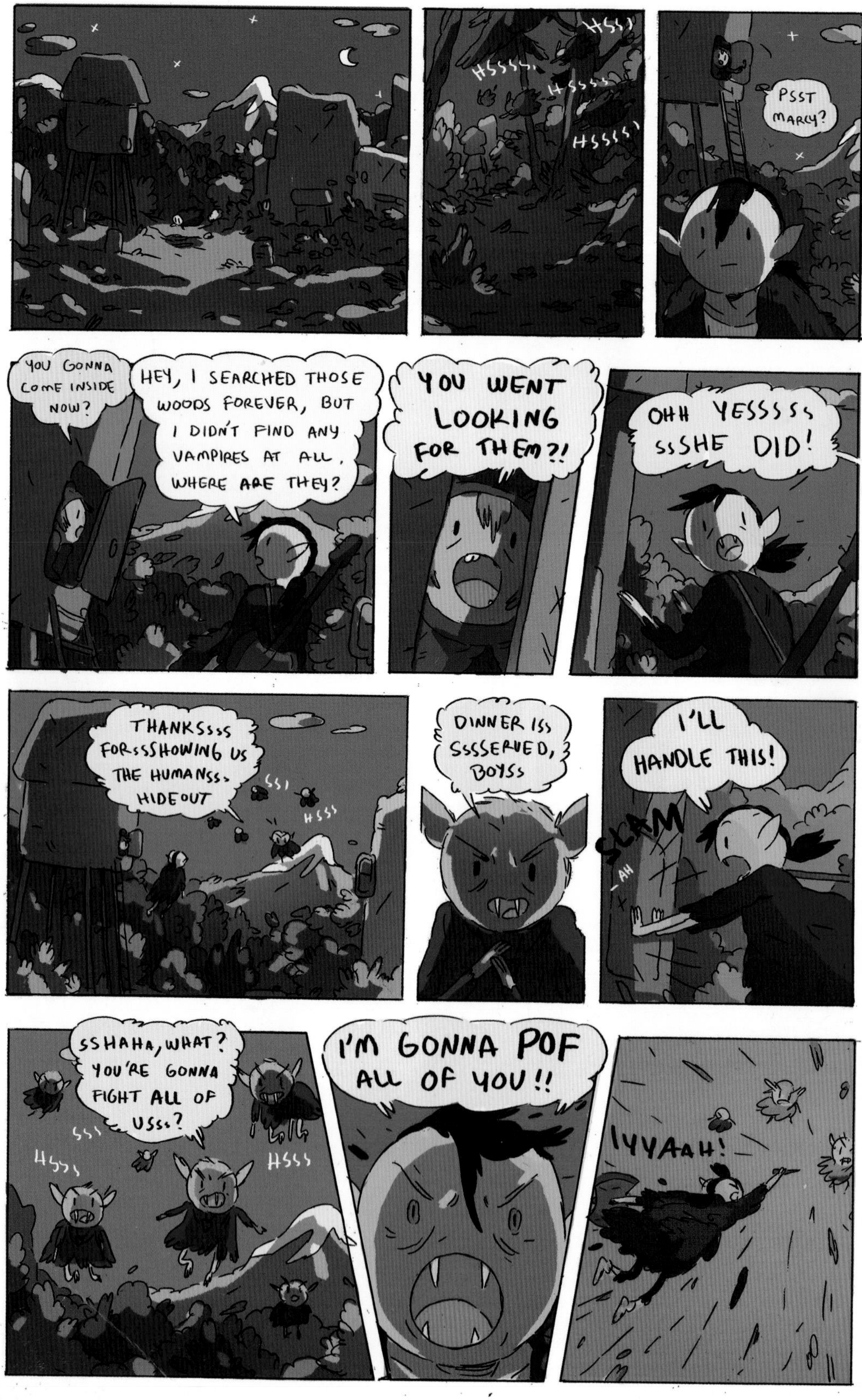
HSSS
HSSSS
HSSSS
HSSSS
PSST MARCY?
YOU GONNA COME INSIDE NOW?
HEY, I SEARCHED THOSE WOODS FOREVER, BUT I DIDN'T FIND ANY VAMPIRES AT ALL. WHERE ARE THEY?
YOU WENT LOOKING FOR THEM?!
OHH YESSSSS SSHE DID!
THANKSSSS FORSSHOWING US THE HUMANSSS HIDEOUT
SSS
HSSS
DINNER ISS SSSSERVED, BOYSS
I'LL HANDLE THIS!
SLAM
AH
SSHAHA, WHAT? YOU'RE GONNA FIGHT ALL OF USSS?
SSS
HSSS
HSSS
I'M GONNA POF ALL OF YOU!!
IYYAAH!

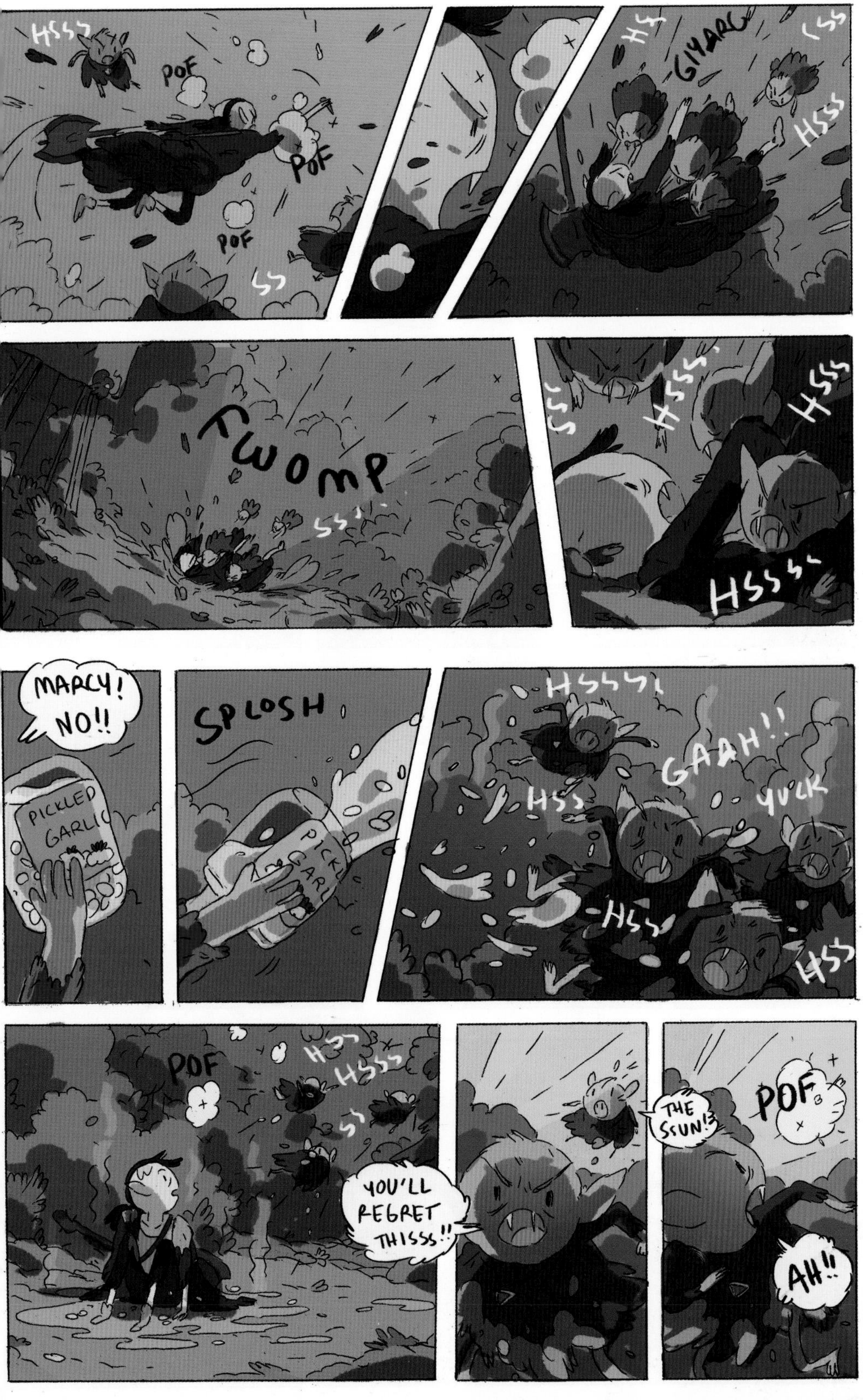
HSSS
POF
POF
POF
SS
HSS
GIYARG
SSS
HSSS
FWOMP
SSS
SSS
HSSS
HSSS
HSSSS
MARCY! NO!!
PICKLED GARLIC
SPLOSH
HSSS
GAAH!!
HSS
YUCK
HSS
HSS
POF
HSS
HSSS
SS
YOU'LL REGRET THISSS!!
THE SSUN!
POF
AH!!

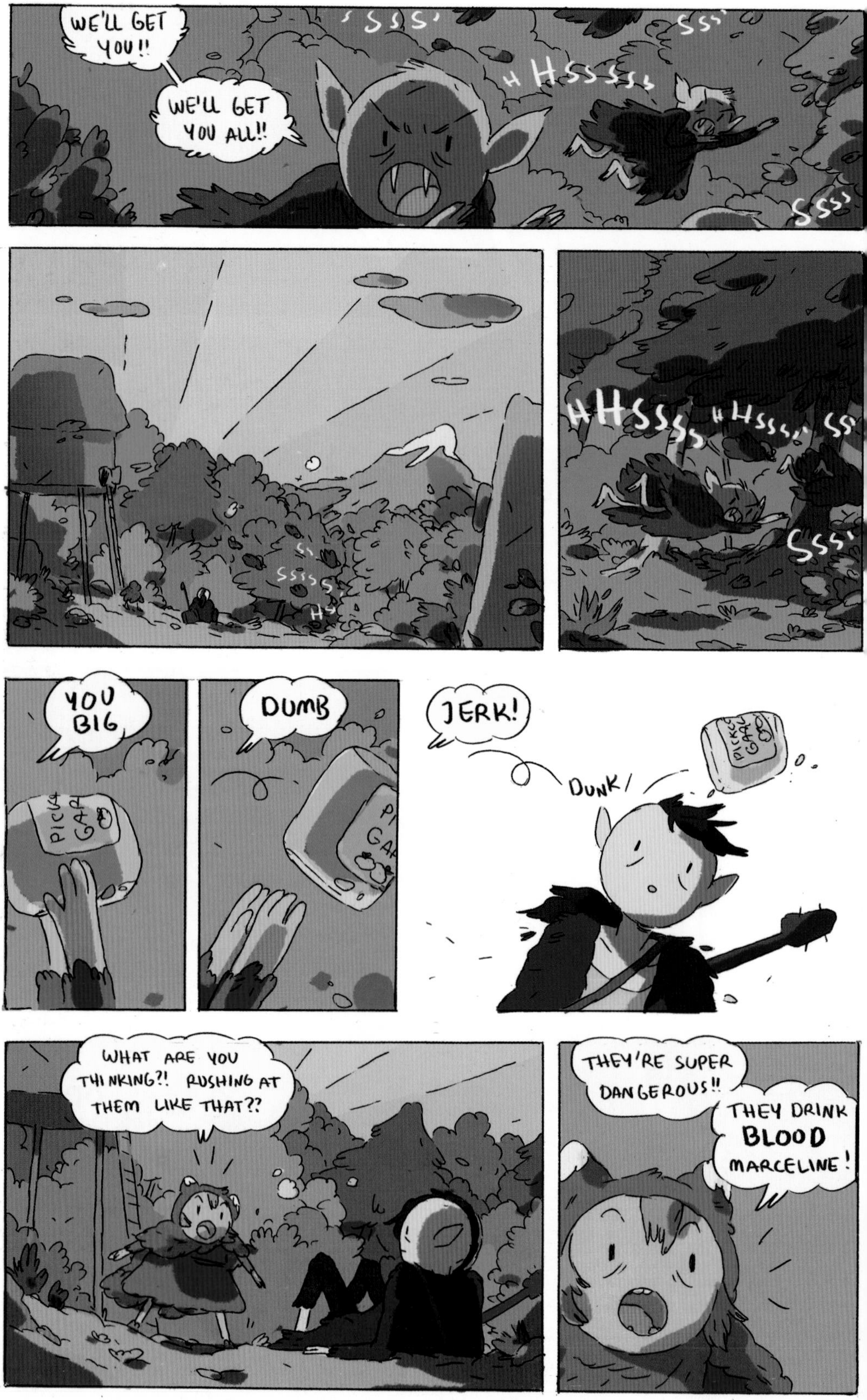
WE'LL GET YOU!!
WE'LL GET YOU ALL!!
SSS
SSS
HSSSSSS
SSS
SSSSS
H
HHSSSS
HHSSSS
SS
SSS
YOU BIG
DUMB
JERK!
DUNK!
WHAT ARE YOU THINKING?! RUSHING AT THEM LIKE THAT??
THEY'RE SUPER DANGEROUS!!
THEY DRINK **BLOOD** MARCELINE!

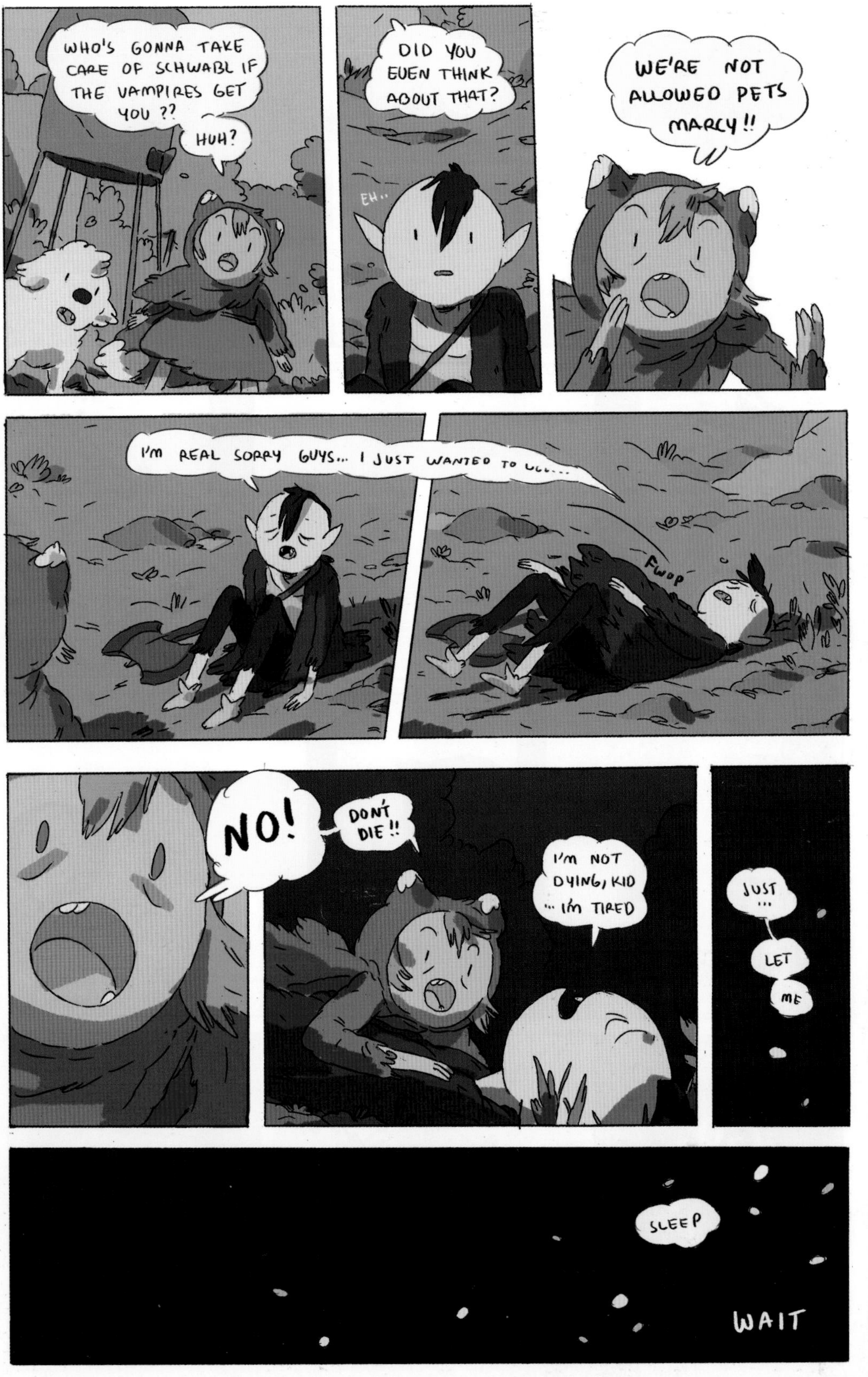
WHO'S GONNA TAKE CARE OF SCHWABL IF THE VAMPIRES GET YOU ??
HUH?
DID YOU EVEN THINK ABOUT THAT?
EH..
WE'RE NOT ALLOWED PETS MARCY!!
I'M REAL SORRY GUYS... I JUST WANTED TO UUU...
FWOP
NO!
DON'T DIE!!
I'M NOT DYING, KID ... I'M TIRED
JUST ...
LET
ME
SLEEP
WAIT

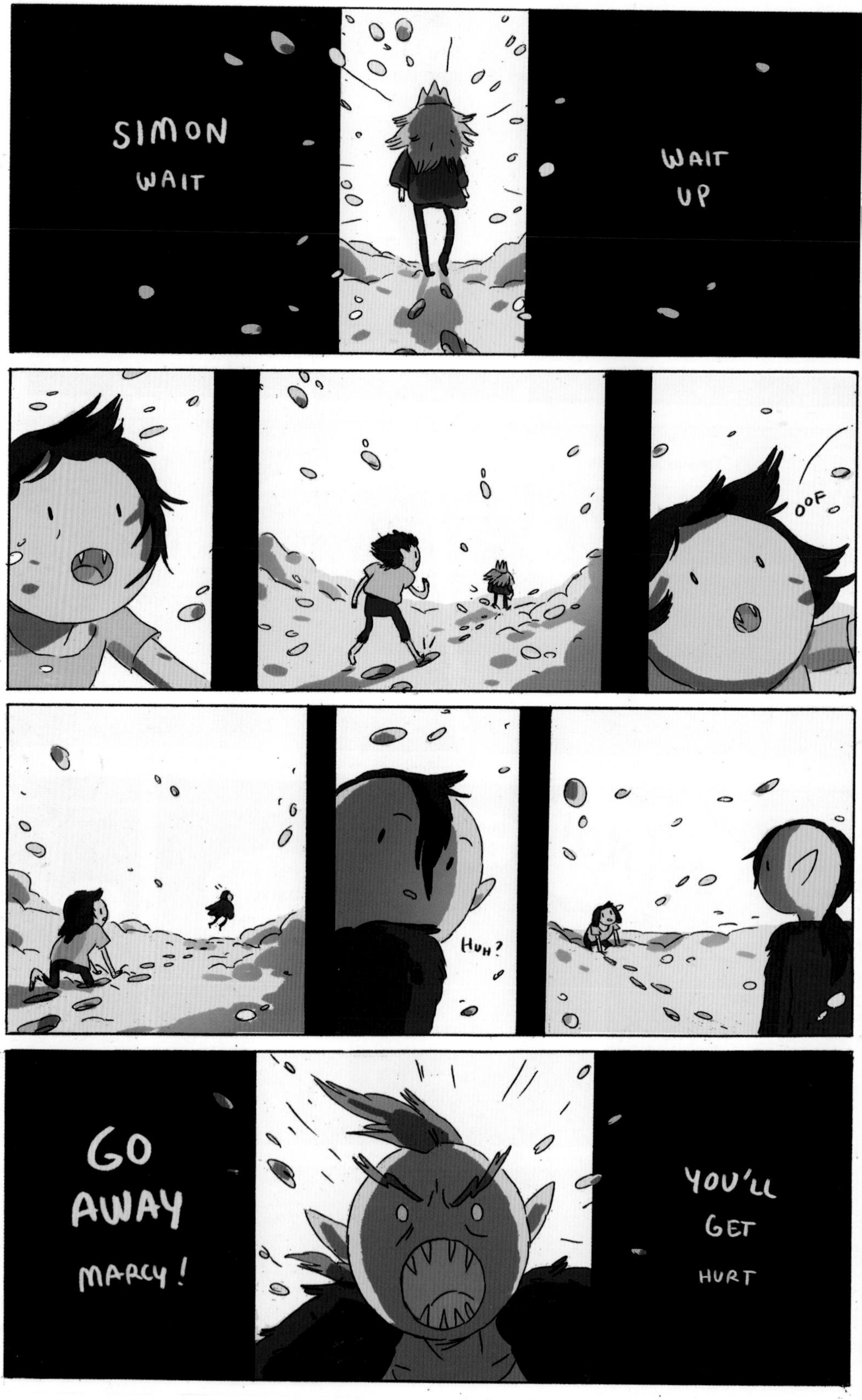
SIMON
WAIT
WAIT
UP
OOF
HUH?
GO
AWAY
MARCY!
YOU'LL
GET
HURT

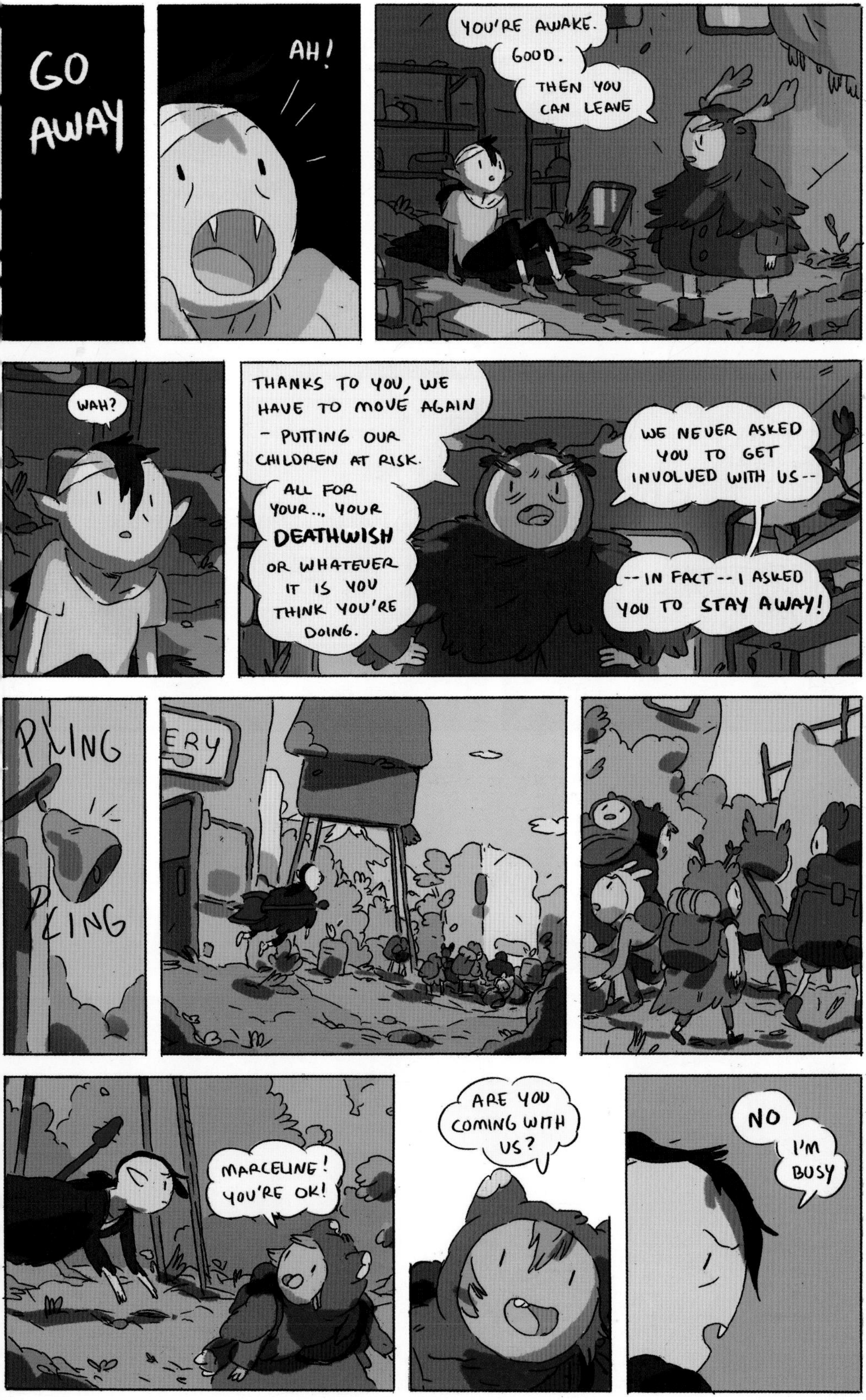
GO AWAY
AH!
YOU'RE AWAKE. GOOD.
THEN YOU CAN LEAVE
WAH?
THANKS TO YOU, WE HAVE TO MOVE AGAIN - PUTTING OUR CHILDREN AT RISK.
ALL FOR YOUR... YOUR DEATHWISH OR WHATEVER IT IS YOU THINK YOU'RE DOING.
WE NEVER ASKED YOU TO GET INVOLVED WITH US--
--IN FACT--I ASKED YOU TO STAY AWAY!
PLING
PLING
ERY
MARCELINE! YOU'RE OK!
ARE YOU COMING WITH US?
NO
I'M BUSY

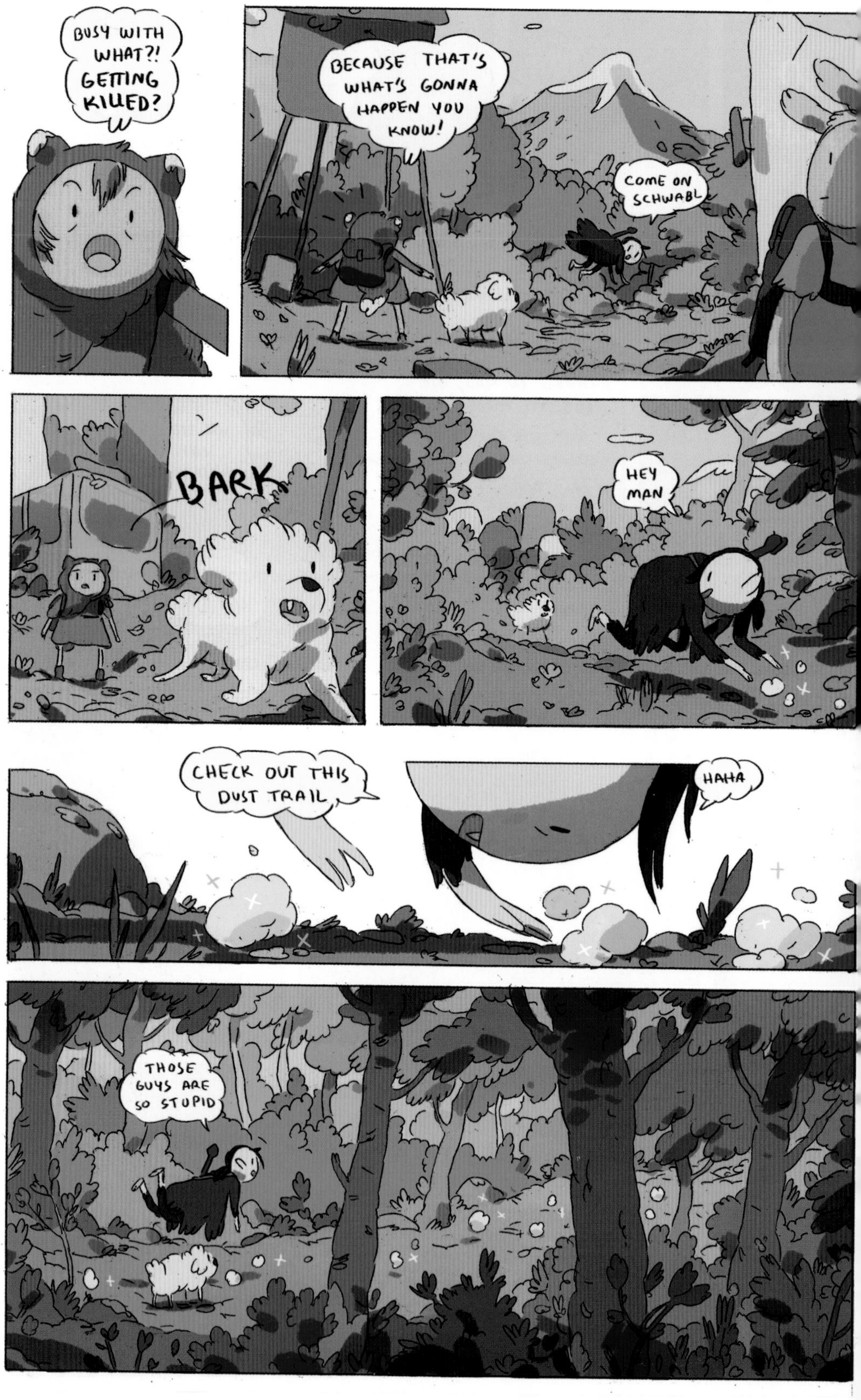
BUSY WITH WHAT?! GETTING KILLED?
BECAUSE THAT'S WHAT'S GONNA HAPPEN YOU KNOW!
COME ON SCHWABL
BARK
HEY MAN
CHECK OUT THIS DUST TRAIL
HAHA
THOSE GUYS ARE SO STUPID

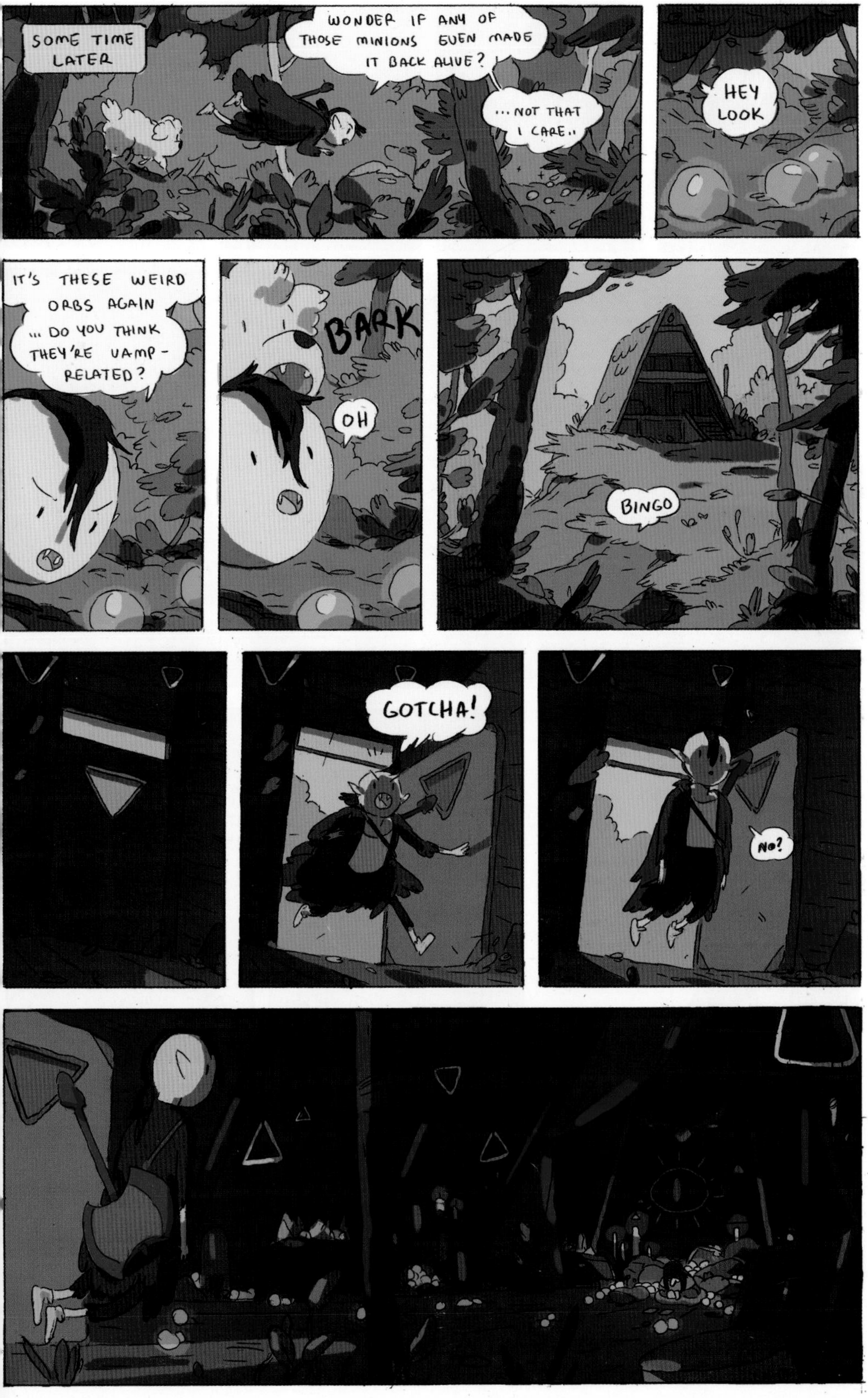
SOME TIME LATER
WONDER IF ANY OF THOSE MINIONS EVEN MADE IT BACK ALIVE?
... NOT THAT I CARE..
HEY LOOK
IT'S THESE WEIRD ORBS AGAIN ... DO YOU THINK THEY'RE VAMP-RELATED?
BARK
OH
BINGO
GOTCHA!
NO?

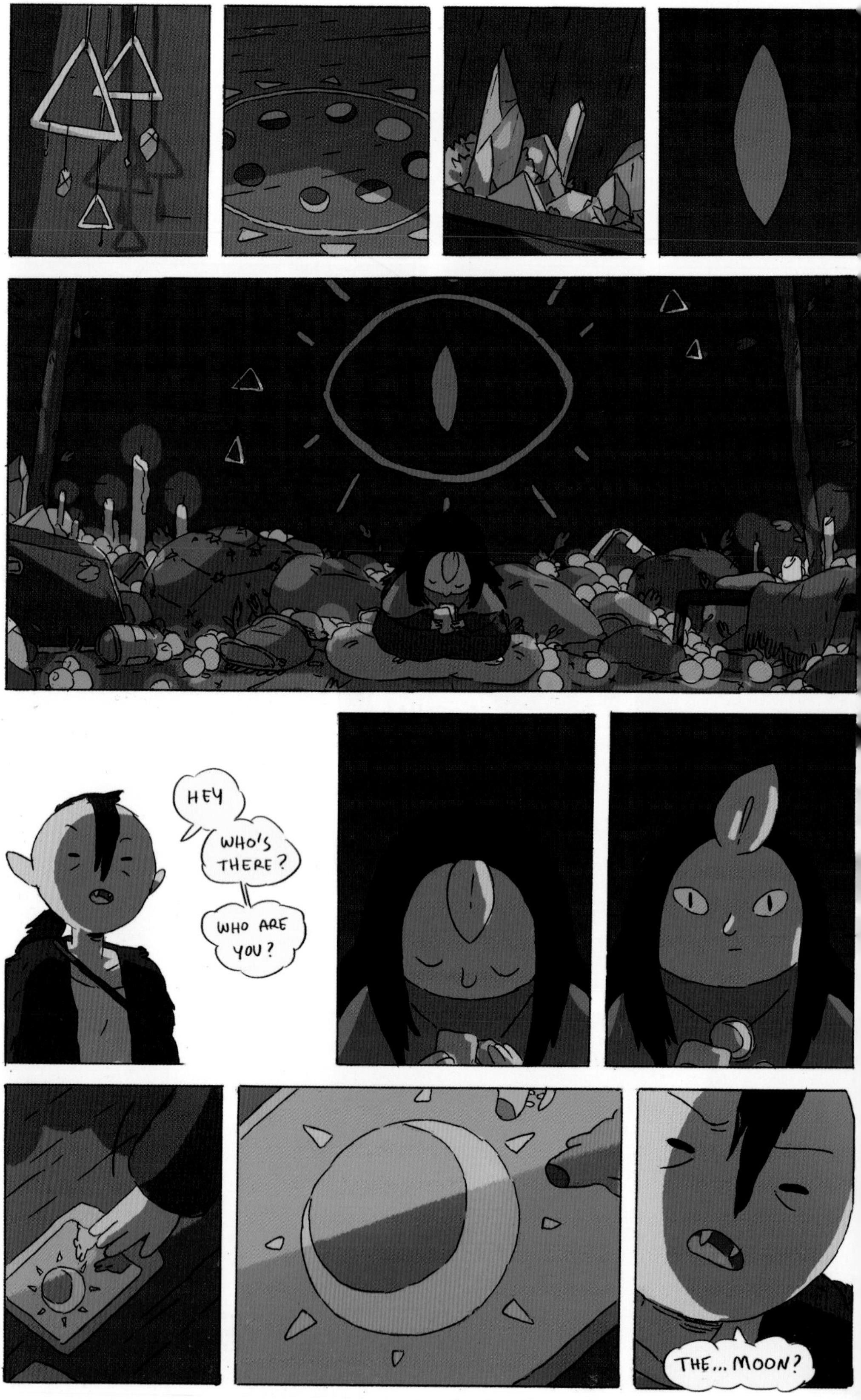
HEY
WHO'S THERE?
WHO ARE YOU?
THE... MOON?

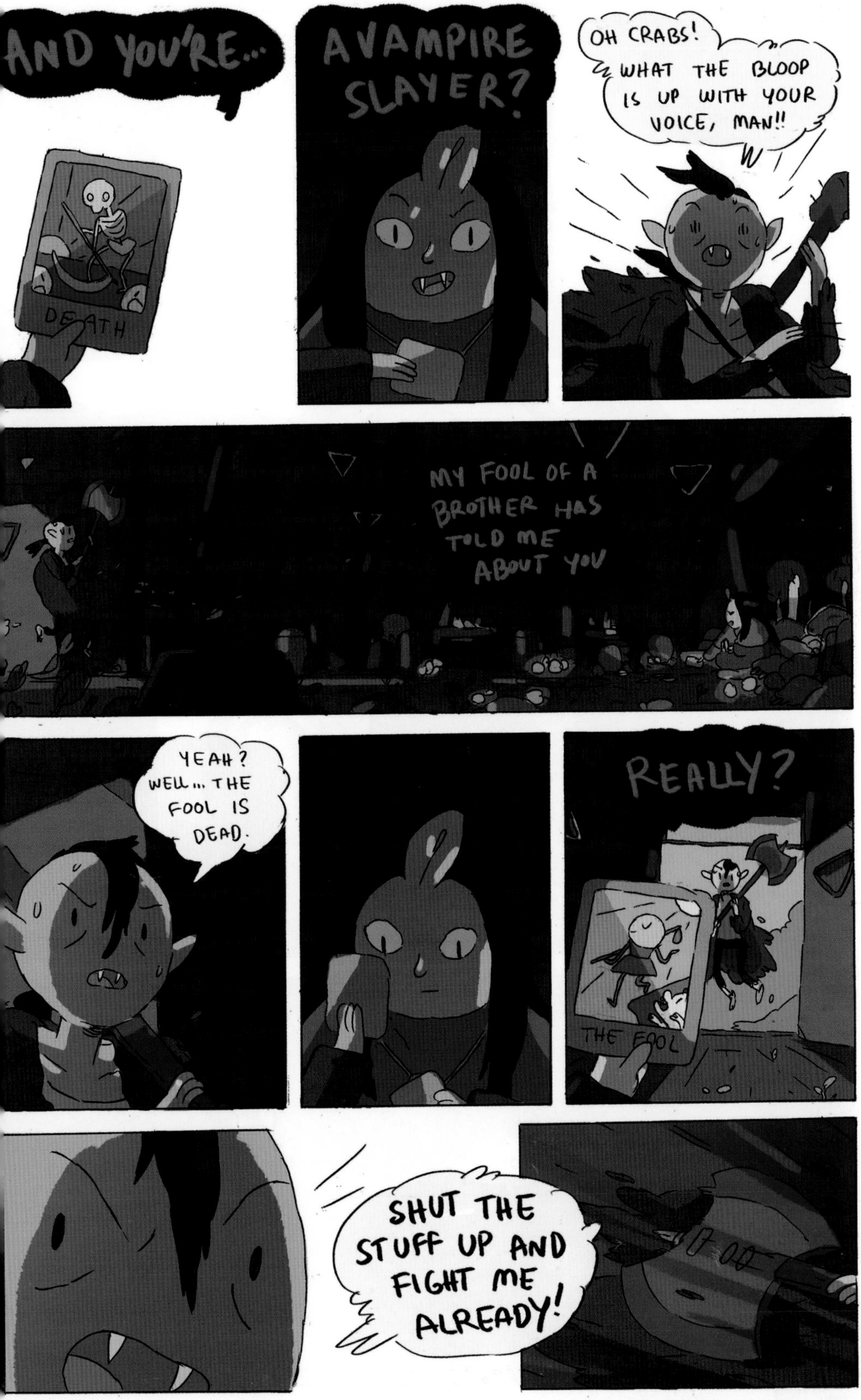
AND YOU'RE...
DEATH
A VAMPIRE SLAYER?
OH CRABS!
WHAT THE BLOOP IS UP WITH YOUR VOICE, MAN!!
MY FOOL OF A BROTHER HAS TOLD ME ABOUT YOU
YEAH? WELL... THE FOOL IS DEAD.
REALLY?
THE FOOL
SHUT THE STUFF UP AND FIGHT ME ALREADY!

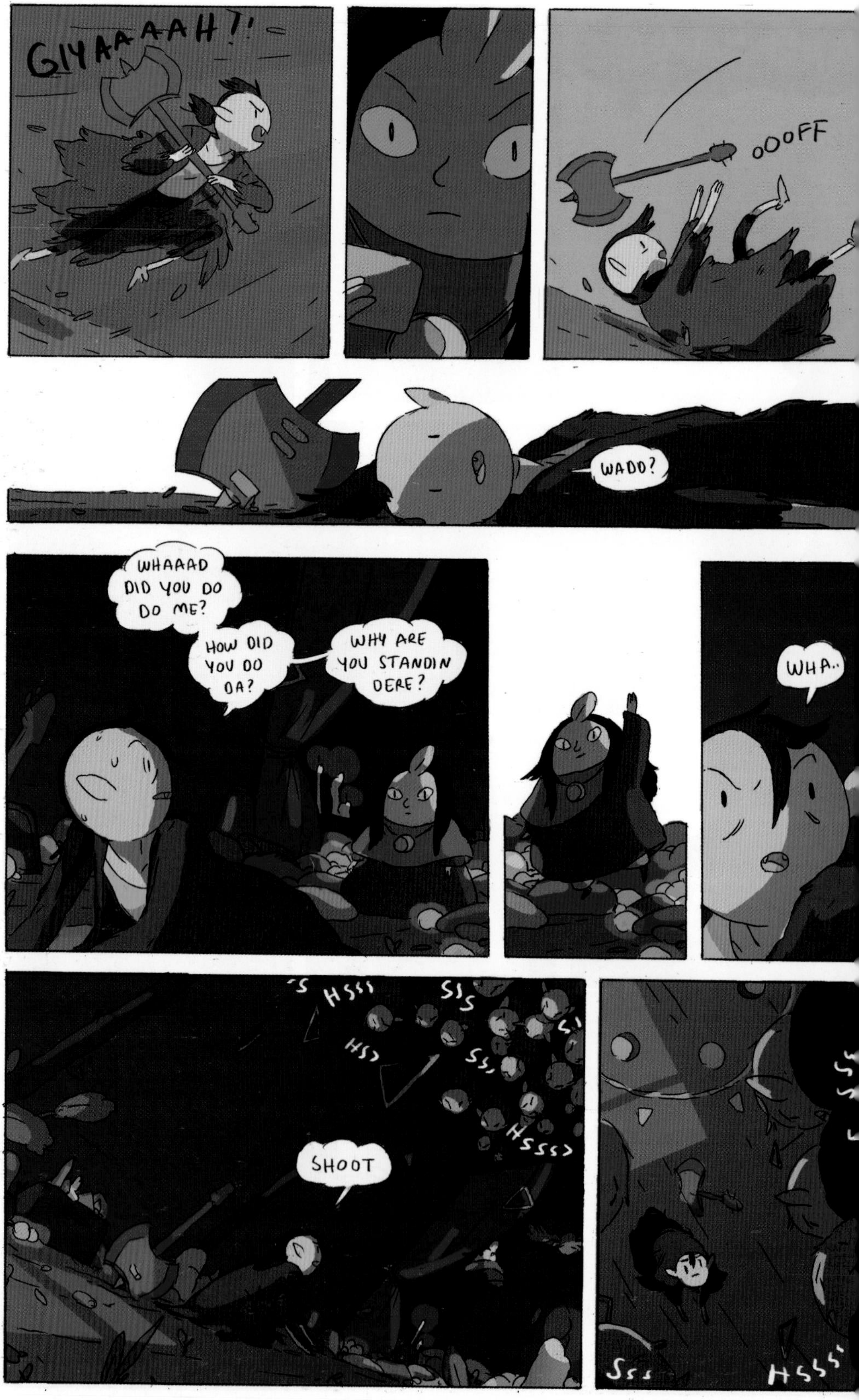
GIYAAAAAH!!
OOOFF
WADO?
WHAAAD DID YOU DO DO ME?
HOW DID YOU DO DA?
WHY ARE YOU STANDIN DERE?
WHA..
HSSS
HSS
SSS
HSSSS
SHOOT
SSS
HSSS

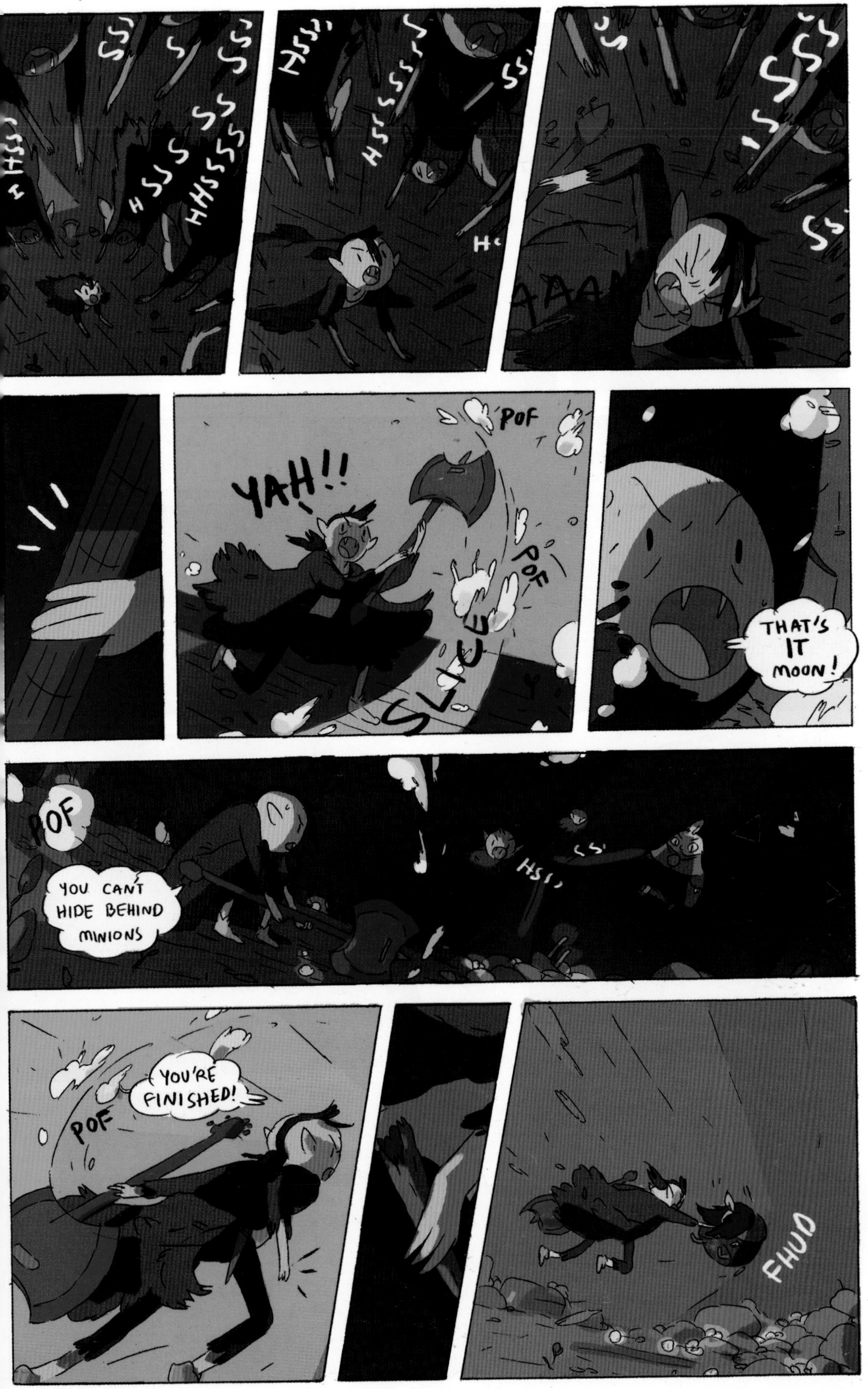

YAH!!
POF
POF
SLICE
THAT'S IT MOON!
POF
YOU CAN'T HIDE BEHIND MINIONS
YOU'RE FINISHED!
POF
FHUD

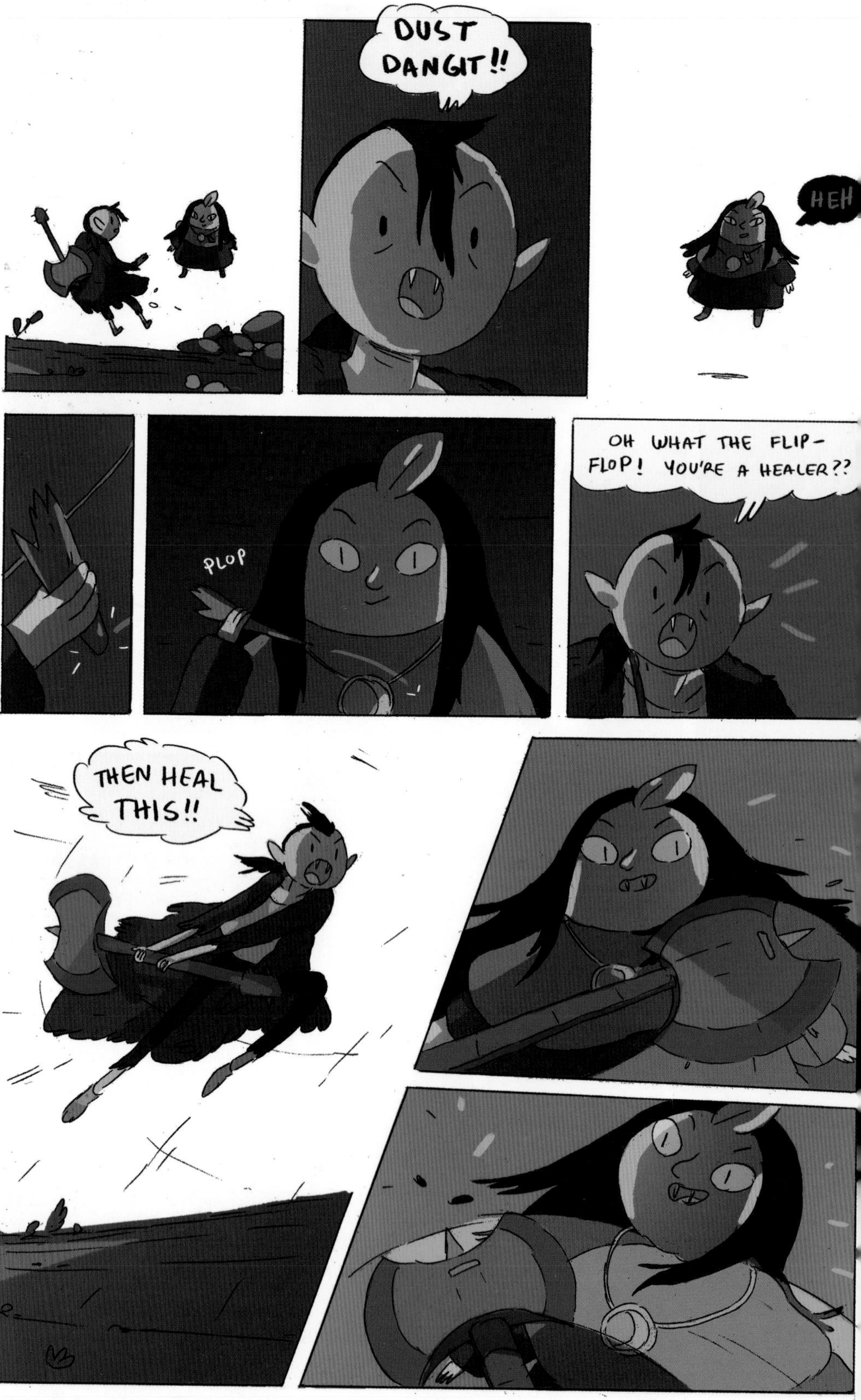
DUST DANGIT!!
HEH
PLOP
OH WHAT THE FLIP-FLOP! YOU'RE A HEALER??
THEN HEAL THIS!!

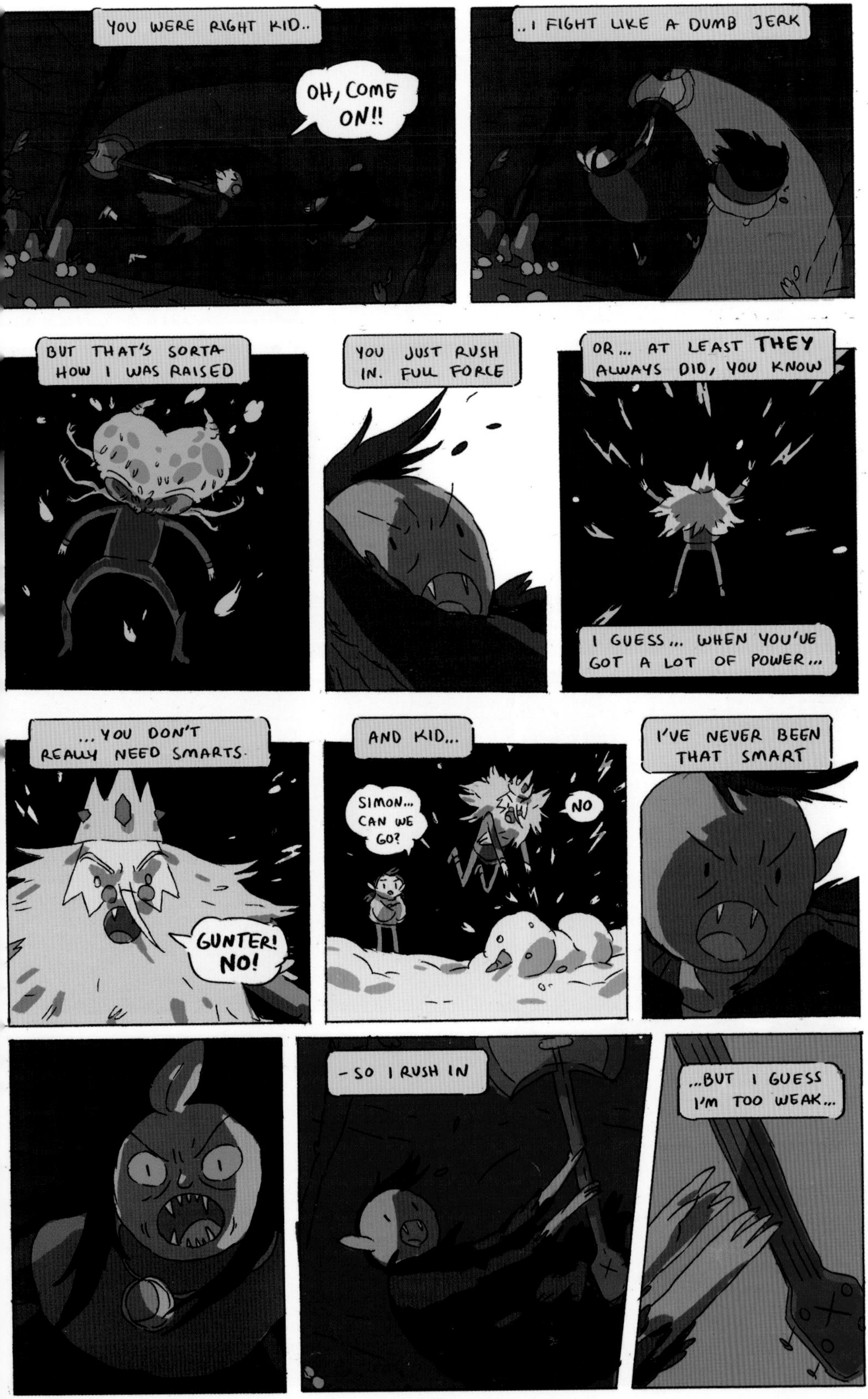
YOU WERE RIGHT KID..
OH, COME ON!!
..I FIGHT LIKE A DUMB JERK
BUT THAT'S SORTA HOW I WAS RAISED
YOU JUST RUSH IN. FULL FORCE
OR... AT LEAST THEY ALWAYS DID, YOU KNOW
I GUESS... WHEN YOU'VE GOT A LOT OF POWER...
...YOU DON'T REALLY NEED SMARTS.
GUNTER! NO!
AND KID...
SIMON... CAN WE GO?
NO
I'VE NEVER BEEN THAT SMART
-SO I RUSH IN
...BUT I GUESS I'M TOO WEAK...

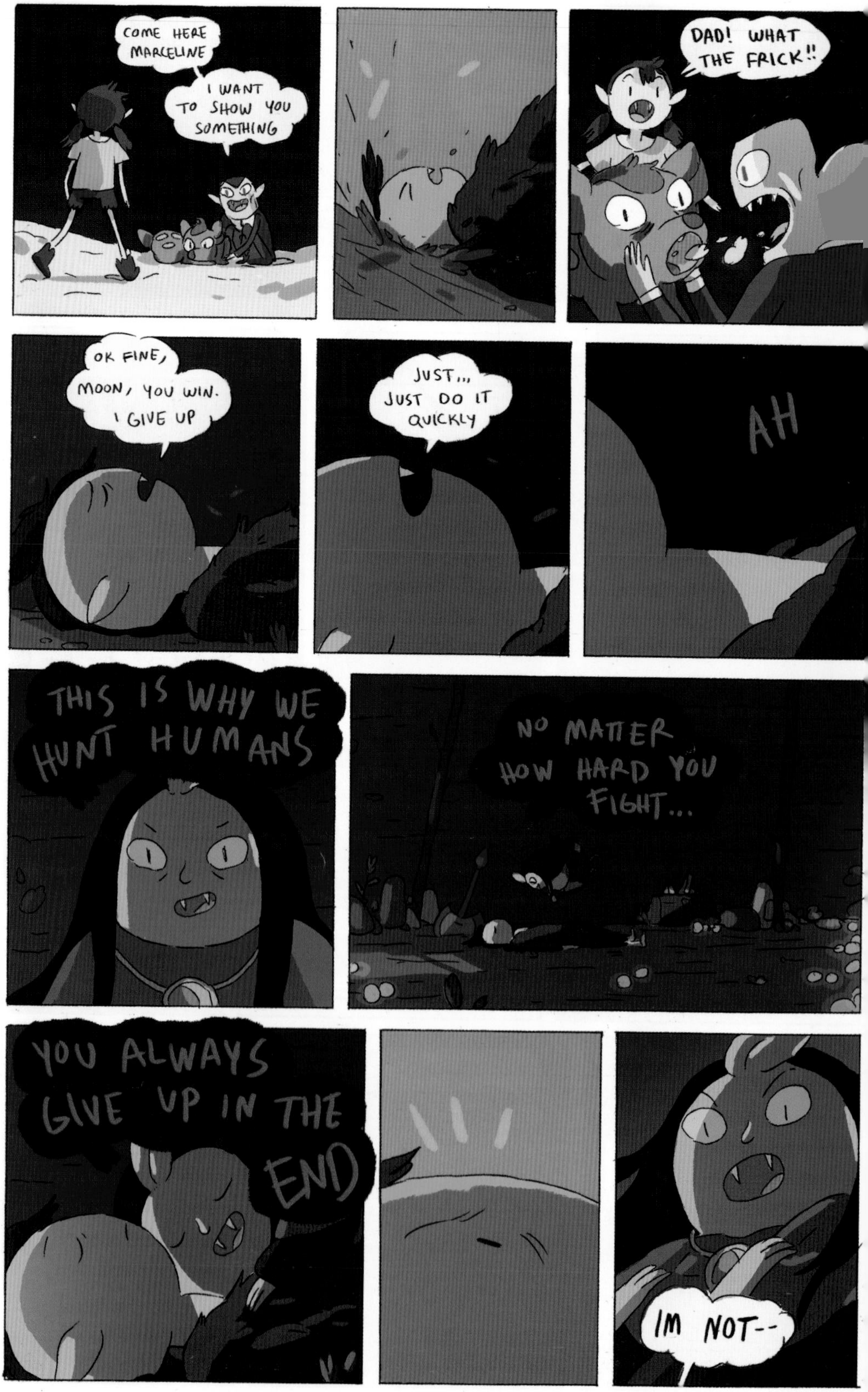
COME HERE MARCELINE
I WANT TO SHOW YOU SOMETHING
DAD! WHAT THE FRICK!!
OK FINE, MOON, YOU WIN. I GIVE UP
JUST... JUST DO IT QUICKLY
AH
THIS IS WHY WE HUNT HUMANS
NO MATTER HOW HARD YOU FIGHT...
YOU ALWAYS GIVE UP IN THE END
IM NOT--

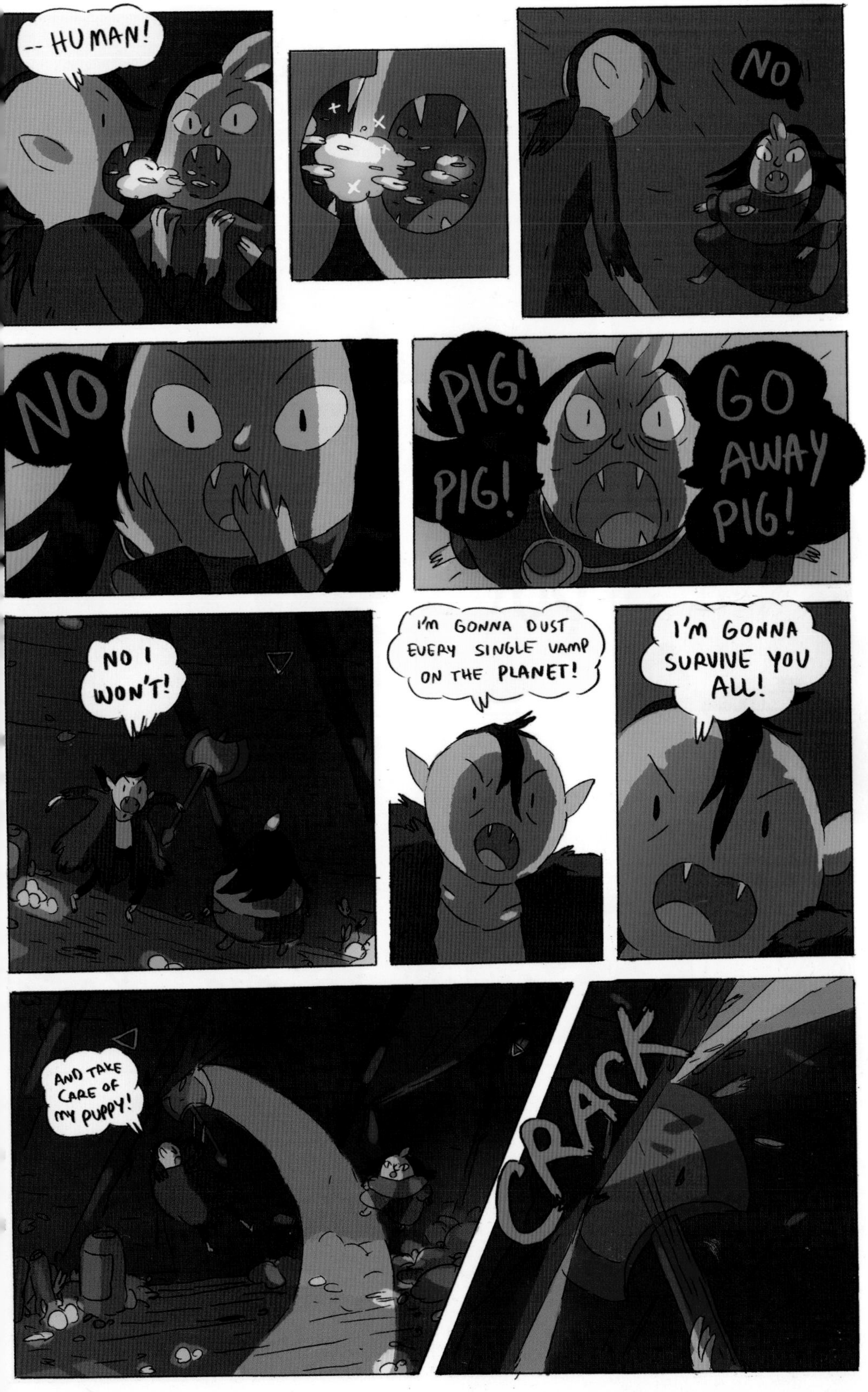

-- HUMAN!
NO
NO
PIG!
PIG!
GO AWAY PIG!
NO I WON'T!
I'M GONNA DUST EVERY SINGLE VAMP ON THE PLANET!
I'M GONNA SURVIVE YOU ALL!
AND TAKE CARE OF MY PUPPY!
CRACK

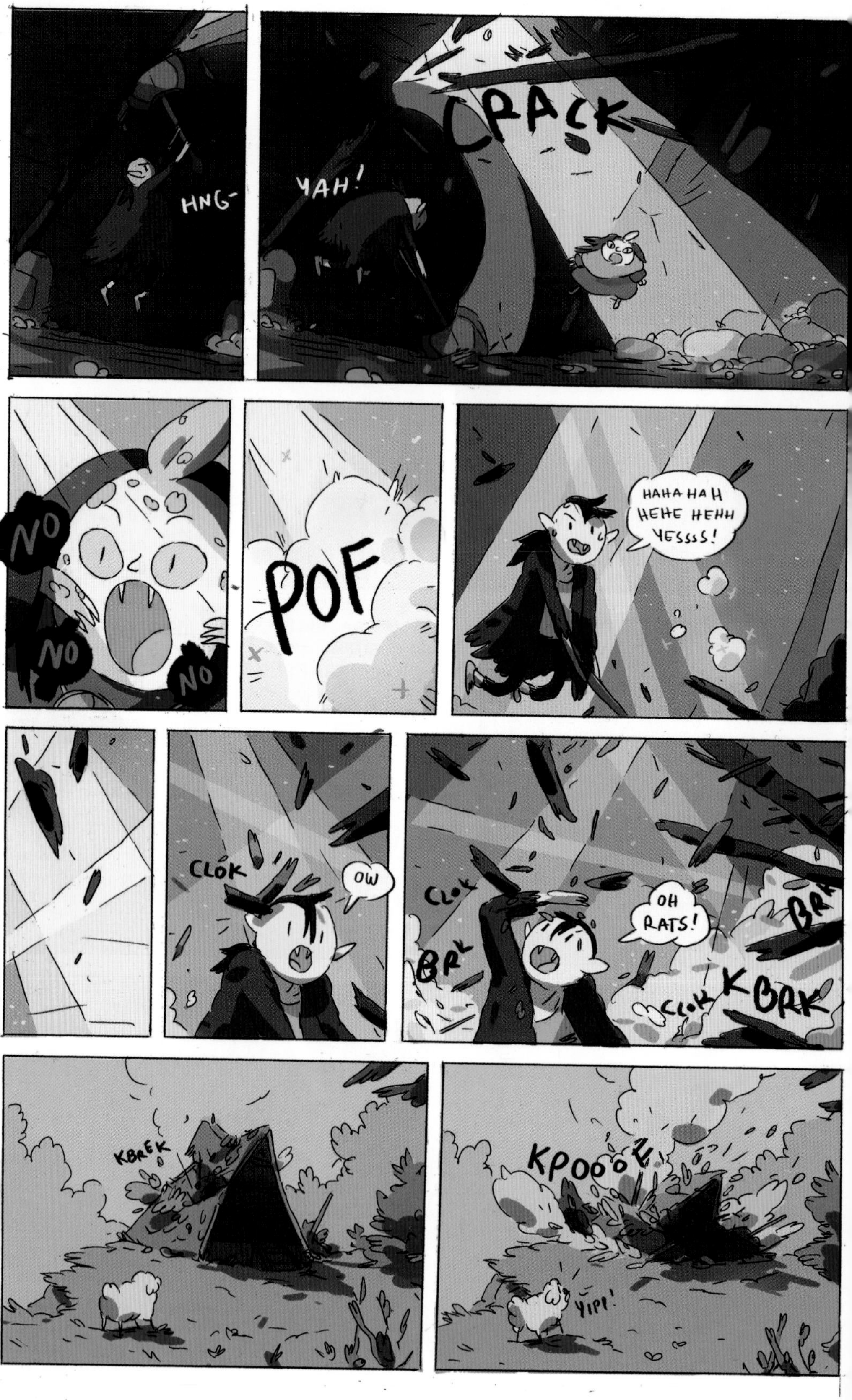
HNG-
YAH!
CRACK
NO
NO
NO
POF
HAHAHAH HEHE HEHH YESSSS!
CLOK
OW
CLOK
OH RATS!
BR
CLOK
KBRK
KBREK
KPOOOF
YIPP!

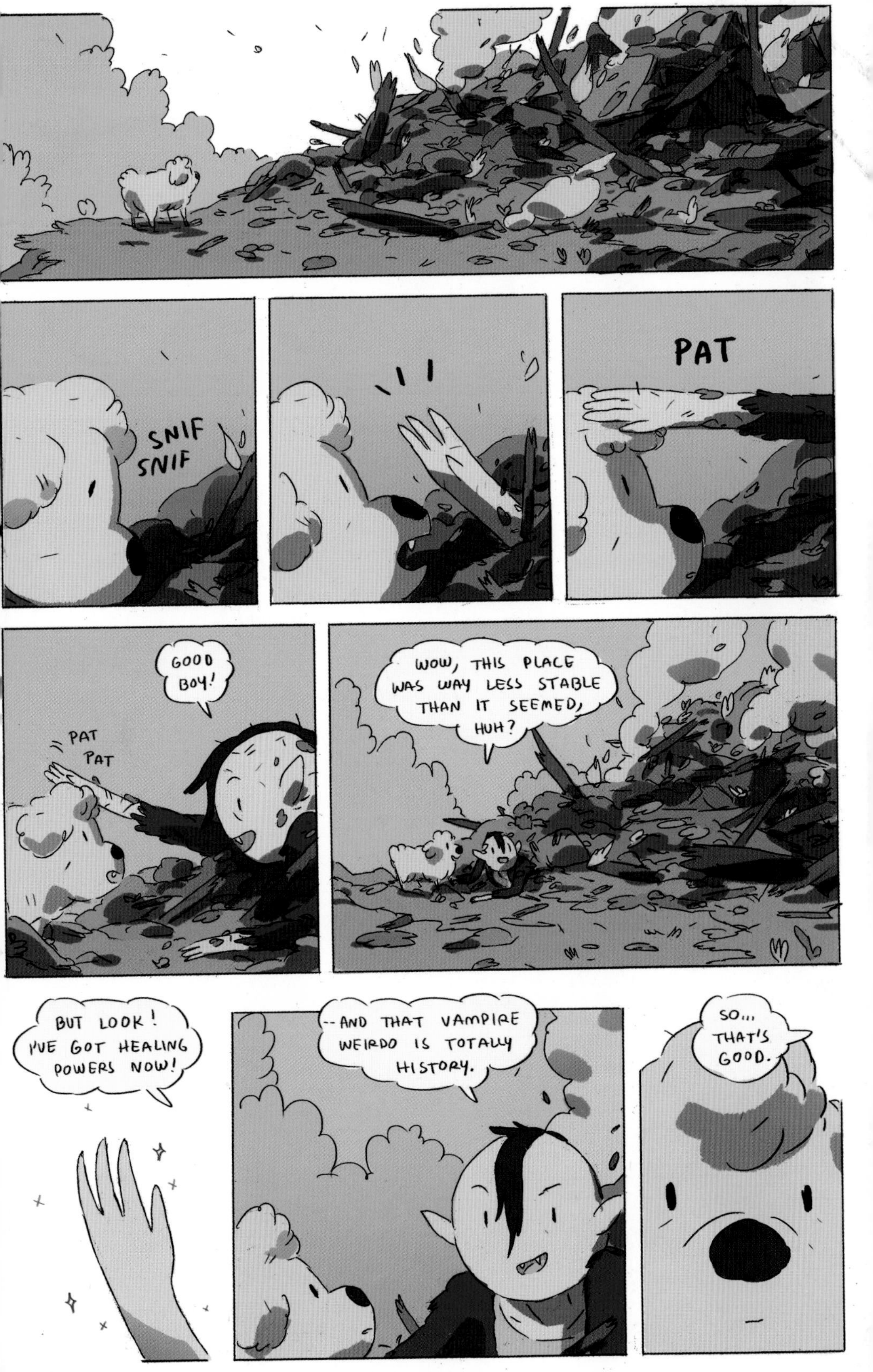
SNIF
SNIF
PAT
GOOD BOY!
PAT
PAT
WOW, THIS PLACE WAS WAY LESS STABLE THAN IT SEEMED, HUH?
BUT LOOK! I'VE GOT HEALING POWERS NOW!
--AND THAT VAMPIRE WEIRDO IS TOTALLY HISTORY.
SO... THAT'S GOOD.

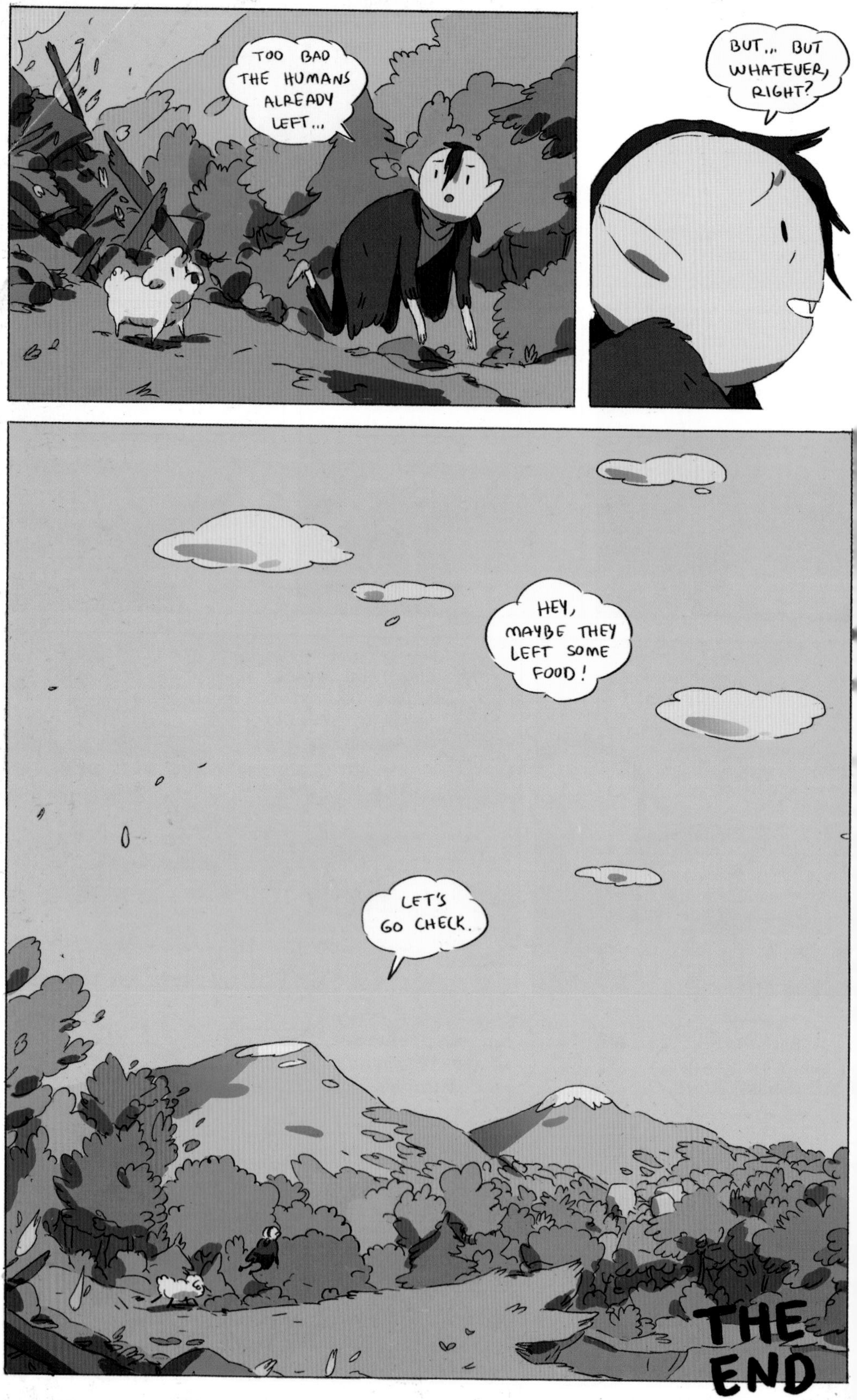
TOO BAD THE HUMANS ALREADY LEFT...
BUT... BUT WHATEVER, RIGHT?
HEY, MAYBE THEY LEFT SOME FOOD!
LET'S GO CHECK.
THE END

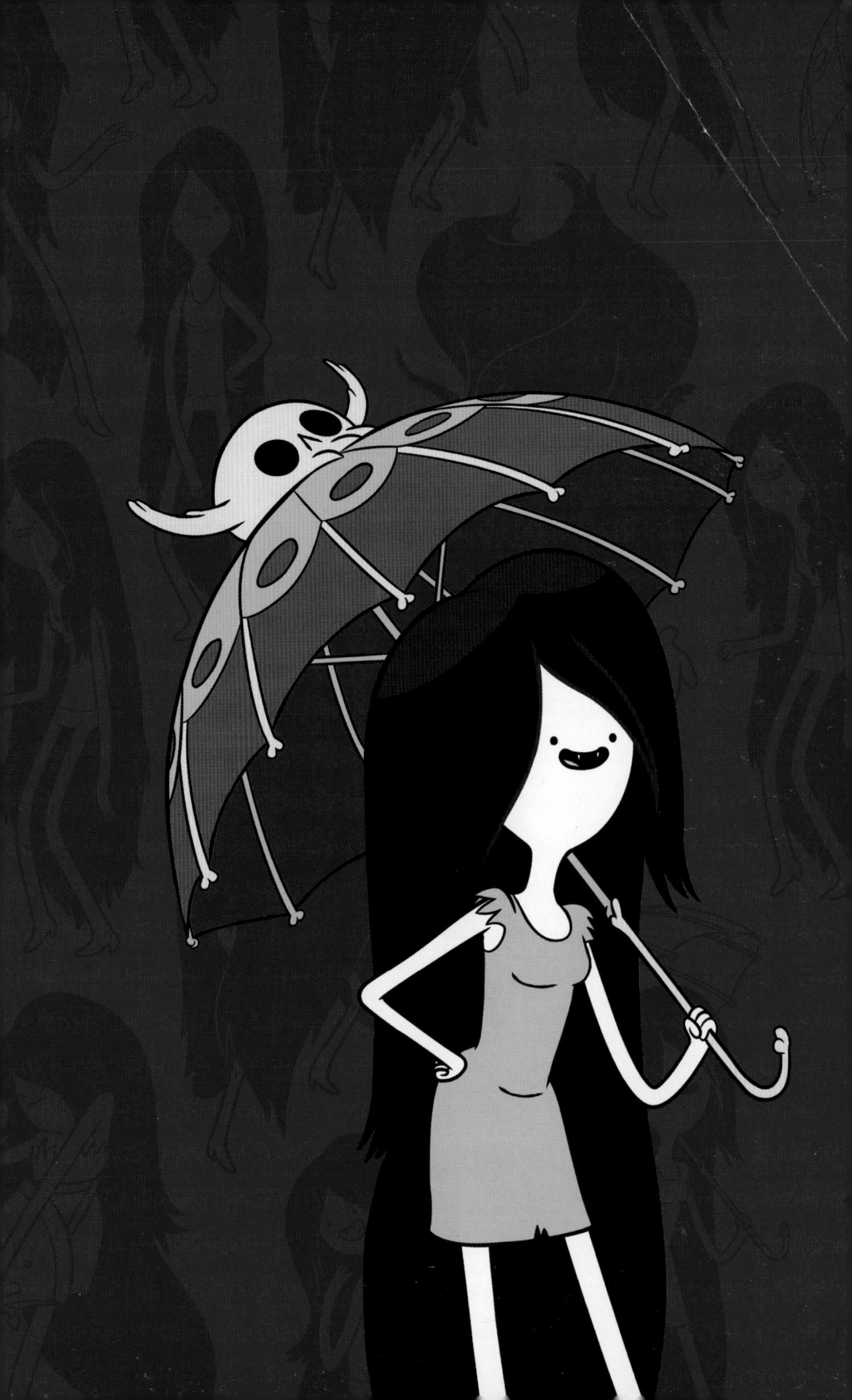

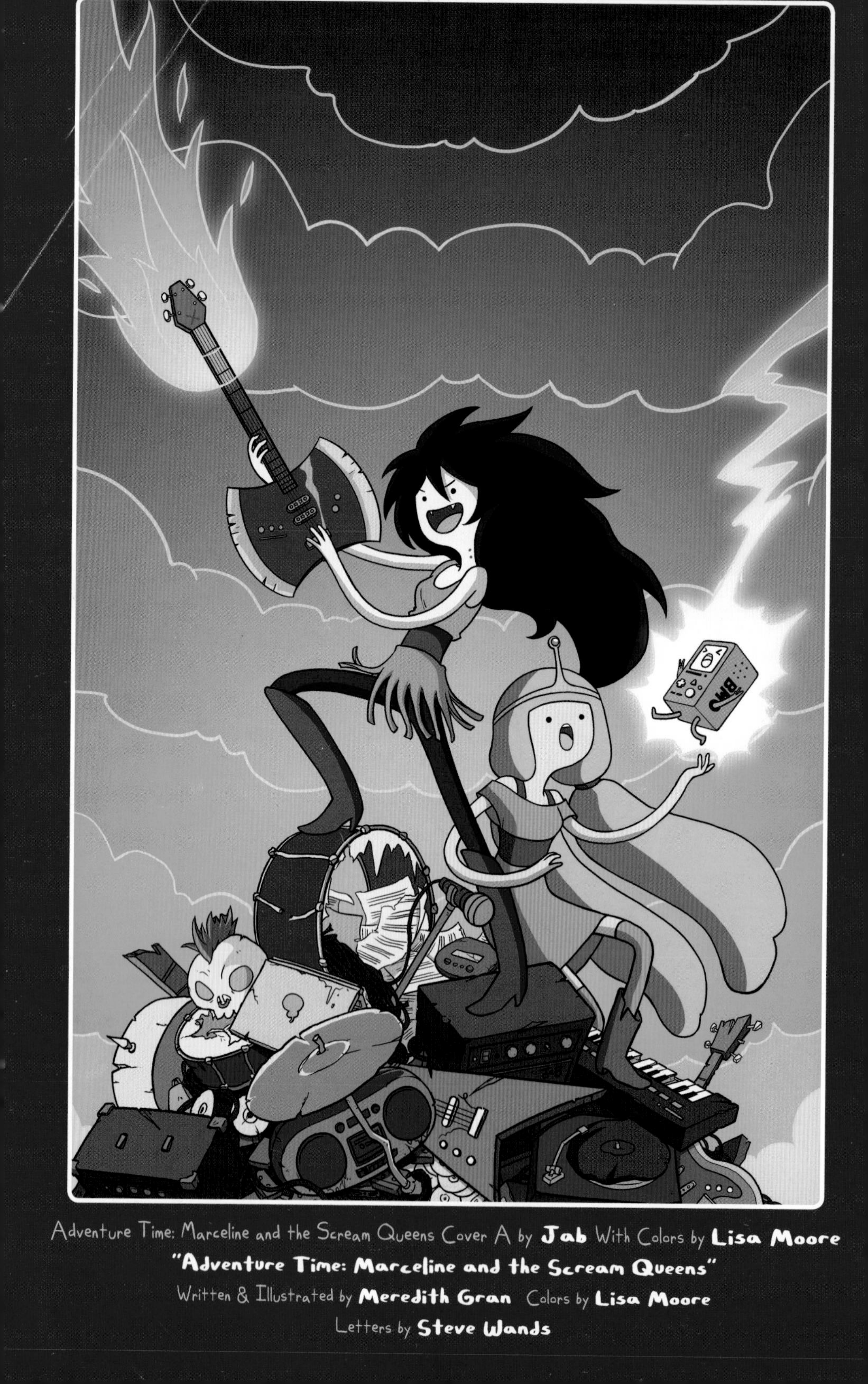

Adventure Time: Marceline and the Scream Queens Cover A by **Jab** With Colors by **Lisa Moore**

"Adventure Time: Marceline and the Scream Queens"

Written & Illustrated by **Meredith Gran** Colors by **Lisa Moore**

Letters by **Steve Wands**

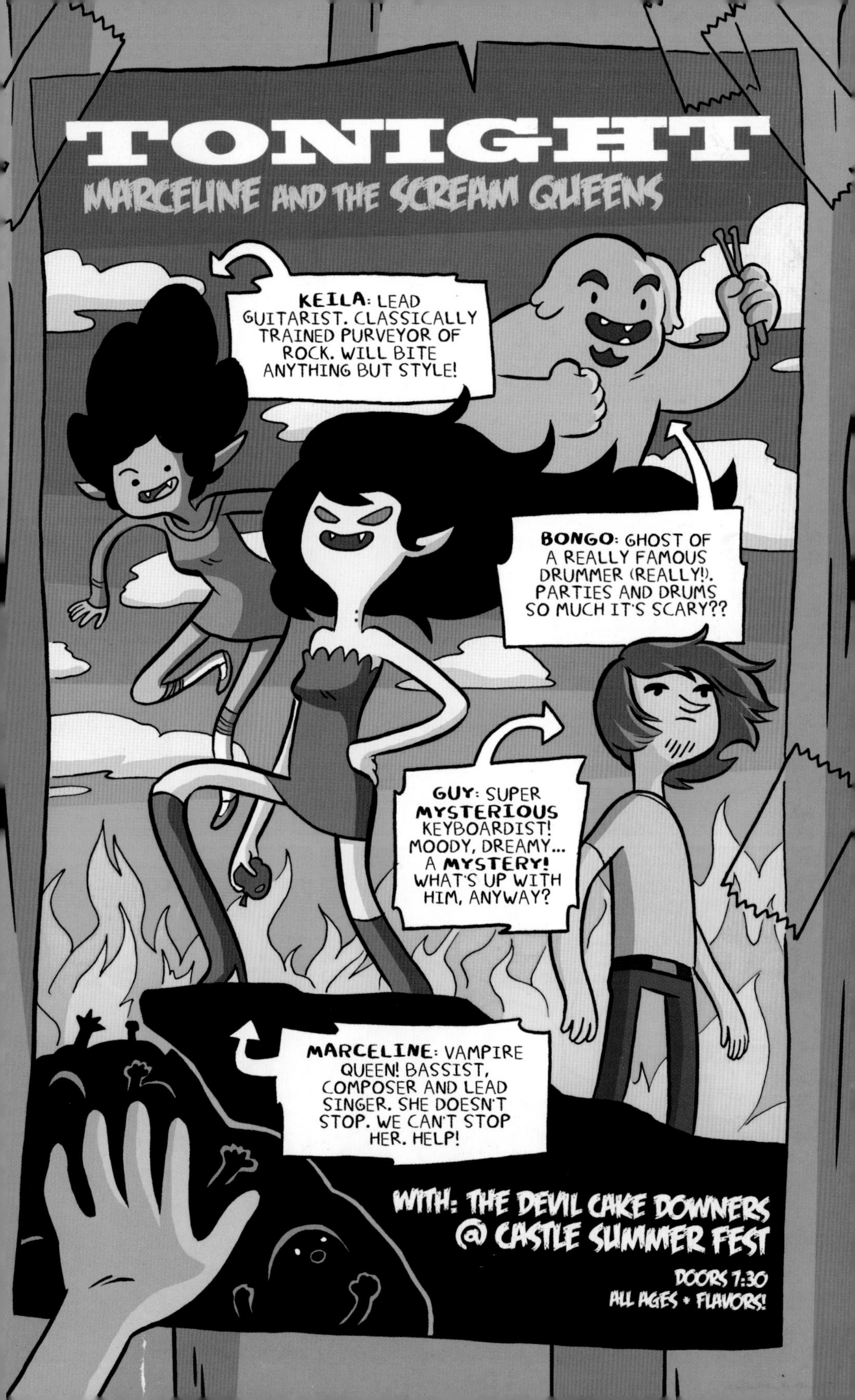
TONIGHT
MARCELINE AND THE SCREAM QUEENS
KEILA: LEAD GUITARIST. CLASSICALLY TRAINED PURVEYOR OF ROCK. WILL BITE ANYTHING BUT STYLE!
BONGO: GHOST OF A REALLY FAMOUS DRUMMER (REALLY!). PARTIES AND DRUMS SO MUCH IT'S SCARY??
GUY: SUPER MYSTERIOUS KEYBOARDIST! MOODY, DREAMY... A MYSTERY! WHAT'S UP WITH HIM, ANYWAY?
MARCELINE: VAMPIRE QUEEN! BASSIST, COMPOSER AND LEAD SINGER. SHE DOESN'T STOP. WE CAN'T STOP HER. HELP!
WITH: THE DEVIL CAKE DOWNERS
@ CASTLE SUMMER FEST
DOORS 7:30
ALL AGES + FLAVORS!

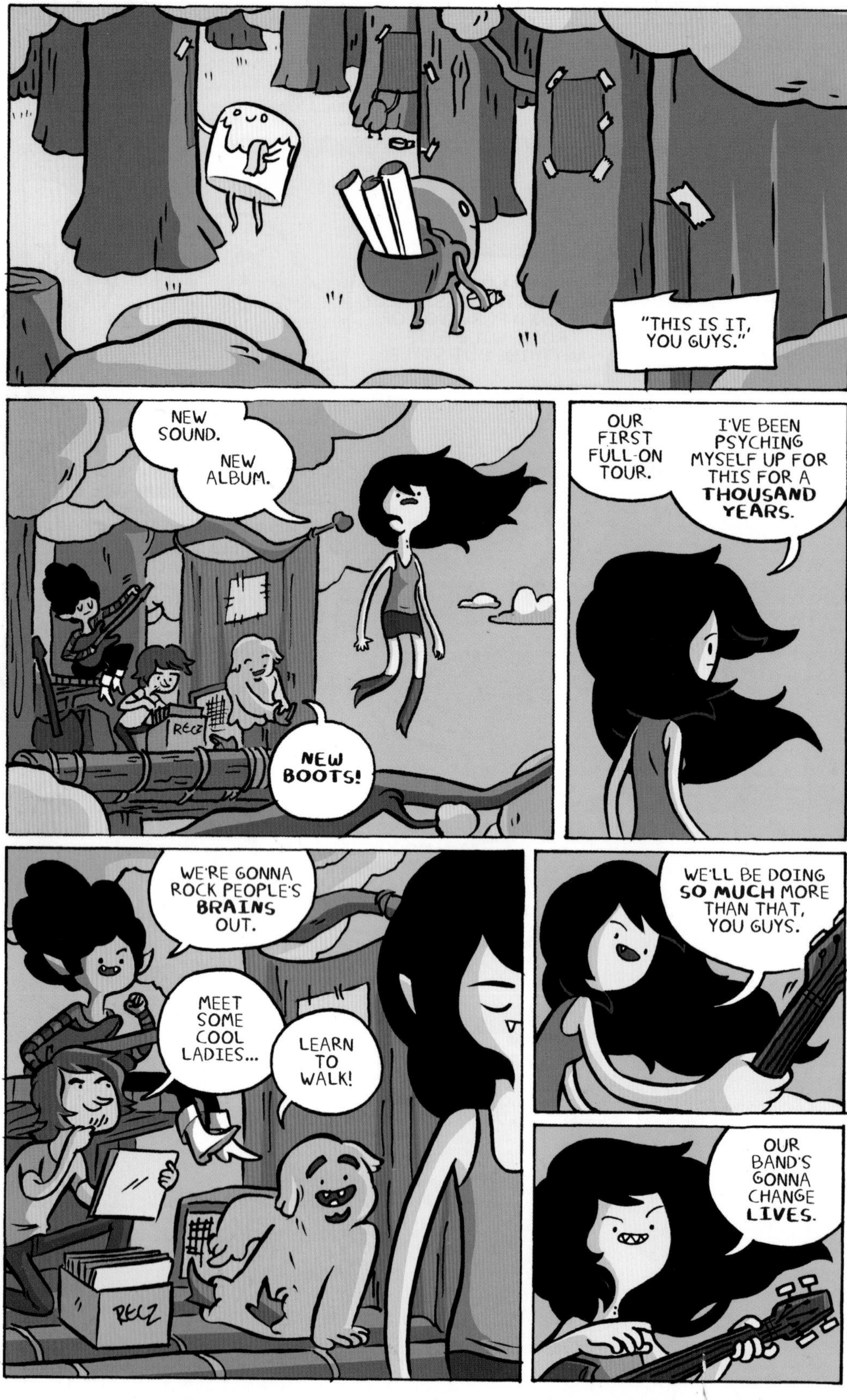
"THIS IS IT, YOU GUYS."
NEW SOUND.
NEW ALBUM.
RECZ
NEW BOOTS!
OUR FIRST FULL-ON TOUR.
I'VE BEEN PSYCHING MYSELF UP FOR THIS FOR A THOUSAND YEARS.
WE'RE GONNA ROCK PEOPLE'S BRAINS OUT.
MEET SOME COOL LADIES...
LEARN TO WALK!
RECZ
WE'LL BE DOING SO MUCH MORE THAN THAT, YOU GUYS.
OUR BAND'S GONNA CHANGE LIVES.

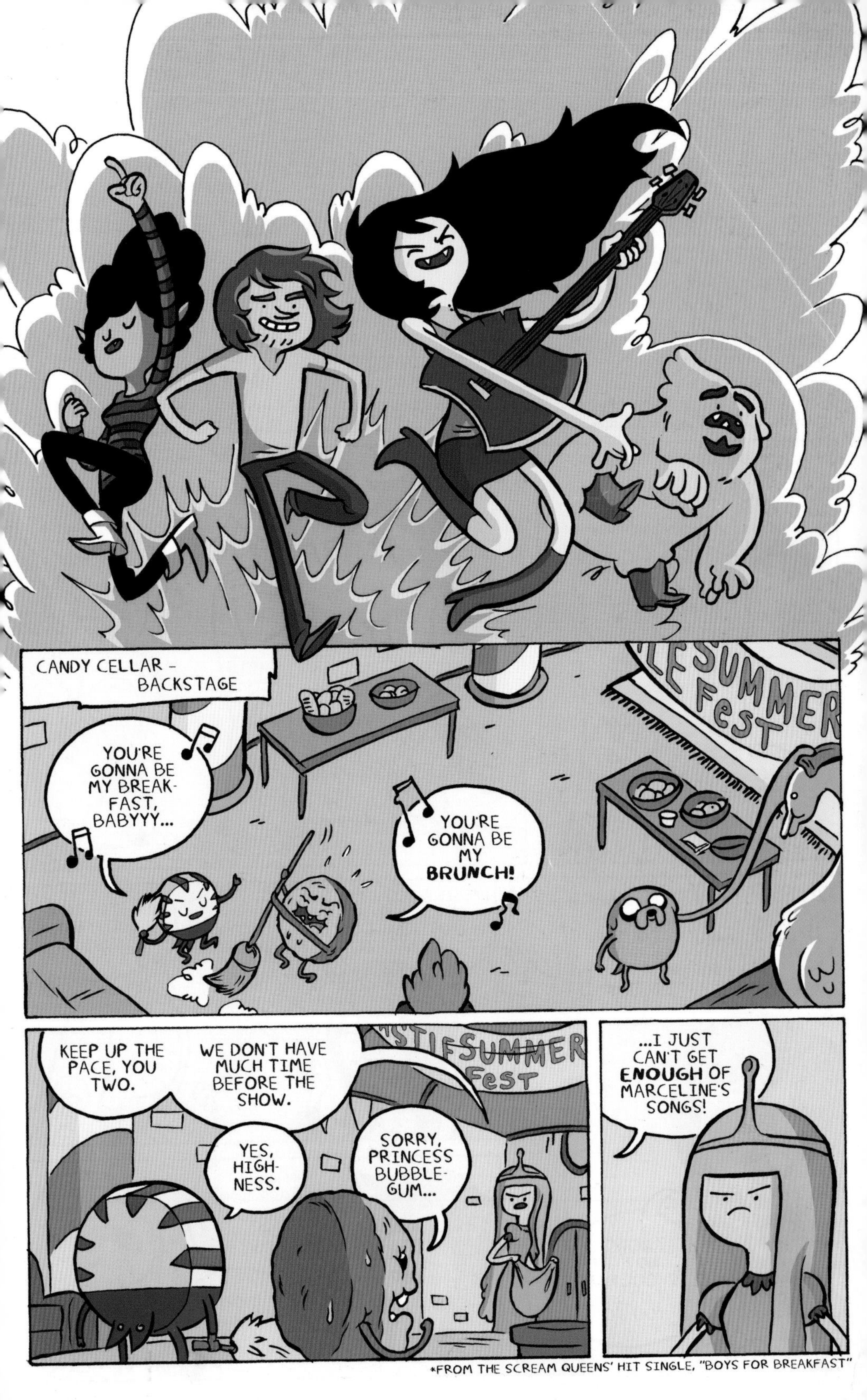
CANDY CELLAR – BACKSTAGE
YOU'RE GONNA BE MY BREAK-FAST, BABYYY...
YOU'RE GONNA BE MY **BRUNCH!**
SUMMER Fest
KEEP UP THE PACE, YOU TWO.
WE DON'T HAVE MUCH TIME BEFORE THE SHOW.
YES, HIGH-NESS.
SORRY, PRINCESS BUBBLE-GUM...
...I JUST CAN'T GET **ENOUGH** OF MARCELINE'S SONGS!

*FROM THE SCREAM QUEENS' HIT SINGLE, "BOYS FOR BREAKFAST"

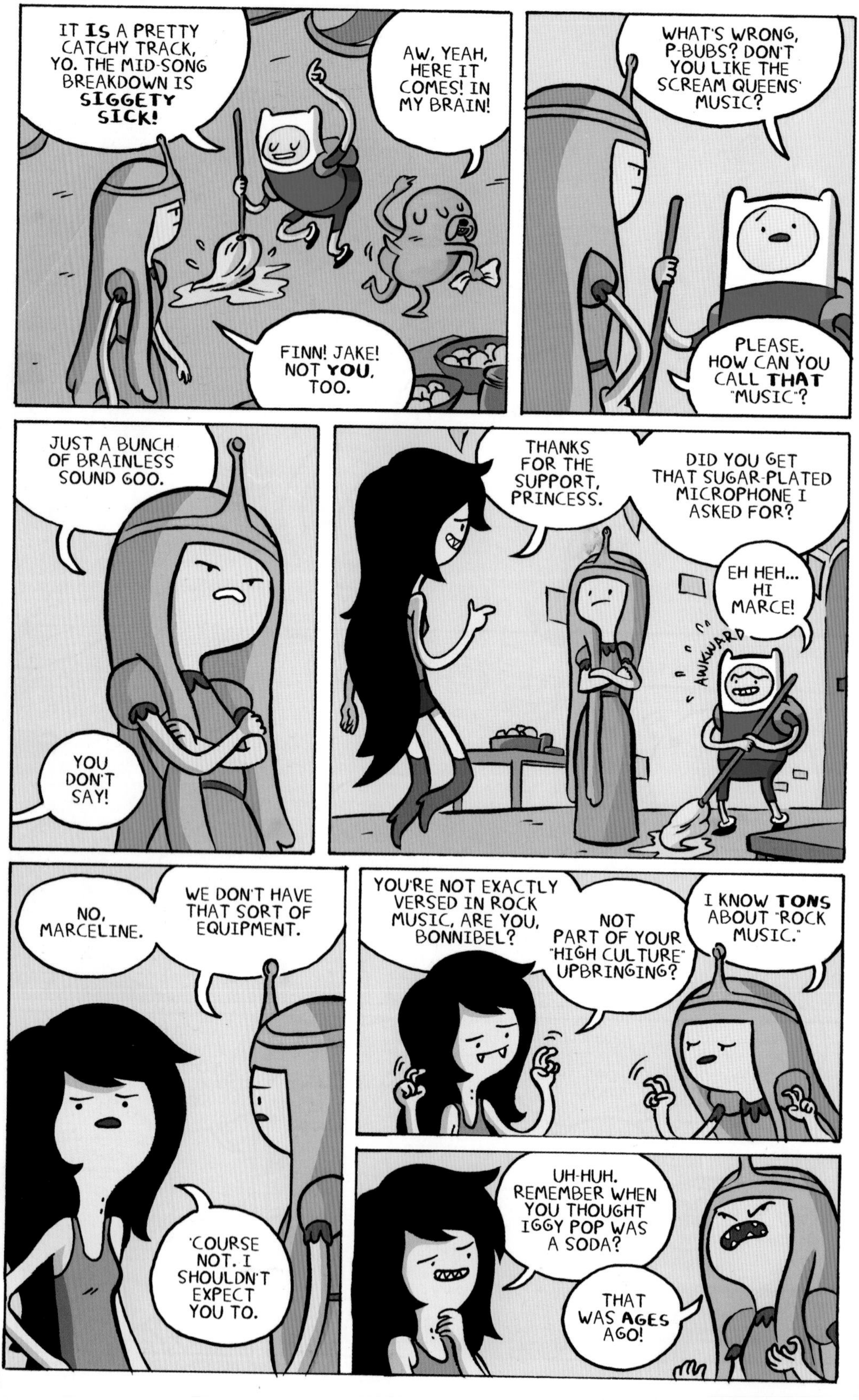
IT IS A PRETTY CATCHY TRACK, YO. THE MID-SONG BREAKDOWN IS SIGGETY SICK!
AW, YEAH, HERE IT COMES! IN MY BRAIN!
FINN! JAKE! NOT YOU, TOO.
WHAT'S WRONG, P-BUBS? DON'T YOU LIKE THE SCREAM QUEENS' MUSIC?
PLEASE. HOW CAN YOU CALL THAT "MUSIC"?
JUST A BUNCH OF BRAINLESS SOUND GOO.
YOU DON'T SAY!
THANKS FOR THE SUPPORT, PRINCESS.
DID YOU GET THAT SUGAR-PLATED MICROPHONE I ASKED FOR?
EH HEH... HI MARCE!
AWKWARD
NO, MARCELINE.
WE DON'T HAVE THAT SORT OF EQUIPMENT.
'COURSE NOT. I SHOULDN'T EXPECT YOU TO.
YOU'RE NOT EXACTLY VERSED IN ROCK MUSIC, ARE YOU, BONNIBEL?
NOT PART OF YOUR "HIGH CULTURE" UPBRINGING?
I KNOW TONS ABOUT "ROCK MUSIC."
UH-HUH. REMEMBER WHEN YOU THOUGHT IGGY POP WAS A SODA?
THAT WAS AGES AGO!

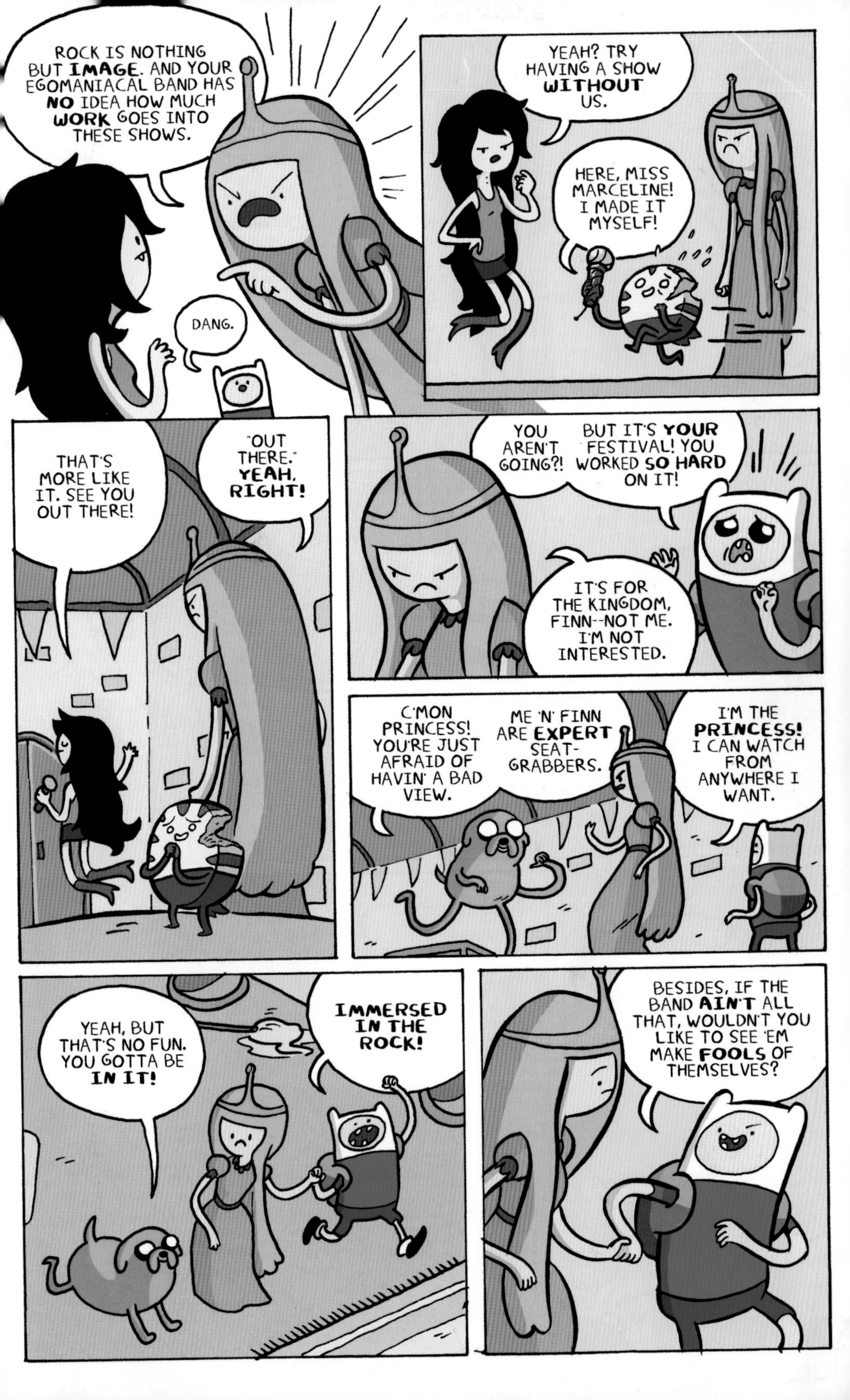
ROCK IS NOTHING BUT **IMAGE**. AND YOUR EGOMANIACAL BAND HAS **NO** IDEA HOW MUCH **WORK** GOES INTO THESE SHOWS.
DANG.
YEAH? TRY HAVING A SHOW **WITHOUT** US.
HERE, MISS MARCELINE! I MADE IT MYSELF!
THAT'S MORE LIKE IT. SEE YOU OUT THERE!
"OUT THERE." **YEAH, RIGHT!**
YOU AREN'T GOING?!
BUT IT'S **YOUR** FESTIVAL! YOU WORKED **SO HARD** ON IT!
IT'S FOR THE KINGDOM, FINN--NOT ME. I'M NOT INTERESTED.
C'MON PRINCESS! YOU'RE JUST AFRAID OF HAVIN' A BAD VIEW.
ME 'N' FINN ARE **EXPERT** SEAT-GRABBERS.
I'M THE **PRINCESS!** I CAN WATCH FROM ANYWHERE I WANT.
YEAH, BUT THAT'S NO FUN. YOU GOTTA BE **IN IT!**
IMMERSED IN THE ROCK!
BESIDES, IF THE BAND **AIN'T** ALL THAT, WOULDN'T YOU LIKE TO SEE 'EM MAKE **FOOLS** OF THEMSELVES?

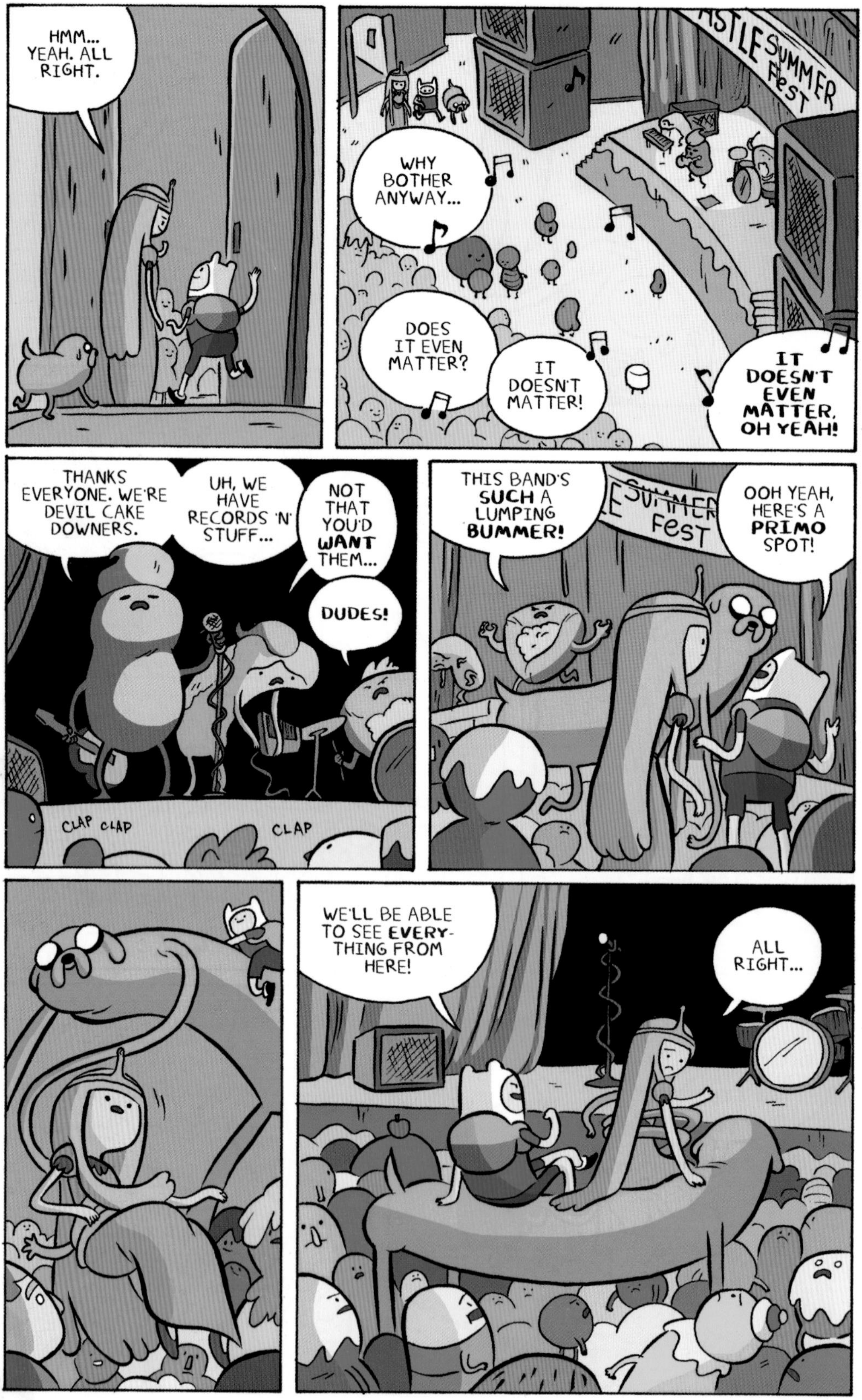
HMM... YEAH. ALL RIGHT.
WHY BOTHER ANYWAY...
DOES IT EVEN MATTER?
IT DOESN'T MATTER!
IT DOESN'T EVEN MATTER, OH YEAH!
THANKS EVERYONE. WE'RE DEVIL CAKE DOWNERS.
UH, WE HAVE RECORDS 'N' STUFF...
NOT THAT YOU'D **WANT** THEM...
DUDES!
CLAP CLAP
CLAP
THIS BAND'S **SUCH** A LUMPING **BUMMER!**
OOH YEAH, HERE'S A **PRIMO** SPOT!
WE'LL BE ABLE TO SEE **EVERY**-THING FROM HERE!
ALL RIGHT...

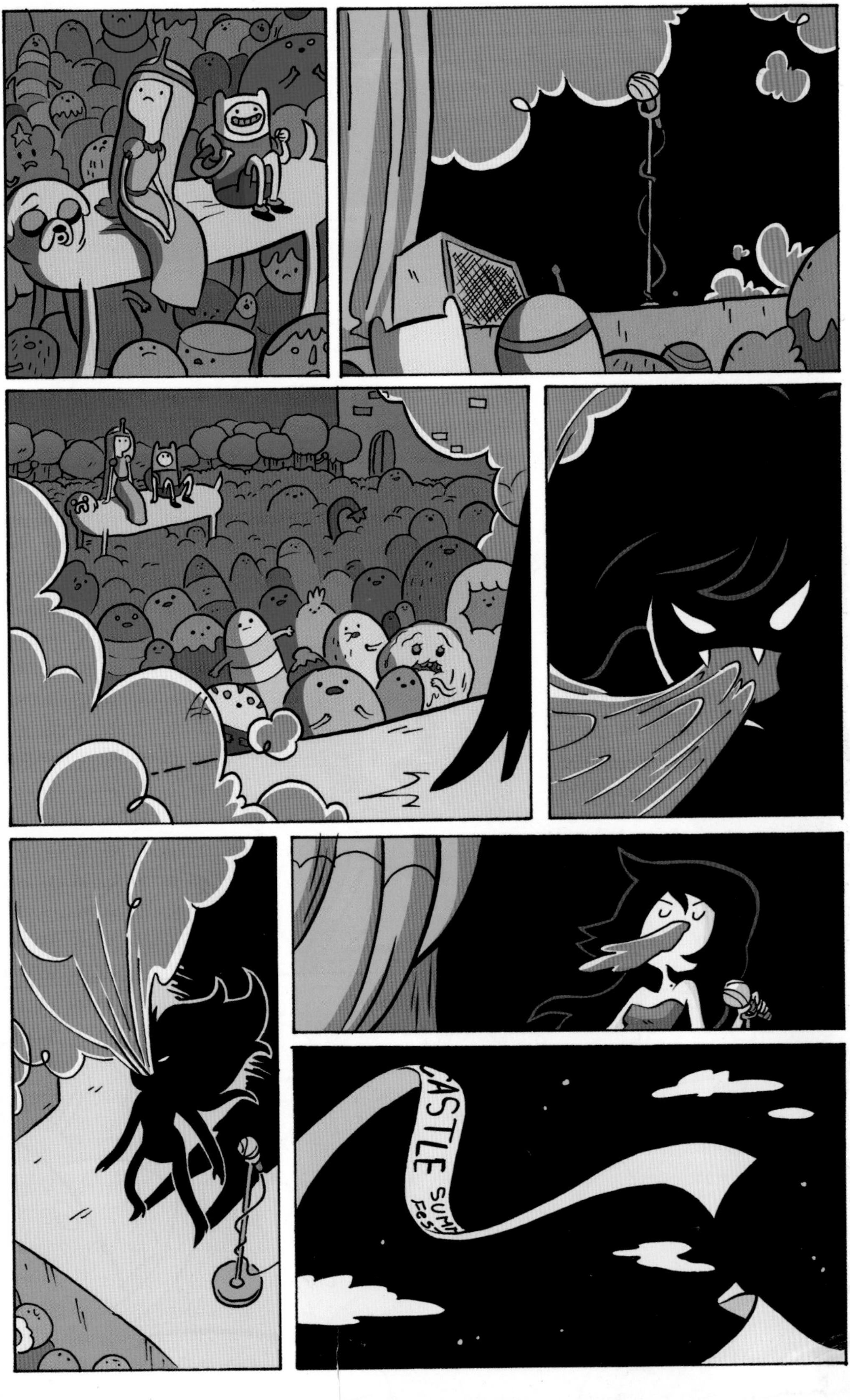
CASTLE SUMM
FES

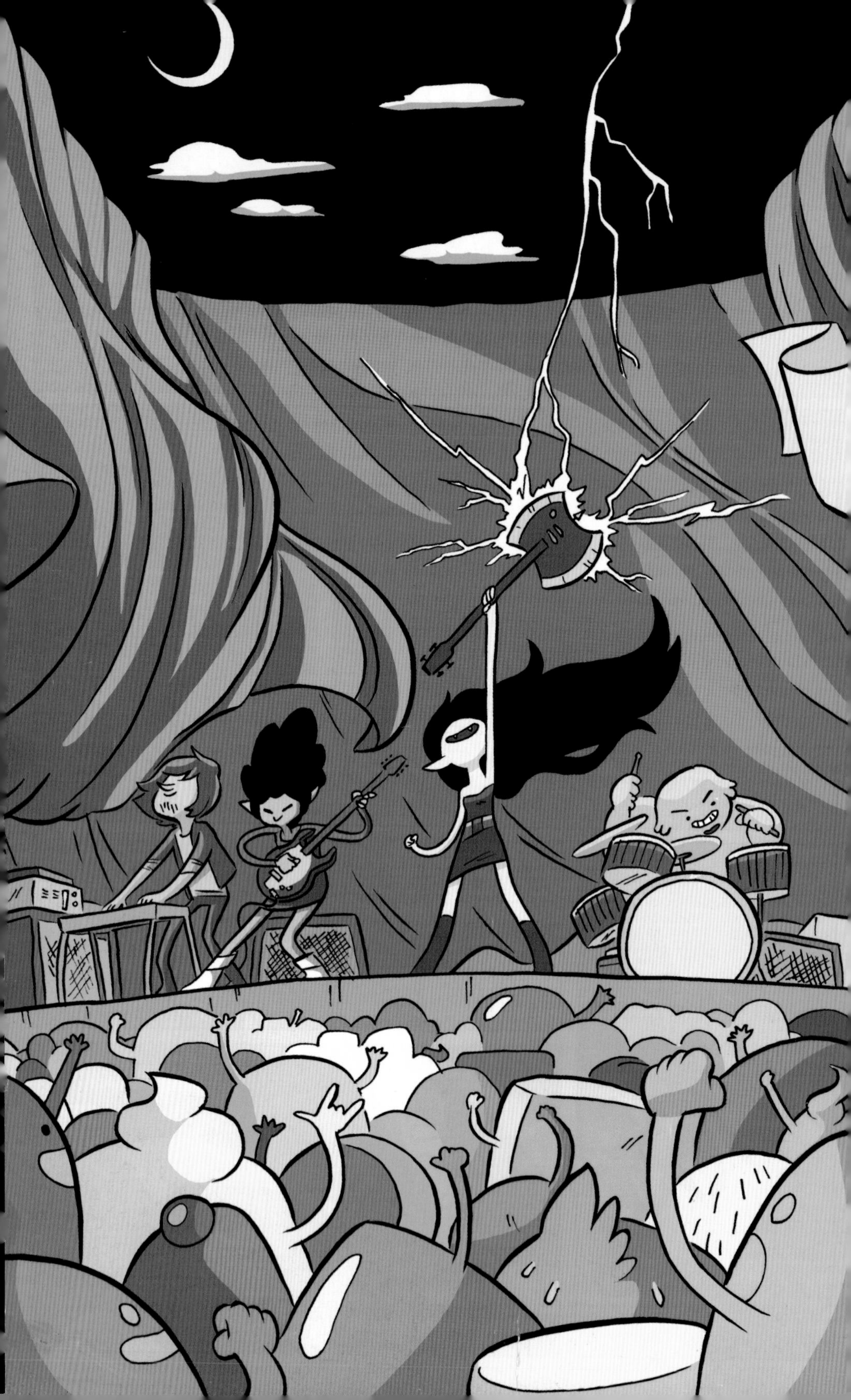

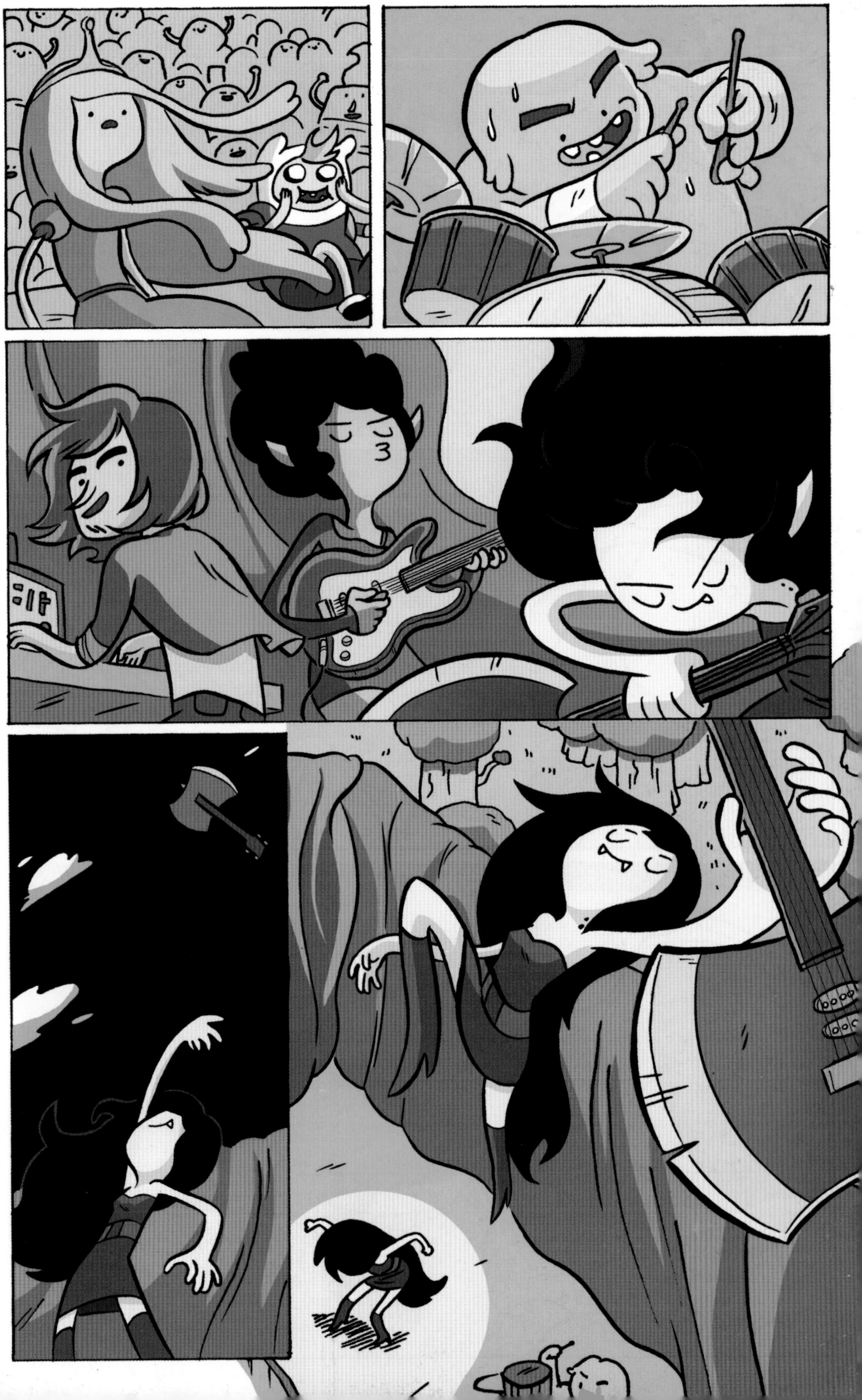

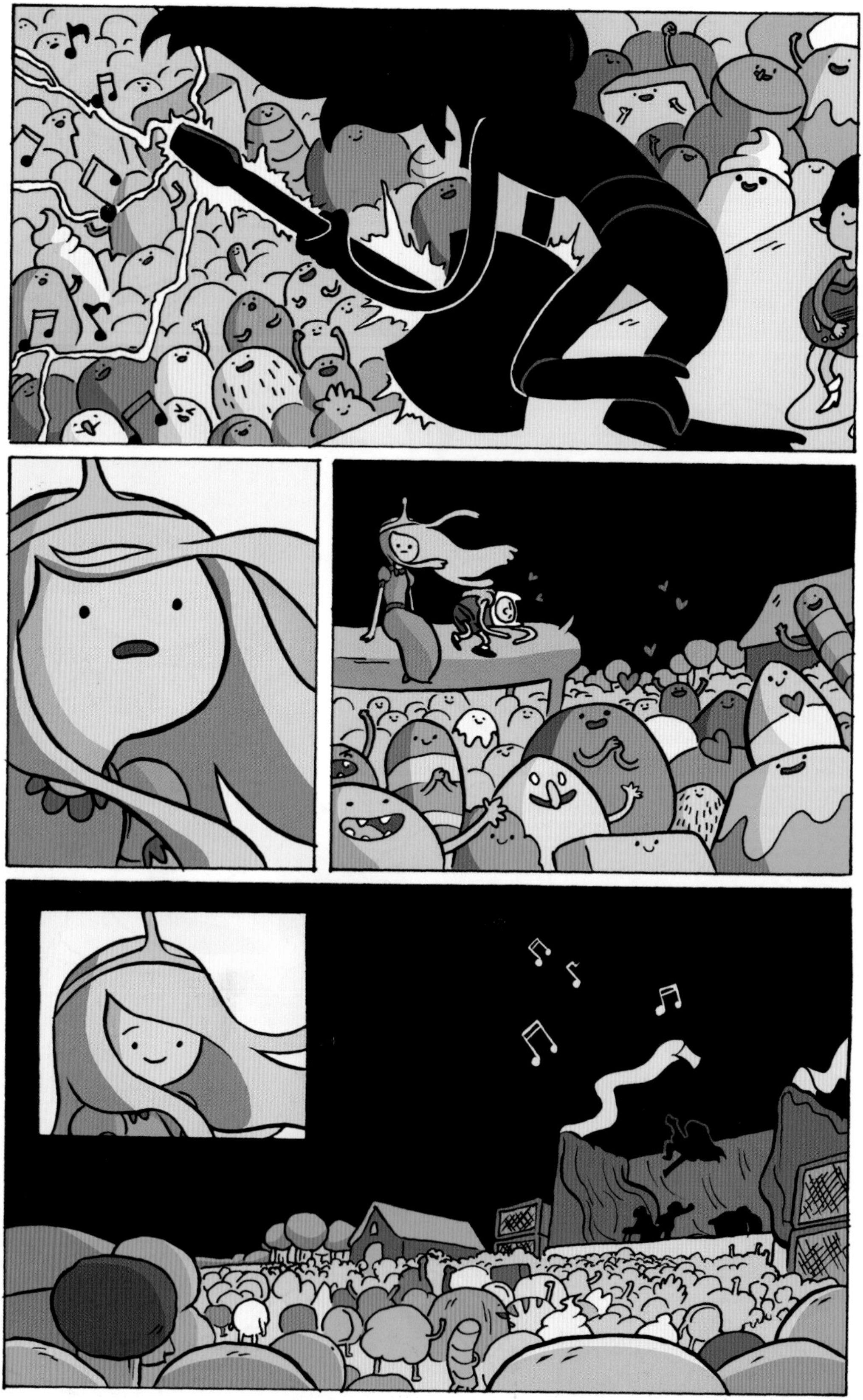

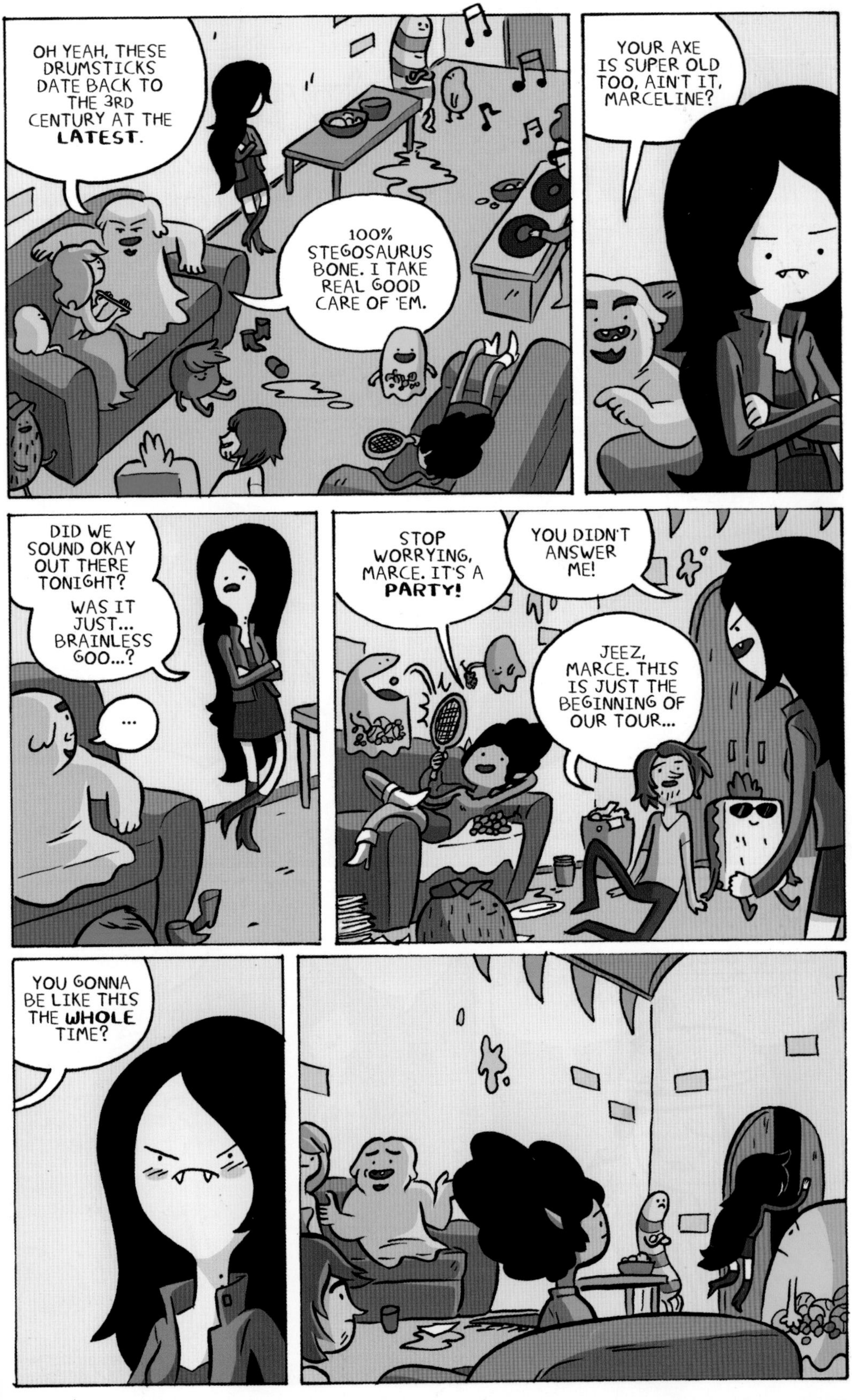
OH YEAH, THESE DRUMSTICKS DATE BACK TO THE 3RD CENTURY AT THE LATEST.
100% STEGOSAURUS BONE. I TAKE REAL GOOD CARE OF 'EM.
YOUR AXE IS SUPER OLD TOO, AIN'T IT, MARCELINE?
DID WE SOUND OKAY OUT THERE TONIGHT?
WAS IT JUST... BRAINLESS GOO...?
...
STOP WORRYING, MARCE. IT'S A PARTY!
YOU DIDN'T ANSWER ME!
JEEZ, MARCE. THIS IS JUST THE BEGINNING OF OUR TOUR...
YOU GONNA BE LIKE THIS THE WHOLE TIME?

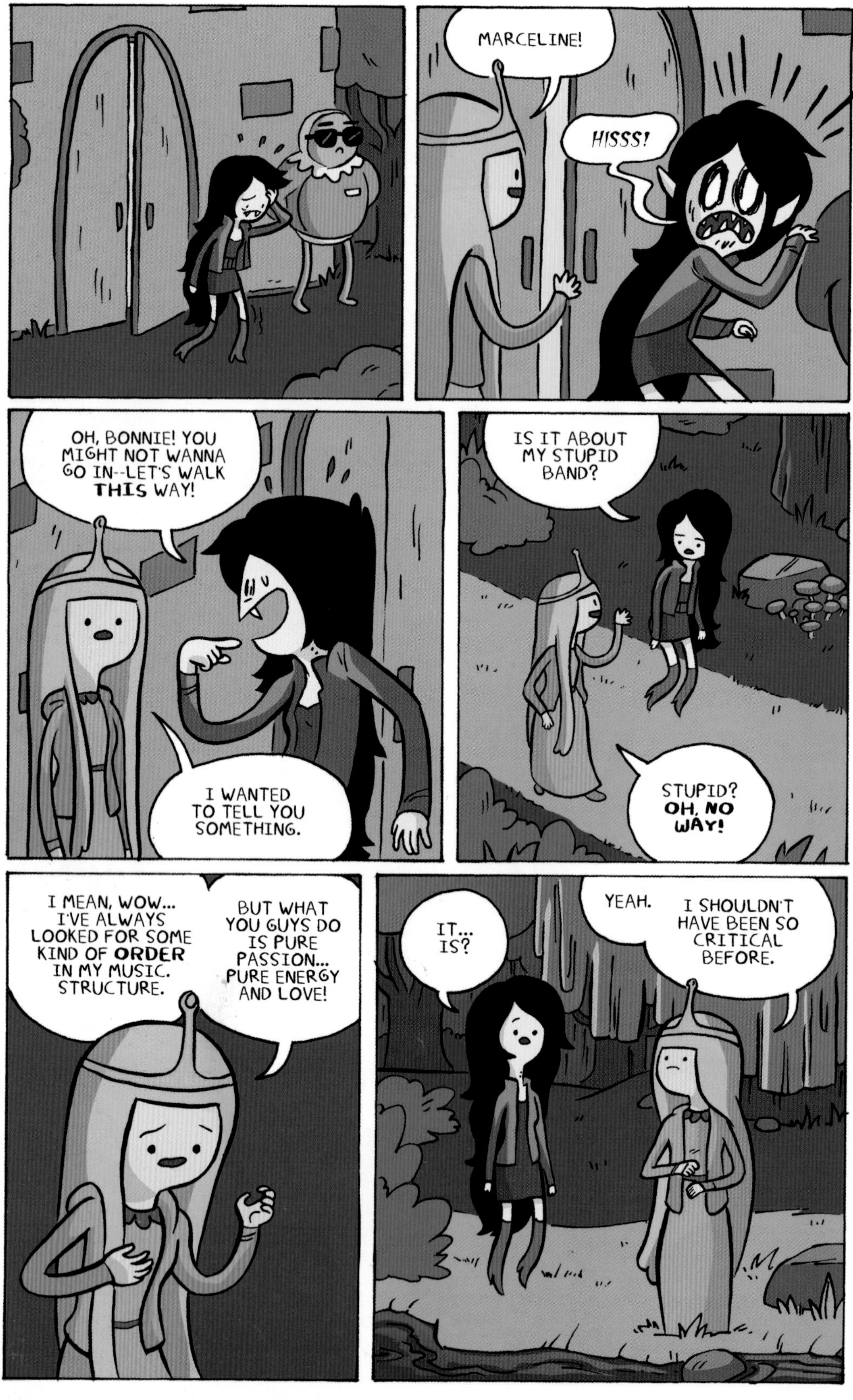
MARCELINE!
HISSS!
OH, BONNIE! YOU MIGHT NOT WANNA GO IN--LET'S WALK **THIS** WAY!
I WANTED TO TELL YOU SOMETHING.
IS IT ABOUT MY STUPID BAND?
STUPID? **OH, NO WAY!**
I MEAN, WOW... I'VE ALWAYS LOOKED FOR SOME KIND OF **ORDER** IN MY MUSIC. STRUCTURE.
BUT WHAT YOU GUYS DO IS PURE PASSION... PURE ENERGY AND LOVE!
IT... IS?
YEAH.
I SHOULDN'T HAVE BEEN SO CRITICAL BEFORE.

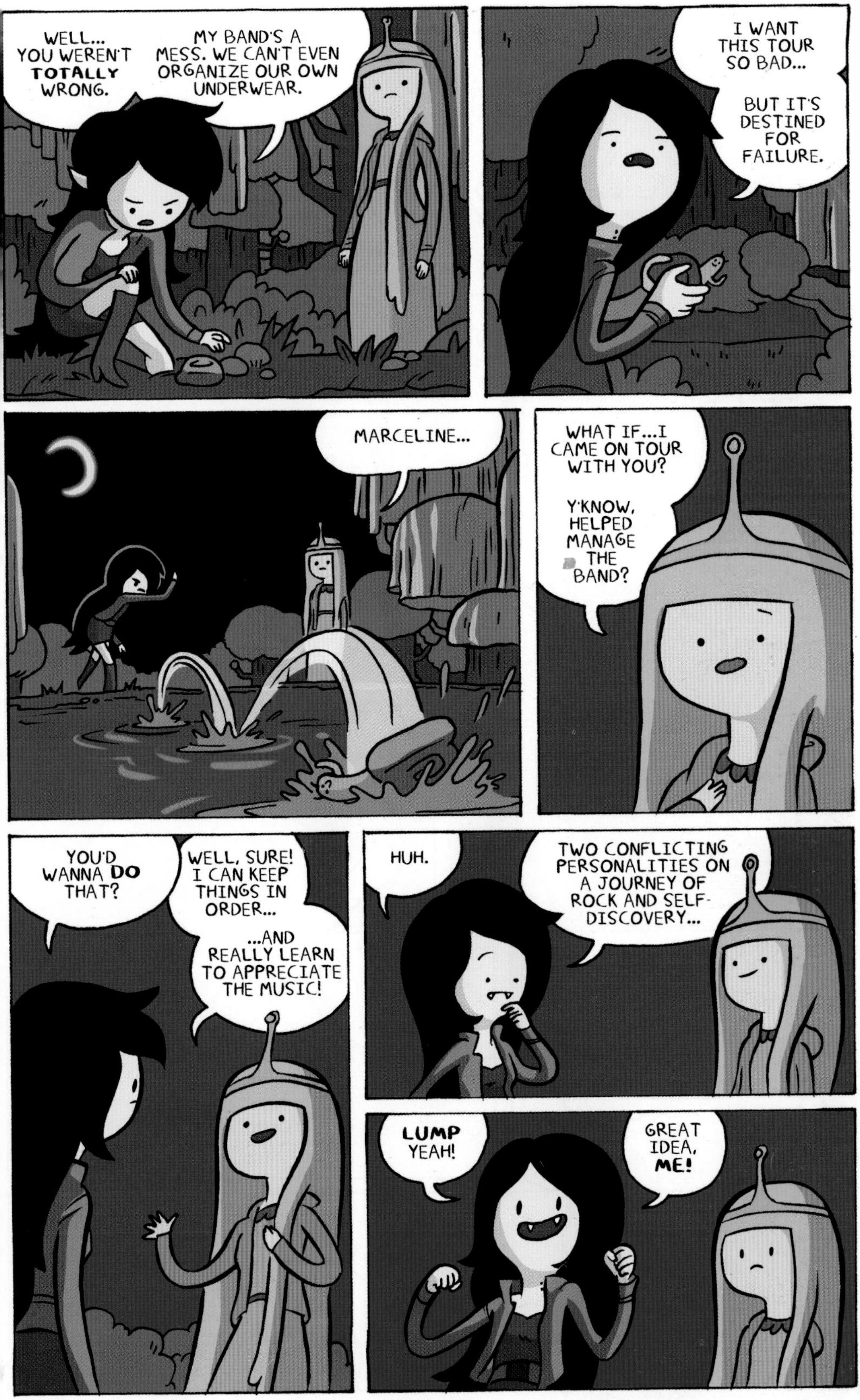
WELL... YOU WEREN'T **TOTALLY** WRONG.
MY BAND'S A MESS. WE CAN'T EVEN ORGANIZE OUR OWN UNDERWEAR.
I WANT THIS TOUR SO BAD...
BUT IT'S DESTINED FOR FAILURE.
MARCELINE...
WHAT IF...I CAME ON TOUR WITH YOU?
Y'KNOW, HELPED MANAGE THE BAND?
YOU'D WANNA **DO** THAT?
WELL, SURE! I CAN KEEP THINGS IN ORDER...
...AND REALLY LEARN TO APPRECIATE THE MUSIC!
HUH.
TWO CONFLICTING PERSONALITIES ON A JOURNEY OF ROCK AND SELF-DISCOVERY...
LUMP YEAH!
GREAT IDEA, **ME!**

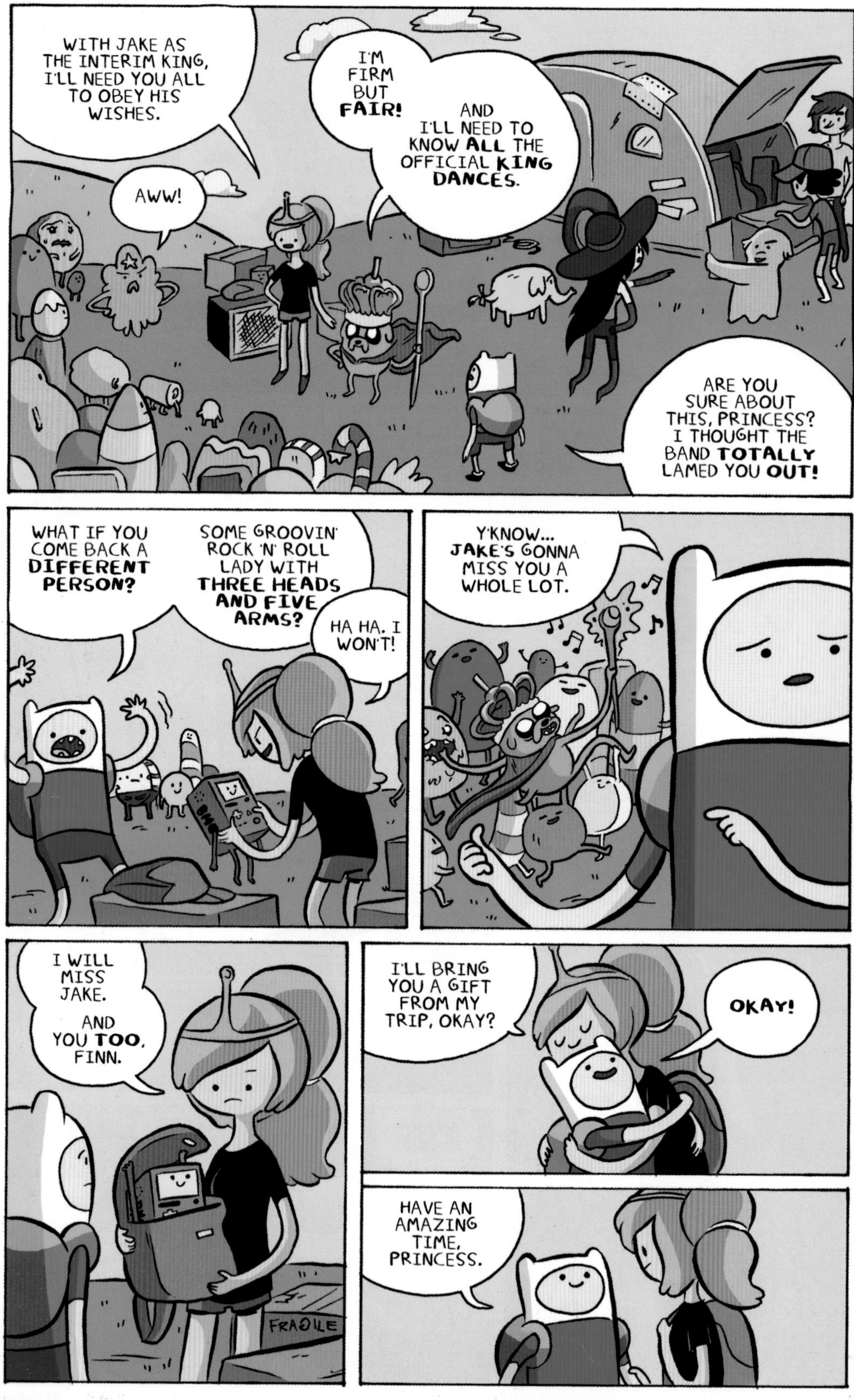
WITH JAKE AS THE INTERIM KING, I'LL NEED YOU ALL TO OBEY HIS WISHES.
AWW!
I'M FIRM BUT FAIR!
AND I'LL NEED TO KNOW ALL THE OFFICIAL KING DANCES.
ARE YOU SURE ABOUT THIS, PRINCESS? I THOUGHT THE BAND TOTALLY LAMED YOU OUT!
WHAT IF YOU COME BACK A DIFFERENT PERSON?
SOME GROOVIN' ROCK 'N' ROLL LADY WITH THREE HEADS AND FIVE ARMS?
HA HA. I WON'T!
Y'KNOW... JAKE'S GONNA MISS YOU A WHOLE LOT.
I WILL MISS JAKE.
AND YOU TOO, FINN.
FRAGILE
I'LL BRING YOU A GIFT FROM MY TRIP, OKAY?
OKAY!
HAVE AN AMAZING TIME, PRINCESS.

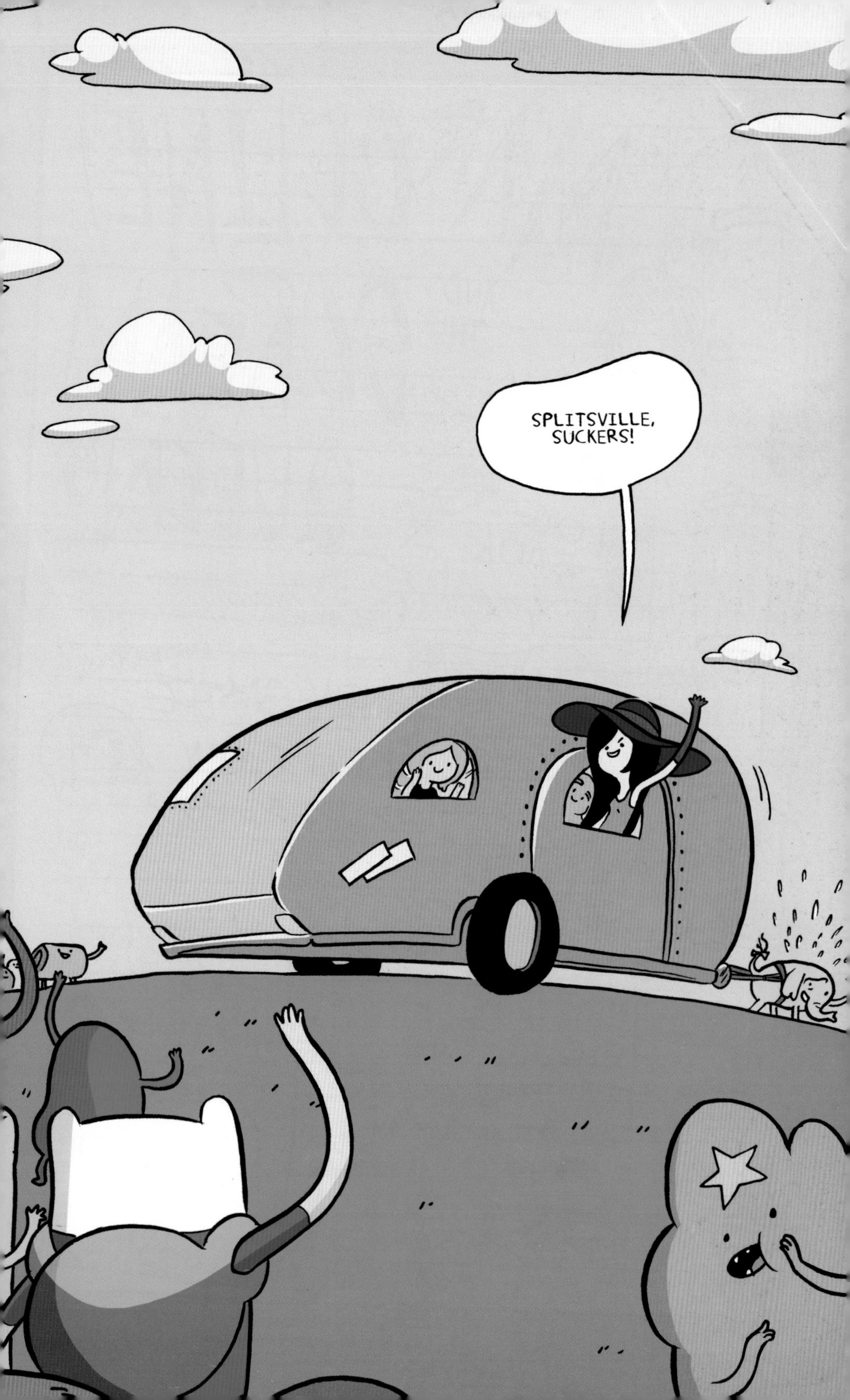
SPLITSVILLE, SUCKERS!

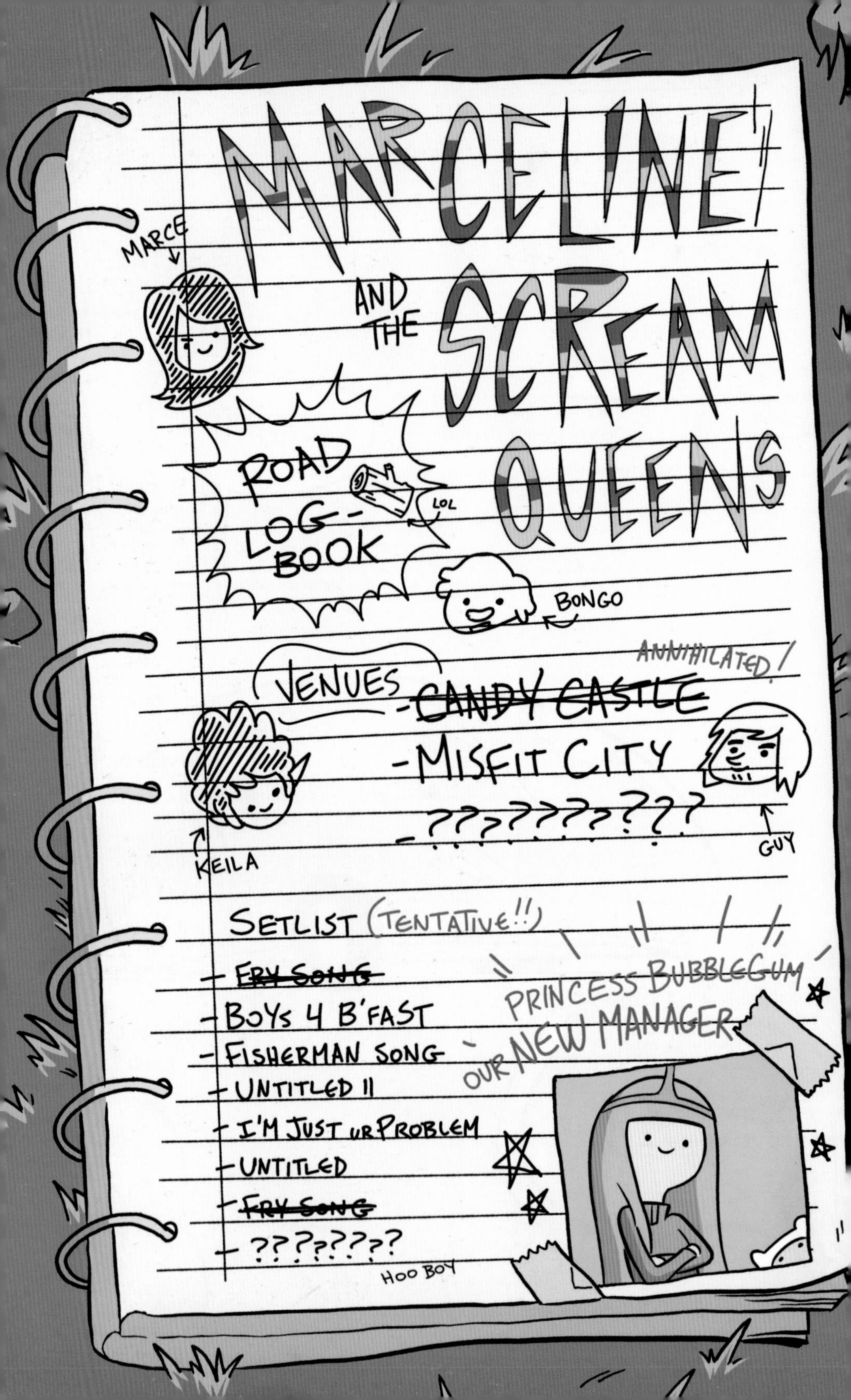
MARCELINE AND THE SCREAM QUEENS
MARCE
ROAD -LOG- BOOK
LOL
BONGO
VENUES
-CANDY CASTLE
ANNIHILATED!
-MISFIT CITY
-??????????
GUY
KEILA
SETLIST (TENTATIVE!!)
-FRY SONG
-BOYS 4 B'FAST
-FISHERMAN SONG
-UNTITLED II
-I'M JUST UR PROBLEM
-UNTITLED
-FRY SONG
-????????
HOO BOY
PRINCESS BUBBLEGUM
OUR NEW MANAGER

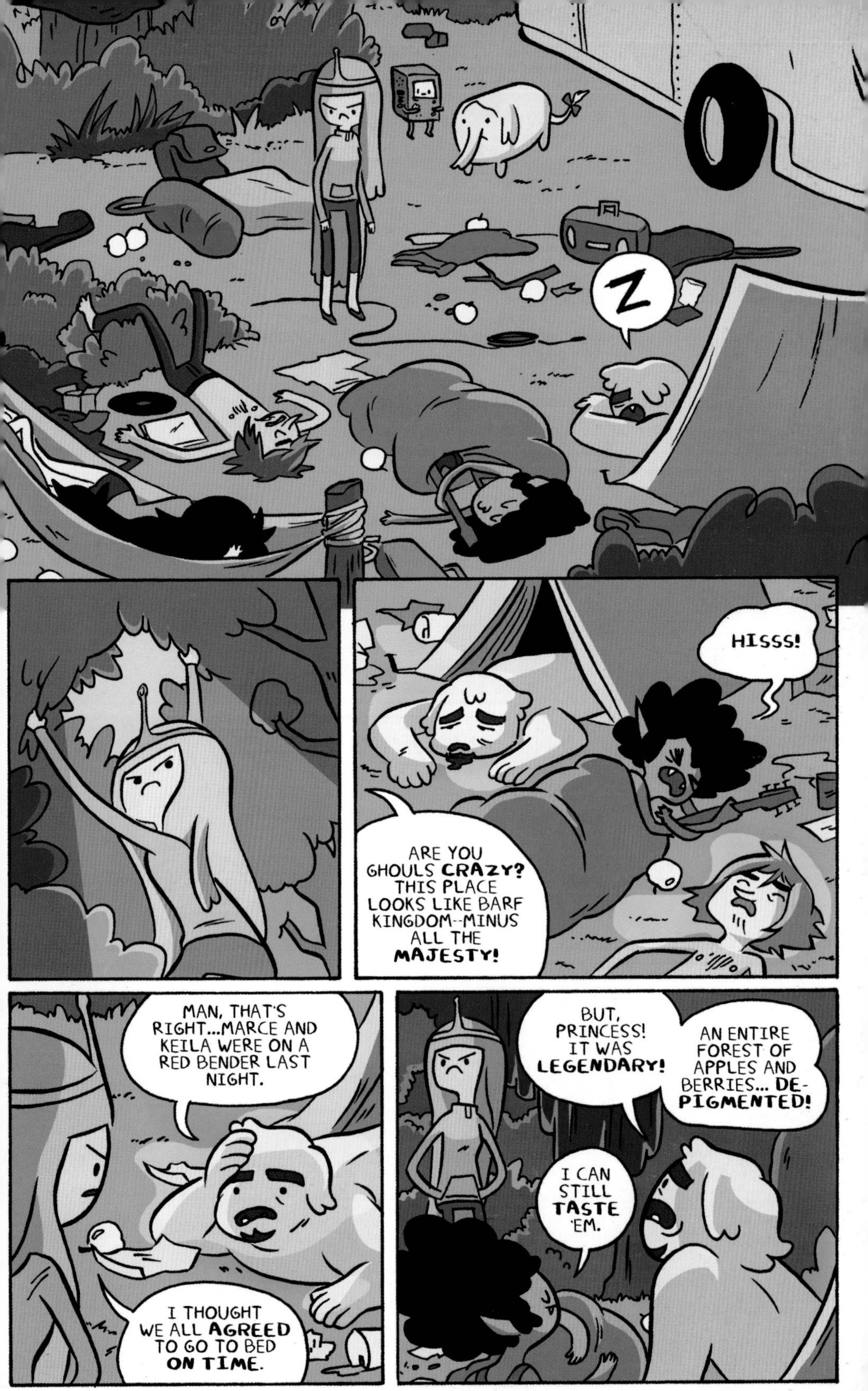
Z
HISSS!
ARE YOU GHOULS CRAZY? THIS PLACE LOOKS LIKE BARF KINGDOM--MINUS ALL THE MAJESTY!
MAN, THAT'S RIGHT...MARCE AND KEILA WERE ON A RED BENDER LAST NIGHT.
I THOUGHT WE ALL AGREED TO GO TO BED ON TIME.
BUT, PRINCESS! IT WAS LEGENDARY!
AN ENTIRE FOREST OF APPLES AND BERRIES... DE-PIGMENTED!
I CAN STILL TASTE 'EM.

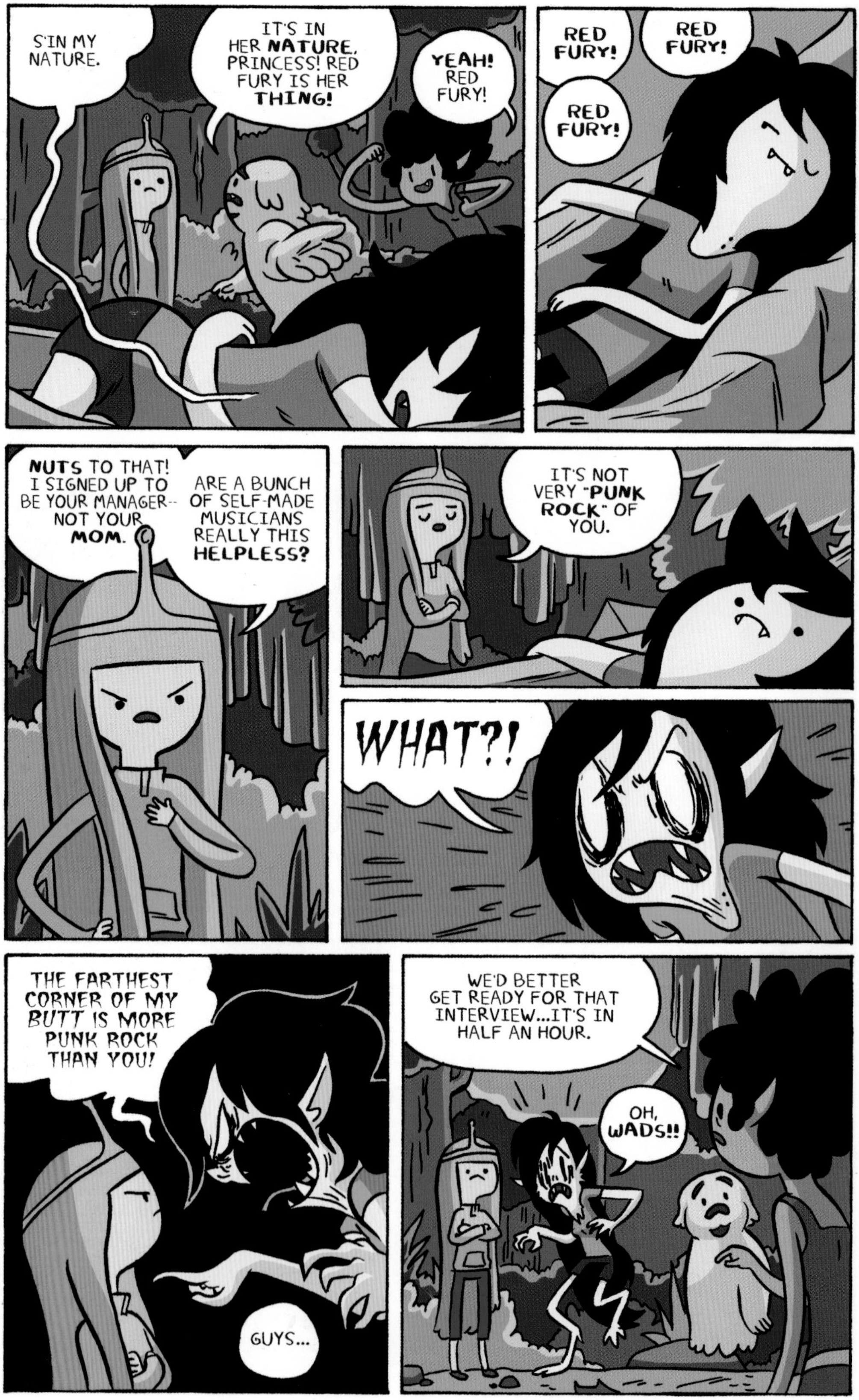
S'IN MY NATURE.
IT'S IN HER NATURE, PRINCESS! RED FURY IS HER THING!
YEAH! RED FURY!
RED FURY!
RED FURY!
RED FURY!
NUTS TO THAT! I SIGNED UP TO BE YOUR MANAGER-- NOT YOUR MOM.
ARE A BUNCH OF SELF-MADE MUSICIANS REALLY THIS HELPLESS?
IT'S NOT VERY "PUNK ROCK" OF YOU.
WHAT?!
THE FARTHEST CORNER OF MY BUTT IS MORE PUNK ROCK THAN YOU!
GUYS...
WE'D BETTER GET READY FOR THAT INTERVIEW...IT'S IN HALF AN HOUR.
OH, WADS!!

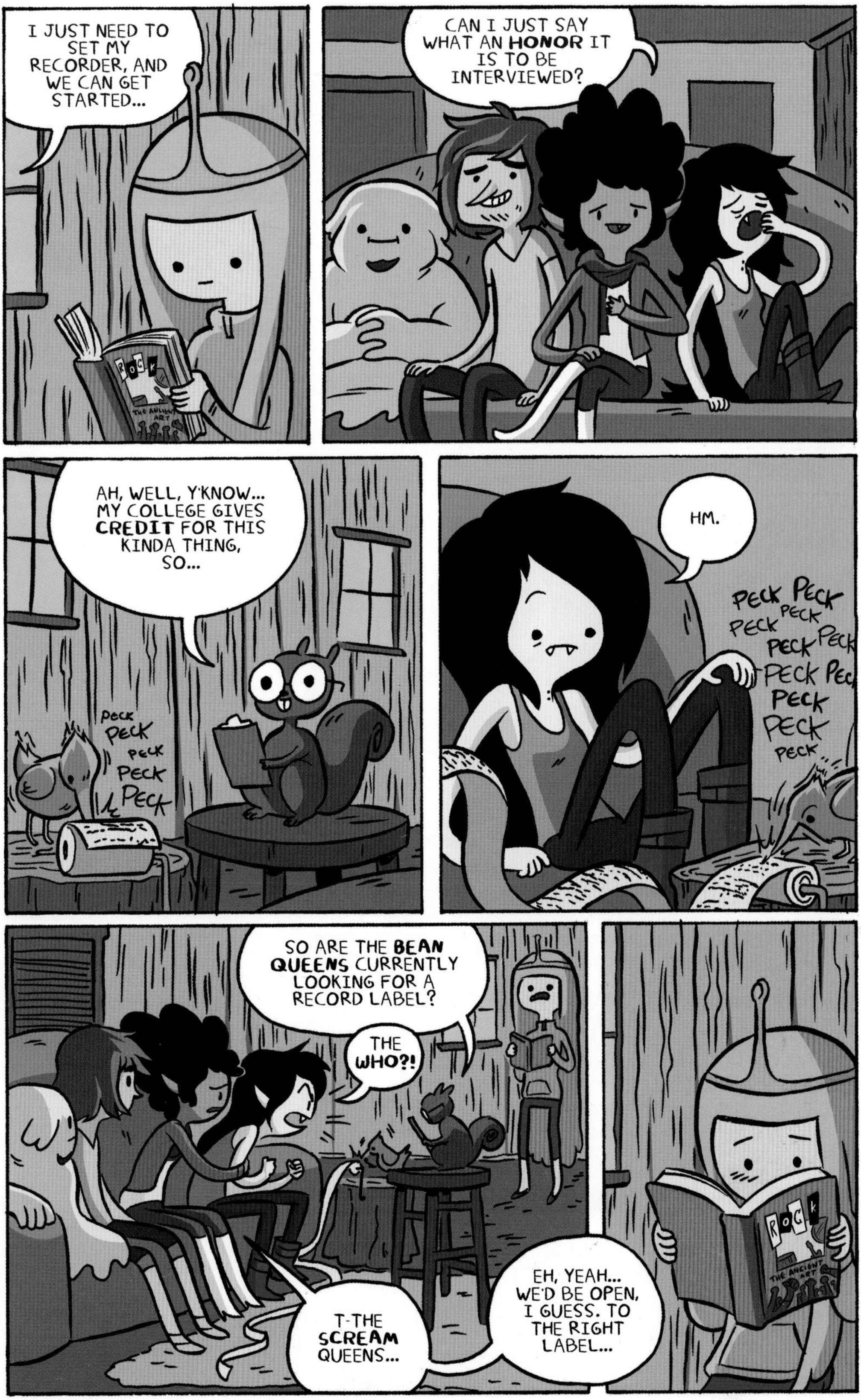
I JUST NEED TO SET MY RECORDER, AND WE CAN GET STARTED...
ROCK
THE ANCIENT ART
CAN I JUST SAY WHAT AN **HONOR** IT IS TO BE INTERVIEWED?
AH, WELL, Y'KNOW... MY COLLEGE GIVES **CREDIT** FOR THIS KINDA THING, SO...
PECK PECK PECK PECK PECK
HM.
PECK PECK PECK PECK PECK PECK PECK PECK PECK PECK
SO ARE THE **BEAN QUEENS** CURRENTLY LOOKING FOR A RECORD LABEL?
THE **WHO?!**
T-THE **SCREAM** QUEENS...
EH, YEAH... WE'D BE OPEN, I GUESS. TO THE RIGHT LABEL...
ROCK
THE ANCIENT ART

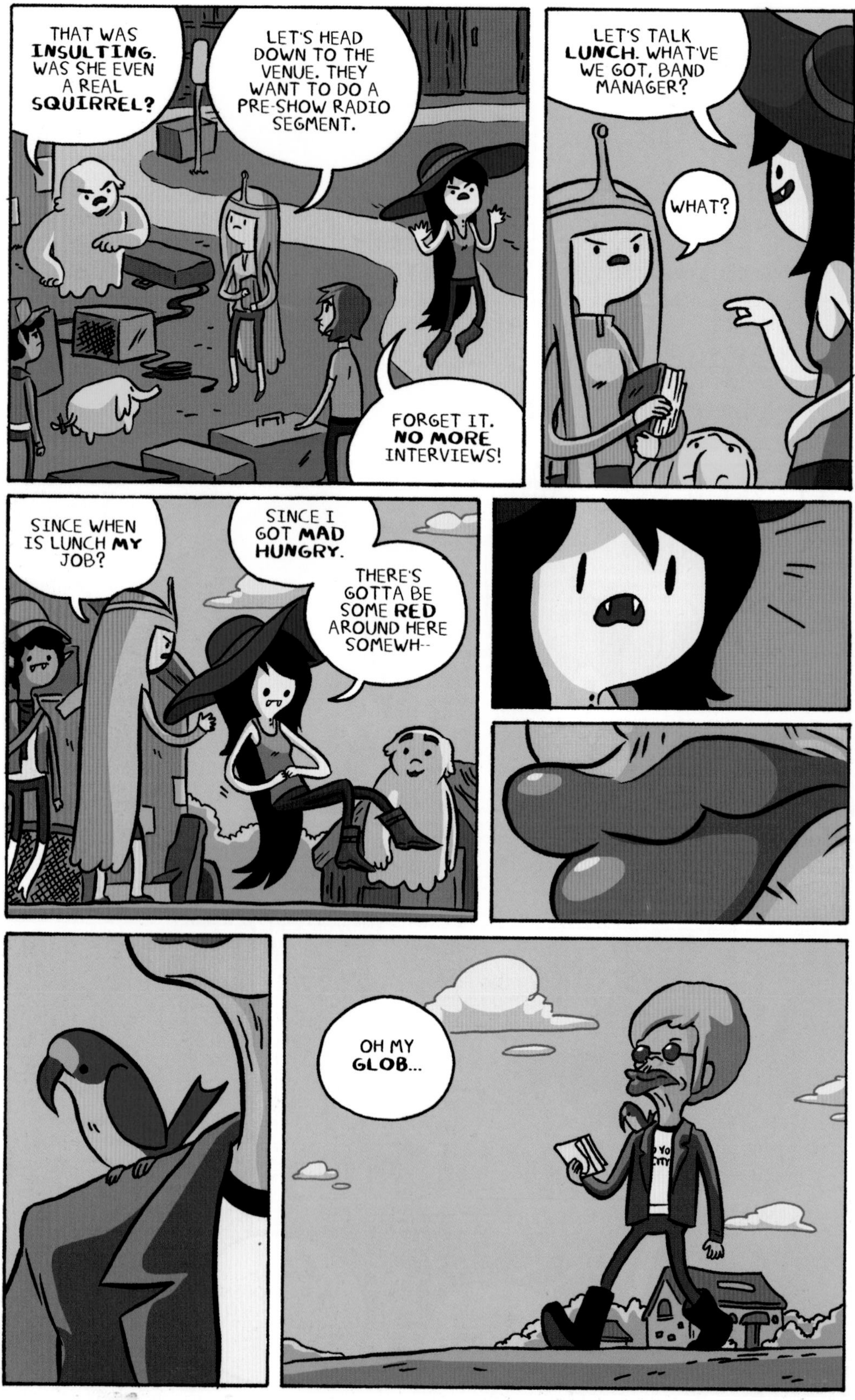
THAT WAS **INSULTING**. WAS SHE EVEN A REAL **SQUIRREL?**
LET'S HEAD DOWN TO THE VENUE. THEY WANT TO DO A PRE-SHOW RADIO SEGMENT.
FORGET IT. **NO MORE** INTERVIEWS!
LET'S TALK **LUNCH**. WHAT'VE WE GOT, BAND MANAGER?
WHAT?
SINCE WHEN IS LUNCH **MY** JOB?
SINCE I GOT **MAD HUNGRY**.
THERE'S GOTTA BE SOME **RED** AROUND HERE SOMEWH--
OH MY **GLOB**...

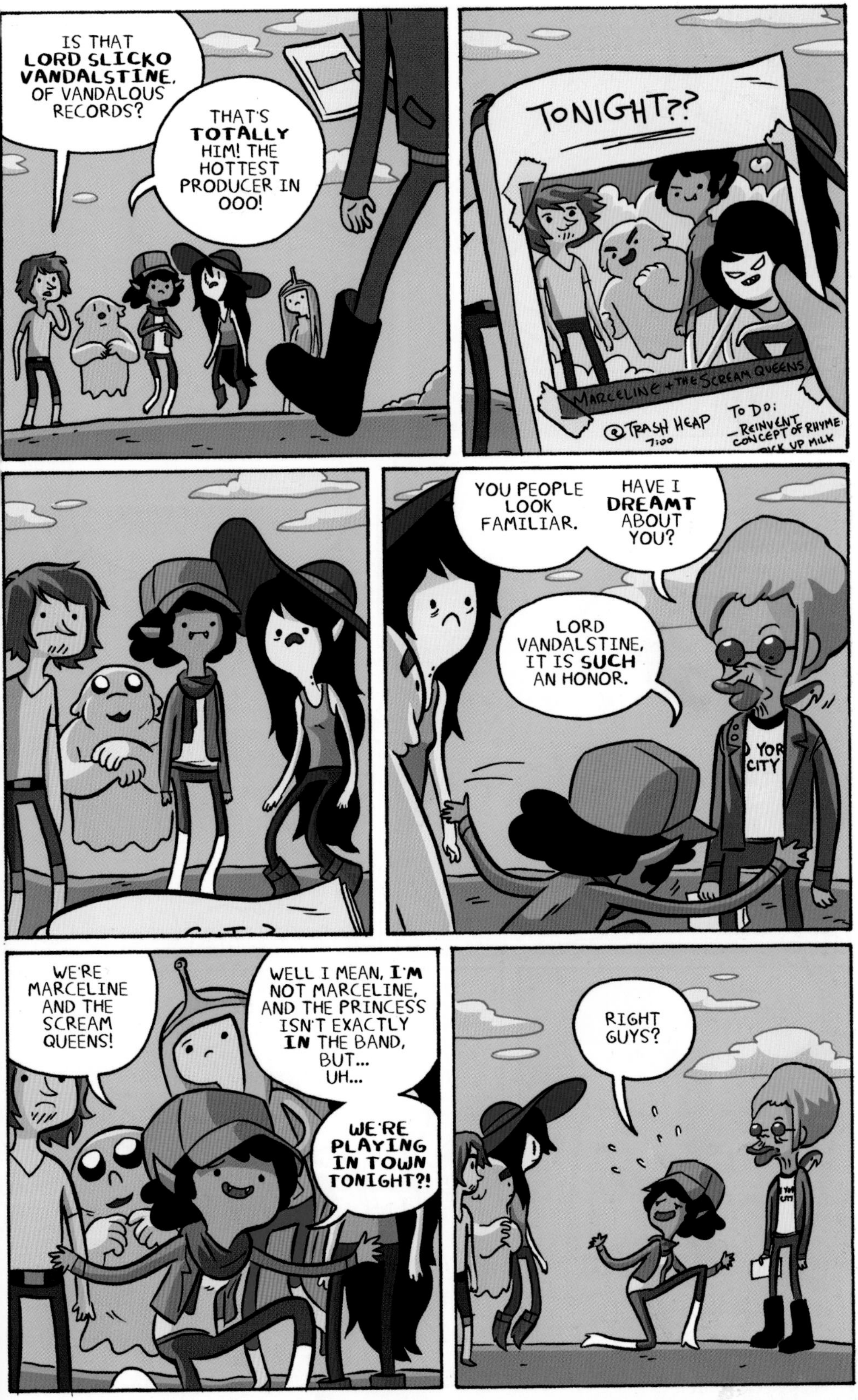
IS THAT **LORD SLICKO VANDALSTINE**, OF VANDALOUS RECORDS?
THAT'S **TOTALLY** HIM! THE HOTTEST PRODUCER IN OOO!
TONIGHT??
MARCELINE + THE SCREAM QUEENS
@ TRASH HEAP 7:00
TO DO: — REINVENT CONCEPT OF RHYME
YOU PEOPLE LOOK FAMILIAR.
HAVE I **DREAMT** ABOUT YOU?
LORD VANDALSTINE, IT IS **SUCH** AN HONOR.
WE'RE MARCELINE AND THE SCREAM QUEENS!
WELL I MEAN, **I'M** NOT MARCELINE, AND THE PRINCESS ISN'T EXACTLY **IN** THE BAND, BUT... UH...
WE'RE PLAYING IN TOWN TONIGHT?!
RIGHT GUYS?

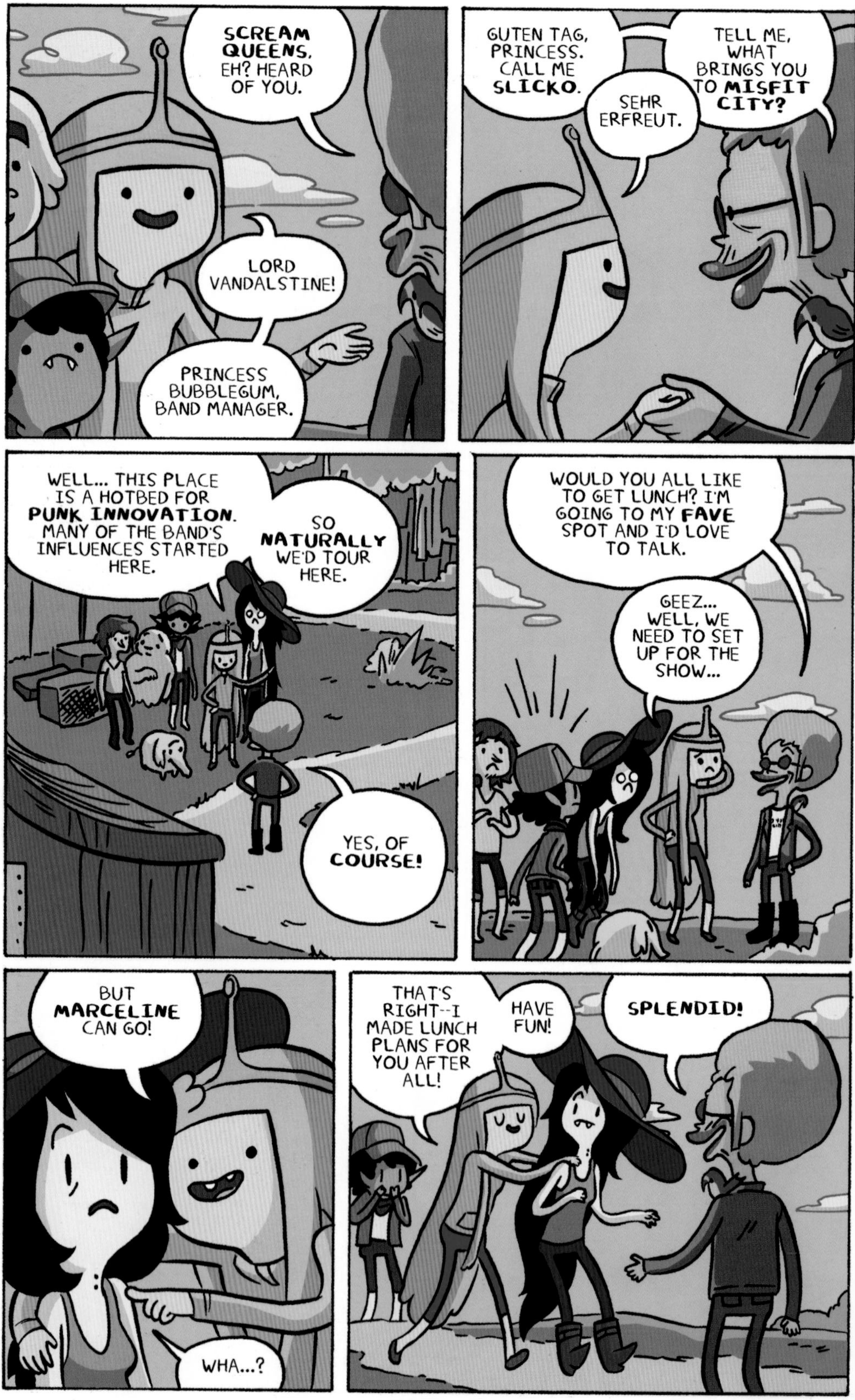
SCREAM QUEENS, EH? HEARD OF YOU.
LORD VANDALSTINE!
PRINCESS BUBBLEGUM, BAND MANAGER.
GUTEN TAG, PRINCESS. CALL ME SLICKO.
SEHR ERFREUT.
TELL ME, WHAT BRINGS YOU TO MISFIT CITY?
WELL... THIS PLACE IS A HOTBED FOR PUNK INNOVATION. MANY OF THE BAND'S INFLUENCES STARTED HERE.
SO NATURALLY WE'D TOUR HERE.
YES, OF COURSE!
WOULD YOU ALL LIKE TO GET LUNCH? I'M GOING TO MY FAVE SPOT AND I'D LOVE TO TALK.
GEEZ... WELL, WE NEED TO SET UP FOR THE SHOW...
BUT MARCELINE CAN GO!
WHA...?
THAT'S RIGHT--I MADE LUNCH PLANS FOR YOU AFTER ALL!
HAVE FUN!
SPLENDID!

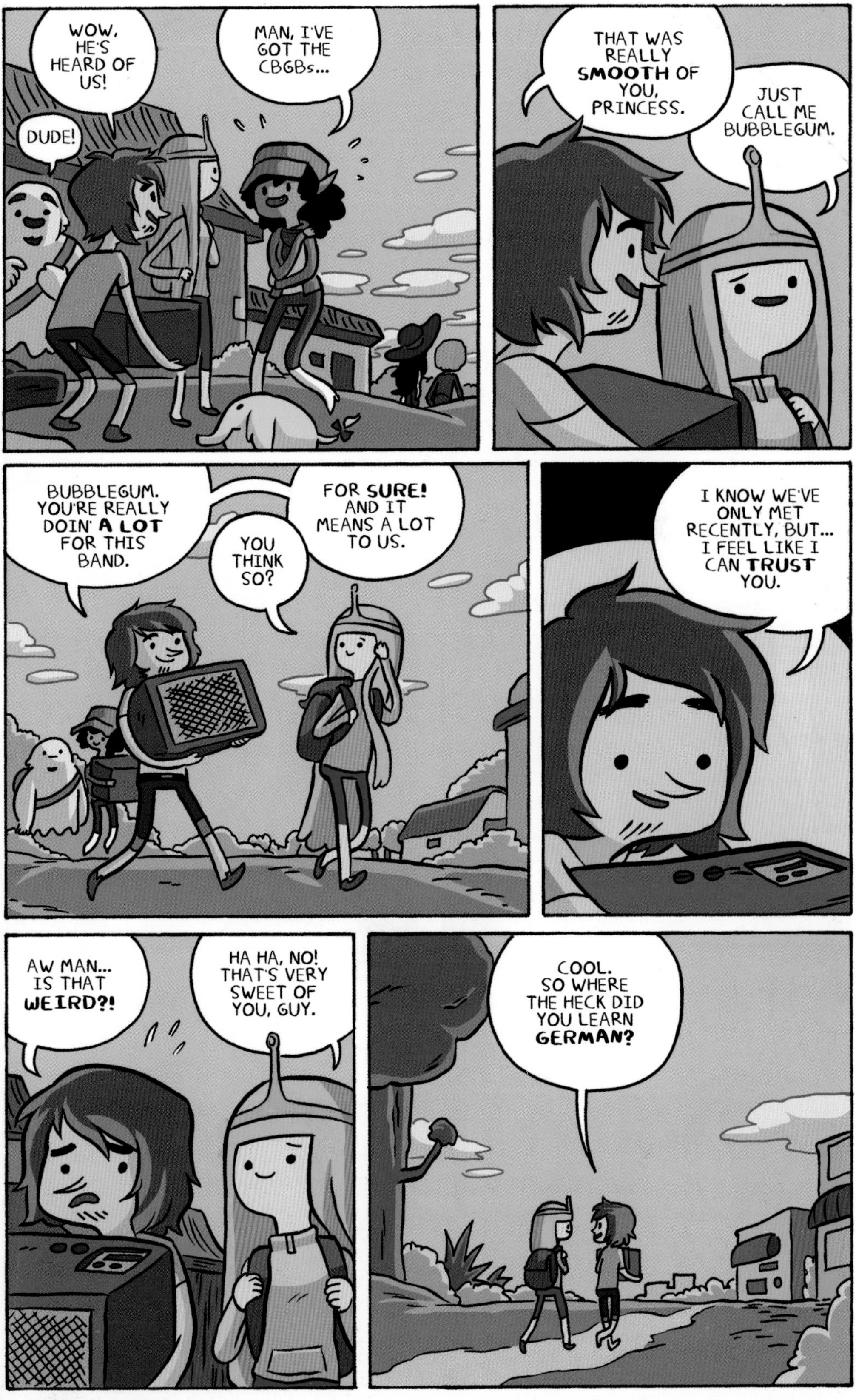

WOW, HE'S HEARD OF US!
DUDE!
MAN, I'VE GOT THE CBGBs...
THAT WAS REALLY **SMOOTH** OF YOU, PRINCESS.
JUST CALL ME BUBBLEGUM.
BUBBLEGUM. YOU'RE REALLY DOIN' **A LOT** FOR THIS BAND.
YOU THINK SO?
FOR **SURE!** AND IT MEANS A LOT TO US.
I KNOW WE'VE ONLY MET RECENTLY, BUT... I FEEL LIKE I CAN **TRUST** YOU.
AW MAN... IS THAT **WEIRD?!**
HA HA, NO! THAT'S VERY SWEET OF YOU, GUY.
COOL. SO WHERE THE HECK DID YOU LEARN **GERMAN?**

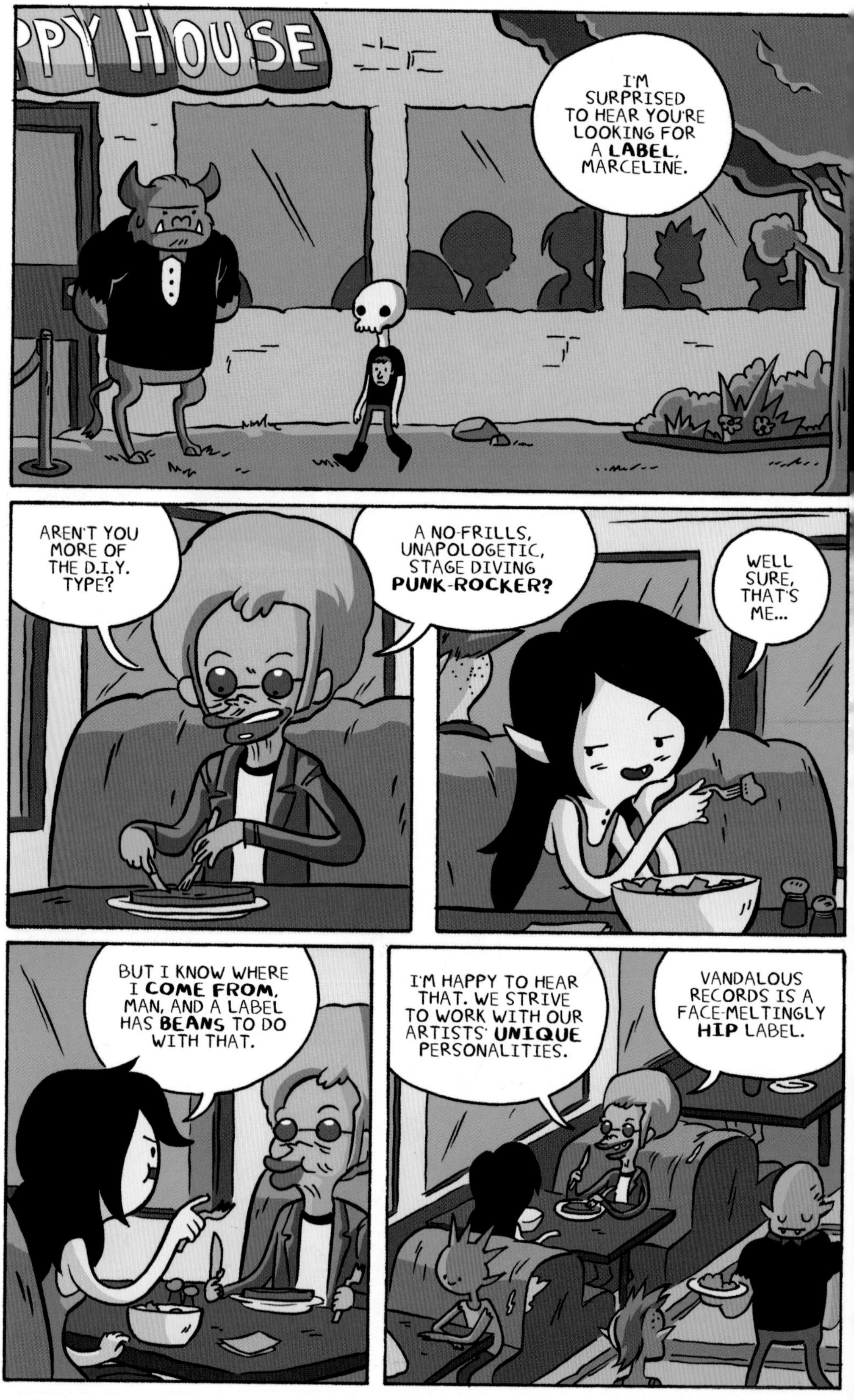
PPY HOUSE
I'M SURPRISED TO HEAR YOU'RE LOOKING FOR A **LABEL**, MARCELINE.
AREN'T YOU MORE OF THE D.I.Y. TYPE?
A NO-FRILLS, UNAPOLOGETIC, STAGE DIVING **PUNK-ROCKER?**
WELL SURE, THAT'S ME...
BUT I KNOW WHERE I **COME FROM**, MAN, AND A LABEL HAS **BEANS** TO DO WITH THAT.
I'M HAPPY TO HEAR THAT. WE STRIVE TO WORK WITH OUR ARTISTS' **UNIQUE** PERSONALITIES.
VANDALOUS RECORDS IS A FACE-MELTINGLY **HIP** LABEL.

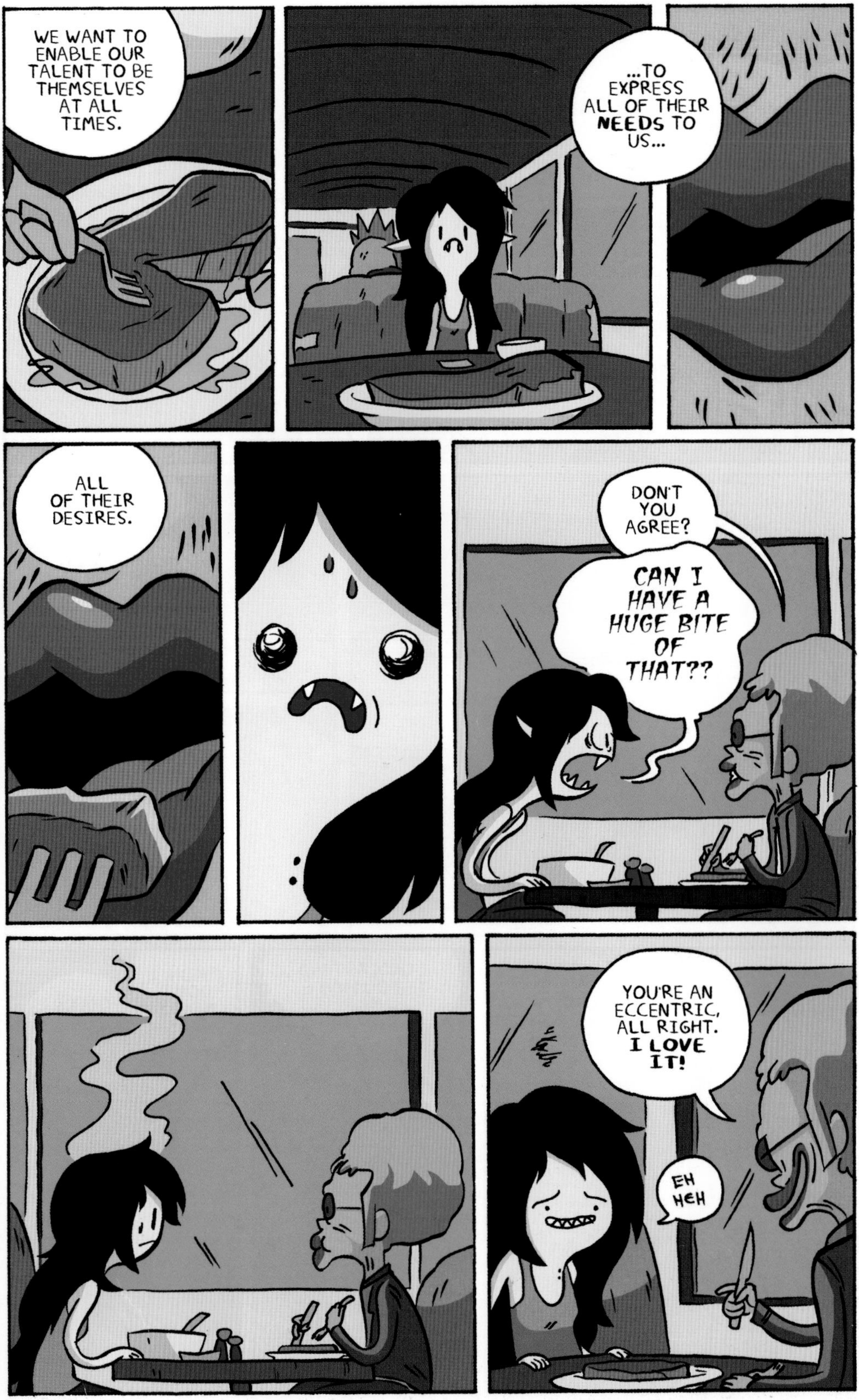
WE WANT TO ENABLE OUR TALENT TO BE THEMSELVES AT ALL TIMES.
...TO EXPRESS ALL OF THEIR **NEEDS** TO US...
ALL OF THEIR DESIRES.
DON'T YOU AGREE?
CAN I HAVE A HUGE BITE OF THAT??
YOU'RE AN ECCENTRIC, ALL RIGHT. **I LOVE IT!**
EH HEH

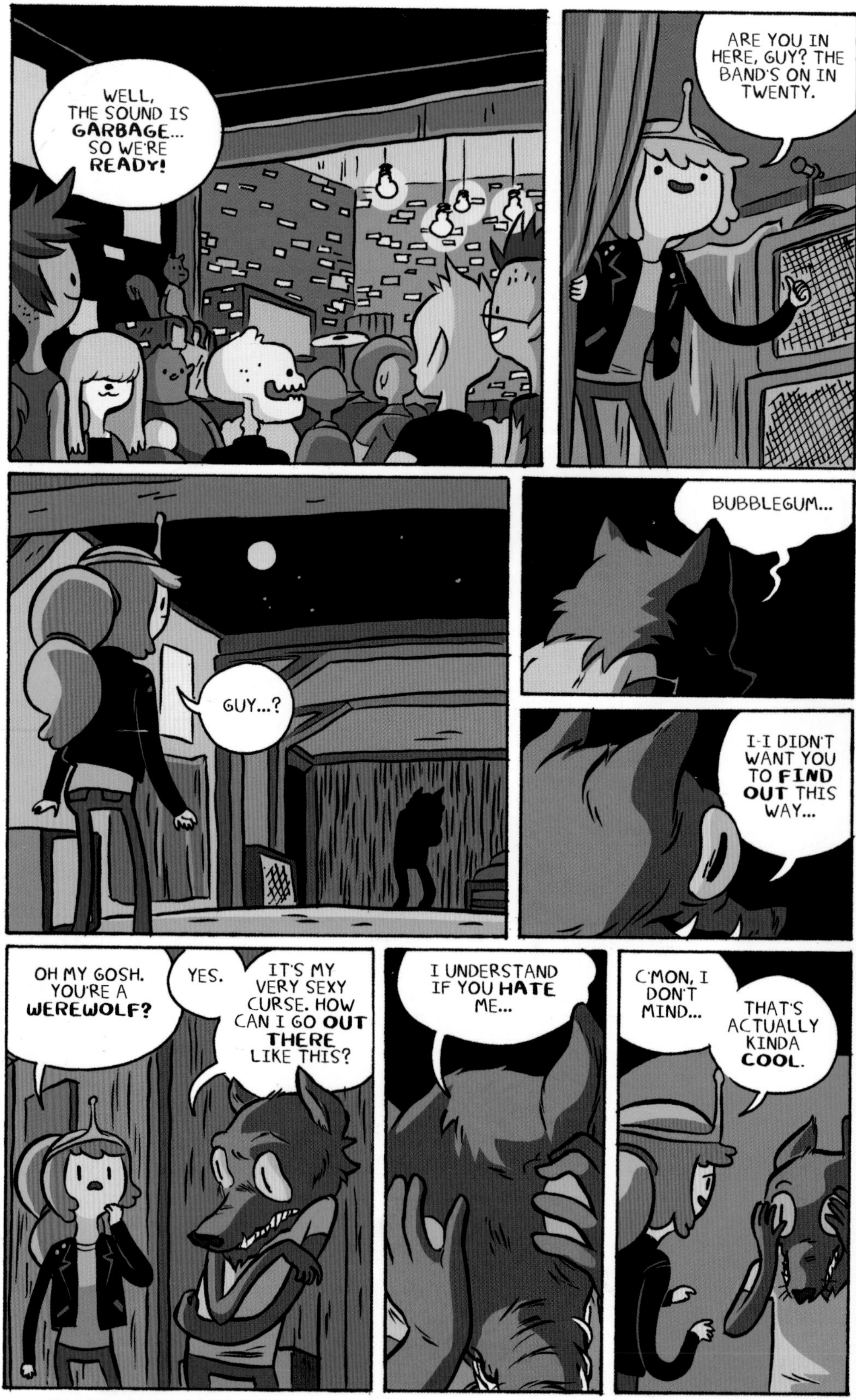
WELL, THE SOUND IS GARBAGE... SO WE'RE READY!
ARE YOU IN HERE, GUY? THE BAND'S ON IN TWENTY.
GUY...?
BUBBLEGUM...
I-I DIDN'T WANT YOU TO FIND OUT THIS WAY...
OH MY GOSH. YOU'RE A WEREWOLF?
YES.
IT'S MY VERY SEXY CURSE. HOW CAN I GO OUT THERE LIKE THIS?
I UNDERSTAND IF YOU HATE ME...
C'MON, I DON'T MIND...
THAT'S ACTUALLY KINDA COOL.

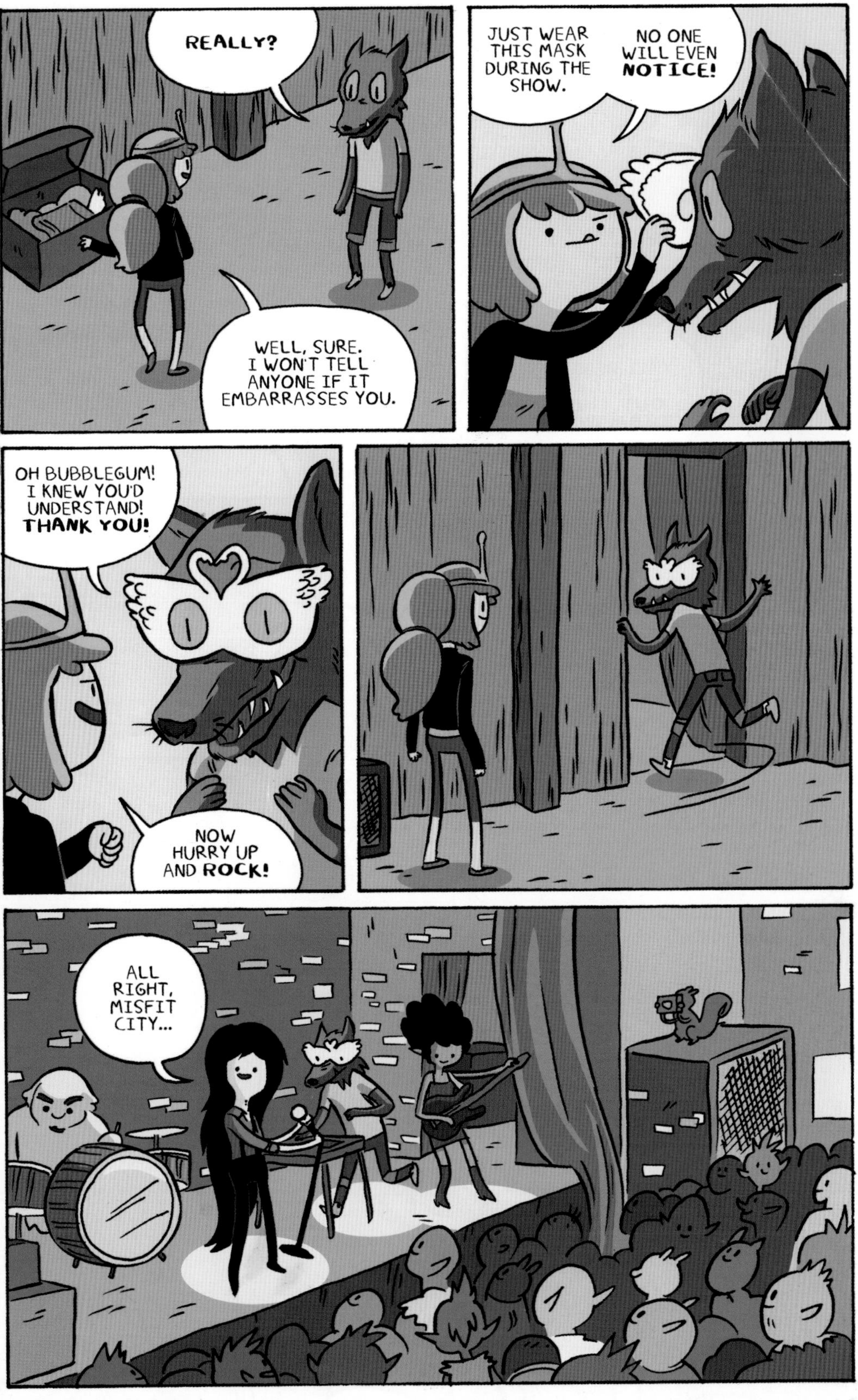
REALLY?
WELL, SURE. I WON'T TELL ANYONE IF IT EMBARRASSES YOU.
JUST WEAR THIS MASK DURING THE SHOW.
NO ONE WILL EVEN NOTICE!
OH BUBBLEGUM! I KNEW YOU'D UNDERSTAND! THANK YOU!
NOW HURRY UP AND ROCK!
ALL RIGHT, MISFIT CITY...

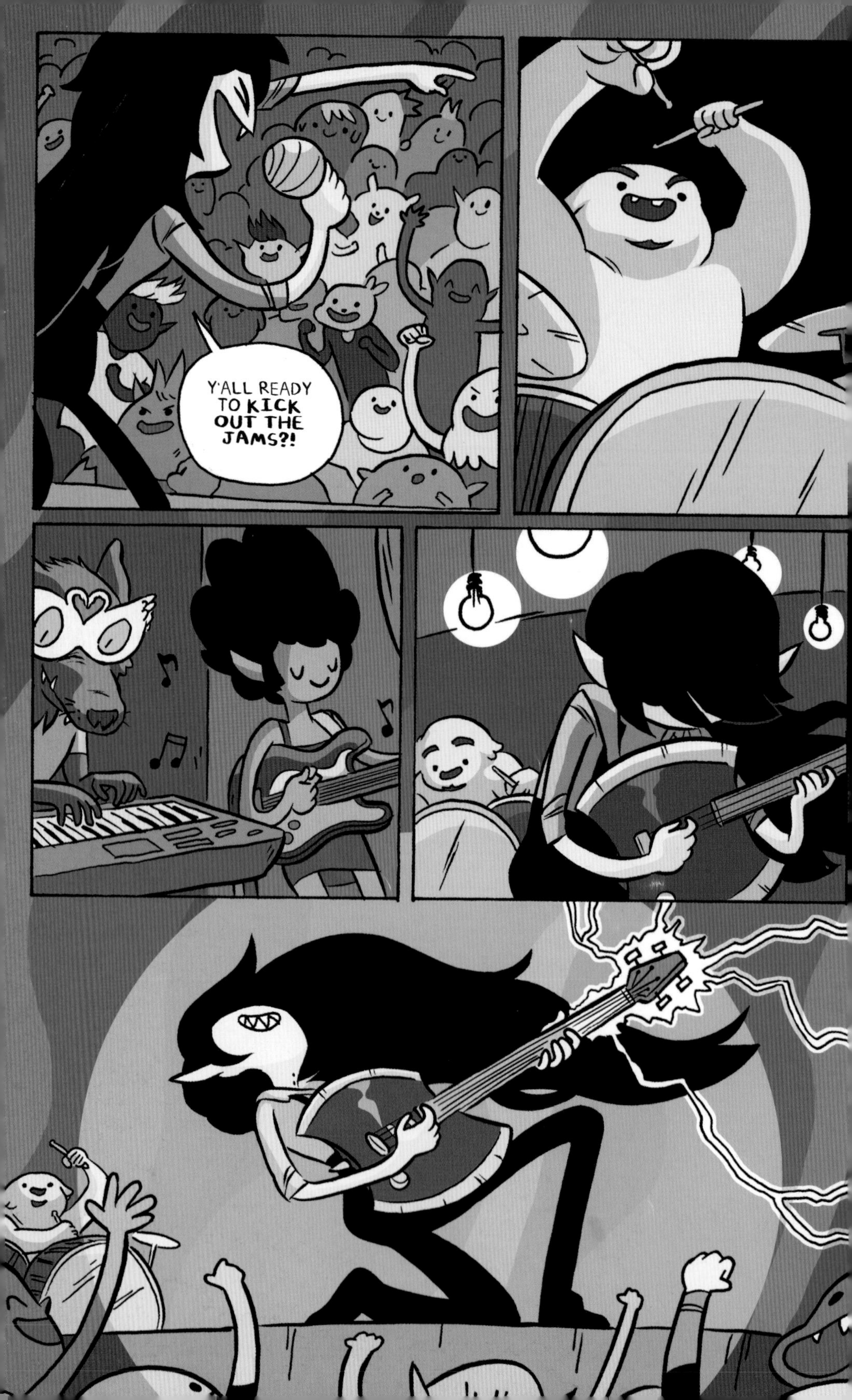
Y'ALL READY TO **KICK OUT THE JAMS?!**

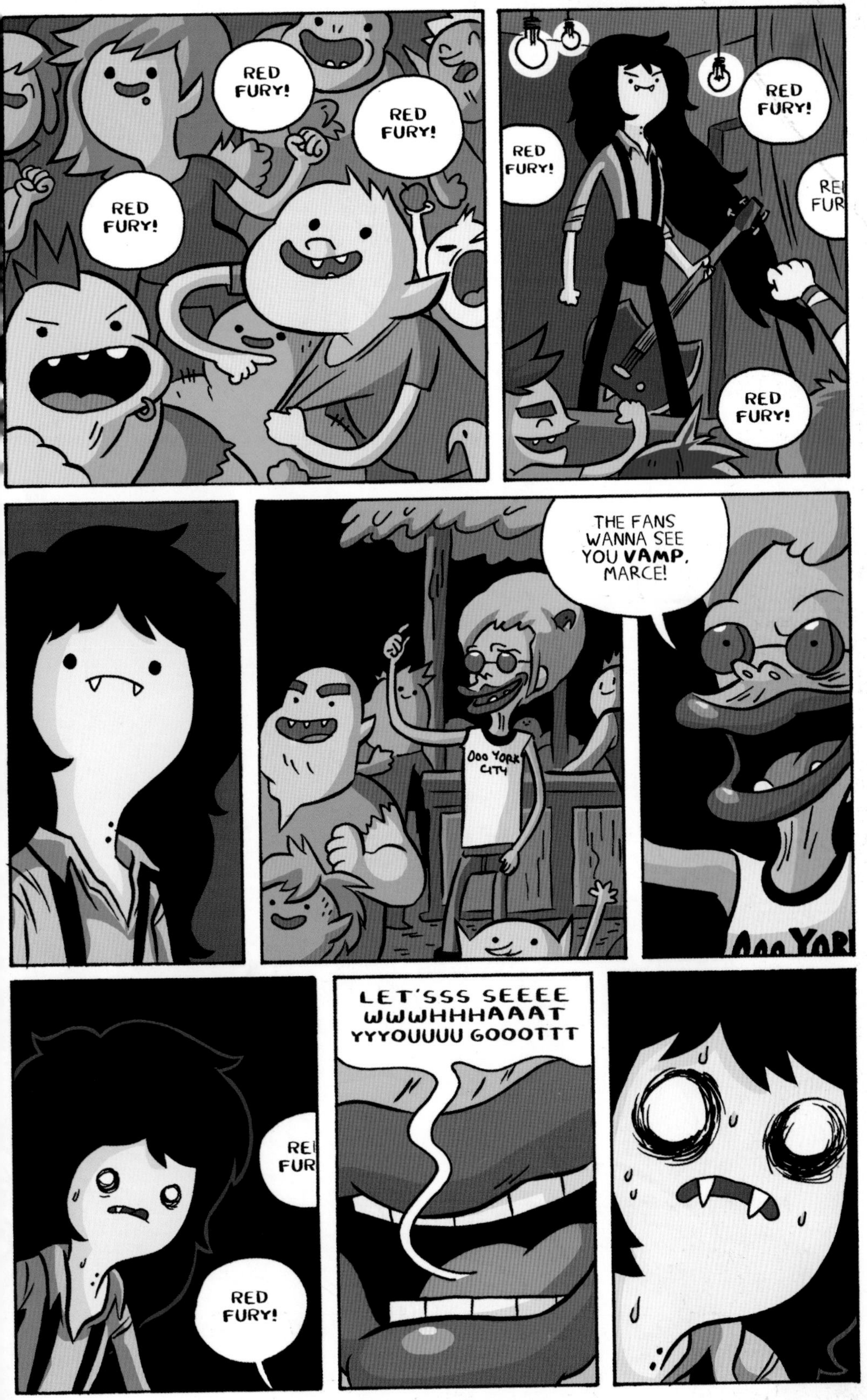
RED FURY!
RED FURY!
RED FURY!
RED FURY!
RED FURY!
RED FURY!
THE FANS WANNA SEE YOU **VAMP**, MARCE!
OOO YORK CITY
RED FURY!
LET'SSS SEEEE WWWHHHAAAT YYYOUUUU GOOOTTT

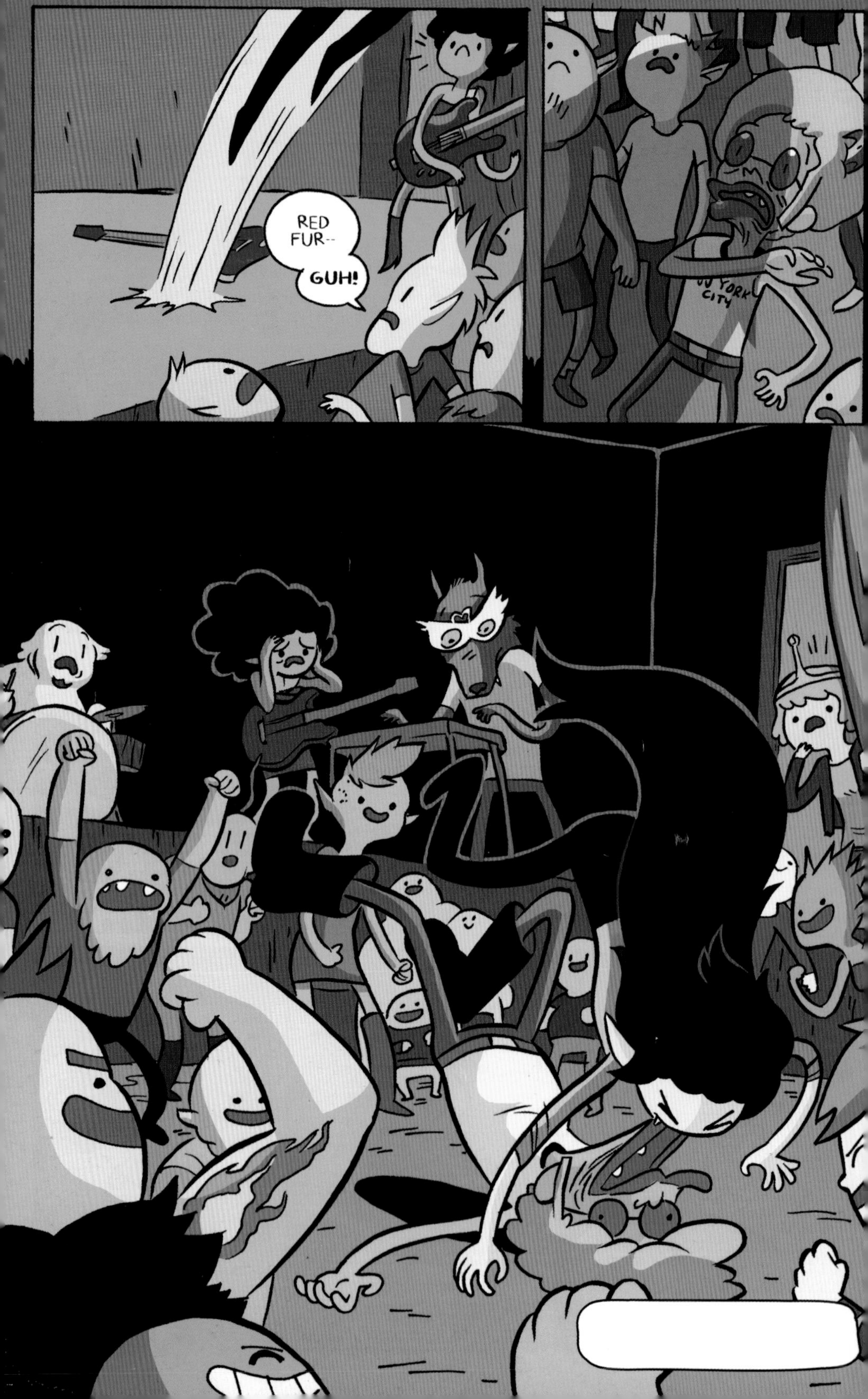
RED FUR--
GUH!
YORK CITY

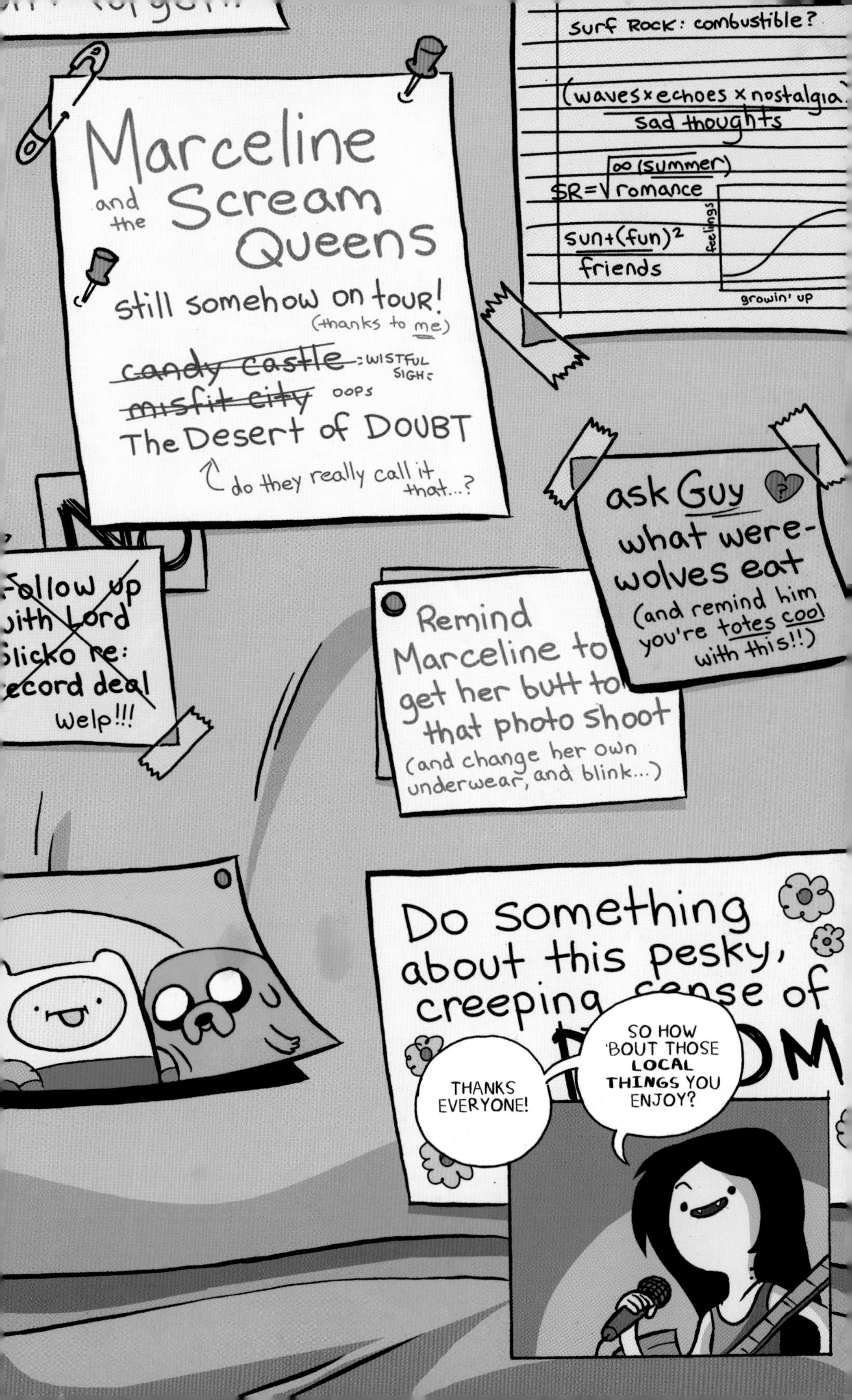

Surf Rock: combustible?
(waves x echoes x nostalgia) / sad thoughts
SR = √(∞(summer) / romance)
sun+(fun)² / friends
feelings
growin' up
Marceline and the Scream Queens
still somehow on tour!
(thanks to me)
candy castle :WISTFUL SIGH:
misfit city OOPS
The Desert of DOUBT
do they really call it that...?
ask Guy what were-wolves eat
(and remind him you're totes cool with this!!)
Follow up with Lord Slicko re: record deal
Welp!!!
Remind Marceline to get her butt to that photo shoot
(and change her own underwear, and blink...)
Do something about this pesky, creeping sense of
THANKS EVERYONE!
SO HOW 'BOUT THOSE LOCAL THINGS YOU ENJOY?

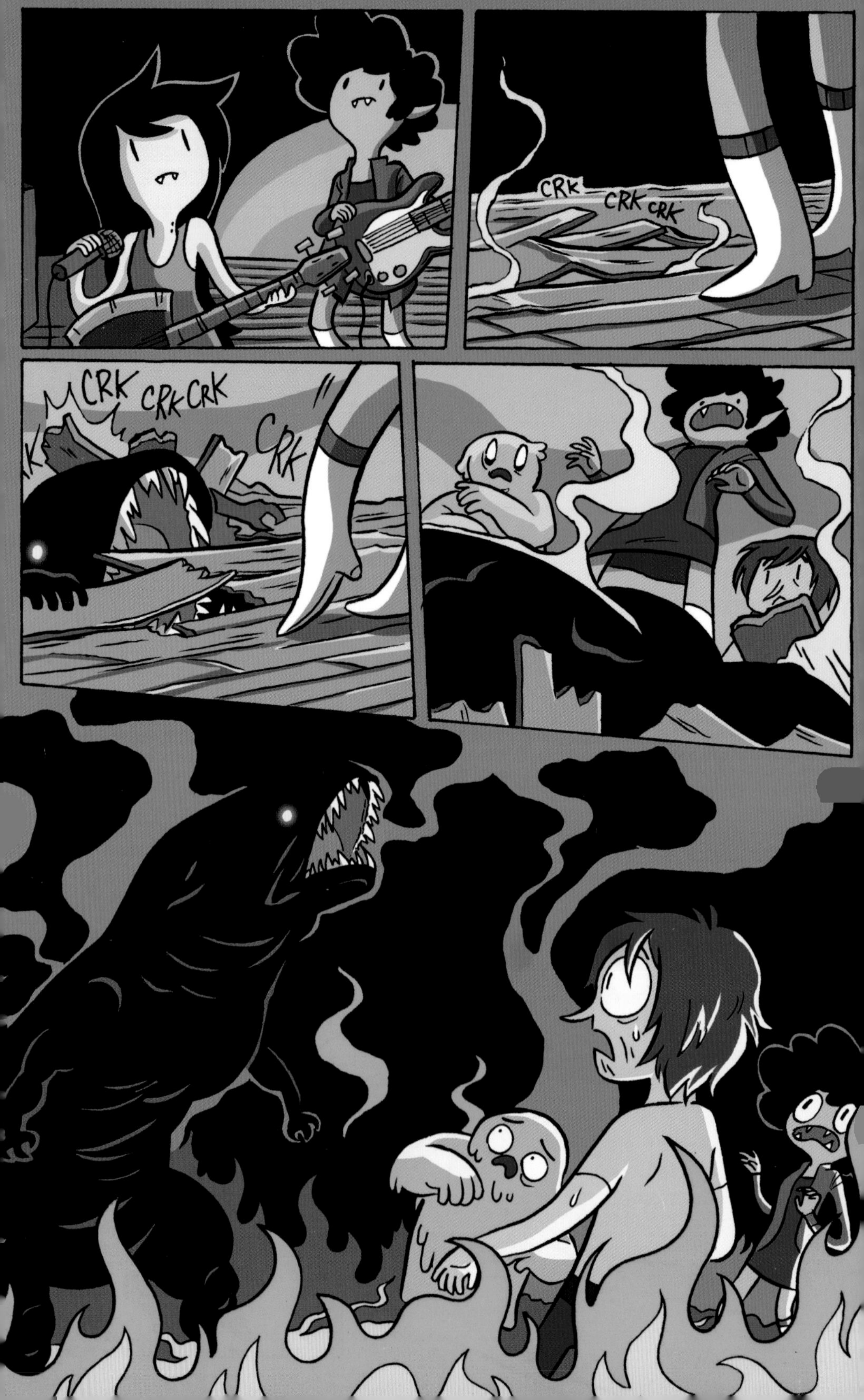
CRK
CRK CRK
CRK
CRK CRK
CRK

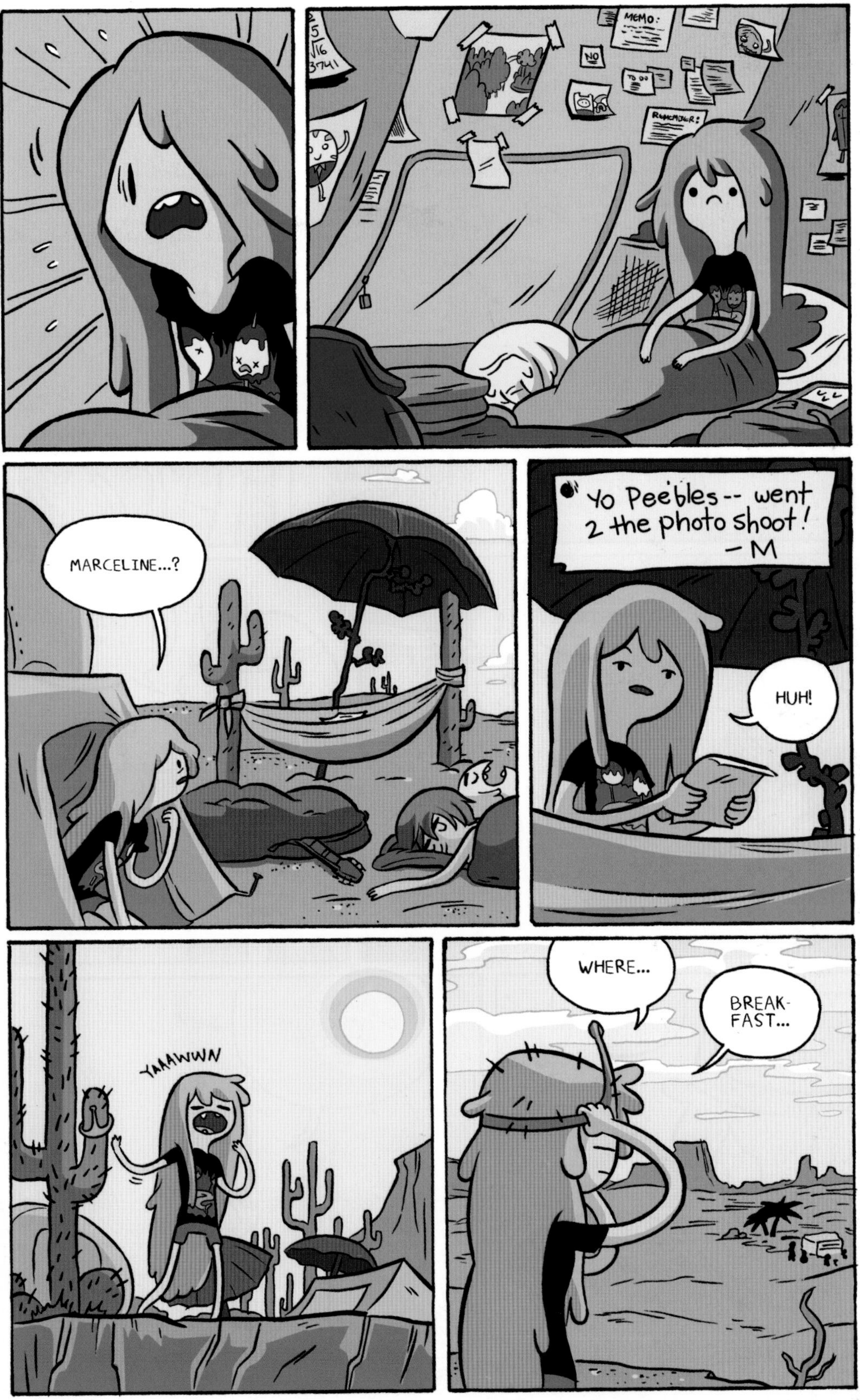
MEMO:
NO
TO DO
MARCELINE...?
Yo Peebles -- went 2 the photo shoot! -M
HUH!
YAAAWWN
WHERE...
BREAK-FAST...

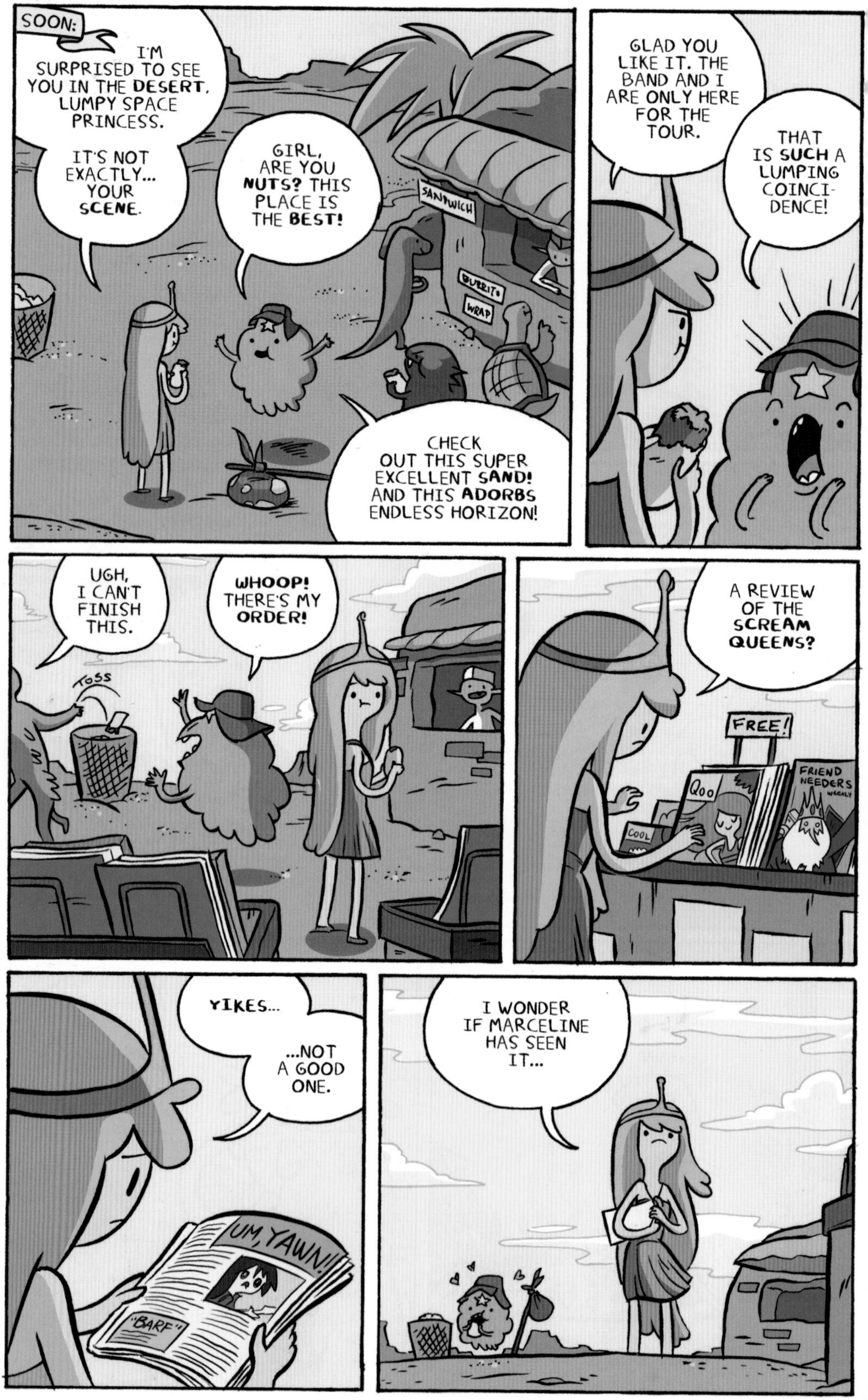
SOON:
I'M SURPRISED TO SEE YOU IN THE DESERT, LUMPY SPACE PRINCESS.
IT'S NOT EXACTLY... YOUR SCENE.
GIRL, ARE YOU NUTS? THIS PLACE IS THE BEST!
SANDWICH
BURRITO
WRAP
CHECK OUT THIS SUPER EXCELLENT SAND! AND THIS ADORBS ENDLESS HORIZON!
GLAD YOU LIKE IT. THE BAND AND I ARE ONLY HERE FOR THE TOUR.
THAT IS SUCH A LUMPING COINCI-DENCE!
UGH, I CAN'T FINISH THIS.
TOSS
WHOOP! THERE'S MY ORDER!
A REVIEW OF THE SCREAM QUEENS?
FREE!
QOO
COOL
FRIEND NEEDERS WEEKLY
YIKES...
...NOT A GOOD ONE.
UM, YAWN!!
"BARF"
I WONDER IF MARCELINE HAS SEEN IT...

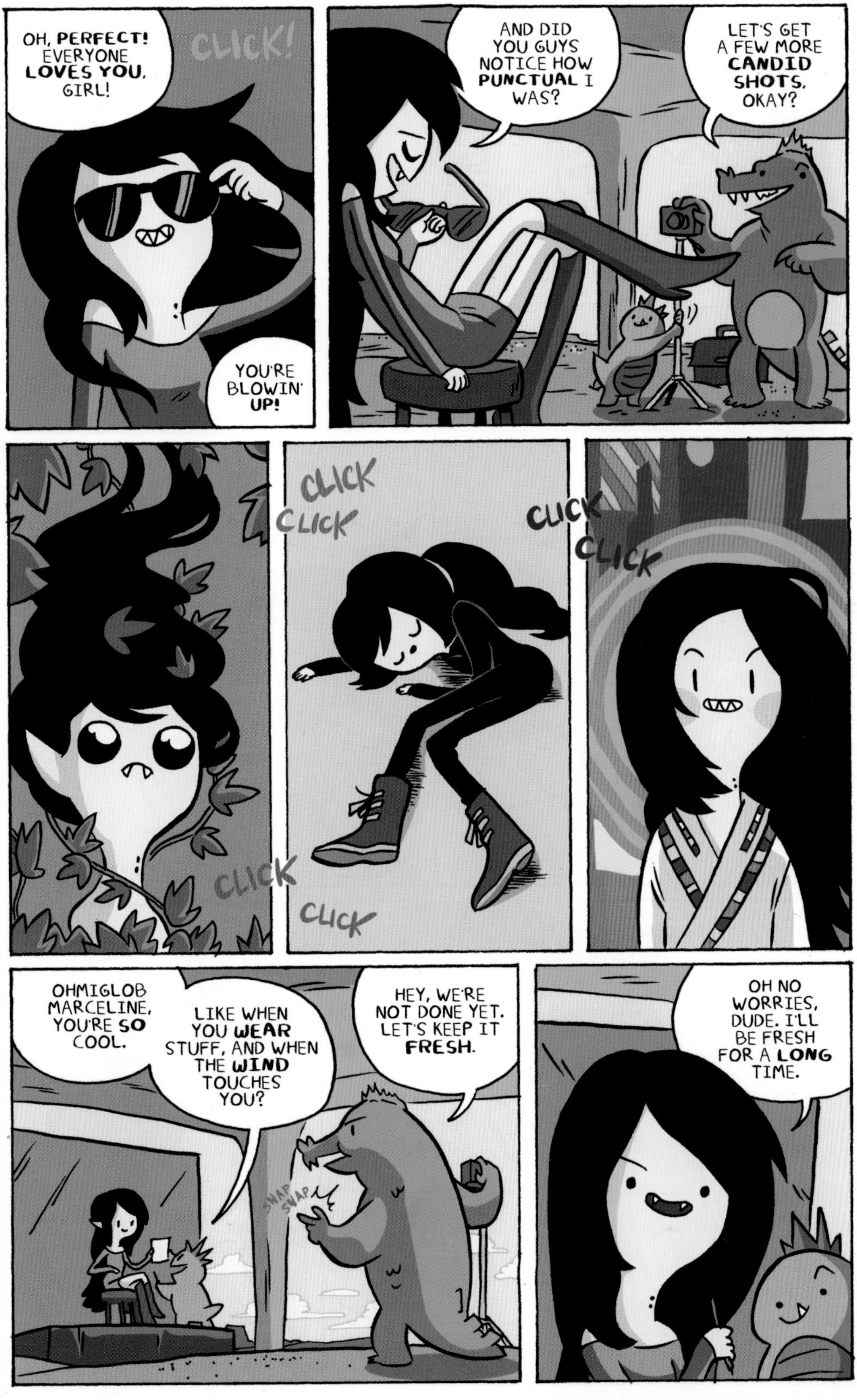

OH, **PERFECT!** EVERYONE **LOVES YOU**, GIRL!
CLICK!
YOU'RE BLOWIN' **UP!**
AND DID YOU GUYS NOTICE HOW **PUNCTUAL** I WAS?
LET'S GET A FEW MORE **CANDID SHOTS**, OKAY?
CLICK
CLICK
CLICK
CLICK
CLICK
CLICK
CLICK
CLICK
OHMIGLOB MARCELINE, YOU'RE **SO** COOL.
LIKE WHEN YOU **WEAR** STUFF, AND WHEN THE **WIND** TOUCHES YOU?
HEY, WE'RE NOT DONE YET. LET'S KEEP IT **FRESH**.
SWAP SWAP
OH NO WORRIES, DUDE. I'LL BE FRESH FOR A **LONG** TIME.

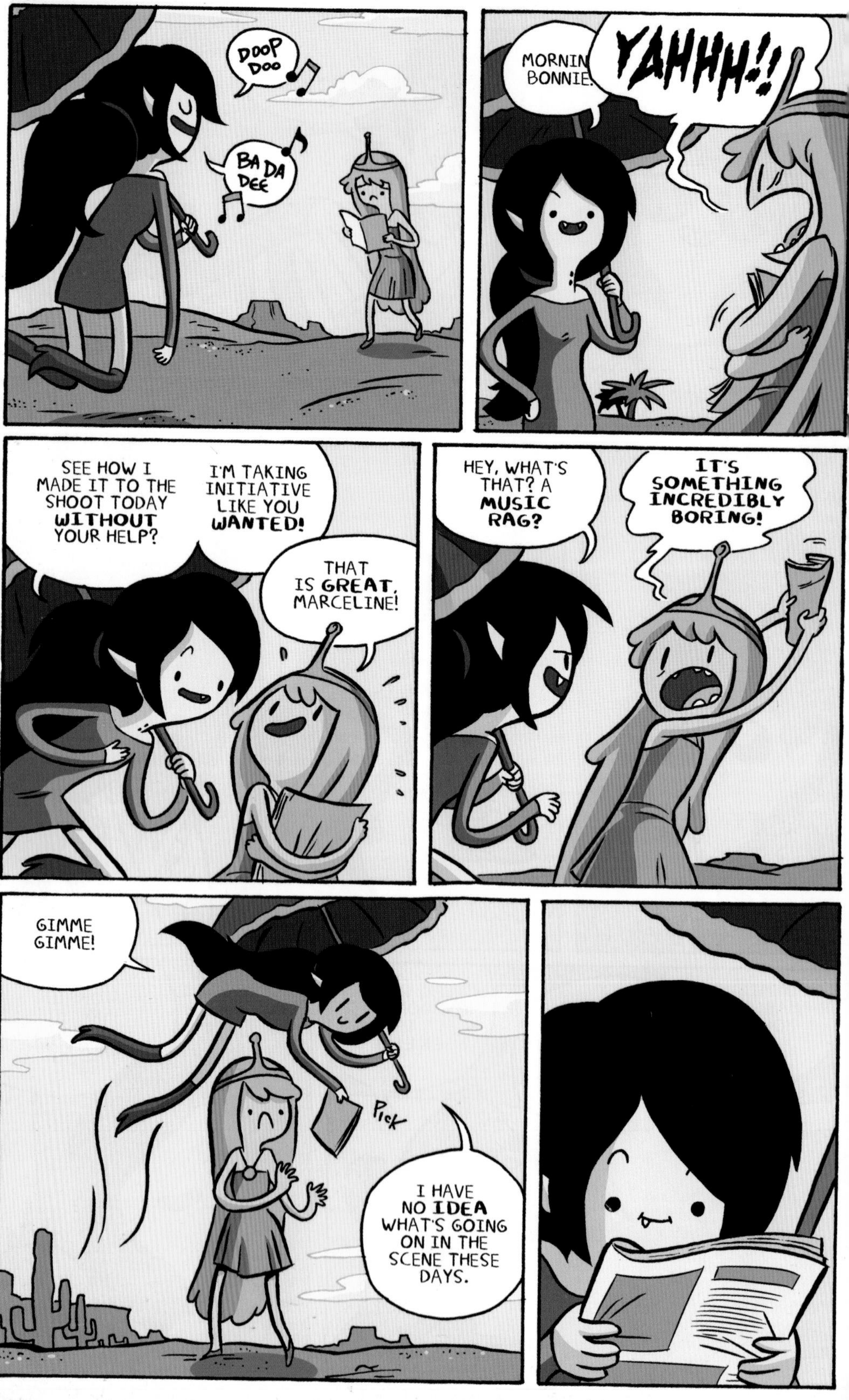

DOOP DOO
BA DA DEE
MORNIN' BONNIE!
YAHHH!!
SEE HOW I MADE IT TO THE SHOOT TODAY **WITHOUT** YOUR HELP?
I'M TAKING INITIATIVE LIKE YOU **WANTED!**
THAT IS **GREAT**, MARCELINE!
HEY, WHAT'S THAT? A **MUSIC RAG?**
IT'S SOMETHING INCREDIBLY BORING!
GIMME GIMME!
PICK
I HAVE NO **IDEA** WHAT'S GOING ON IN THE SCENE THESE DAYS.

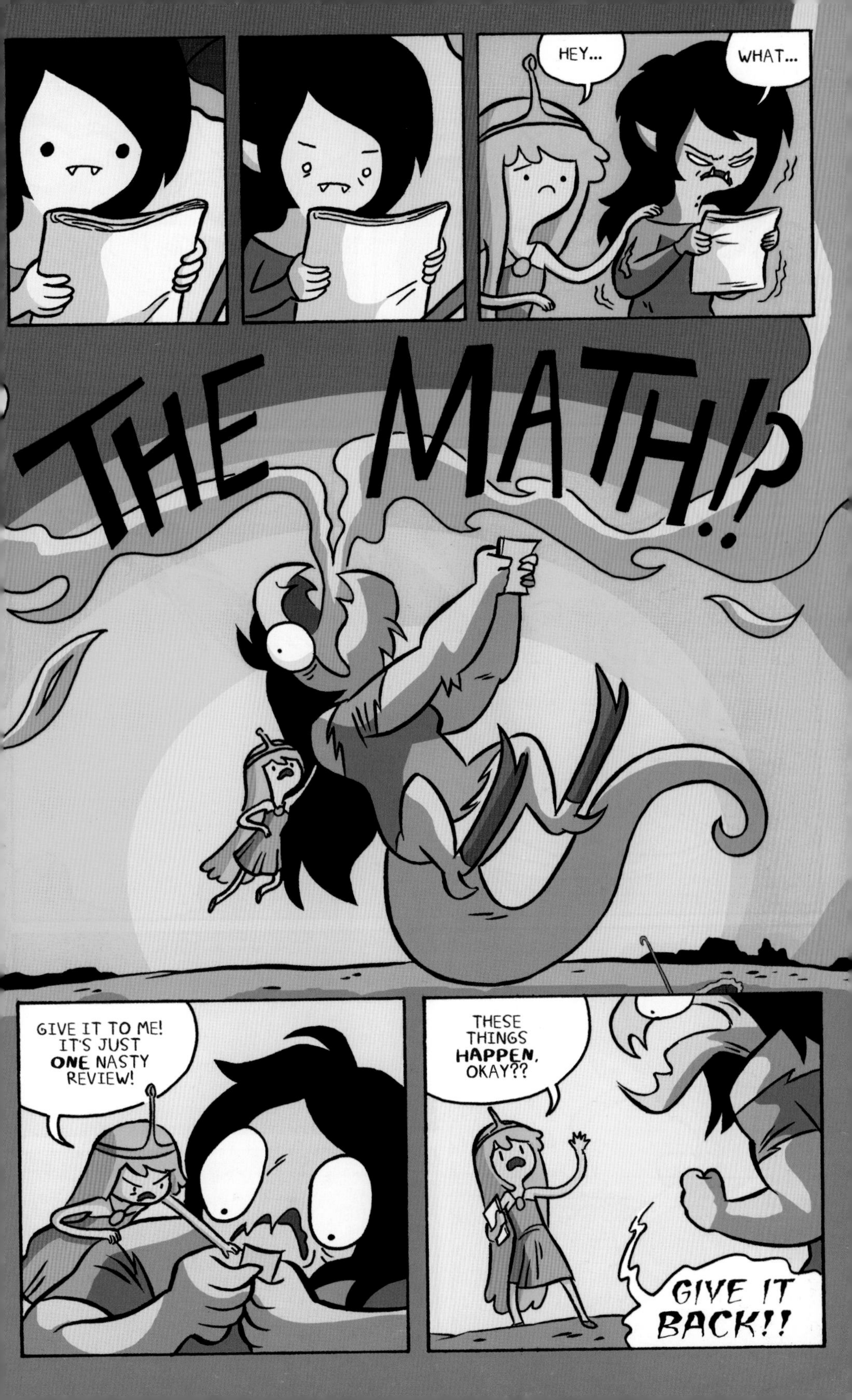
HEY...
WHAT...
THE MATH!?!
GIVE IT TO ME! IT'S JUST **ONE** NASTY REVIEW!
THESE THINGS **HAPPEN**, OKAY??
GIVE IT BACK!!

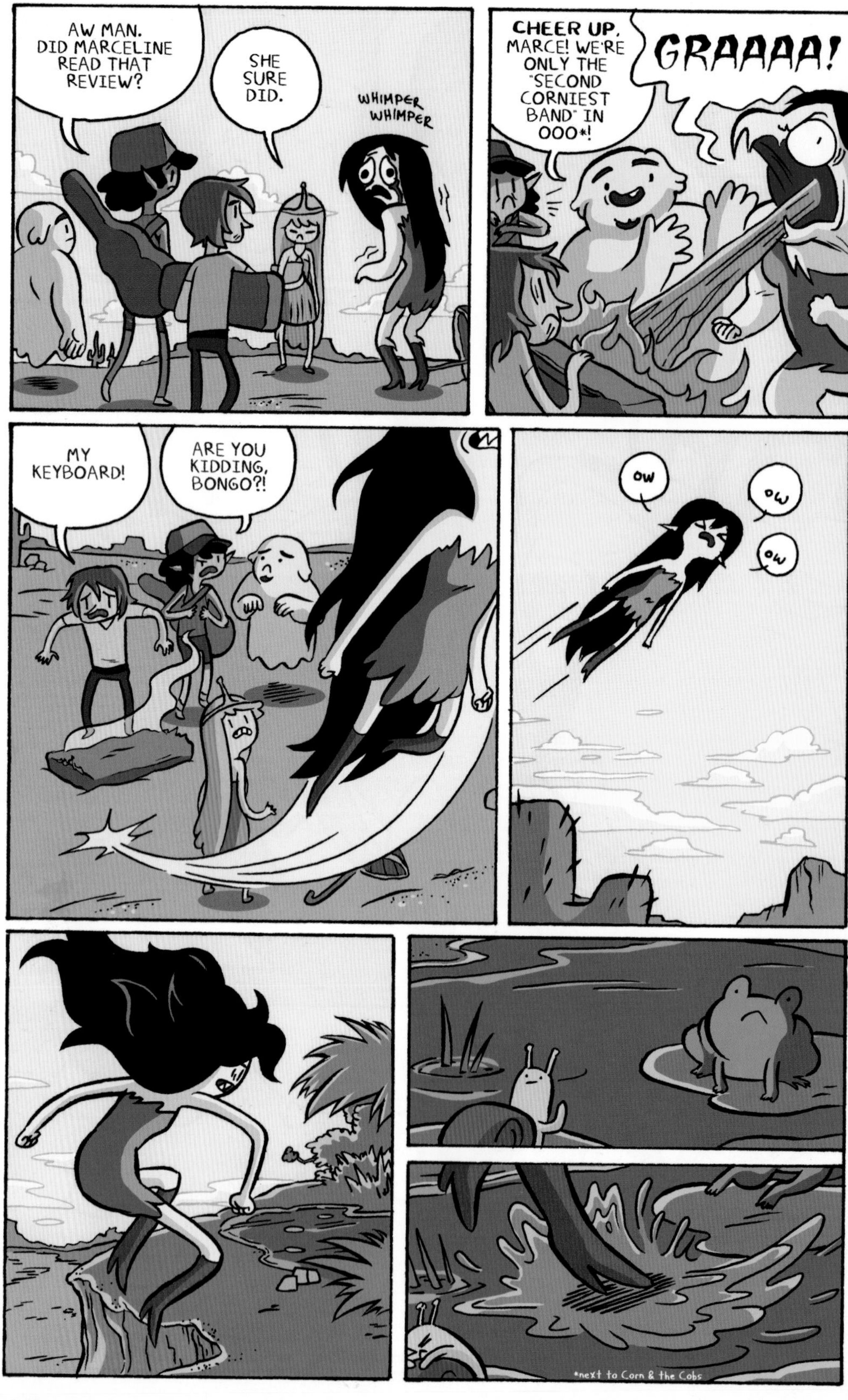
AW MAN. DID MARCELINE READ THAT REVIEW?
SHE SURE DID.
WHIMPER WHIMPER
CHEER UP, MARCE! WE'RE ONLY THE "SECOND CORNIEST BAND" IN OOO*!
GRAAAA!
MY KEYBOARD!
ARE YOU KIDDING, BONGO?!
OW
OW
OW
*next to Corn & the Cobs

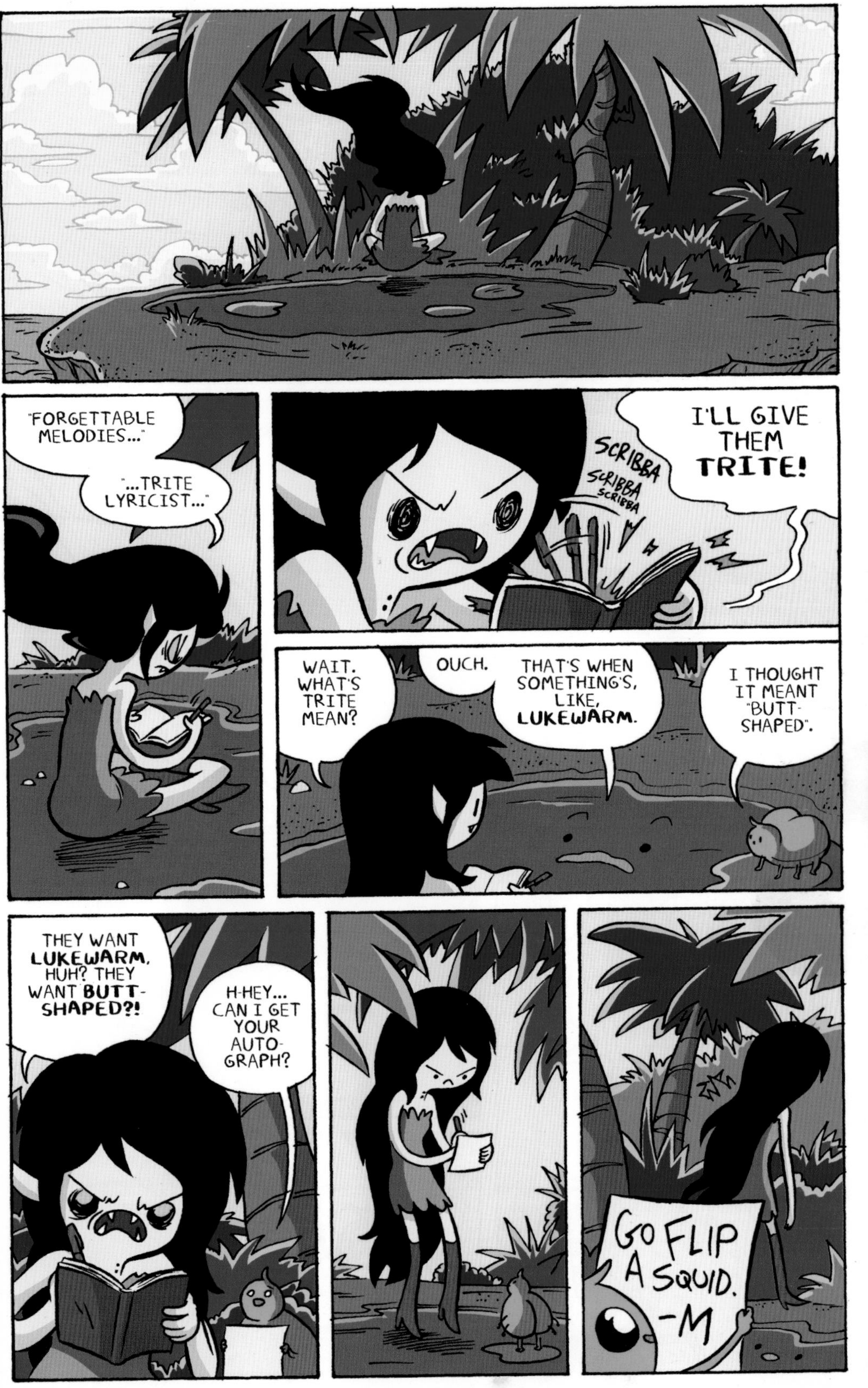
"FORGETTABLE MELODIES..."
"...TRITE LYRICIST..."
SCRIBBA SCRIBBA SCRIBBA
I'LL GIVE THEM TRITE!
WAIT. WHAT'S TRITE MEAN?
OUCH.
THAT'S WHEN SOMETHING'S, LIKE, LUKEWARM.
I THOUGHT IT MEANT "BUTT-SHAPED".
THEY WANT LUKEWARM, HUH? THEY WANT BUTT-SHAPED?!
H-HEY... CAN I GET YOUR AUTO-GRAPH?
GO FLIP A SQUID. -M

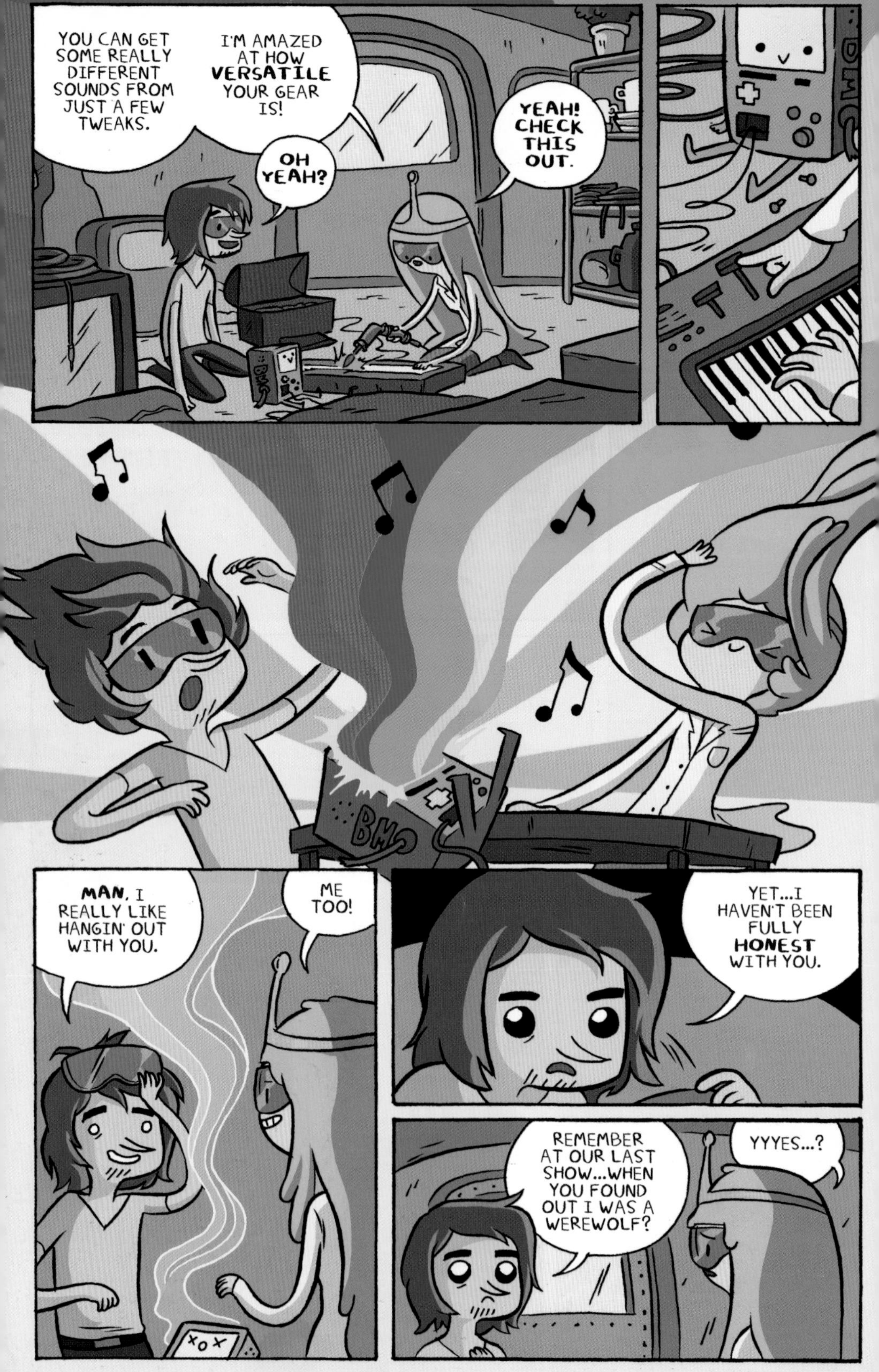
YOU CAN GET SOME REALLY DIFFERENT SOUNDS FROM JUST A FEW TWEAKS.
I'M AMAZED AT HOW VERSATILE YOUR GEAR IS!
OH YEAH?
YEAH! CHECK THIS OUT.
BMO
MAN, I REALLY LIKE HANGIN' OUT WITH YOU.
ME TOO!
YET...I HAVEN'T BEEN FULLY HONEST WITH YOU.
REMEMBER AT OUR LAST SHOW...WHEN YOU FOUND OUT I WAS A WEREWOLF?
YYYES...?

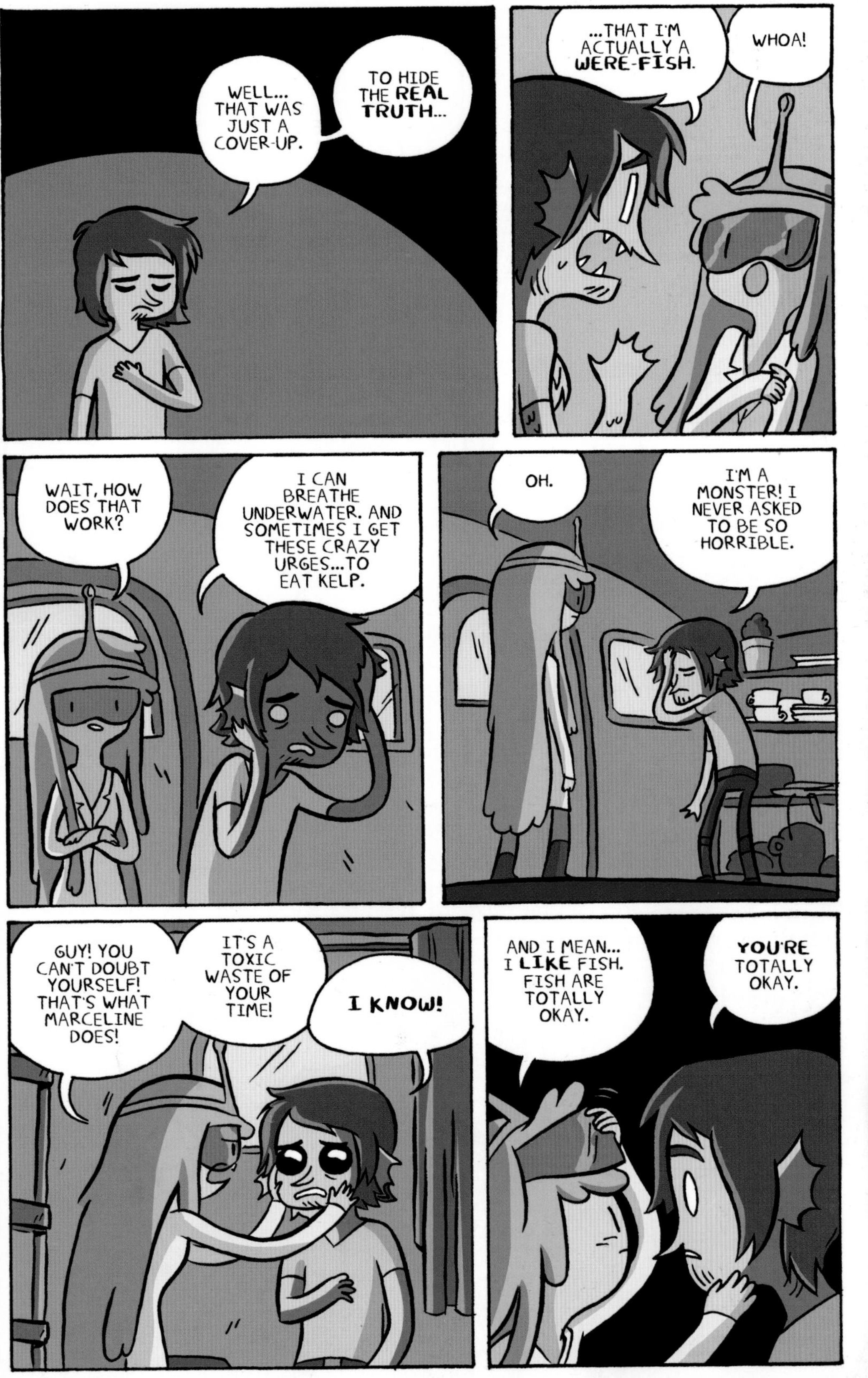
WELL... THAT WAS JUST A COVER-UP.
TO HIDE THE REAL TRUTH...
...THAT I'M ACTUALLY A WERE-FISH.
WHOA!
WAIT, HOW DOES THAT WORK?
I CAN BREATHE UNDERWATER. AND SOMETIMES I GET THESE CRAZY URGES...TO EAT KELP.
OH.
I'M A MONSTER! I NEVER ASKED TO BE SO HORRIBLE.
GUY! YOU CAN'T DOUBT YOURSELF! THAT'S WHAT MARCELINE DOES!
IT'S A TOXIC WASTE OF YOUR TIME!
I KNOW!
AND I MEAN... I LIKE FISH. FISH ARE TOTALLY OKAY.
YOU'RE TOTALLY OKAY.

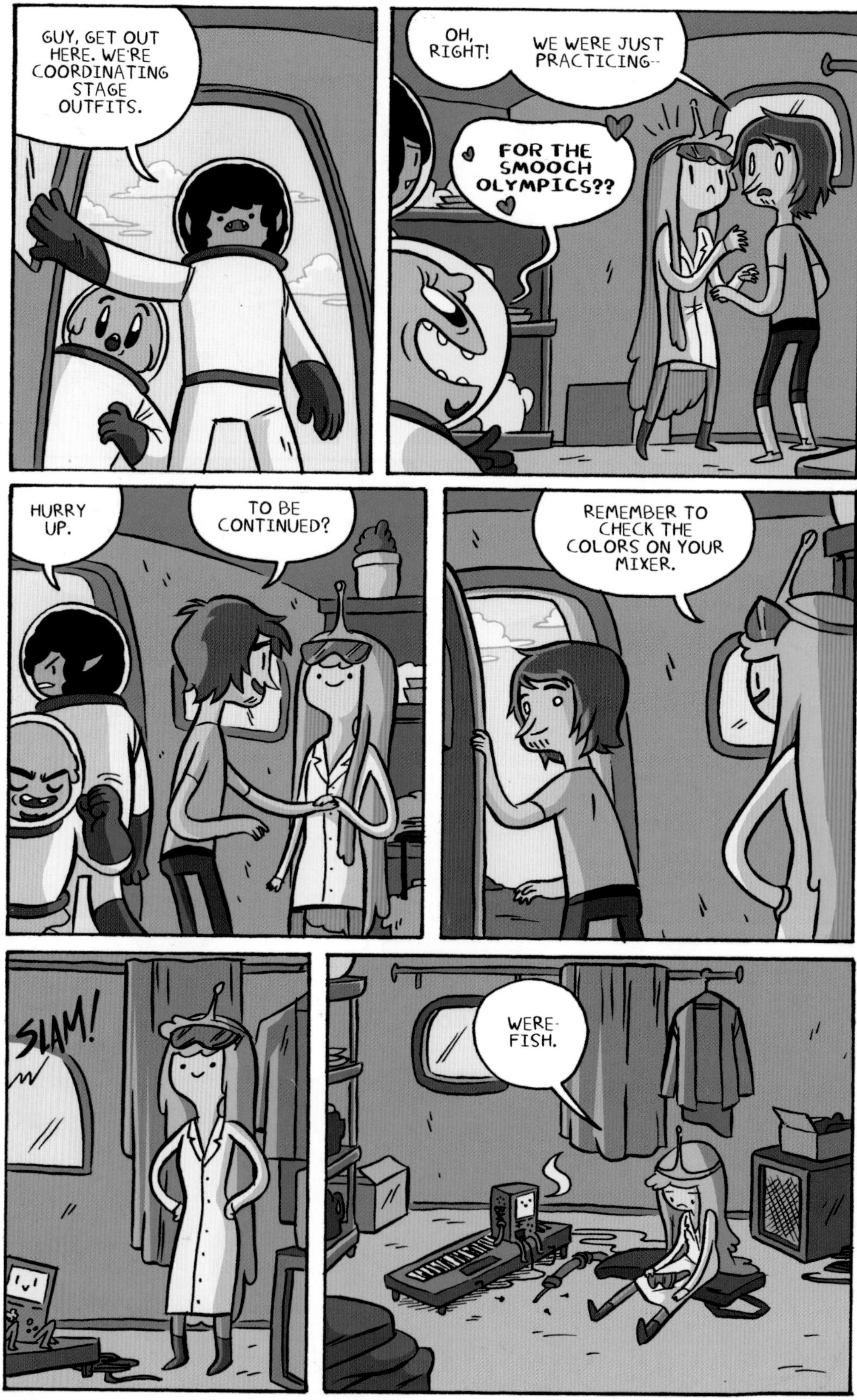
GUY, GET OUT HERE. WE'RE COORDINATING STAGE OUTFITS.
OH, RIGHT!
WE WERE JUST PRACTICING--
FOR THE SMOOCH OLYMPICS??
HURRY UP.
TO BE CONTINUED?
REMEMBER TO CHECK THE COLORS ON YOUR MIXER.
SLAM!
WERE-FISH.

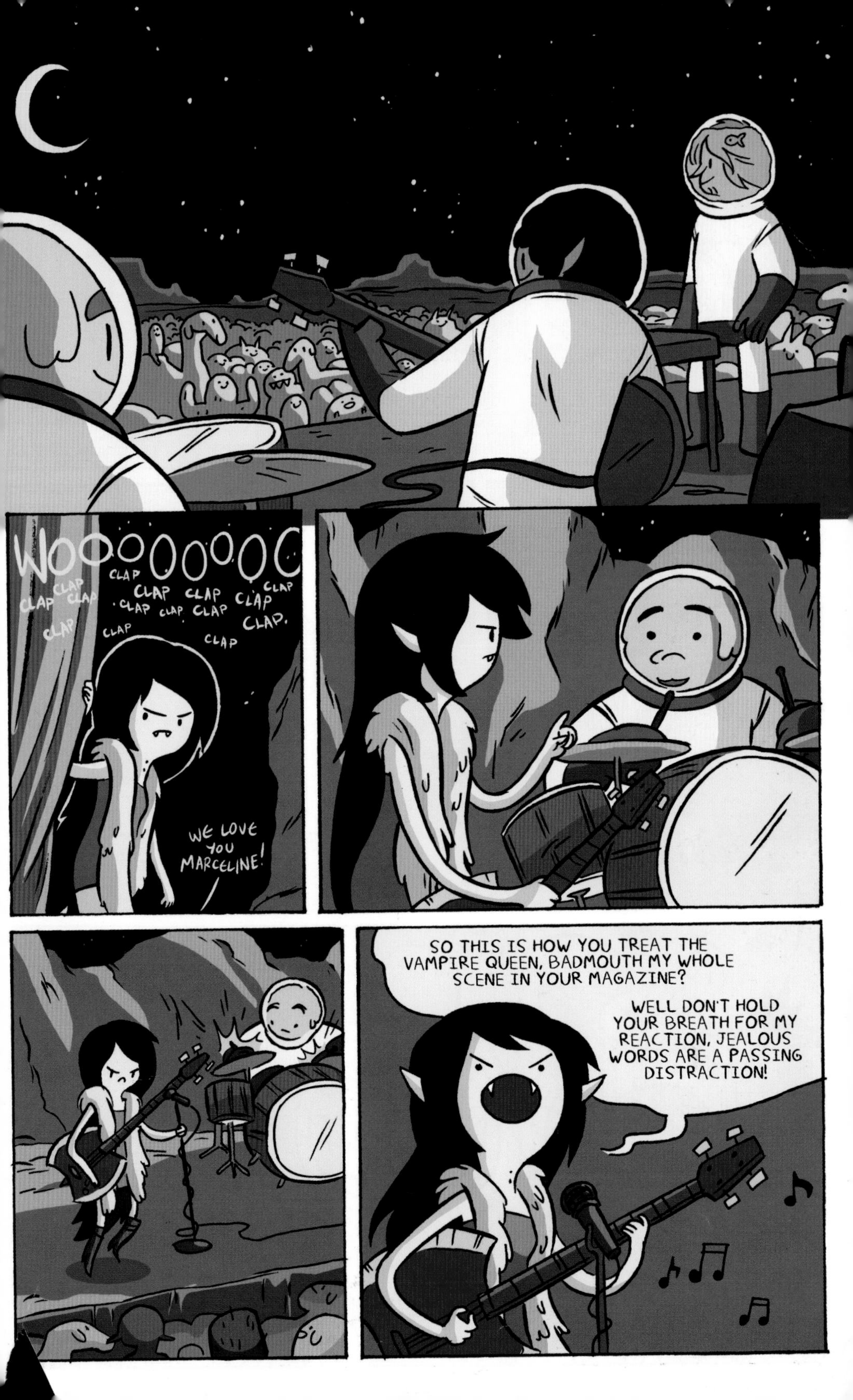
WOOOOOOOOO
CLAP CLAP CLAP CLAP CLAP CLAP CLAP CLAP CLAP CLAP CLAP CLAP CLAP CLAP
WE LOVE YOU MARCELINE!
SO THIS IS HOW YOU TREAT THE VAMPIRE QUEEN, BADMOUTH MY WHOLE SCENE IN YOUR MAGAZINE?
WELL DON'T HOLD YOUR BREATH FOR MY REACTION, JEALOUS WORDS ARE A PASSING DISTRACTION!

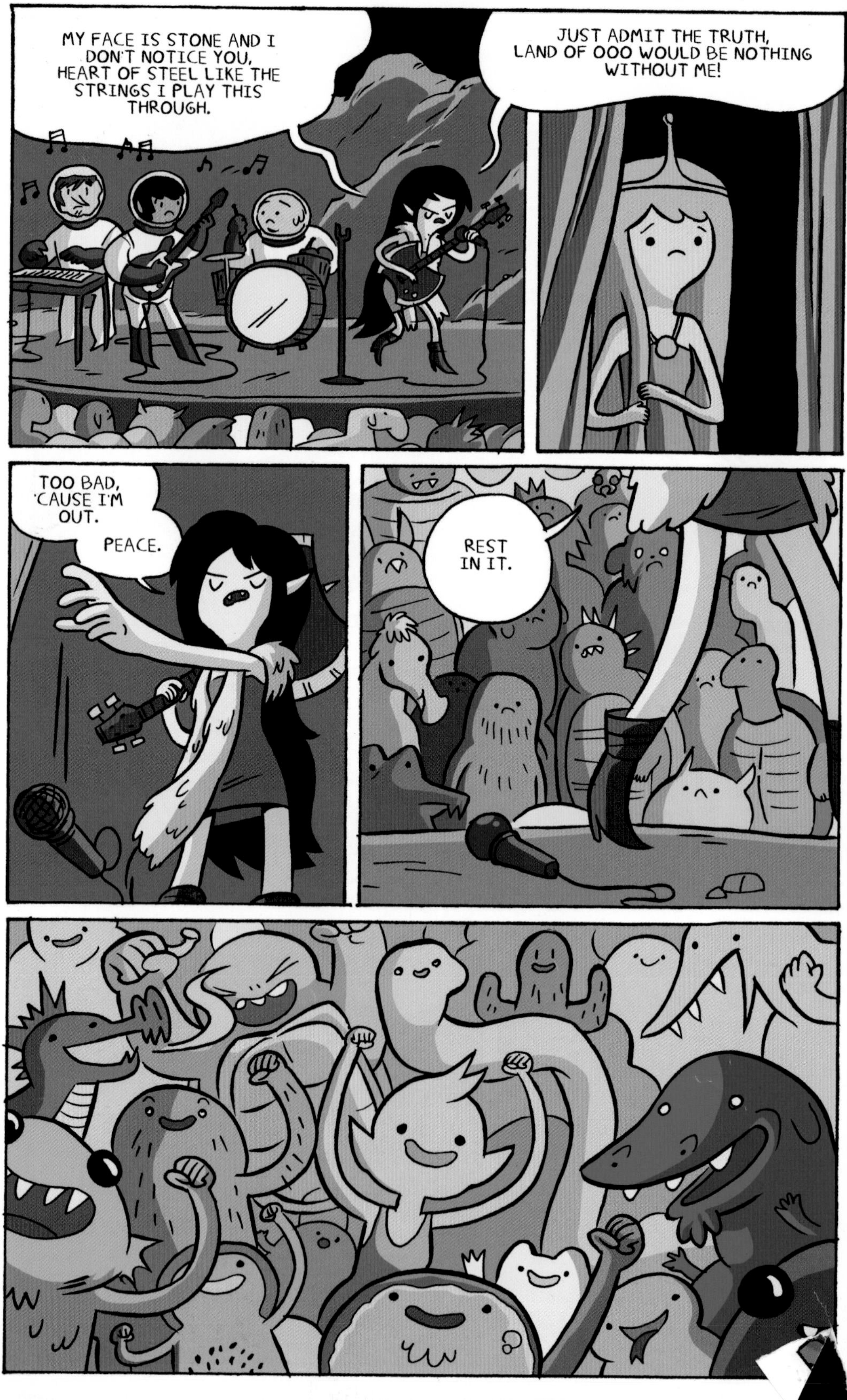
MY FACE IS STONE AND I DON'T NOTICE YOU, HEART OF STEEL LIKE THE STRINGS I PLAY THIS THROUGH.
JUST ADMIT THE TRUTH, LAND OF OOO WOULD BE NOTHING WITHOUT ME!
TOO BAD, 'CAUSE I'M OUT.
PEACE.
REST IN IT.

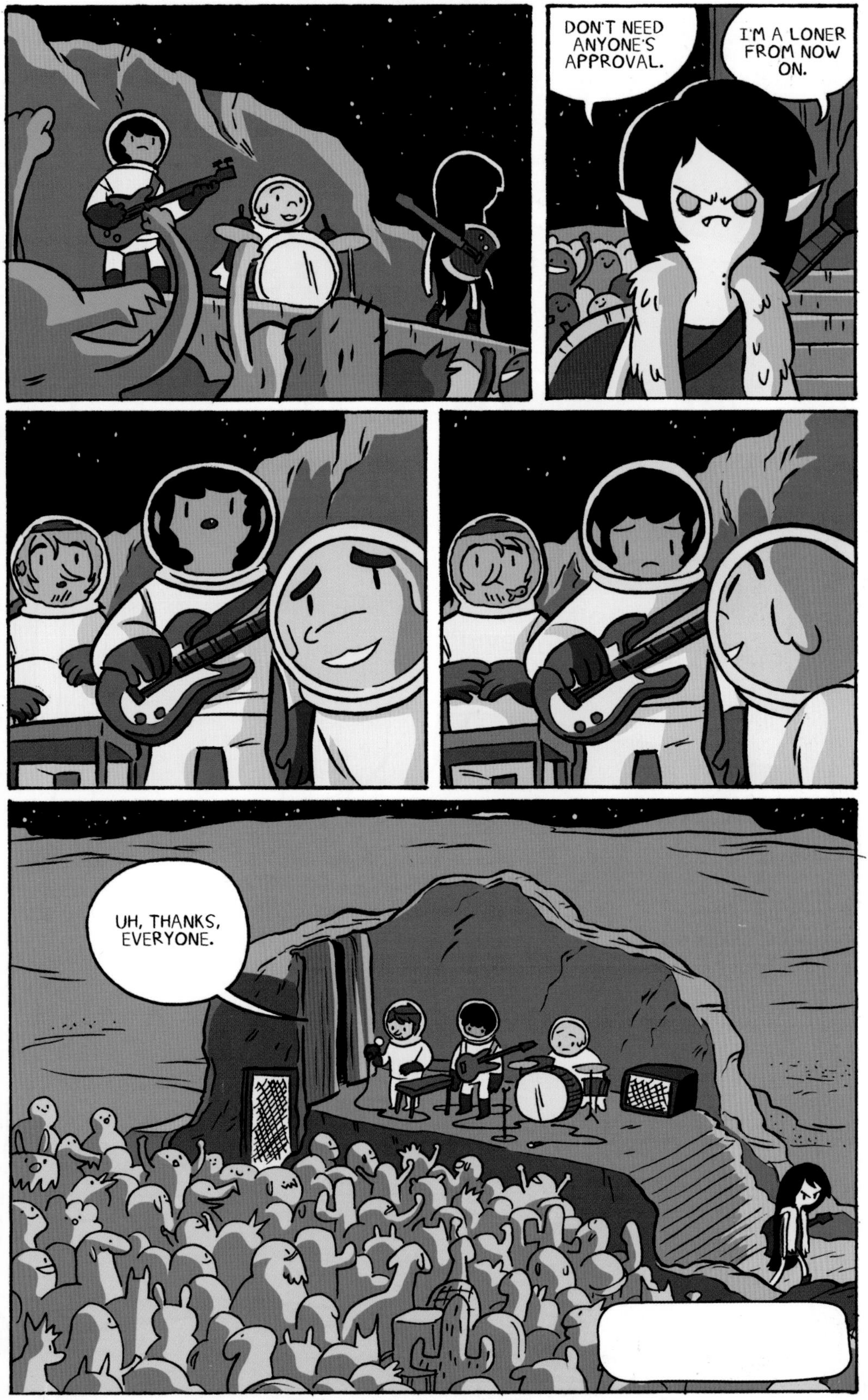
DON'T NEED ANYONE'S APPROVAL.
I'M A LONER FROM NOW ON.
UH, THANKS, EVERYONE.

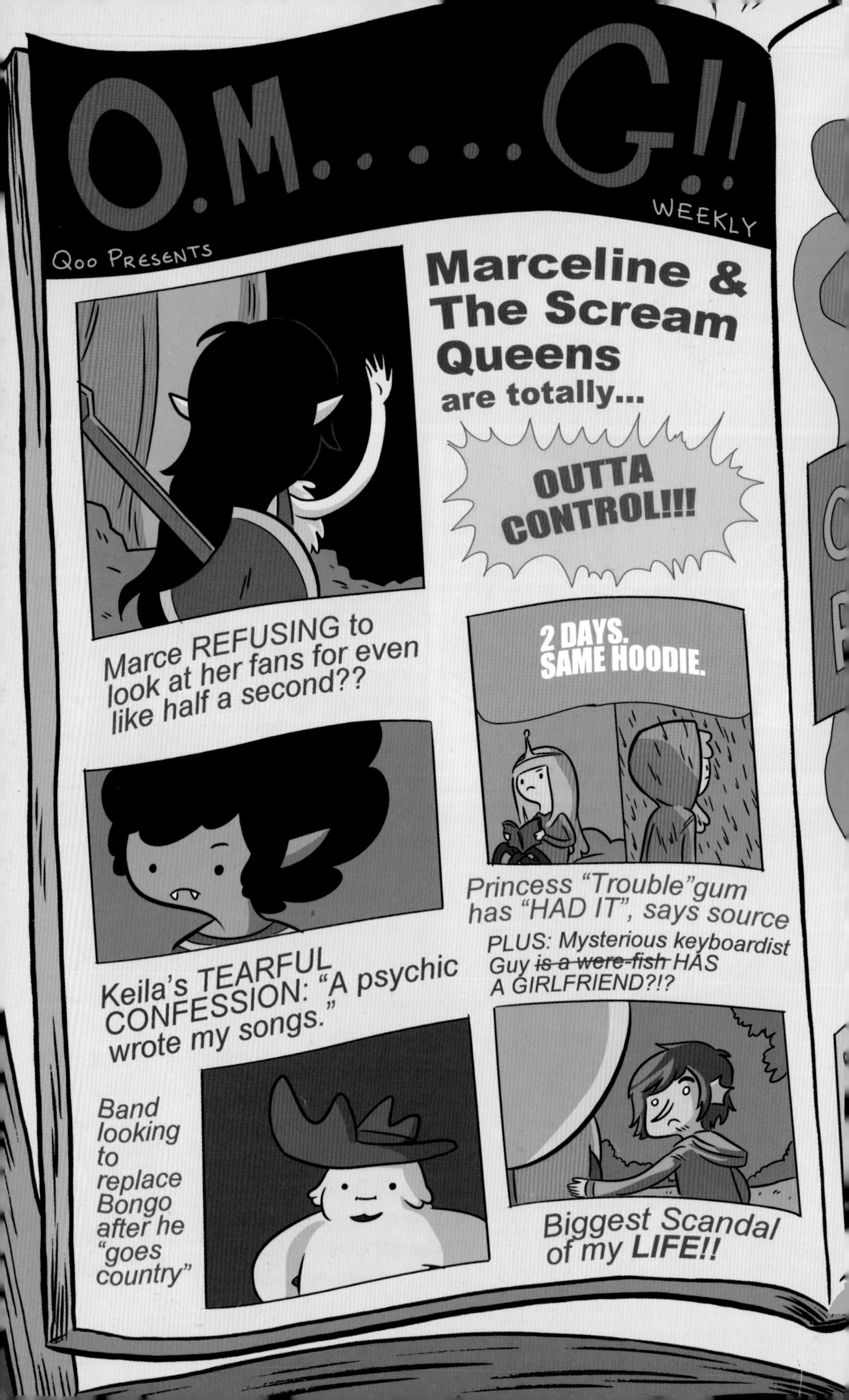

O.M....G!!
WEEKLY
Qoo PRESENTS
Marceline & The Scream Queens
are totally...
OUTTA CONTROL!!!
Marce REFUSING to look at her fans for even like half a second??
2 DAYS. SAME HOODIE.
Princess "Trouble"gum has "HAD IT", says source
PLUS: Mysterious keyboardist Guy ~~is a were-fish~~ HAS A GIRLFRIEND?!?
Keila's TEARFUL CONFESSION: "A psychic wrote my songs."
Band looking to replace Bongo after he "goes country"
Biggest Scandal of my LIFE!!

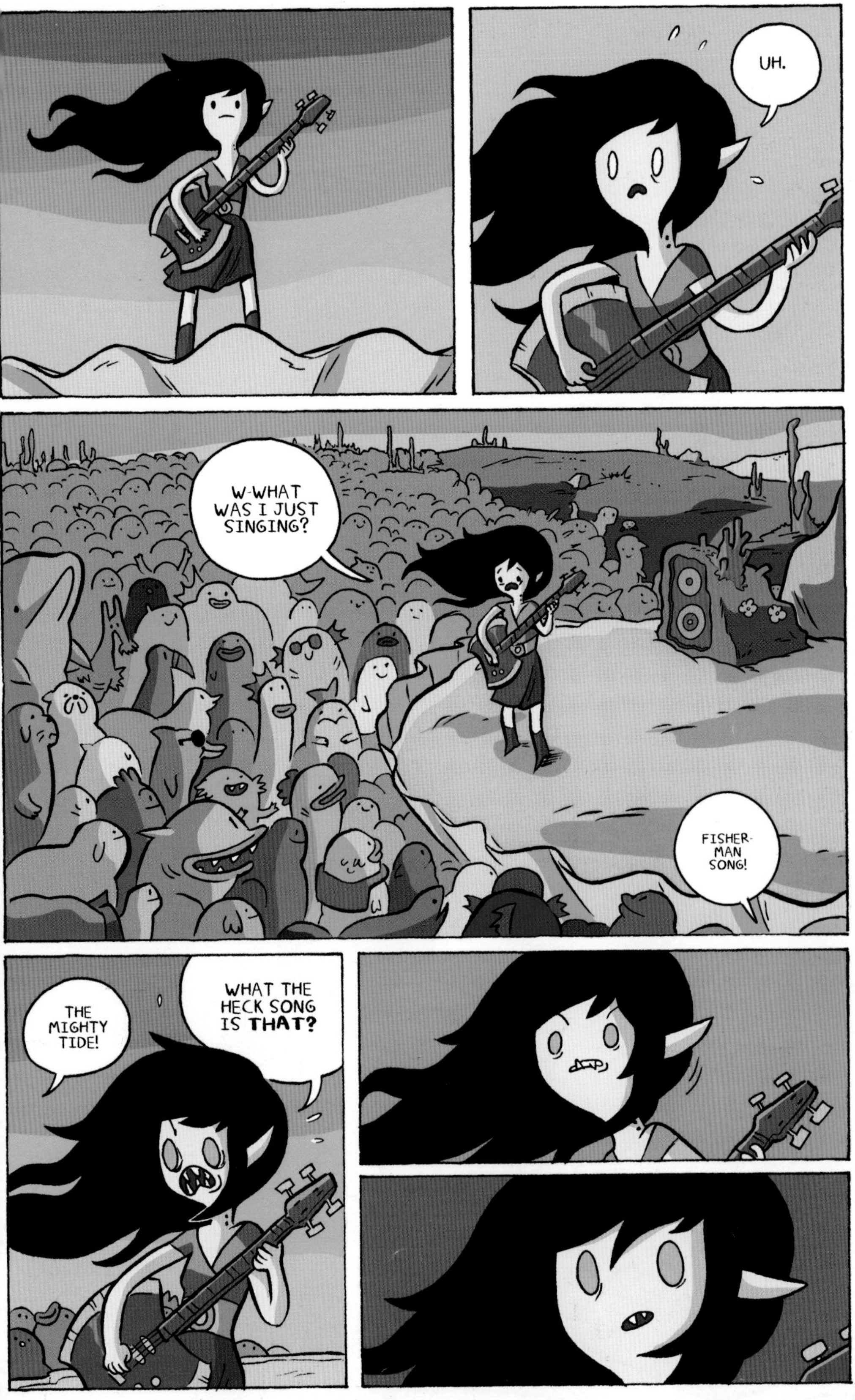
UH.
W-WHAT WAS I JUST SINGING?
FISHER-MAN SONG!
THE MIGHTY TIDE!
WHAT THE HECK SONG IS THAT?

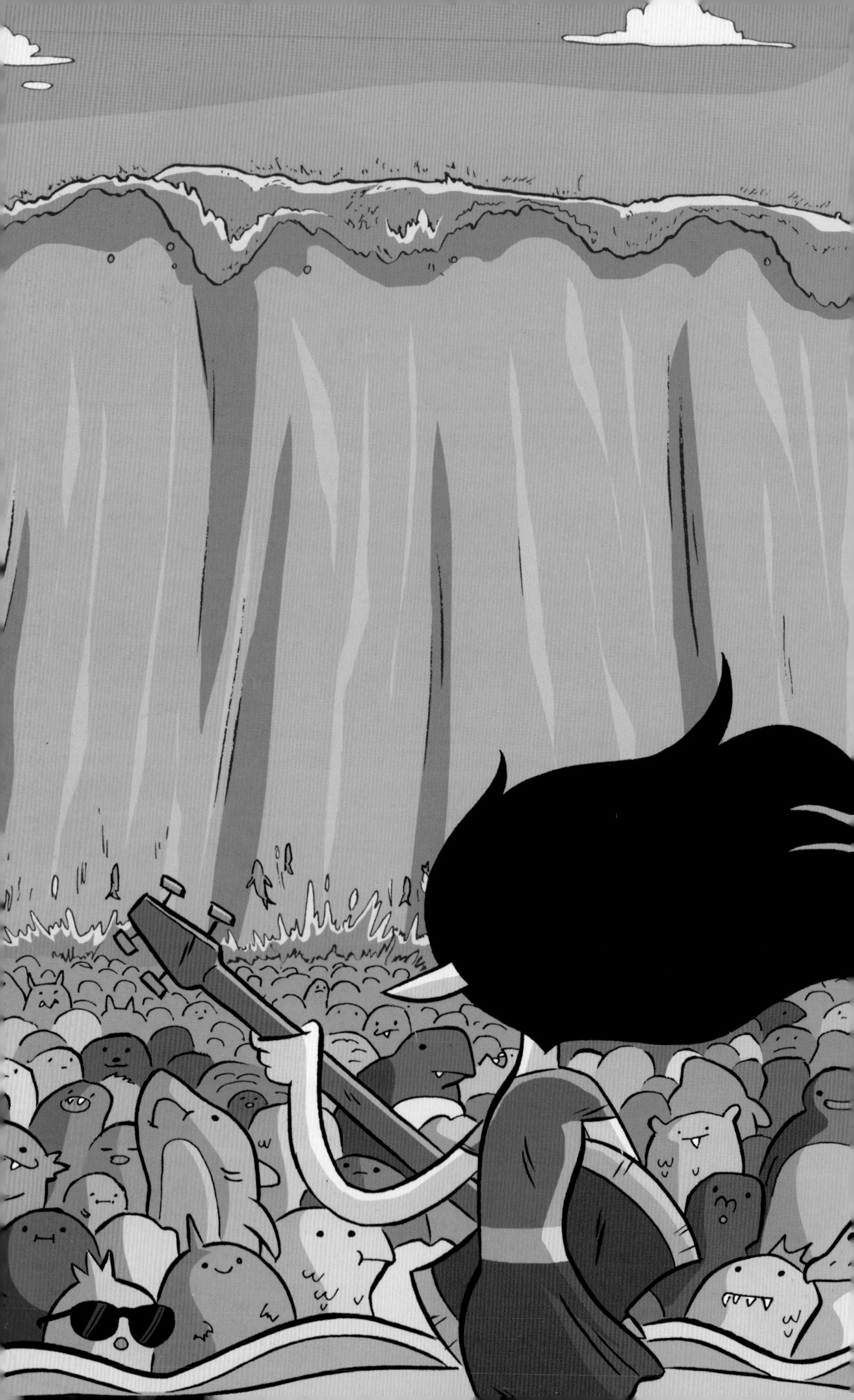

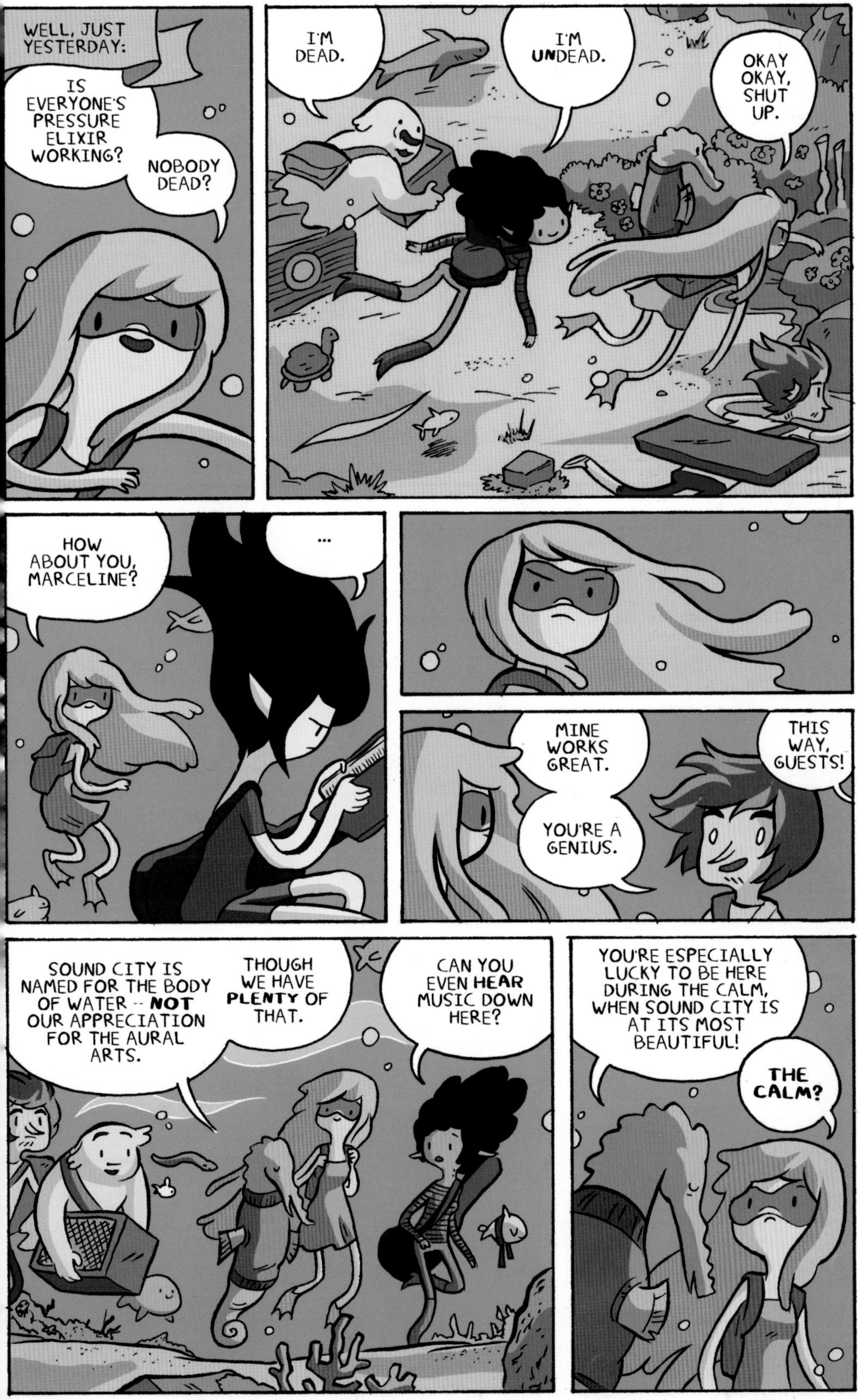
WELL, JUST YESTERDAY:
IS EVERYONE'S PRESSURE ELIXIR WORKING?
NOBODY DEAD?
I'M DEAD.
I'M **UN**DEAD.
OKAY OKAY, SHUT UP.
HOW ABOUT YOU, MARCELINE?
...
MINE WORKS GREAT.
YOU'RE A GENIUS.
THIS WAY, GUESTS!
SOUND CITY IS NAMED FOR THE BODY OF WATER -- **NOT** OUR APPRECIATION FOR THE AURAL ARTS.
THOUGH WE HAVE **PLENTY** OF THAT.
CAN YOU EVEN **HEAR** MUSIC DOWN HERE?
YOU'RE ESPECIALLY LUCKY TO BE HERE DURING THE CALM, WHEN SOUND CITY IS AT ITS MOST BEAUTIFUL!
THE CALM?

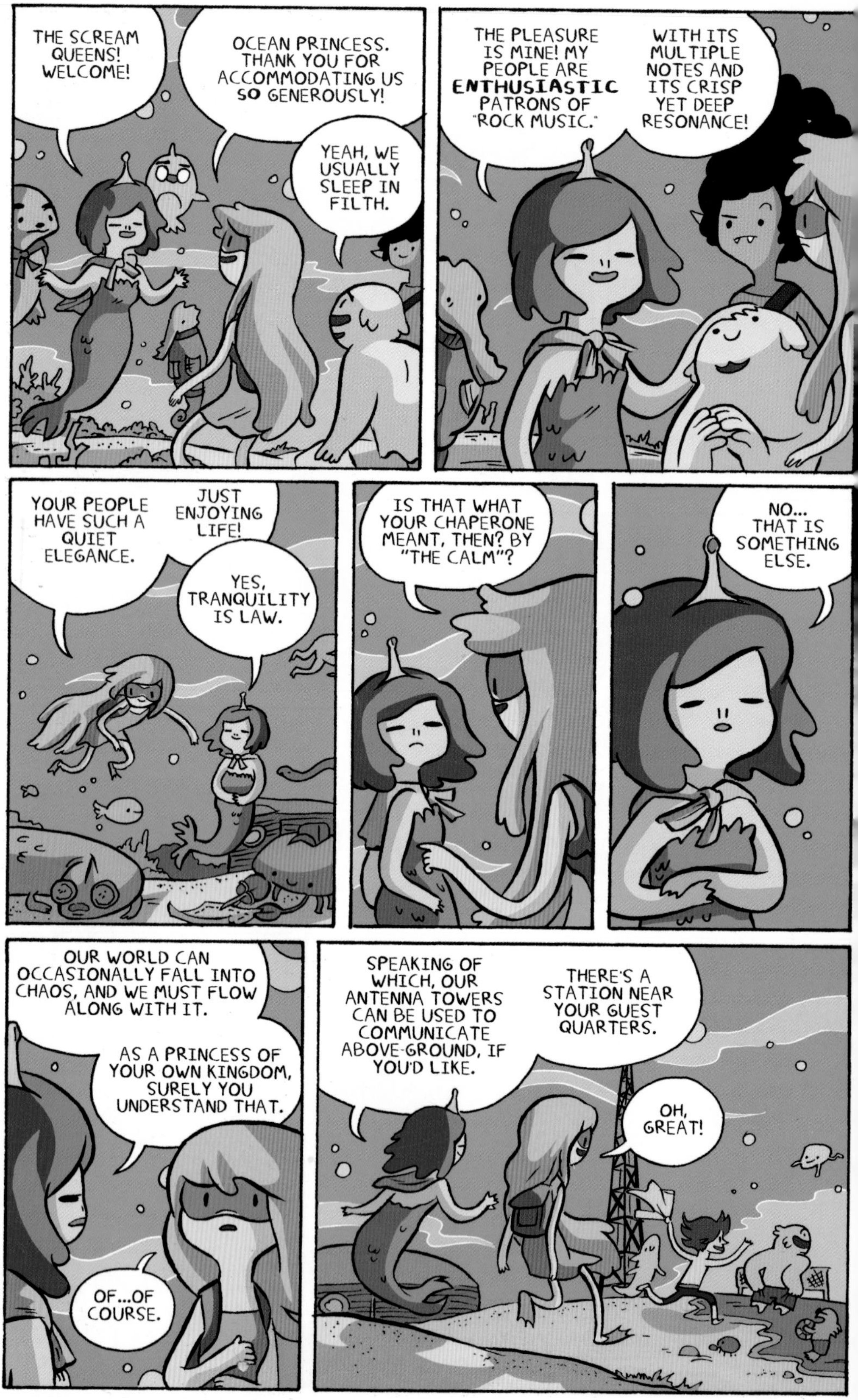
THE SCREAM QUEENS! WELCOME!
OCEAN PRINCESS. THANK YOU FOR ACCOMMODATING US SO GENEROUSLY!
YEAH, WE USUALLY SLEEP IN FILTH.
THE PLEASURE IS MINE! MY PEOPLE ARE **ENTHUSIASTIC** PATRONS OF "ROCK MUSIC."
WITH ITS MULTIPLE NOTES AND ITS CRISP YET DEEP RESONANCE!
YOUR PEOPLE HAVE SUCH A QUIET ELEGANCE.
JUST ENJOYING LIFE!
YES, TRANQUILITY IS LAW.
IS THAT WHAT YOUR CHAPERONE MEANT, THEN? BY "THE CALM"?
NO... THAT IS SOMETHING ELSE.
OUR WORLD CAN OCCASIONALLY FALL INTO CHAOS, AND WE MUST FLOW ALONG WITH IT.
AS A PRINCESS OF YOUR OWN KINGDOM, SURELY YOU UNDERSTAND THAT.
OF...OF COURSE.
SPEAKING OF WHICH, OUR ANTENNA TOWERS CAN BE USED TO COMMUNICATE ABOVE-GROUND, IF YOU'D LIKE.
THERE'S A STATION NEAR YOUR GUEST QUARTERS.
OH, GREAT!

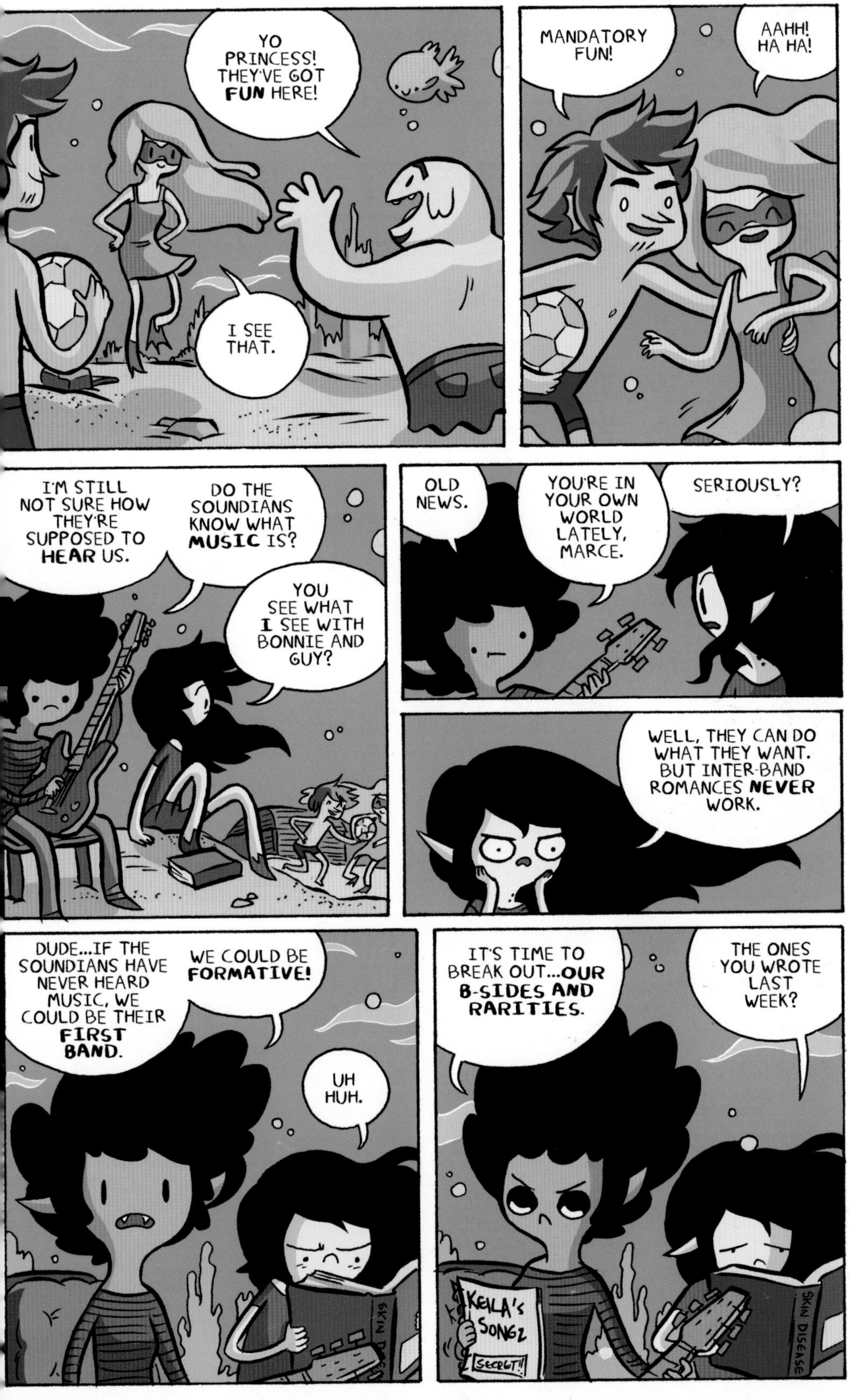
YO PRINCESS! THEY'VE GOT **FUN** HERE!
I SEE THAT.
MANDATORY FUN!
AAHH! HA HA!
I'M STILL NOT SURE HOW THEY'RE SUPPOSED TO **HEAR** US.
DO THE SOUNDIANS KNOW WHAT **MUSIC** IS?
YOU SEE WHAT **I** SEE WITH BONNIE AND GUY?
OLD NEWS.
YOU'RE IN YOUR OWN WORLD LATELY, MARCE.
SERIOUSLY?
WELL, THEY CAN DO WHAT THEY WANT. BUT INTER-BAND ROMANCES **NEVER** WORK.
DUDE...IF THE SOUNDIANS HAVE NEVER HEARD MUSIC, WE COULD BE THEIR **FIRST BAND**.
WE COULD BE **FORMATIVE!**
UH HUH.
SKIN DISEASE
IT'S TIME TO BREAK OUT...**OUR B-SIDES AND RARITIES**.
THE ONES YOU WROTE LAST WEEK?
KEILA's SONGZ
SECRET!!
SKIN DISEASE

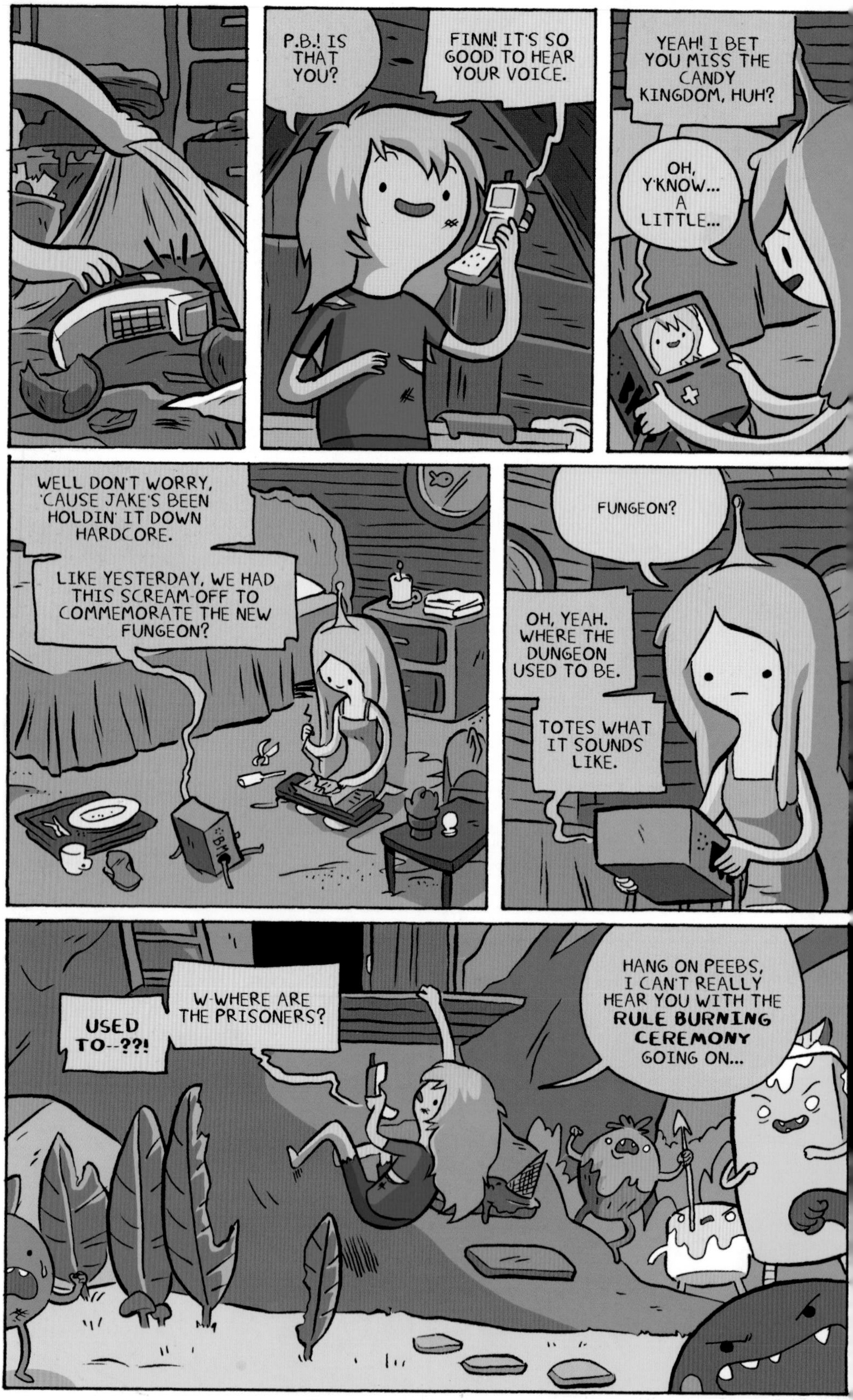
P.B.! IS THAT YOU?
FINN! IT'S SO GOOD TO HEAR YOUR VOICE.
YEAH! I BET YOU MISS THE CANDY KINGDOM, HUH?
OH, Y'KNOW... A LITTLE...
WELL DON'T WORRY, 'CAUSE JAKE'S BEEN HOLDIN' IT DOWN HARDCORE.
LIKE YESTERDAY, WE HAD THIS SCREAM-OFF TO COMMEMORATE THE NEW FUNGEON?
FUNGEON?
OH, YEAH. WHERE THE DUNGEON USED TO BE.
TOTES WHAT IT SOUNDS LIKE.
USED TO--??!
W-WHERE ARE THE PRISONERS?
HANG ON PEEBS, I CAN'T REALLY HEAR YOU WITH THE **RULE BURNING CEREMONY** GOING ON...

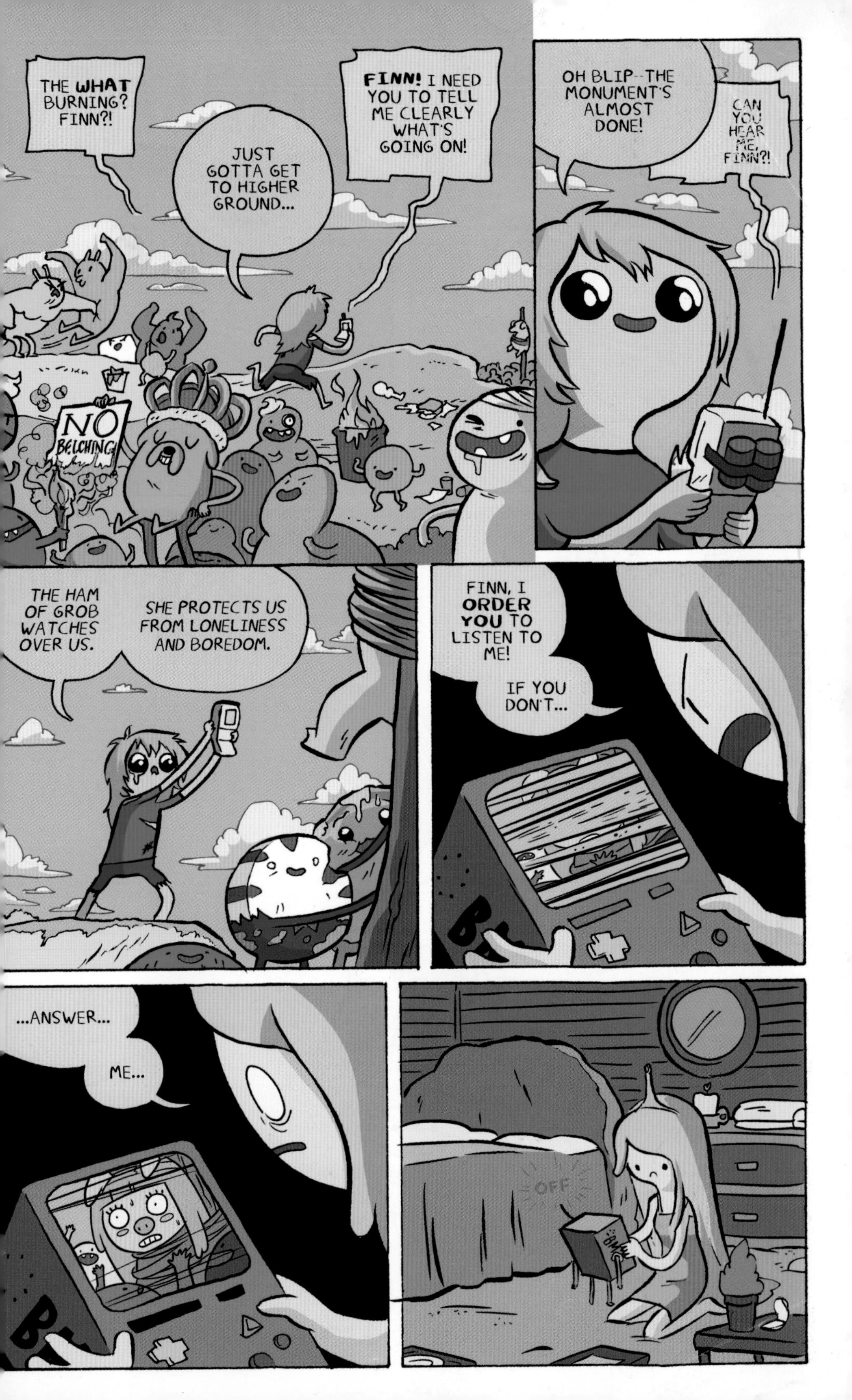
THE WHAT BURNING? FINN?!
JUST GOTTA GET TO HIGHER GROUND...
FINN! I NEED YOU TO TELL ME CLEARLY WHAT'S GOING ON!
NO BELCHING!
OH BLIP--THE MONUMENT'S ALMOST DONE!
CAN YOU HEAR ME, FINN?!
THE HAM OF GROB WATCHES OVER US.
SHE PROTECTS US FROM LONELINESS AND BOREDOM.
FINN, I ORDER YOU TO LISTEN TO ME!
IF YOU DON'T...
...ANSWER...
ME...
OFF

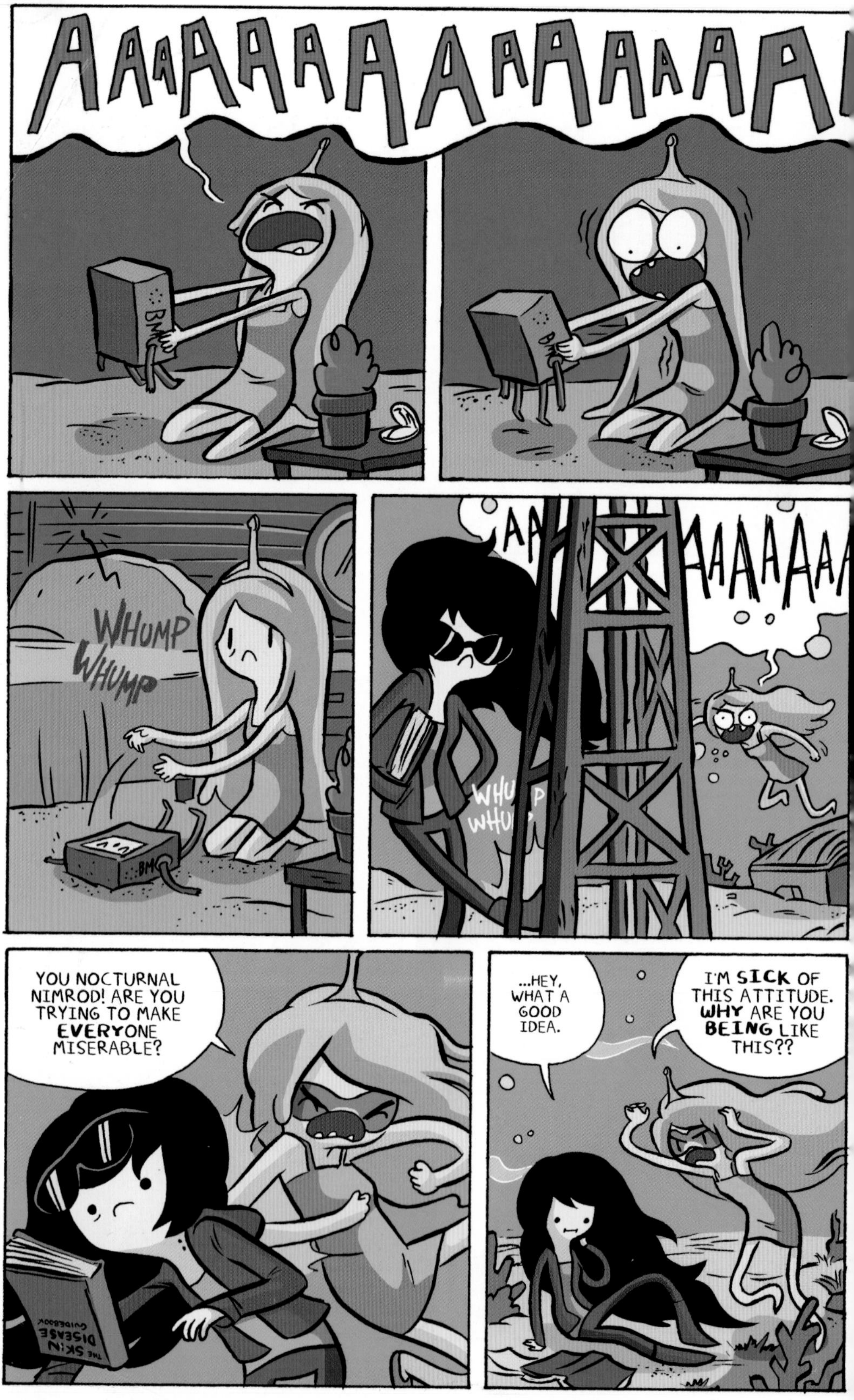
AAAAAAAAAAAAAAAA
BMO
WHUMP
WHUMP
BMO
AAAAAAAAA
WHUMP
WHUMP
YOU NOCTURNAL NIMROD! ARE YOU TRYING TO MAKE EVERYONE MISERABLE?
THE SKIN DISEASE GUIDEBOOK
...HEY, WHAT A GOOD IDEA.
I'M SICK OF THIS ATTITUDE. WHY ARE YOU BEING LIKE THIS??

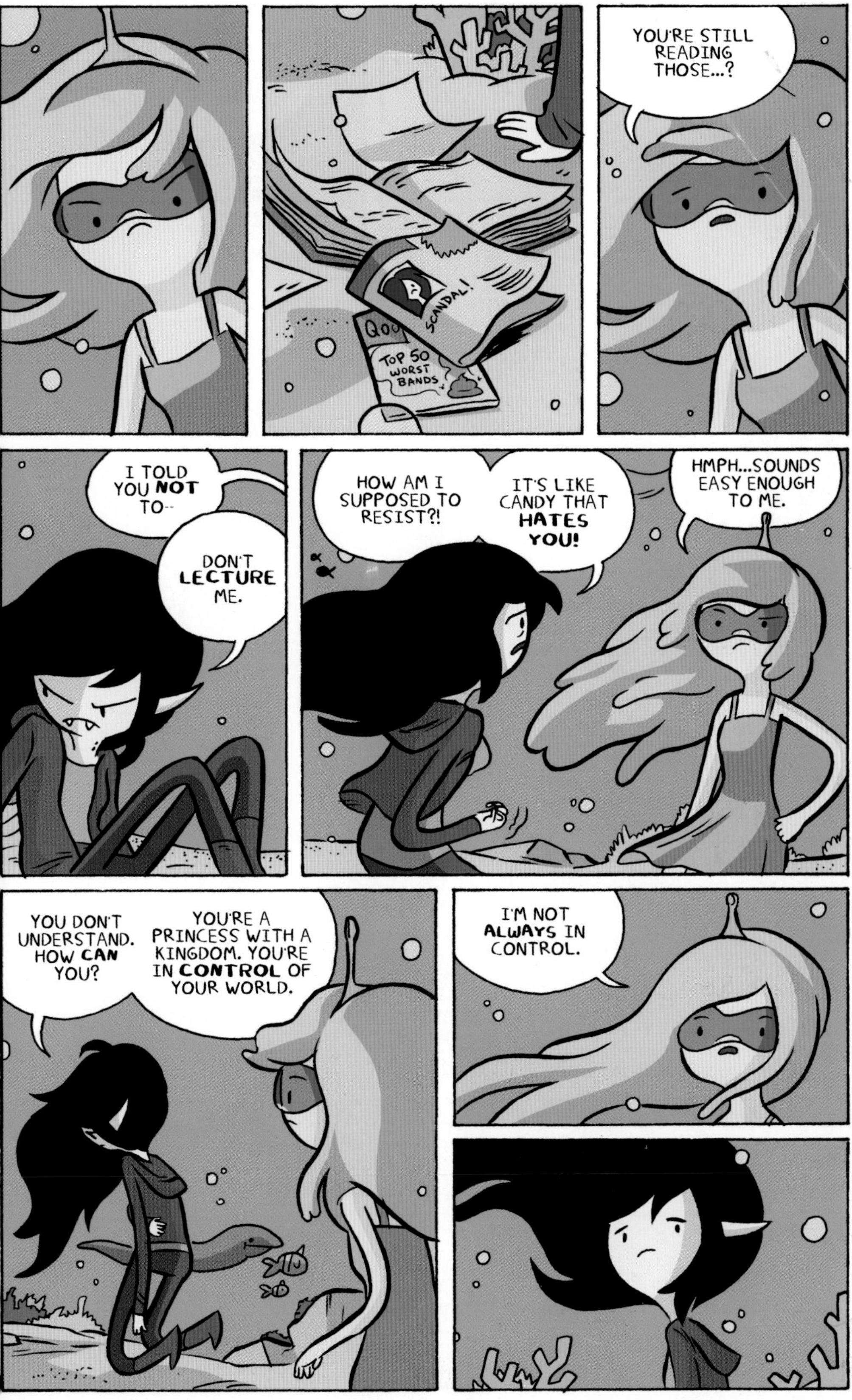
SCANDAL!
QOO
TOP 50 WORST BANDS
YOU'RE STILL READING THOSE...?
I TOLD YOU **NOT** TO--
DON'T **LECTURE** ME.
HOW AM I SUPPOSED TO RESIST?!
IT'S LIKE CANDY THAT **HATES YOU!**
HMPH...SOUNDS EASY ENOUGH TO ME.
YOU DON'T UNDERSTAND. HOW **CAN** YOU?
YOU'RE A PRINCESS WITH A KINGDOM. YOU'RE IN **CONTROL** OF YOUR WORLD.
I'M NOT **ALWAYS** IN CONTROL.

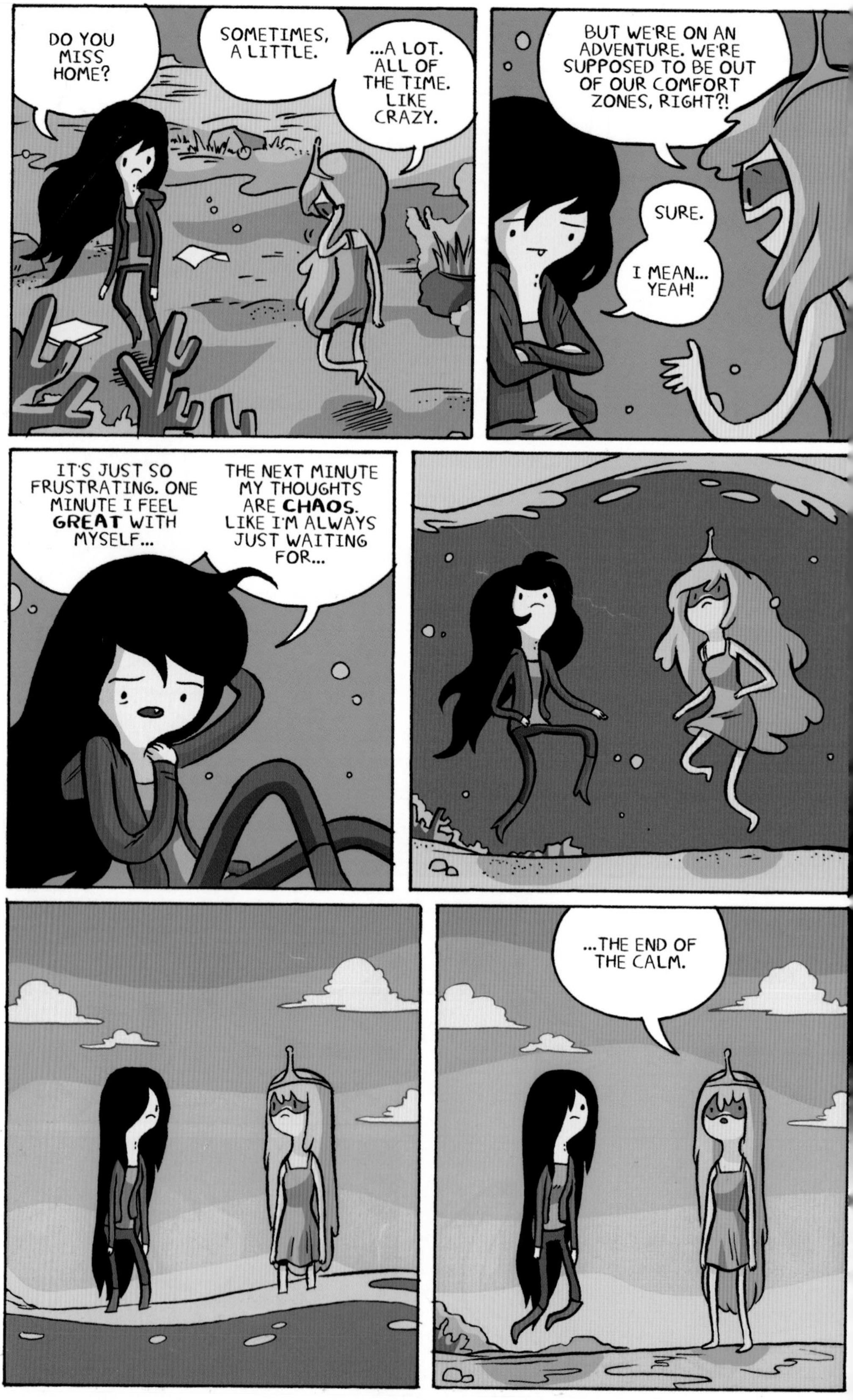
DO YOU MISS HOME?
SOMETIMES, A LITTLE.
...A LOT. ALL OF THE TIME. LIKE CRAZY.
BUT WE'RE ON AN ADVENTURE. WE'RE SUPPOSED TO BE OUT OF OUR COMFORT ZONES, RIGHT?!
SURE.
I MEAN... YEAH!
IT'S JUST SO FRUSTRATING. ONE MINUTE I FEEL GREAT WITH MYSELF...
THE NEXT MINUTE MY THOUGHTS ARE CHAOS. LIKE I'M ALWAYS JUST WAITING FOR...
...THE END OF THE CALM.

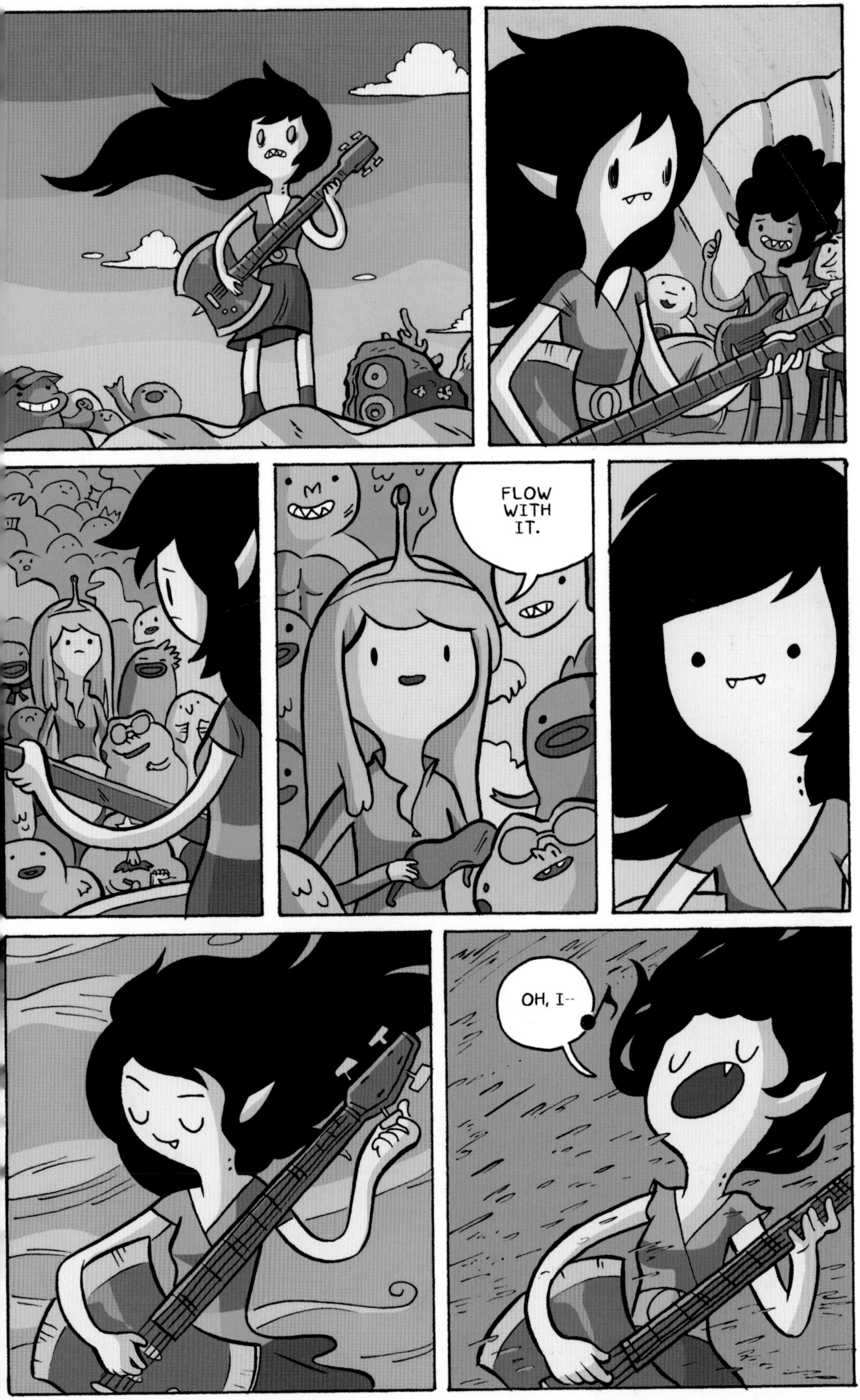
FLOW WITH IT.
OH, I--

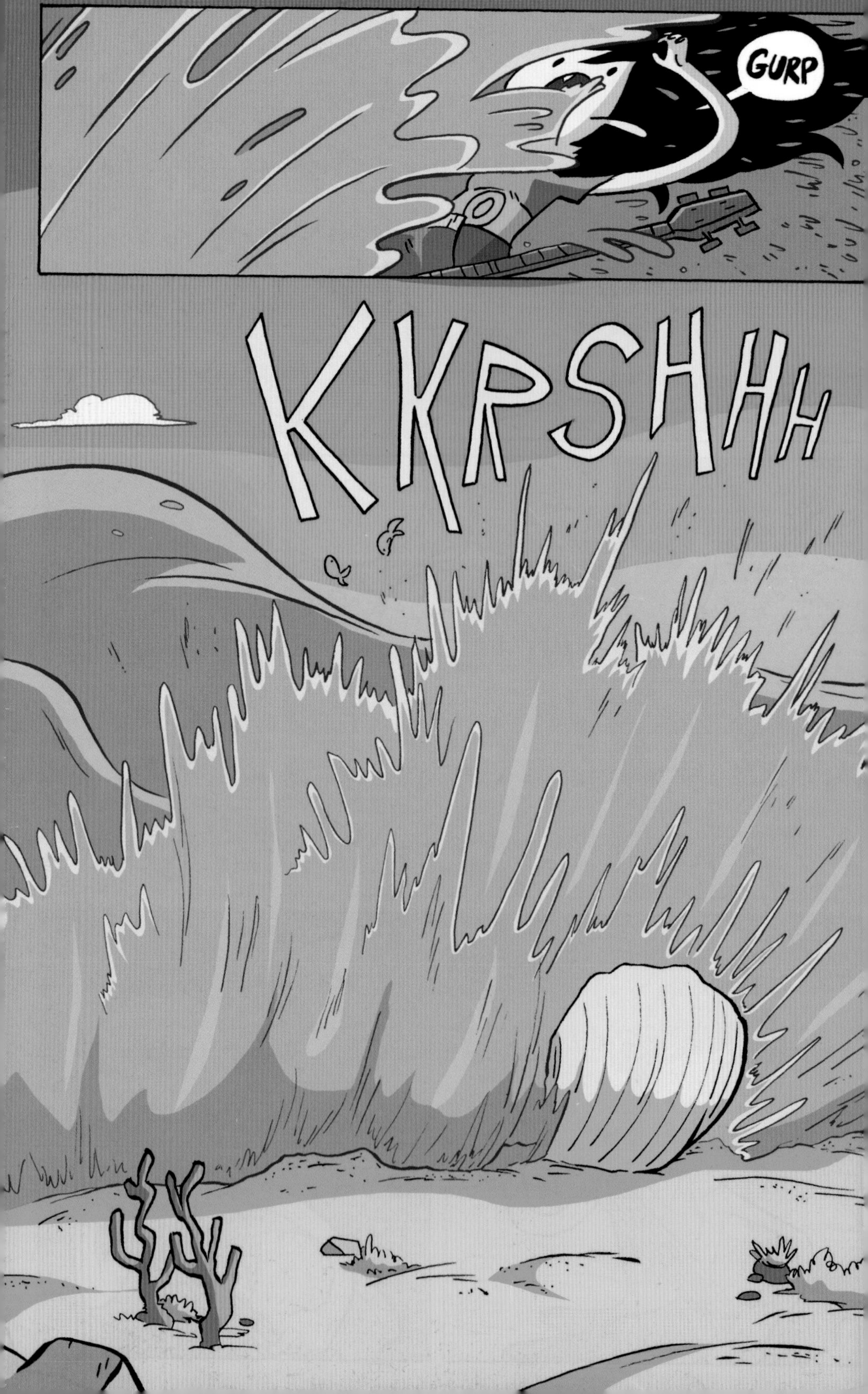
GURP
KKRSHHH

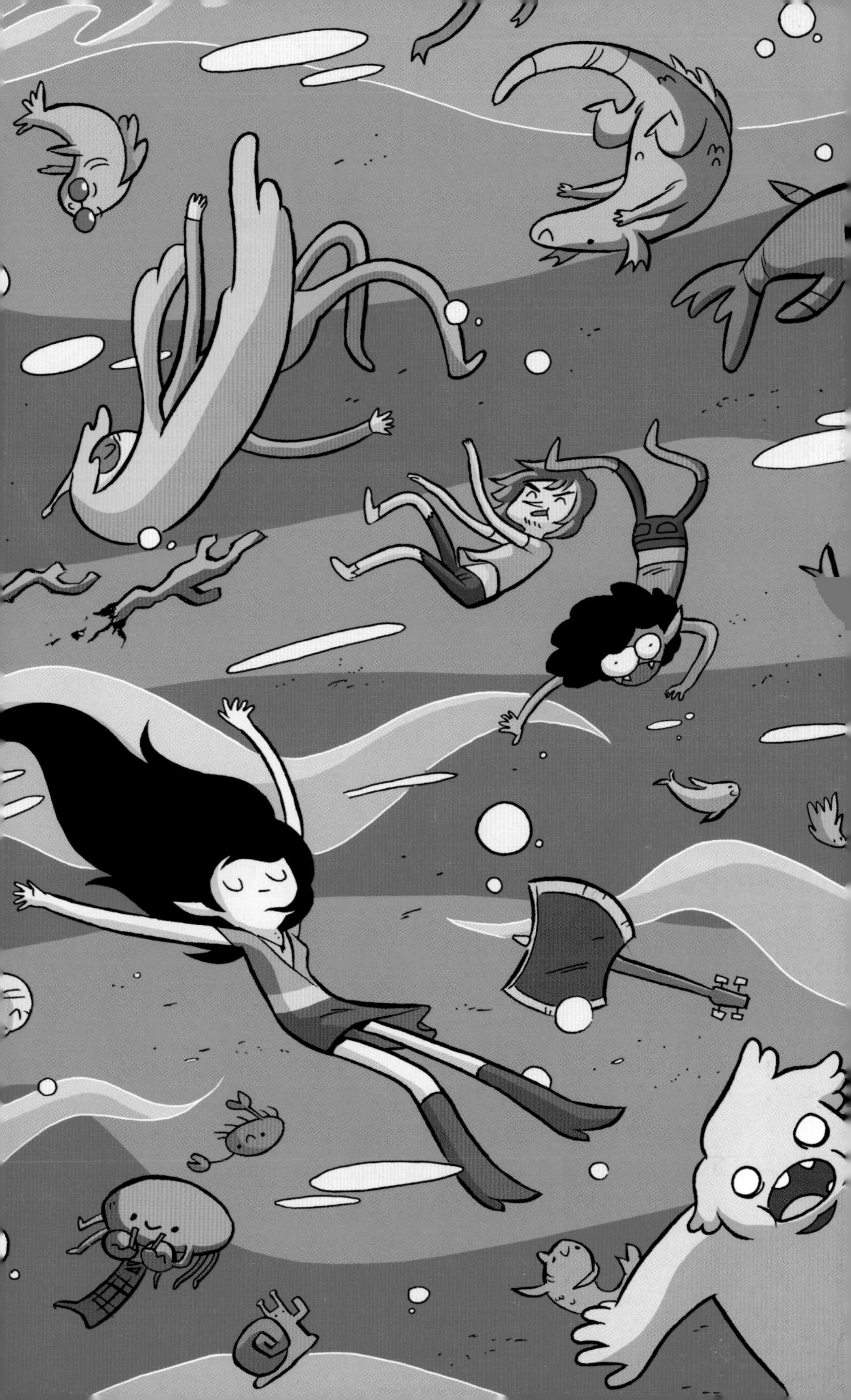

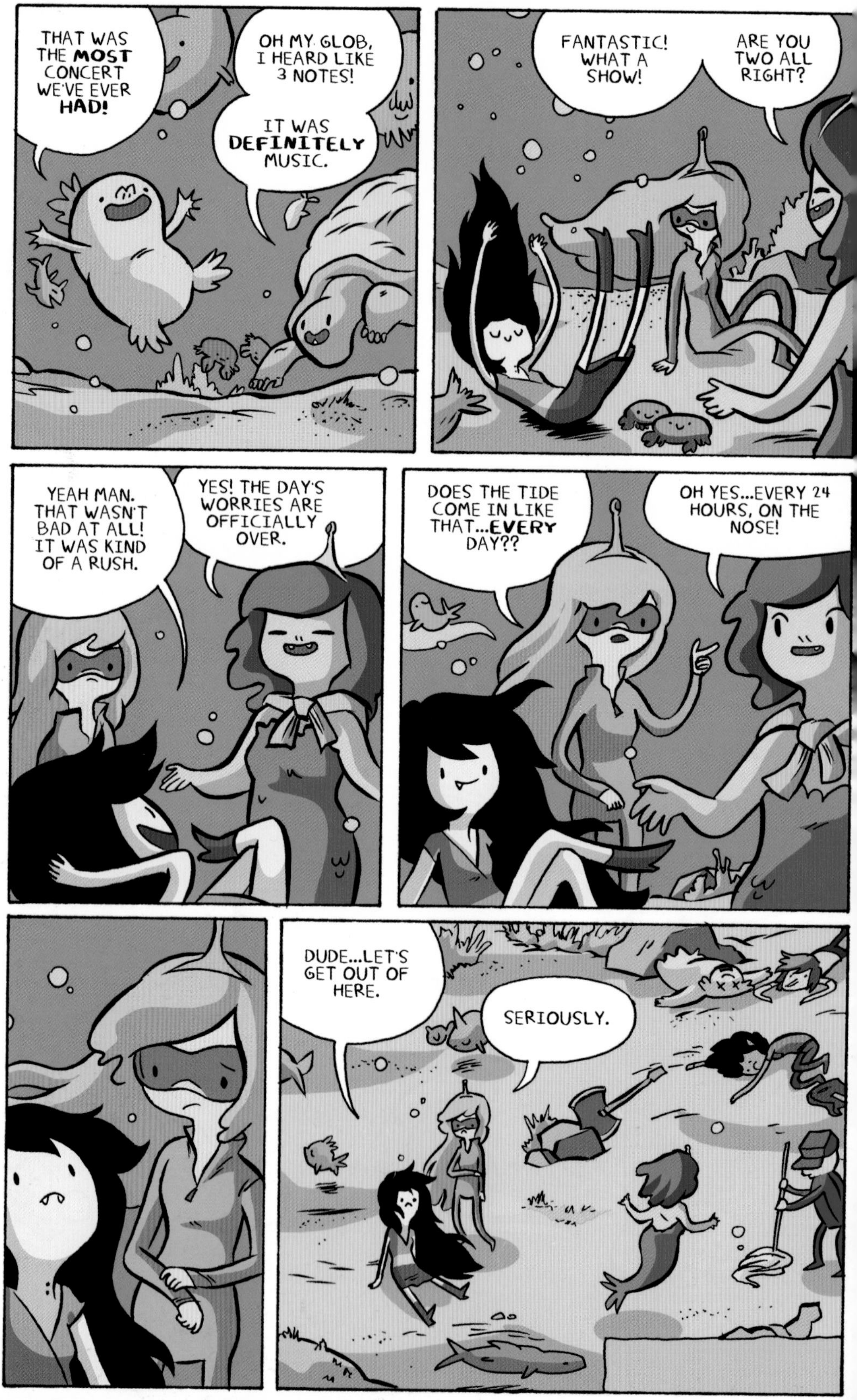
THAT WAS THE MOST CONCERT WE'VE EVER HAD!
OH MY GLOB, I HEARD LIKE 3 NOTES!
IT WAS DEFINITELY MUSIC.
FANTASTIC! WHAT A SHOW!
ARE YOU TWO ALL RIGHT?
YEAH MAN. THAT WASN'T BAD AT ALL! IT WAS KIND OF A RUSH.
YES! THE DAY'S WORRIES ARE OFFICIALLY OVER.
DOES THE TIDE COME IN LIKE THAT...EVERY DAY??
OH YES...EVERY 24 HOURS, ON THE NOSE!
DUDE...LET'S GET OUT OF HERE.
SERIOUSLY.

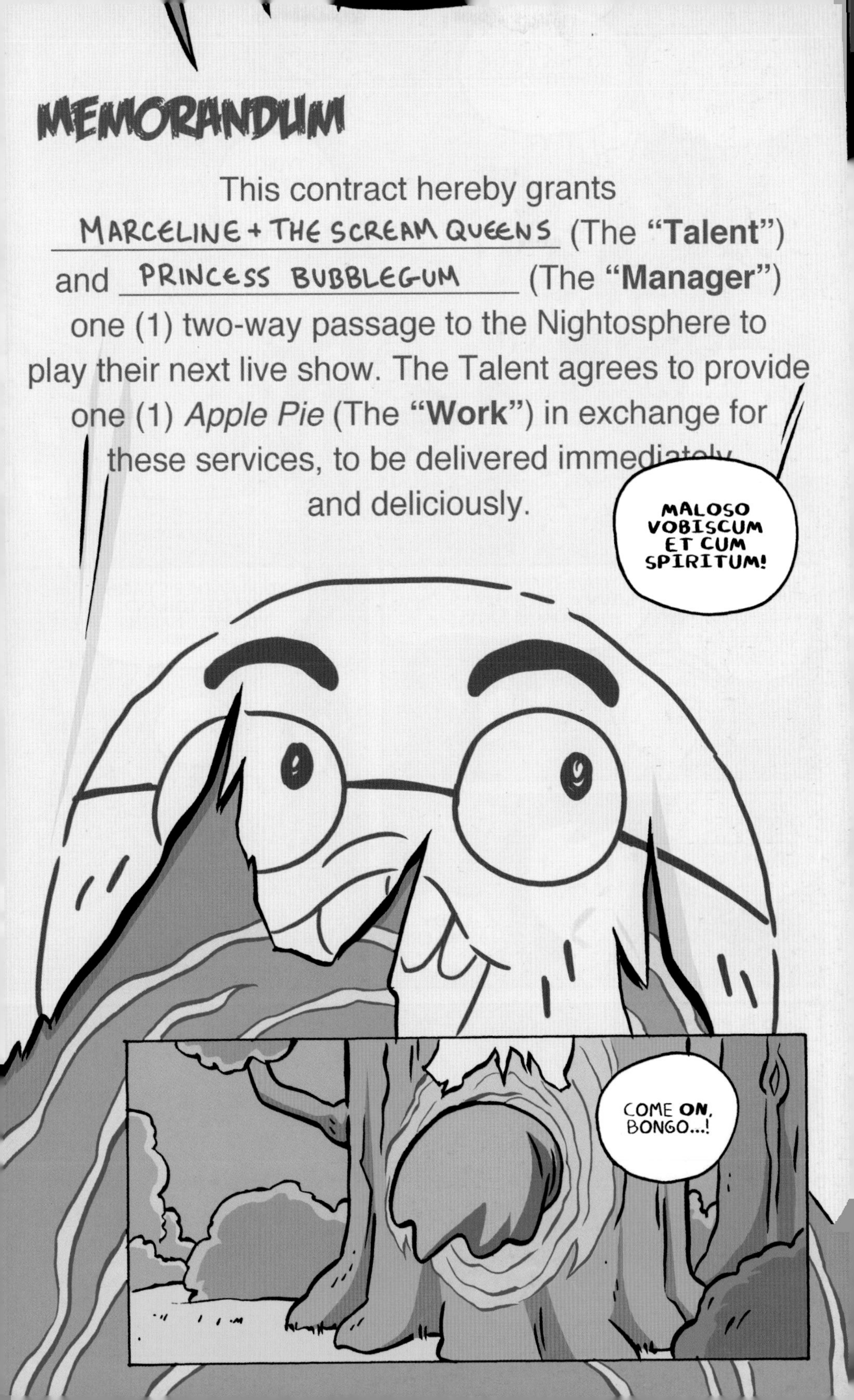
MEMORANDUM
This contract hereby grants
MARCELINE + THE SCREAM QUEENS (The "Talent")
and PRINCESS BUBBLEGUM (The "Manager")
one (1) two-way passage to the Nightosphere to play their next live show. The Talent agrees to provide one (1) Apple Pie (The "Work") in exchange for these services, to be delivered immediately and deliciously.
MALOSO VOBISCUM ET CUM SPIRITUM!
COME ON, BONGO...!

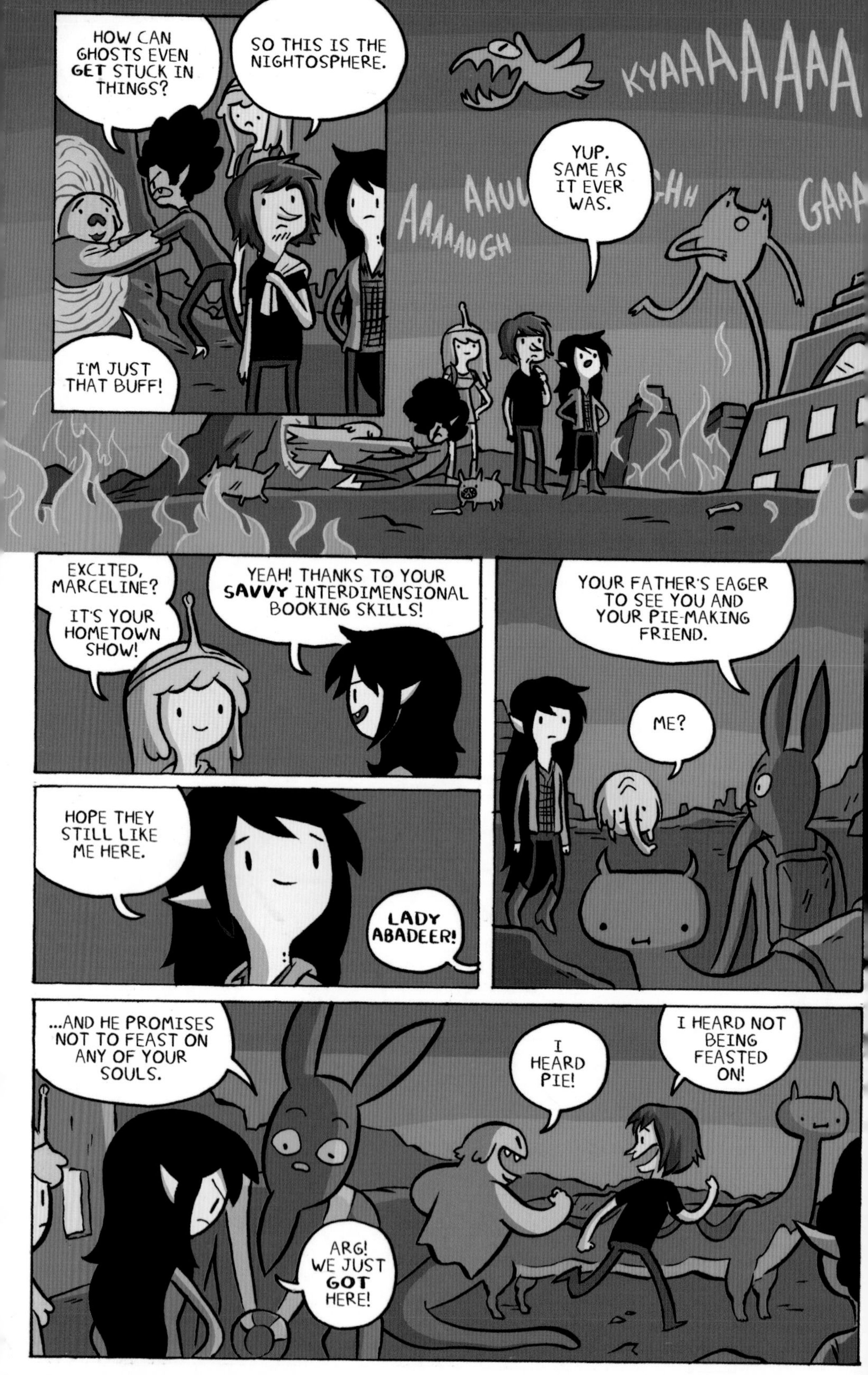
HOW CAN GHOSTS EVEN GET STUCK IN THINGS?
SO THIS IS THE NIGHTOSPHERE.
I'M JUST THAT BUFF!
KYAAAAAAAA
YUP. SAME AS IT EVER WAS.
AAUUGHH
AAAAAUGH
GAAA
EXCITED, MARCELINE?
IT'S YOUR HOMETOWN SHOW!
YEAH! THANKS TO YOUR SAVVY INTERDIMENSIONAL BOOKING SKILLS!
HOPE THEY STILL LIKE ME HERE.
LADY ABADEER!
YOUR FATHER'S EAGER TO SEE YOU AND YOUR PIE-MAKING FRIEND.
ME?
...AND HE PROMISES NOT TO FEAST ON ANY OF YOUR SOULS.
ARG! WE JUST GOT HERE!
I HEARD PIE!
I HEARD NOT BEING FEASTED ON!

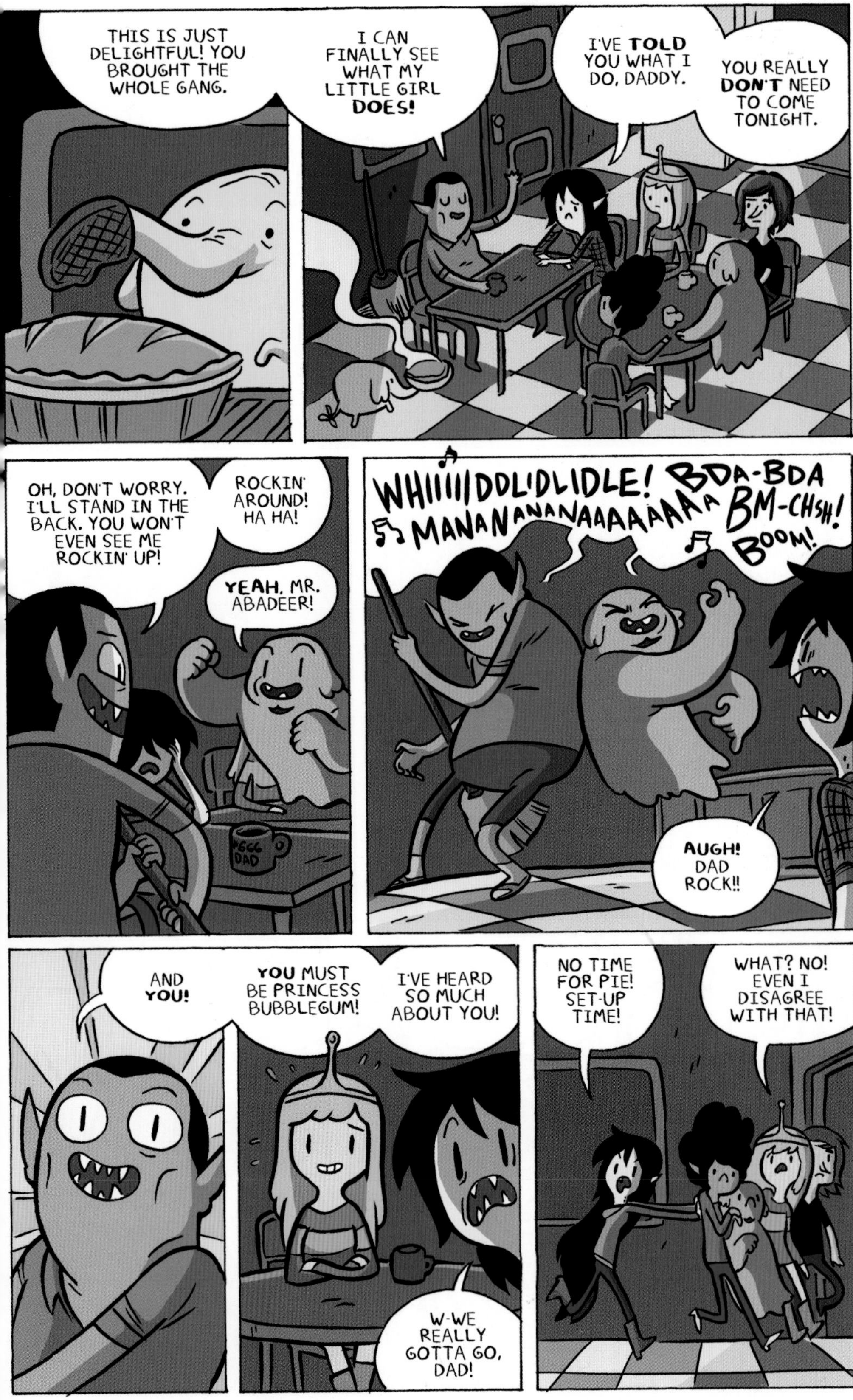

THIS IS JUST DELIGHTFUL! YOU BROUGHT THE WHOLE GANG.
I CAN FINALLY SEE WHAT MY LITTLE GIRL **DOES!**
I'VE **TOLD** YOU WHAT I DO, DADDY.
YOU REALLY **DON'T** NEED TO COME TONIGHT.
OH, DON'T WORRY. I'LL STAND IN THE BACK. YOU WON'T EVEN SEE ME ROCKIN' UP!
ROCKIN' AROUND! HA HA!
YEAH, MR. ABADEER!
#666 DAD
WHIIIIIIDDLIDLIDLE! BDA-BDA MANANANANAAAAAAAA BM-CHSH! BOOM!
AUGH! DAD ROCK!!
AND **YOU!**
YOU MUST BE PRINCESS BUBBLEGUM!
I'VE HEARD SO MUCH ABOUT YOU!
W-WE REALLY GOTTA GO, DAD!
NO TIME FOR PIE! SET-UP TIME!
WHAT? NO! EVEN I DISAGREE WITH THAT!

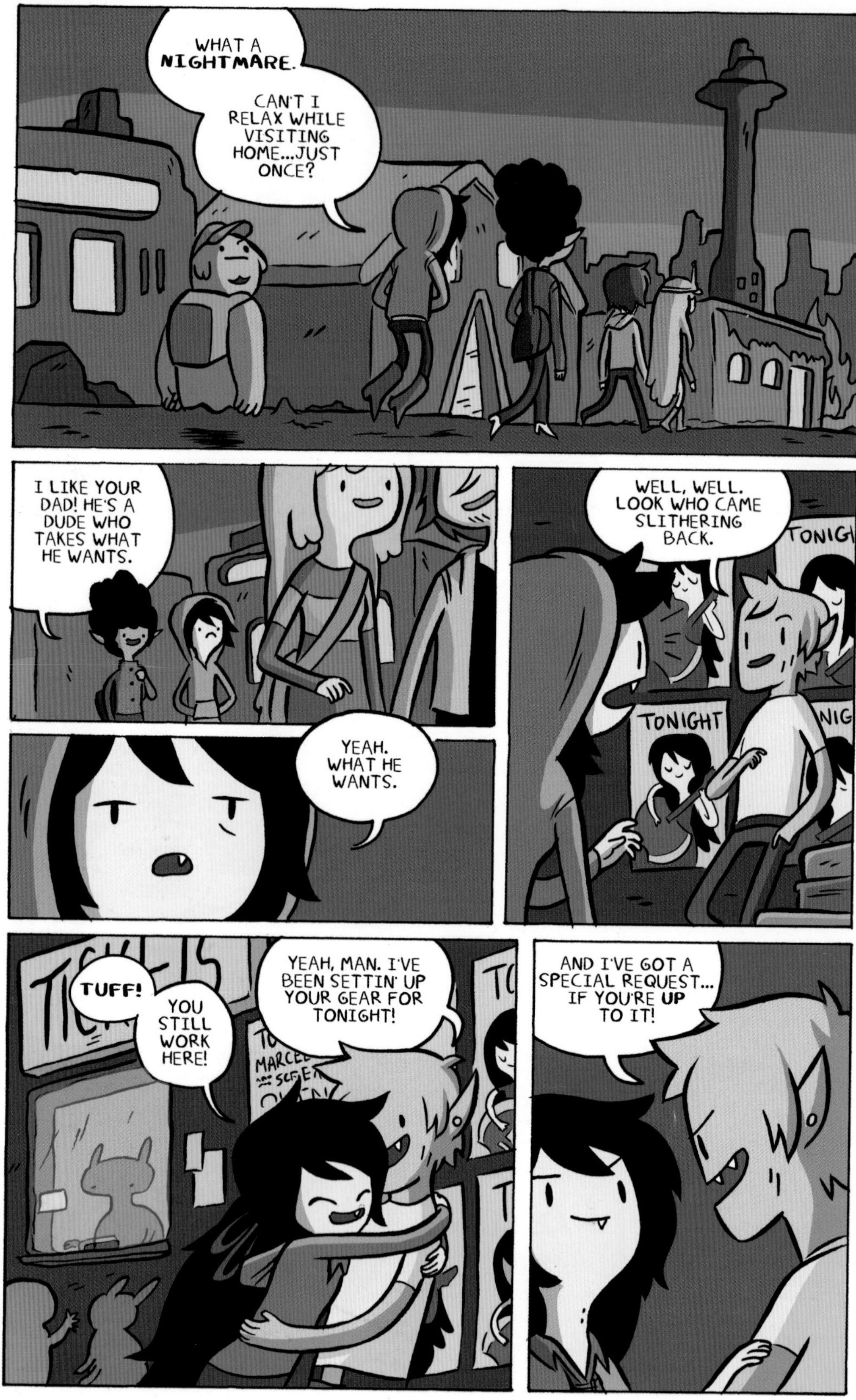

WHAT A **NIGHTMARE**.
CAN'T I RELAX WHILE VISITING HOME...JUST ONCE?
I LIKE YOUR DAD! HE'S A DUDE WHO TAKES WHAT HE WANTS.
YEAH. WHAT HE WANTS.
WELL, WELL. LOOK WHO CAME SLITHERING BACK.
TONIGHT
TUFF!
YOU STILL WORK HERE!
YEAH, MAN. I'VE BEEN SETTIN' UP YOUR GEAR FOR TONIGHT!
AND I'VE GOT A SPECIAL REQUEST... IF YOU'RE **UP** TO IT!

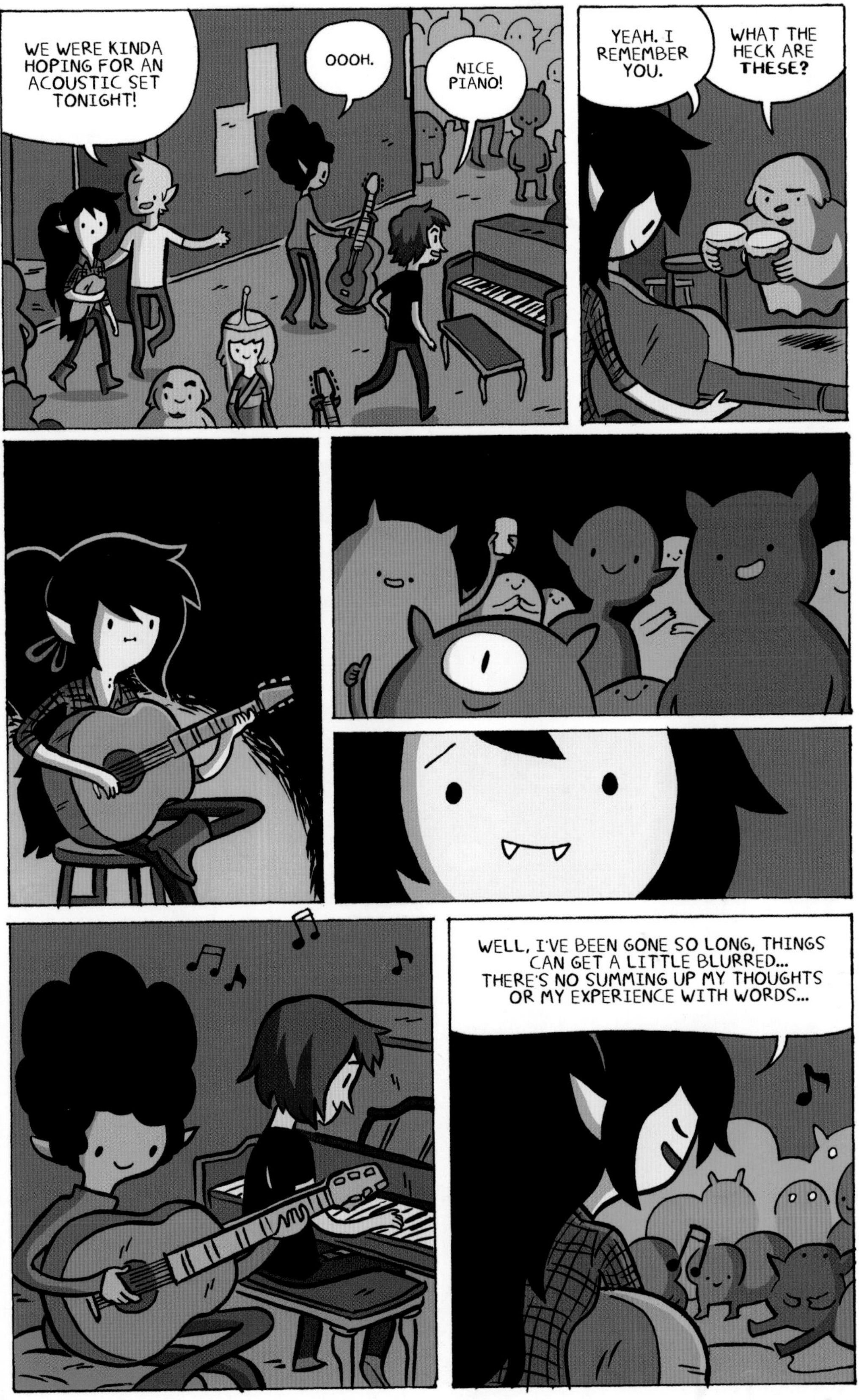
WE WERE KINDA HOPING FOR AN ACOUSTIC SET TONIGHT!
OOOH.
NICE PIANO!
YEAH. I REMEMBER YOU.
WHAT THE HECK ARE **THESE?**
WELL, I'VE BEEN GONE SO LONG, THINGS CAN GET A LITTLE BLURRED...
THERE'S NO SUMMING UP MY THOUGHTS OR MY EXPERIENCE WITH WORDS...

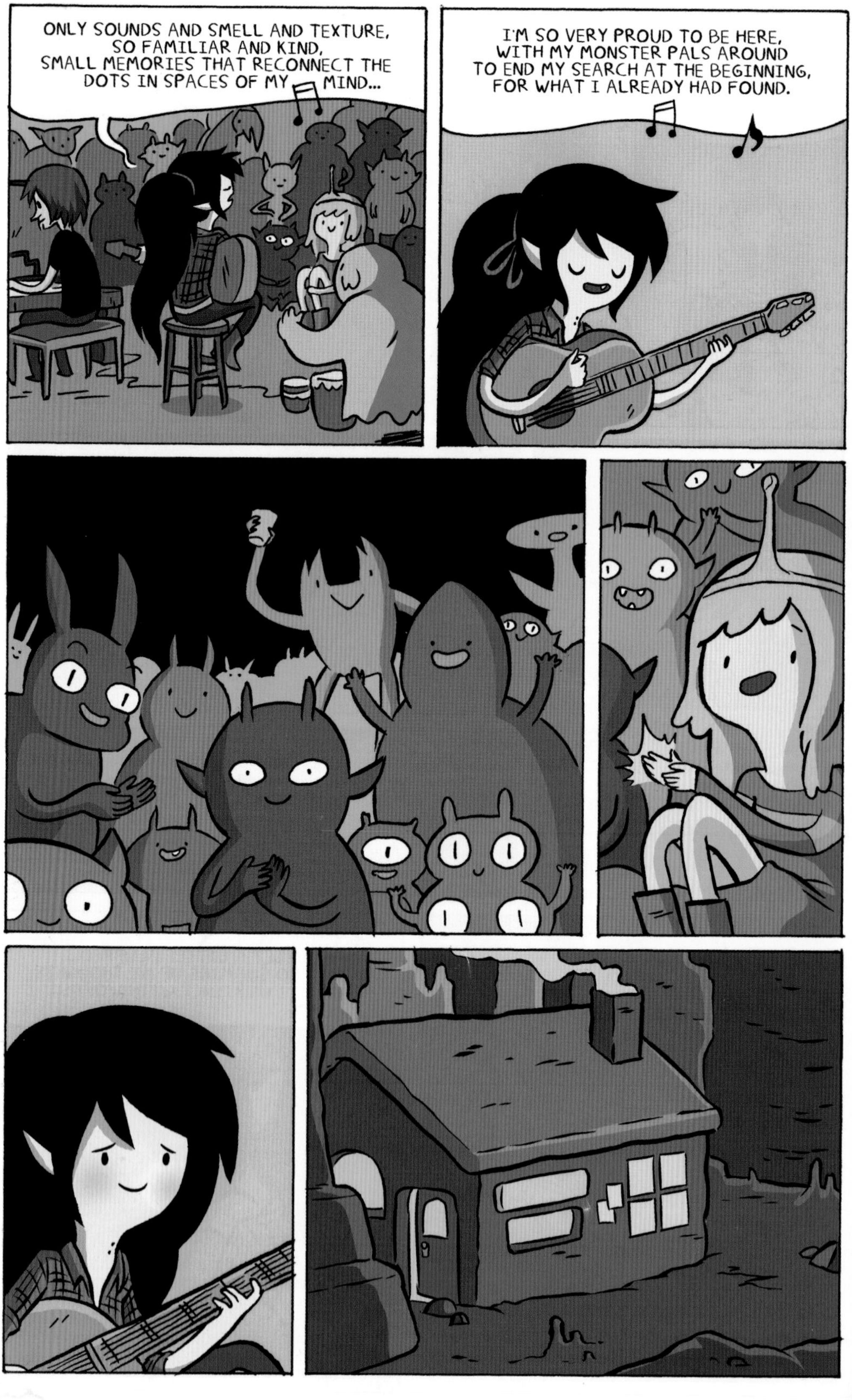
ONLY SOUNDS AND SMELL AND TEXTURE, SO FAMILIAR AND KIND, SMALL MEMORIES THAT RECONNECT THE DOTS IN SPACES OF MY MIND...
I'M SO VERY PROUD TO BE HERE, WITH MY MONSTER PALS AROUND TO END MY SEARCH AT THE BEGINNING, FOR WHAT I ALREADY HAD FOUND.

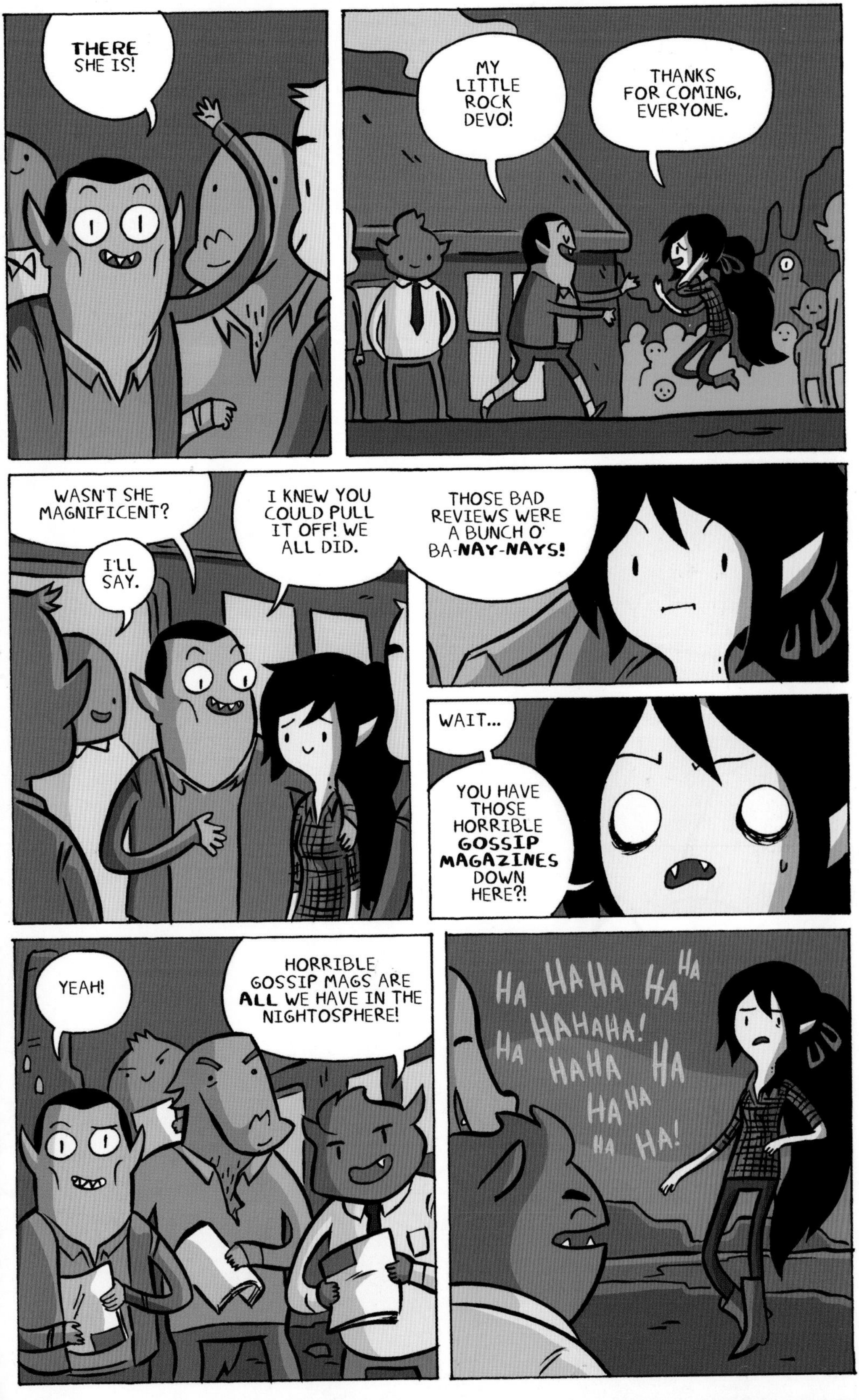

THERE SHE IS!
MY LITTLE ROCK DEVO!
THANKS FOR COMING, EVERYONE.
WASN'T SHE MAGNIFICENT?
I'LL SAY.
I KNEW YOU COULD PULL IT OFF! WE ALL DID.
THOSE BAD REVIEWS WERE A BUNCH O' BA-NAY-NAYS!
WAIT...
YOU HAVE THOSE HORRIBLE GOSSIP MAGAZINES DOWN HERE?!
YEAH!
HORRIBLE GOSSIP MAGS ARE ALL WE HAVE IN THE NIGHTOSPHERE!
HA HAHA HA HA HAHAHA! HA HAHA HA HA HA HA HA!

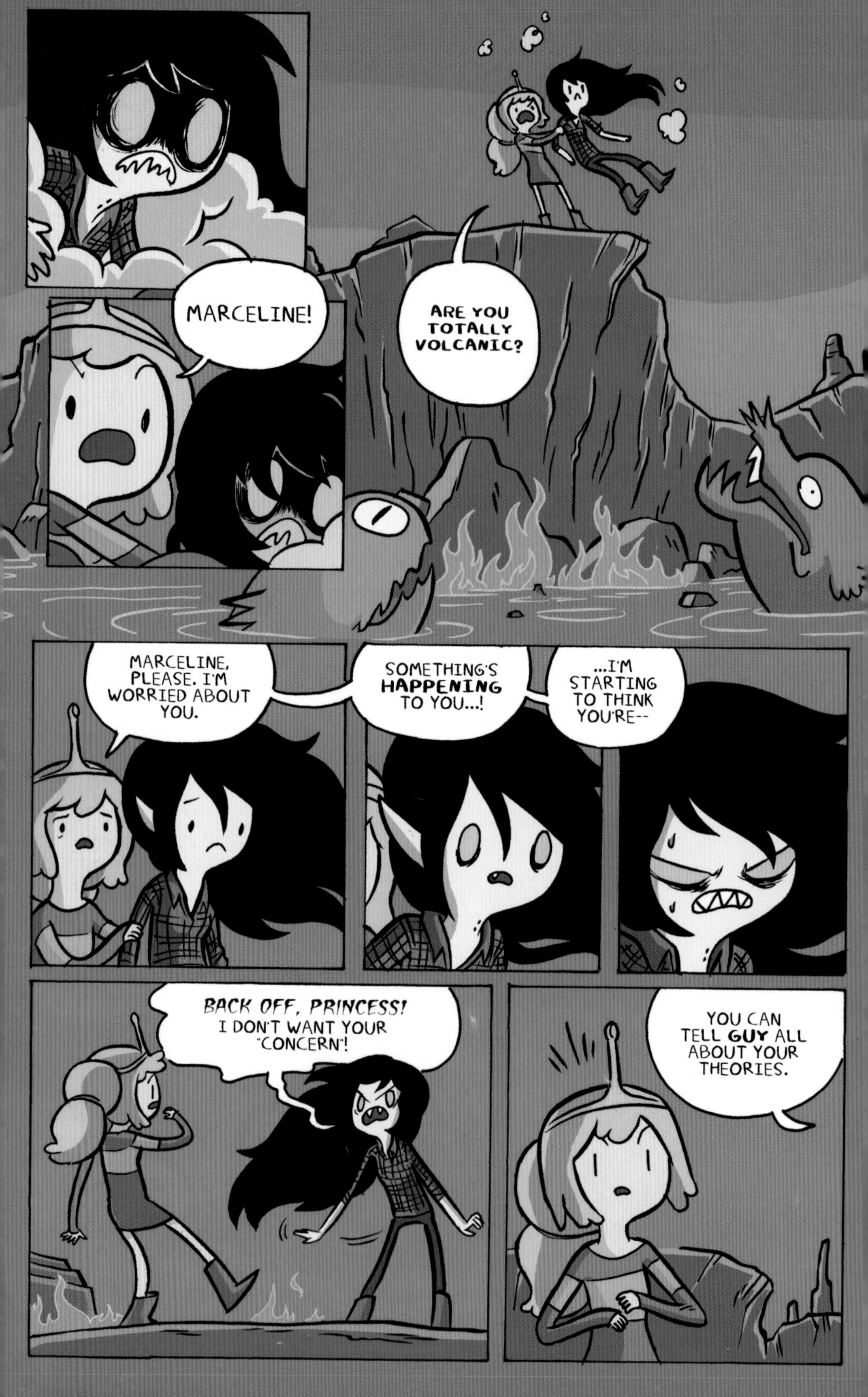
MARCELINE!
ARE YOU TOTALLY VOLCANIC?
MARCELINE, PLEASE. I'M WORRIED ABOUT YOU.
SOMETHING'S **HAPPENING** TO YOU...!
...I'M STARTING TO THINK YOU'RE--
BACK OFF, PRINCESS! I DON'T WANT YOUR "CONCERN"!
YOU CAN TELL **GUY** ALL ABOUT YOUR THEORIES.

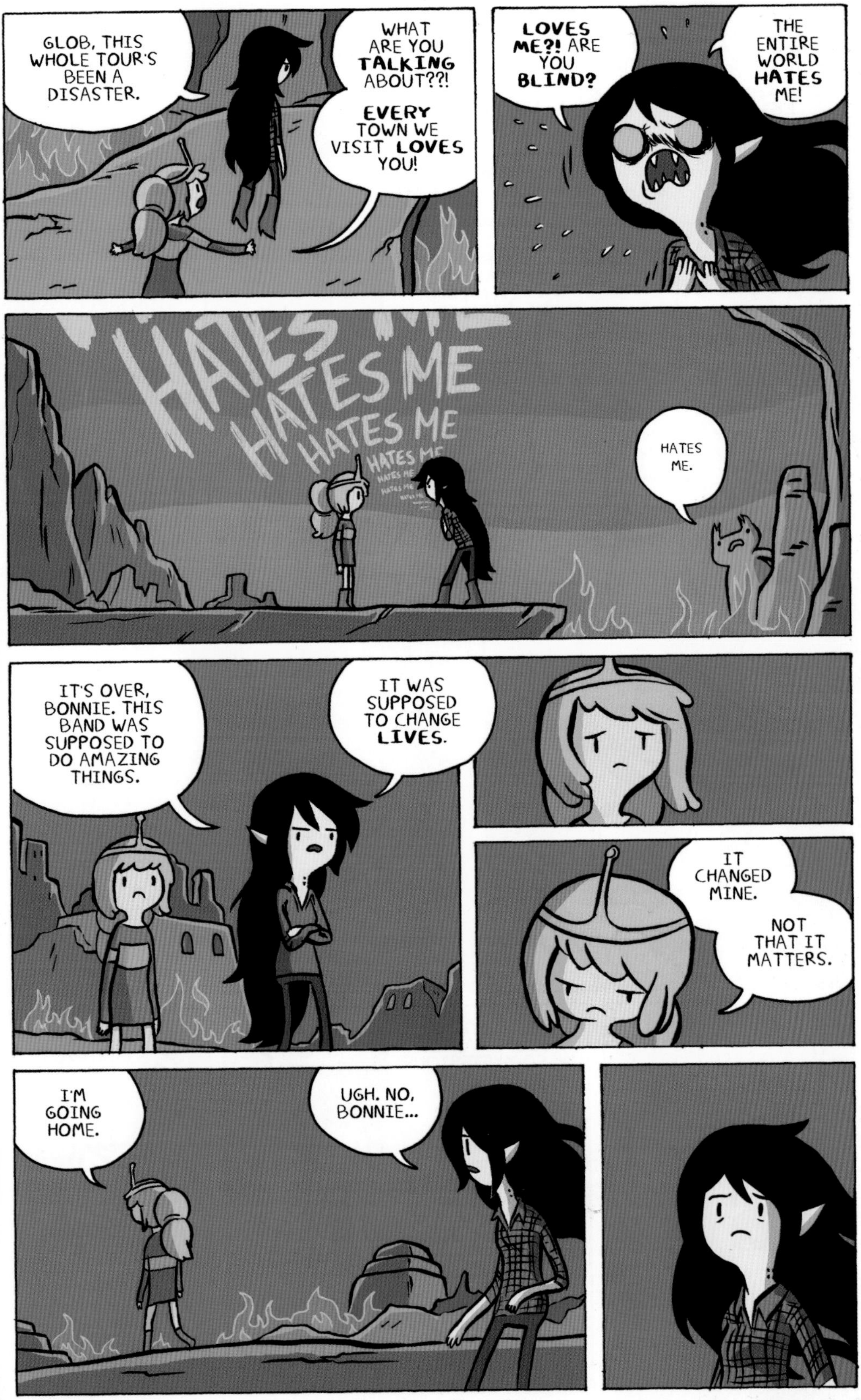

GLOB, THIS WHOLE TOUR'S BEEN A DISASTER.
WHAT ARE YOU **TALKING** ABOUT??!
EVERY TOWN WE VISIT **LOVES** YOU!
LOVES ME?! ARE YOU **BLIND?**
THE ENTIRE WORLD **HATES** ME!
HATES ME
HATES ME
HATES ME
HATES ME
HATES ME.
IT'S OVER, BONNIE. THIS BAND WAS SUPPOSED TO DO AMAZING THINGS.
IT WAS SUPPOSED TO CHANGE **LIVES**.
IT CHANGED MINE.
NOT THAT IT MATTERS.
I'M GOING HOME.
UGH. NO, BONNIE...

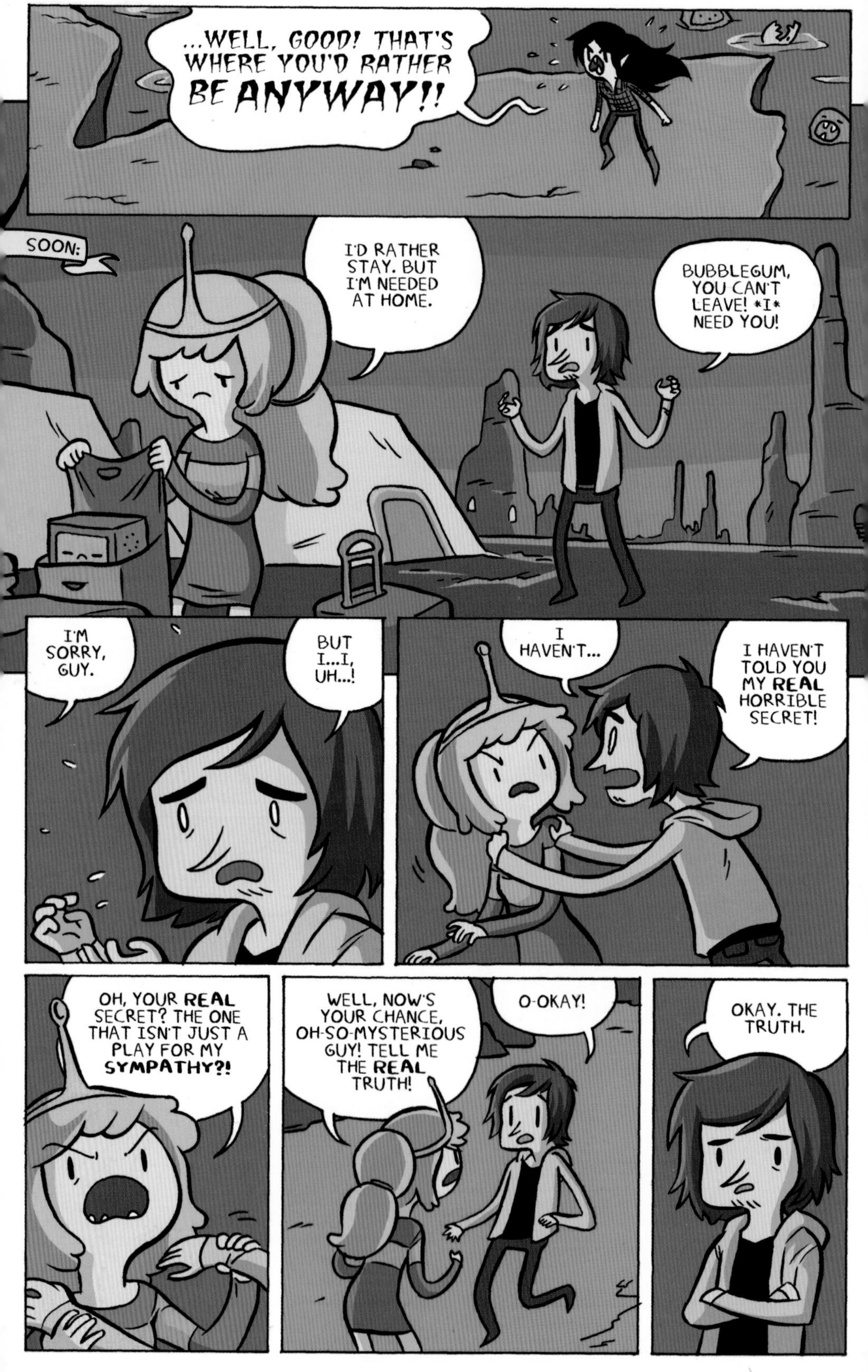
...WELL, GOOD! THAT'S WHERE YOU'D RATHER BE ANYWAY!!
SOON:
I'D RATHER STAY. BUT I'M NEEDED AT HOME.
BUBBLEGUM, YOU CAN'T LEAVE! *I* NEED YOU!
I'M SORRY, GUY.
BUT I...I, UH...!
I HAVEN'T...
I HAVEN'T TOLD YOU MY REAL HORRIBLE SECRET!
OH, YOUR REAL SECRET? THE ONE THAT ISN'T JUST A PLAY FOR MY SYMPATHY?!
WELL, NOW'S YOUR CHANCE, OH-SO-MYSTERIOUS GUY! TELL ME THE REAL TRUTH!
O-OKAY!
OKAY. THE TRUTH.

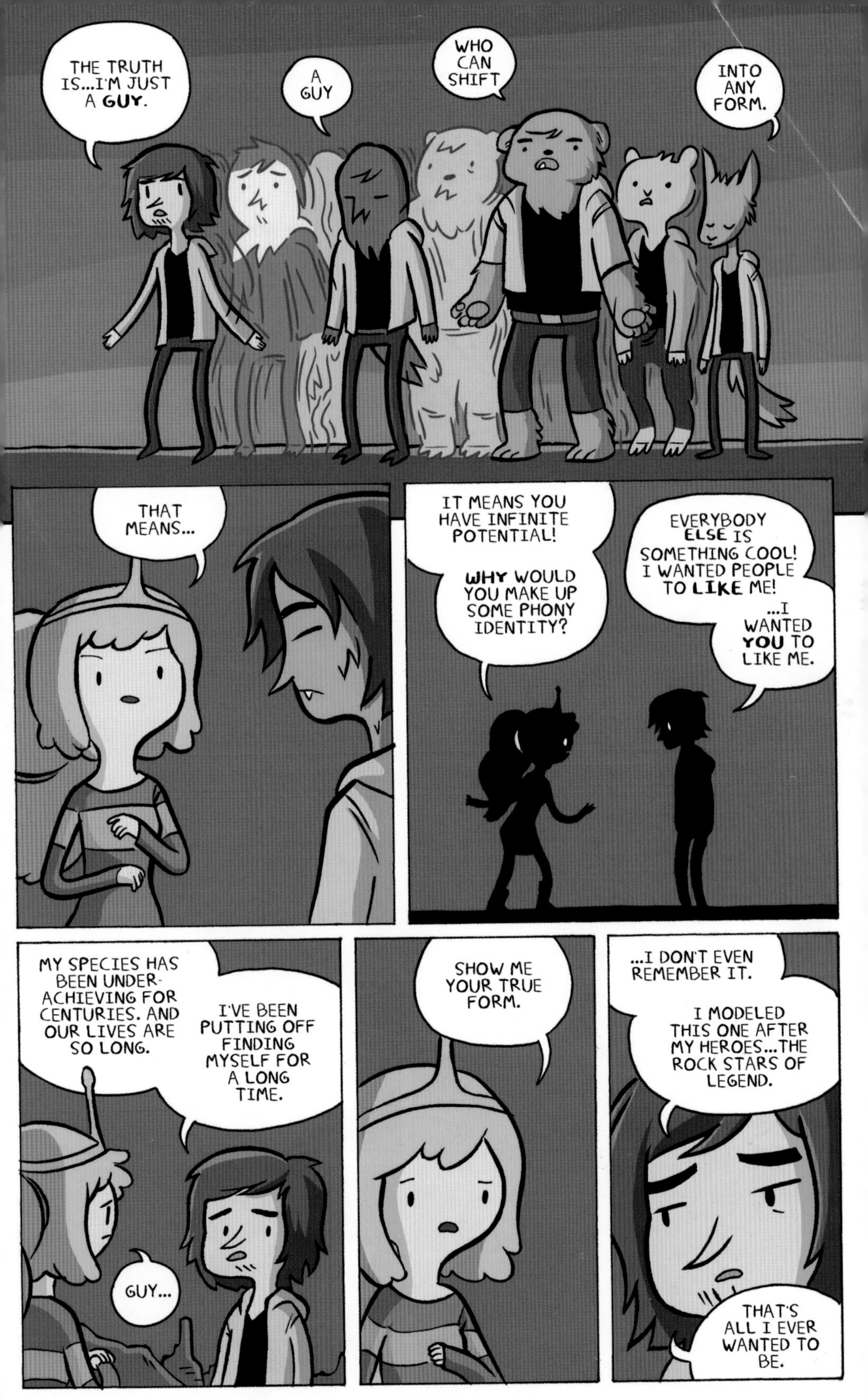
THE TRUTH IS...I'M JUST A **GUY**.
A GUY
WHO CAN SHIFT
INTO ANY FORM.
THAT MEANS...
IT MEANS YOU HAVE INFINITE POTENTIAL!
WHY WOULD YOU MAKE UP SOME PHONY IDENTITY?
EVERYBODY **ELSE** IS SOMETHING COOL! I WANTED PEOPLE TO **LIKE** ME!
...I WANTED **YOU** TO LIKE ME.
MY SPECIES HAS BEEN UNDER-ACHIEVING FOR CENTURIES. AND OUR LIVES ARE SO LONG.
I'VE BEEN PUTTING OFF FINDING MYSELF FOR A LONG TIME.
GUY...
SHOW ME YOUR TRUE FORM.
...I DON'T EVEN REMEMBER IT.
I MODELED THIS ONE AFTER MY HEROES...THE ROCK STARS OF LEGEND.
THAT'S ALL I EVER WANTED TO BE.

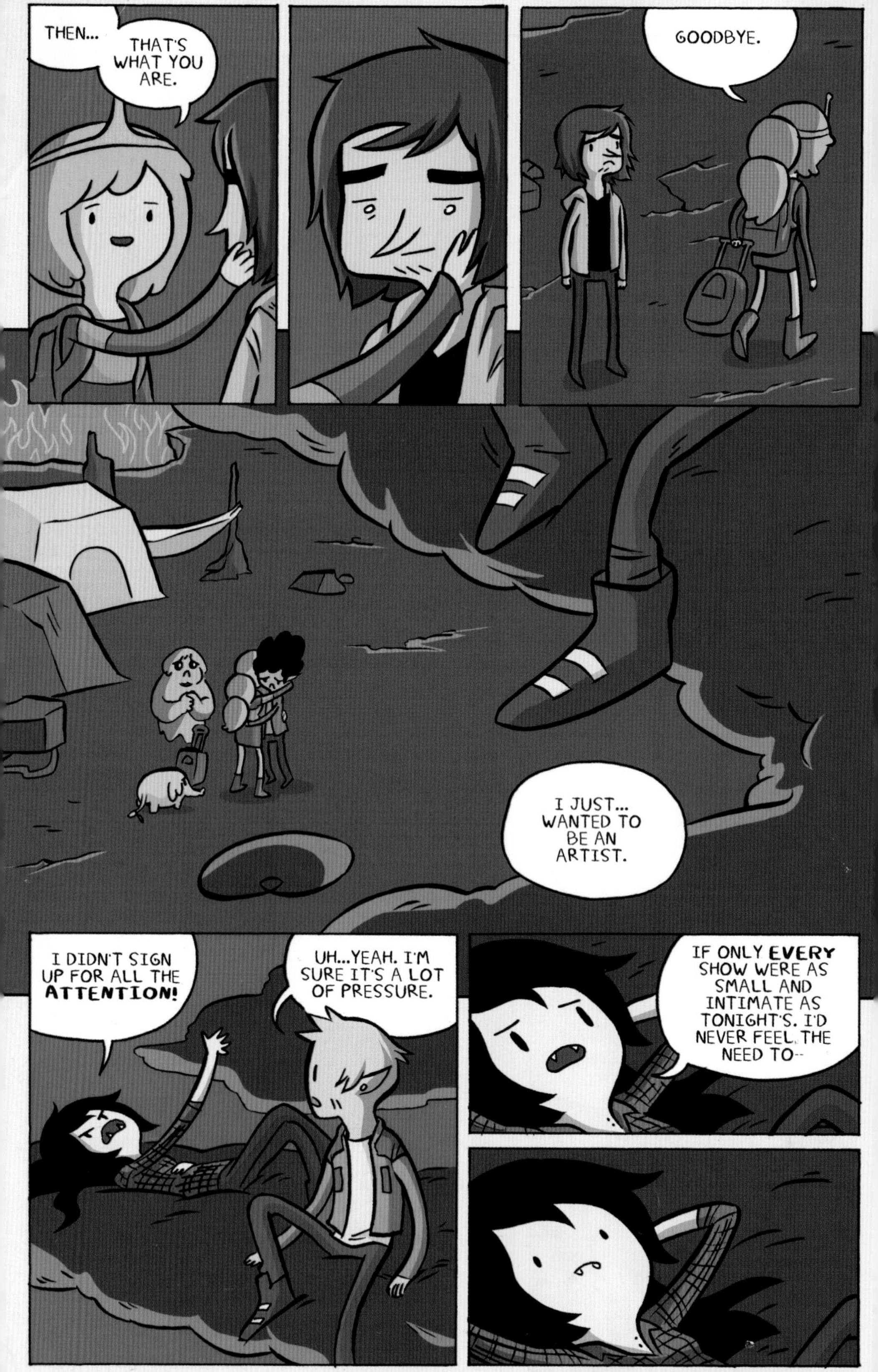
THEN...
THAT'S WHAT YOU ARE.
GOODBYE.
I JUST... WANTED TO BE AN ARTIST.
I DIDN'T SIGN UP FOR ALL THE ATTENTION!
UH...YEAH. I'M SURE IT'S A LOT OF PRESSURE.
IF ONLY EVERY SHOW WERE AS SMALL AND INTIMATE AS TONIGHT'S. I'D NEVER FEEL THE NEED TO--

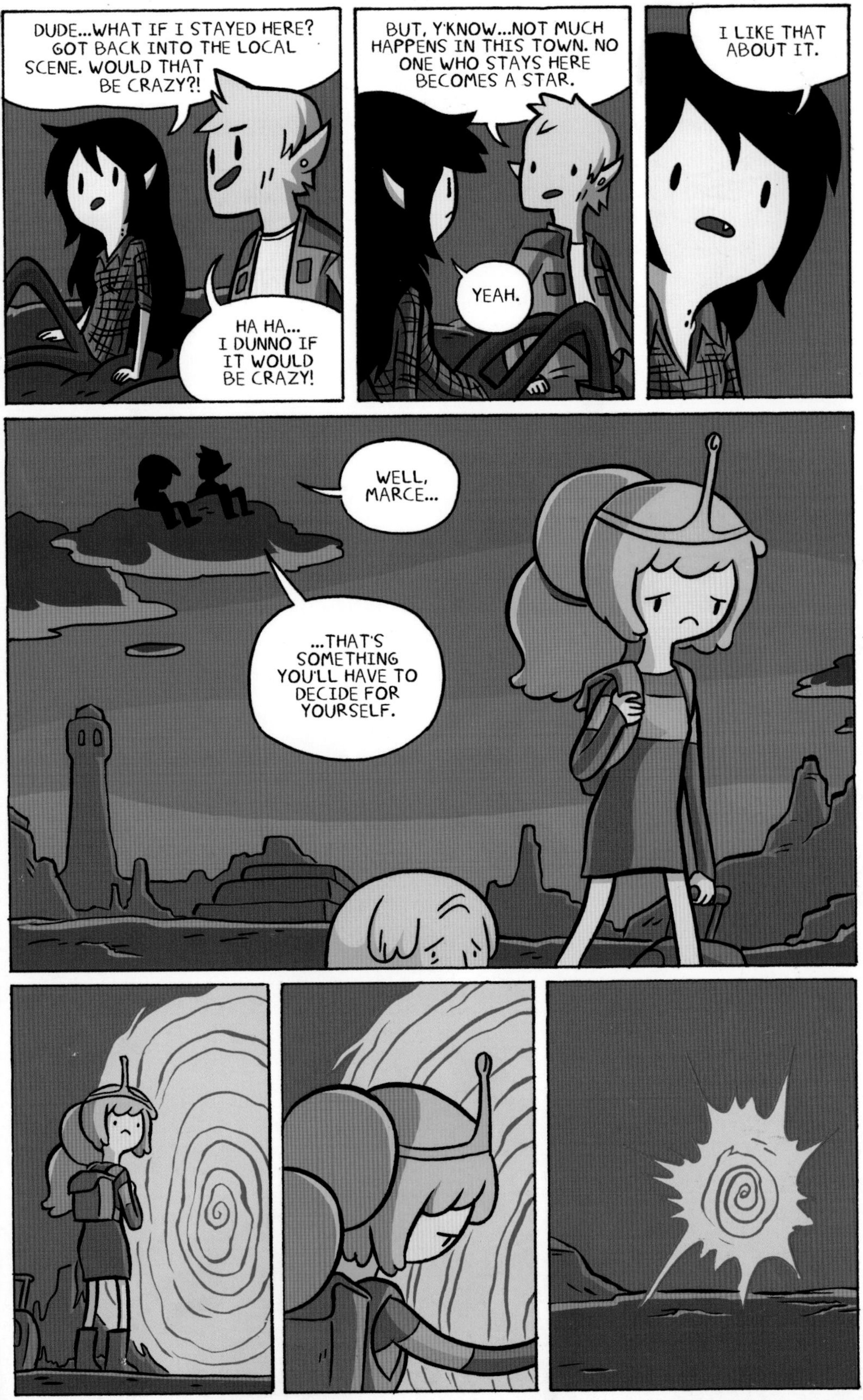
DUDE...WHAT IF I STAYED HERE? GOT BACK INTO THE LOCAL SCENE. WOULD THAT BE CRAZY?!
HA HA... I DUNNO IF IT WOULD BE CRAZY!
BUT, Y'KNOW...NOT MUCH HAPPENS IN THIS TOWN. NO ONE WHO STAYS HERE BECOMES A STAR.
YEAH.
I LIKE THAT ABOUT IT.
WELL, MARCE...
...THAT'S SOMETHING YOU'LL HAVE TO DECIDE FOR YOURSELF.

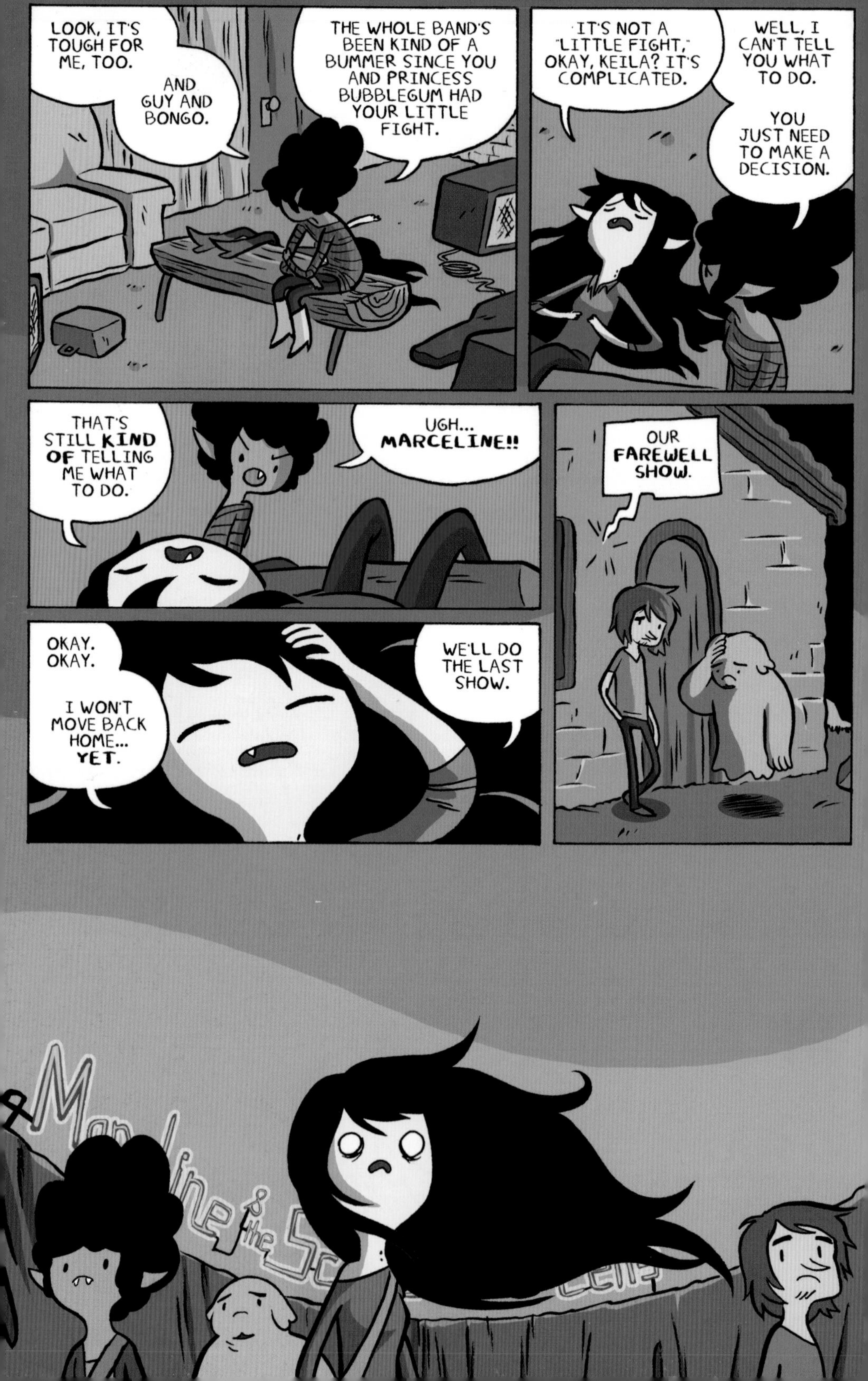
LOOK, IT'S TOUGH FOR ME, TOO.
AND GUY AND BONGO.
THE WHOLE BAND'S BEEN KIND OF A BUMMER SINCE YOU AND PRINCESS BUBBLEGUM HAD YOUR LITTLE FIGHT.
IT'S NOT A "LITTLE FIGHT," OKAY, KEILA? IT'S COMPLICATED.
WELL, I CAN'T TELL YOU WHAT TO DO.
YOU JUST NEED TO MAKE A DECISION.
THAT'S STILL **KIND OF** TELLING ME WHAT TO DO.
UGH... **MARCELINE!!**
OUR **FAREWELL SHOW.**
OKAY. OKAY.
I WON'T MOVE BACK HOME... **YET**.
WE'LL DO THE LAST SHOW.

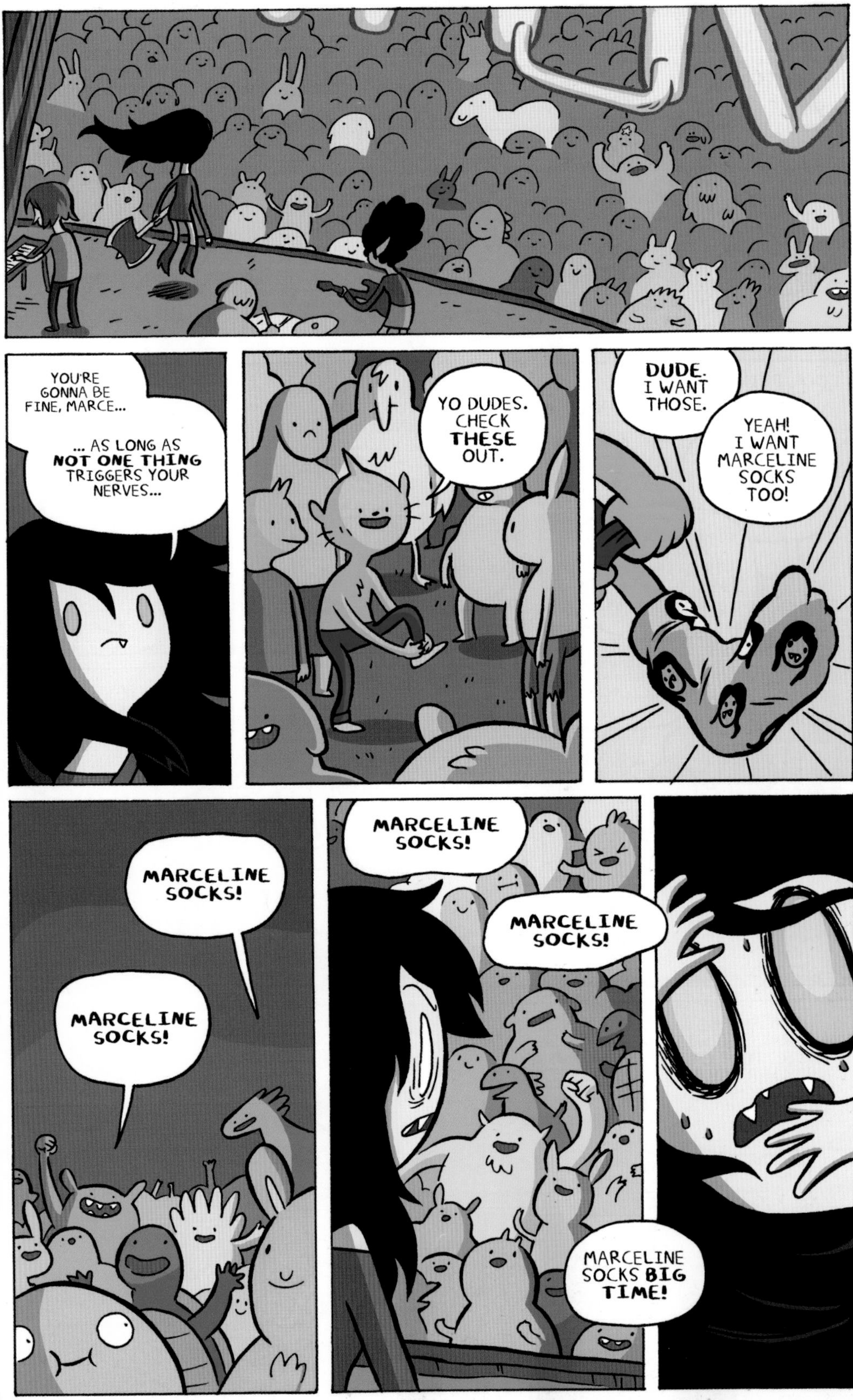
YOU'RE GONNA BE FINE, MARCE...
... AS LONG AS NOT ONE THING TRIGGERS YOUR NERVES...
YO DUDES. CHECK THESE OUT.
DUDE. I WANT THOSE.
YEAH! I WANT MARCELINE SOCKS TOO!
MARCELINE SOCKS!
MARCELINE SOCKS!
MARCELINE SOCKS!
MARCELINE SOCKS!
MARCELINE SOCKS BIG TIME!

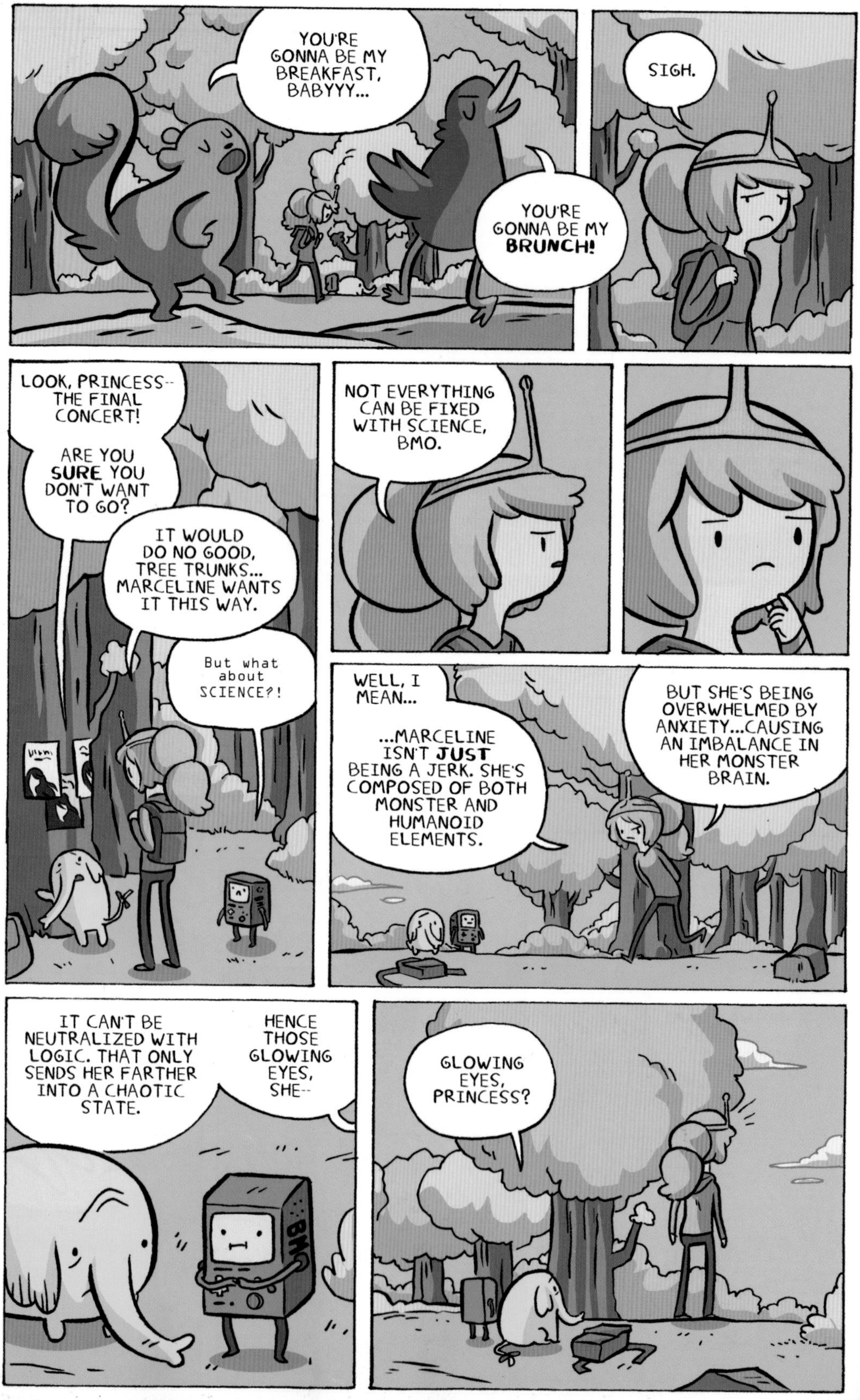
YOU'RE GONNA BE MY BREAKFAST, BABYYY...
YOU'RE GONNA BE MY **BRUNCH!**
SIGH.
LOOK, PRINCESS-- THE FINAL CONCERT!
ARE YOU **SURE** YOU DON'T WANT TO GO?
IT WOULD DO NO GOOD, TREE TRUNKS... MARCELINE WANTS IT THIS WAY.
But what about SCIENCE?!
NOT EVERYTHING CAN BE FIXED WITH SCIENCE, BMO.
WELL, I MEAN...
...MARCELINE ISN'T **JUST** BEING A JERK. SHE'S COMPOSED OF BOTH MONSTER AND HUMANOID ELEMENTS.
BUT SHE'S BEING OVERWHELMED BY ANXIETY...CAUSING AN IMBALANCE IN HER MONSTER BRAIN.
IT CAN'T BE NEUTRALIZED WITH LOGIC. THAT ONLY SENDS HER FARTHER INTO A CHAOTIC STATE.
HENCE THOSE GLOWING EYES, SHE--
GLOWING EYES, PRINCESS?

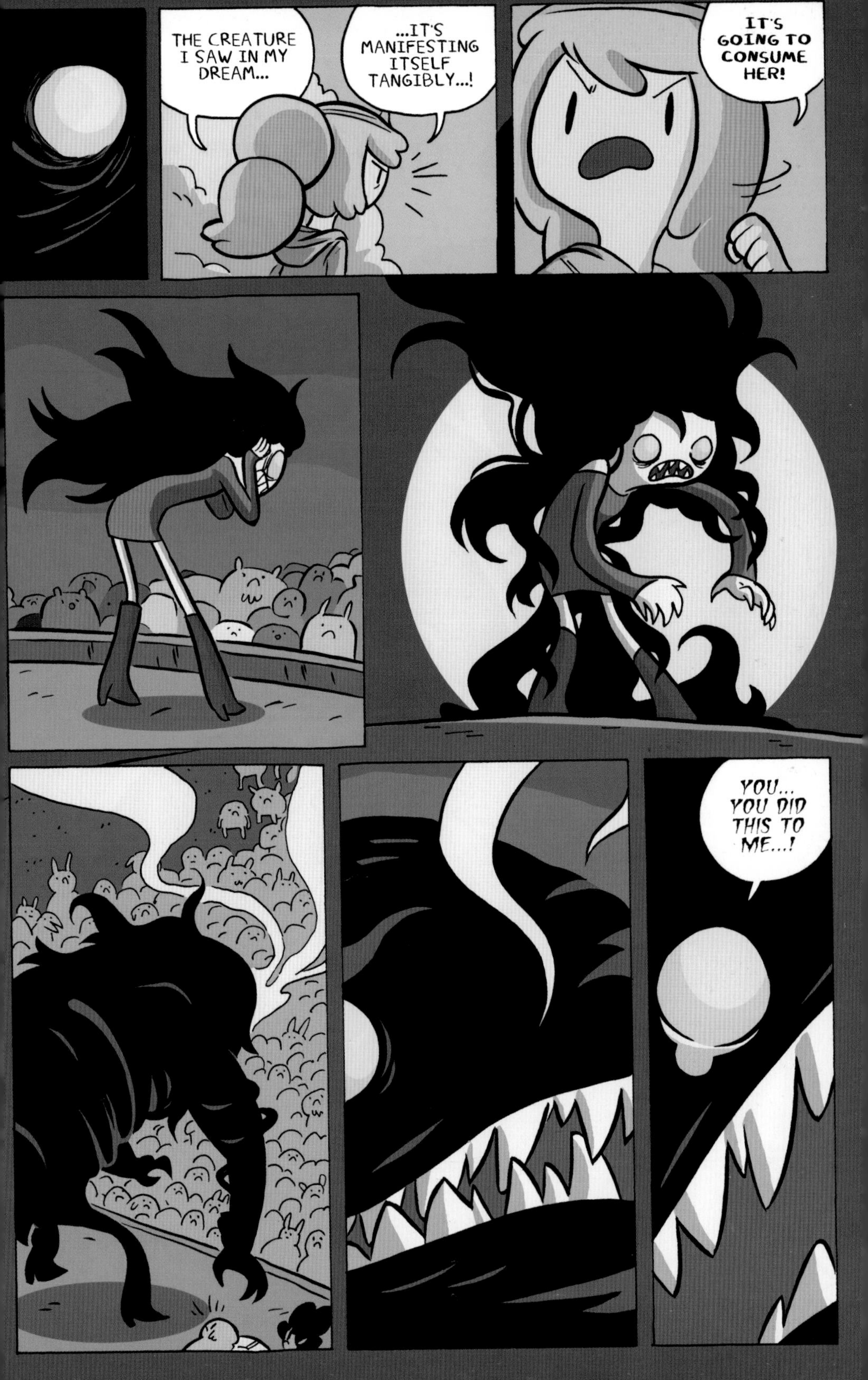
THE CREATURE I SAW IN MY DREAM...
...IT'S MANIFESTING ITSELF TANGIBLY...!
IT'S GOING TO CONSUME HER!
YOU... YOU DID THIS TO ME...!

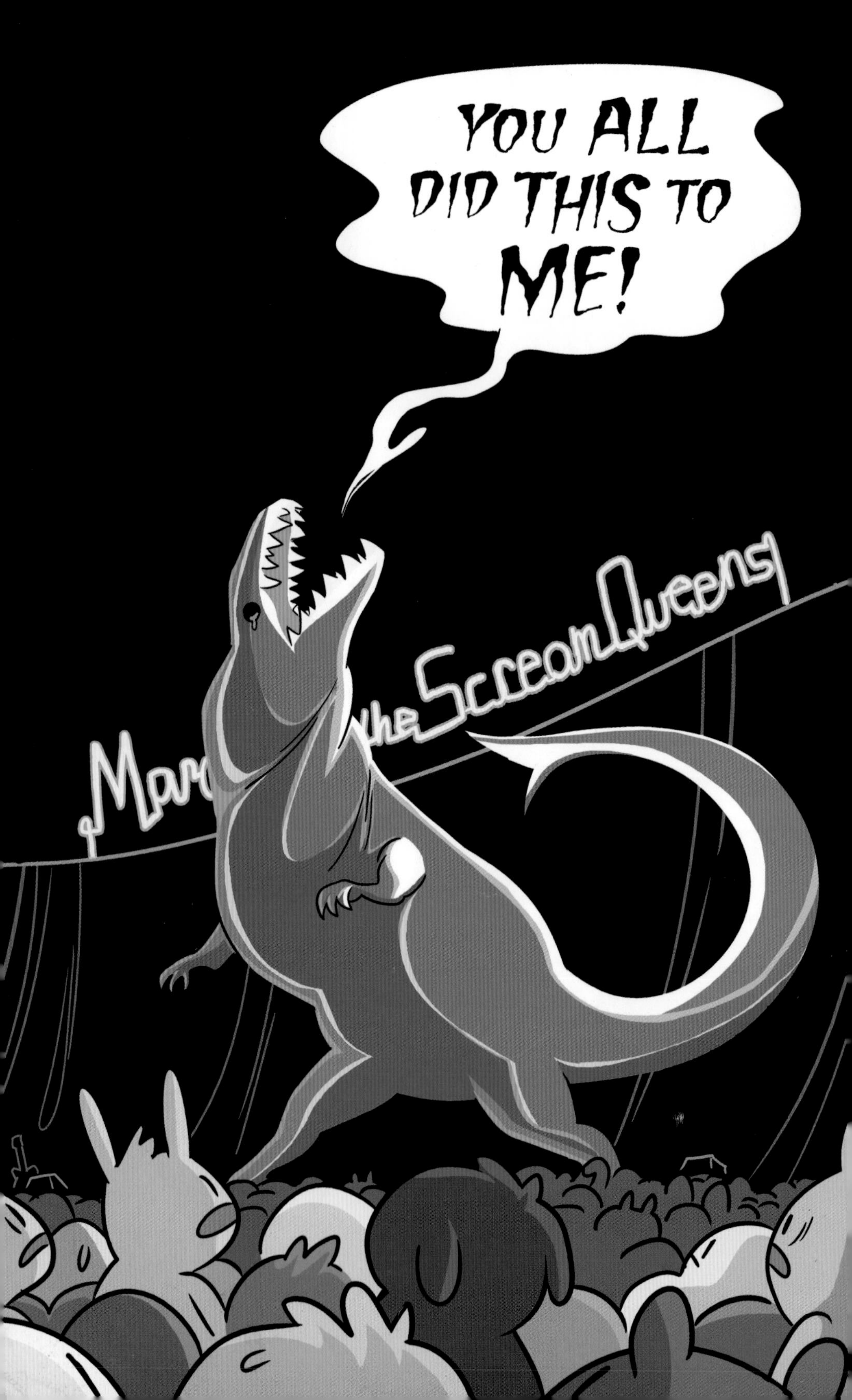
YOU ALL DID THIS TO ME!
Mar
the Scream Queens

MARCE, NO!

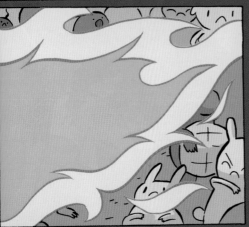

EW.

I DON'T KNOW WHERE THIS IS COMING FROM! WE LOVE YOU!

Y-YEAH GIRL! I DIG THE **FIERCE** LOOK!

I'LL HANDLE THIS...

STOMP

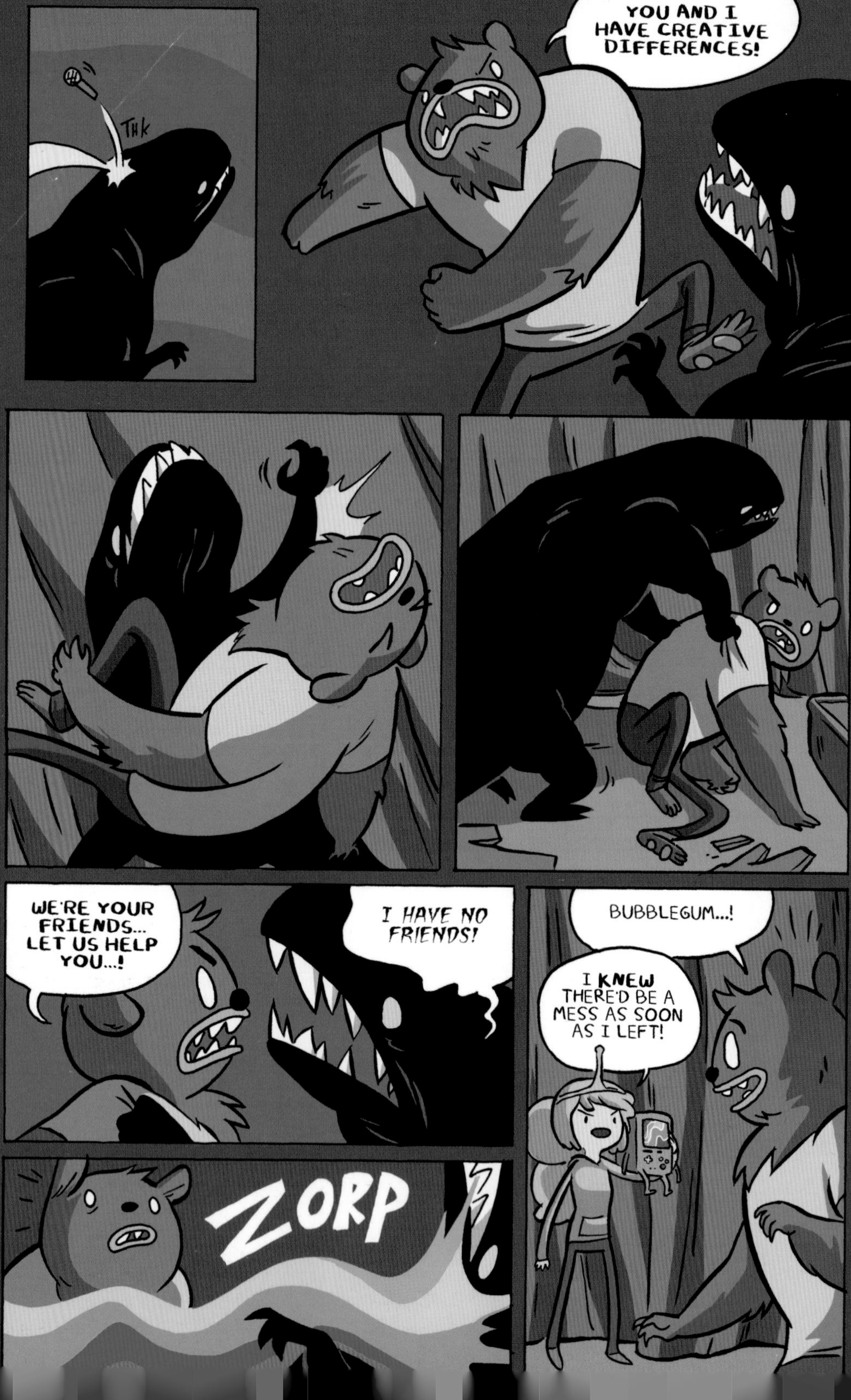

THK
YOU AND I HAVE CREATIVE DIFFERENCES!
WE'RE YOUR FRIENDS... LET US HELP YOU...!
I HAVE NO FRIENDS!
ZORP
BUBBLEGUM...!
I KNEW THERE'D BE A MESS AS SOON AS I LEFT!

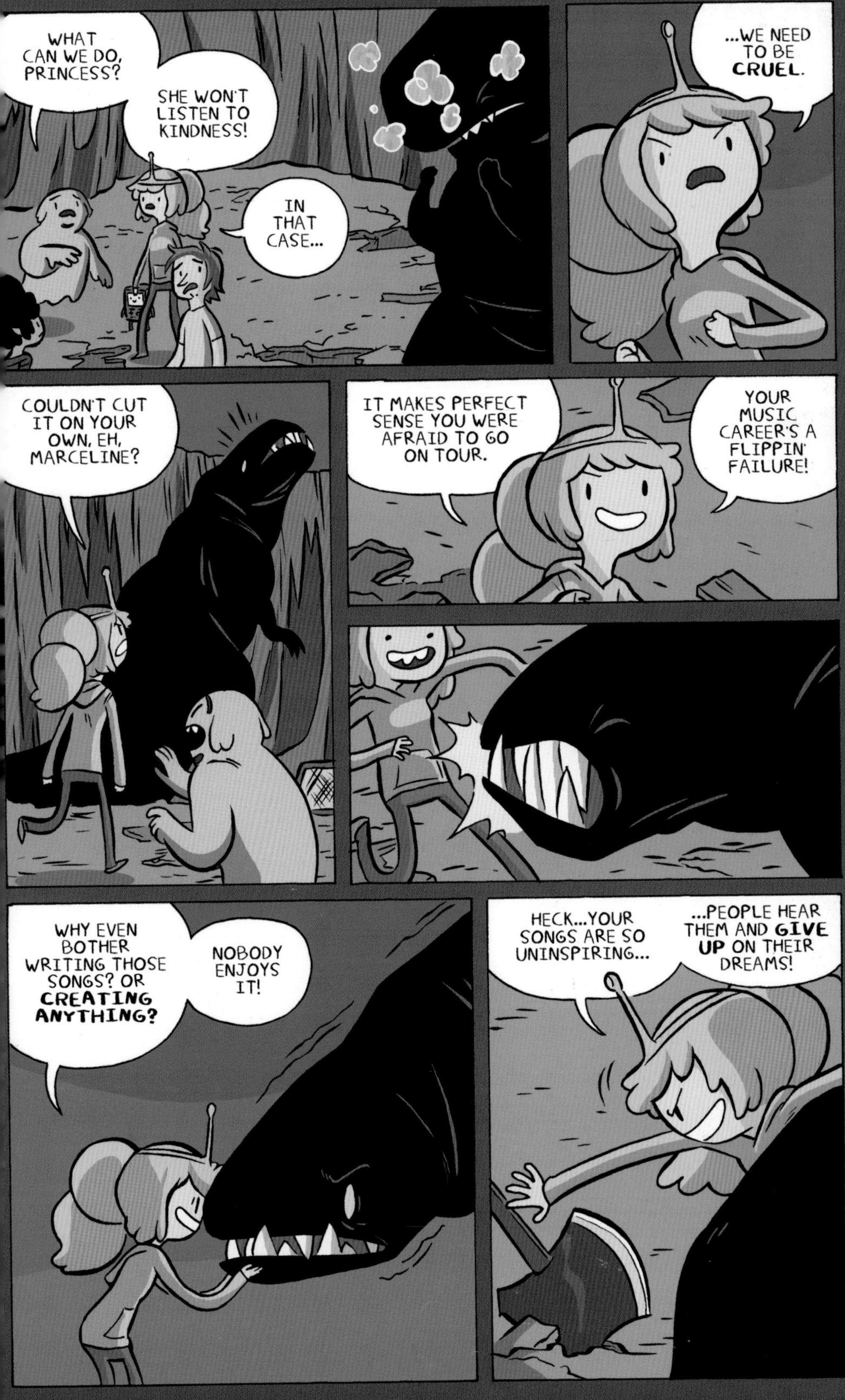
WHAT CAN WE DO, PRINCESS?
SHE WON'T LISTEN TO KINDNESS!
IN THAT CASE...
...WE NEED TO BE **CRUEL**.
COULDN'T CUT IT ON YOUR OWN, EH, MARCELINE?
IT MAKES PERFECT SENSE YOU WERE AFRAID TO GO ON TOUR.
YOUR MUSIC CAREER'S A FLIPPIN' FAILURE!
WHY EVEN BOTHER WRITING THOSE SONGS? OR **CREATING ANYTHING?**
NOBODY ENJOYS IT!
HECK...YOUR SONGS ARE SO UNINSPIRING...
...PEOPLE HEAR THEM AND **GIVE UP** ON THEIR DREAMS!

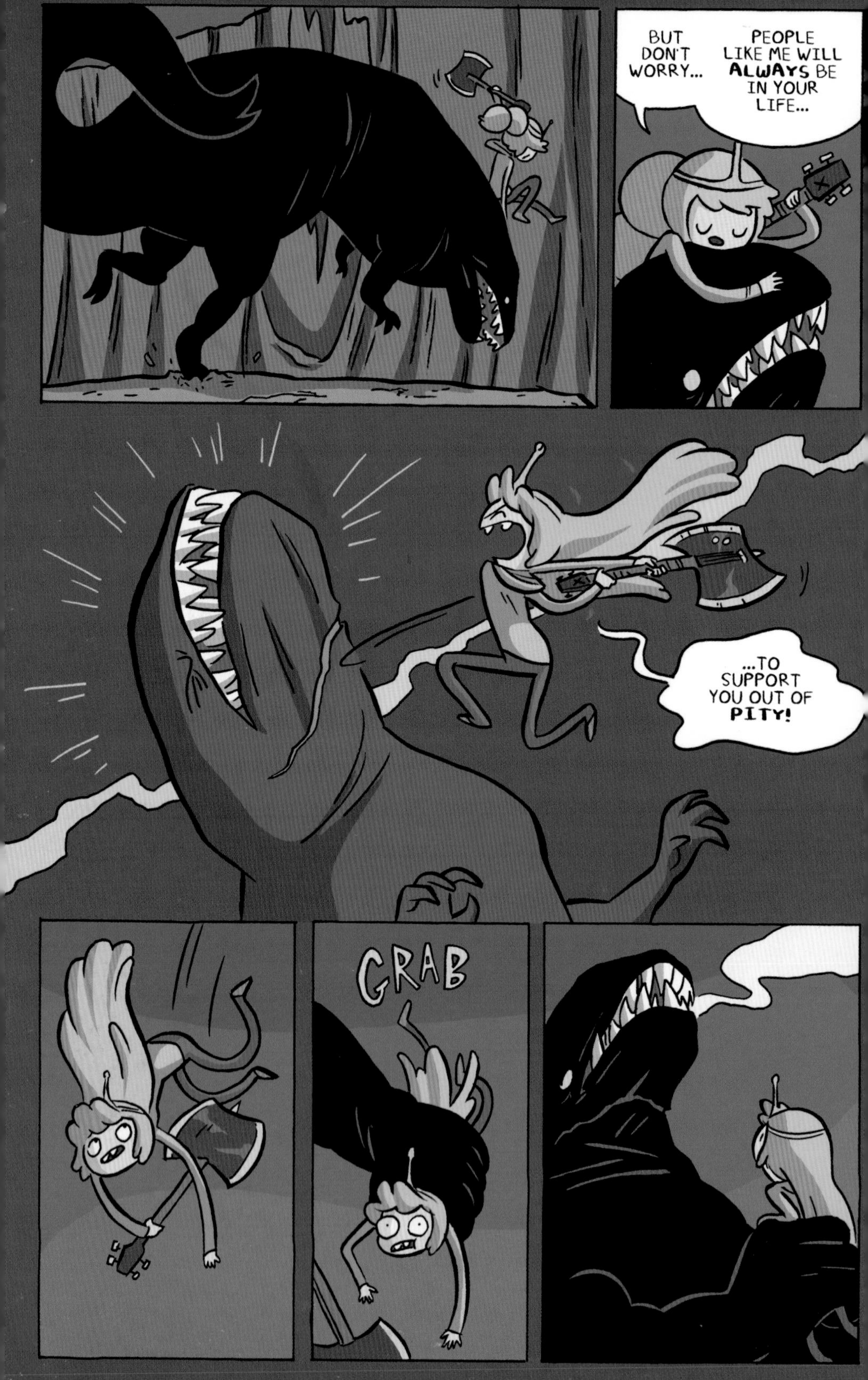
BUT DON'T WORRY...
PEOPLE LIKE ME WILL ALWAYS BE IN YOUR LIFE...
...TO SUPPORT YOU OUT OF PITY!
GRAB

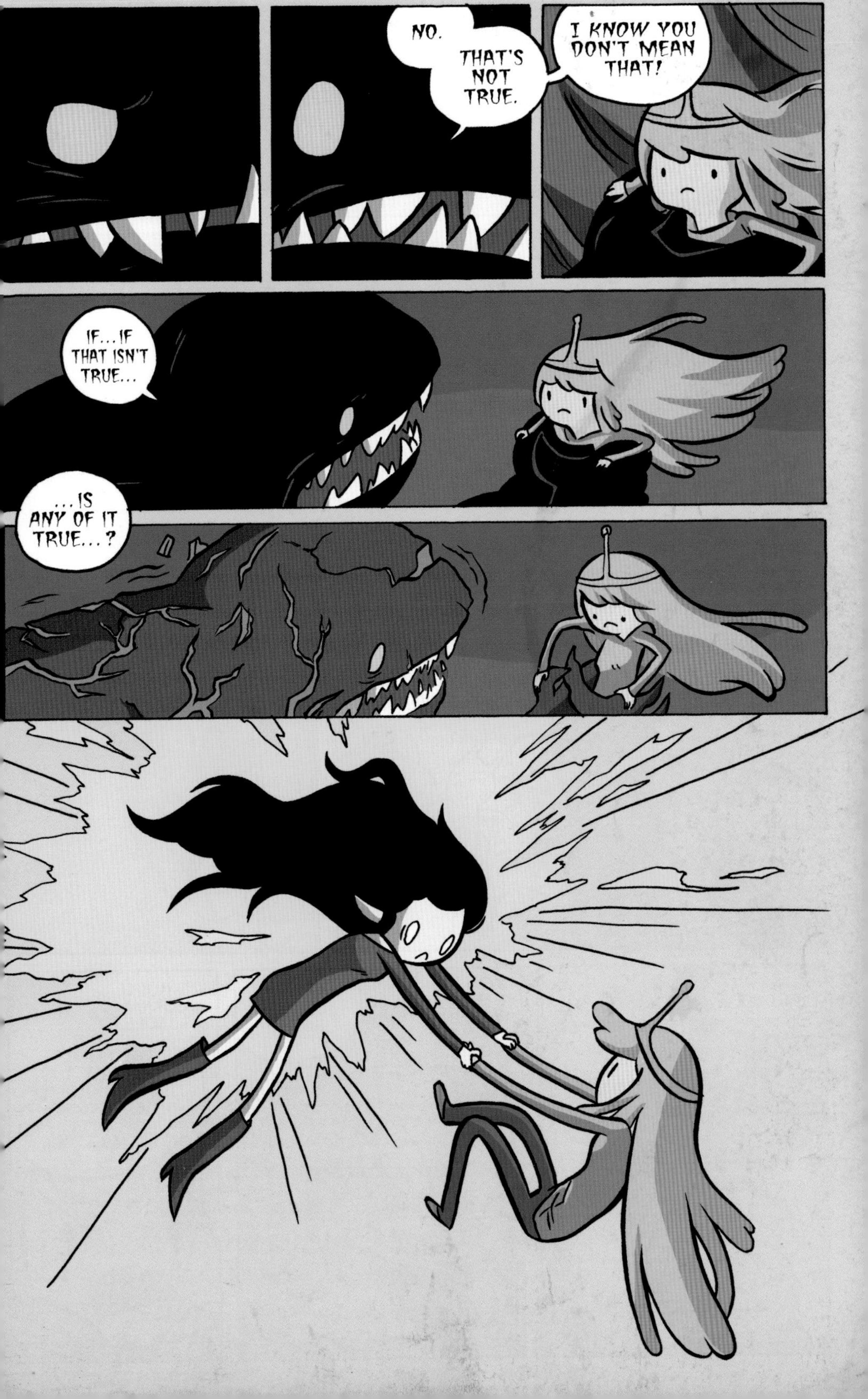
NO.
THAT'S NOT TRUE.
I KNOW YOU DON'T MEAN THAT!
IF...IF THAT ISN'T TRUE...
...IS ANY OF IT TRUE...?

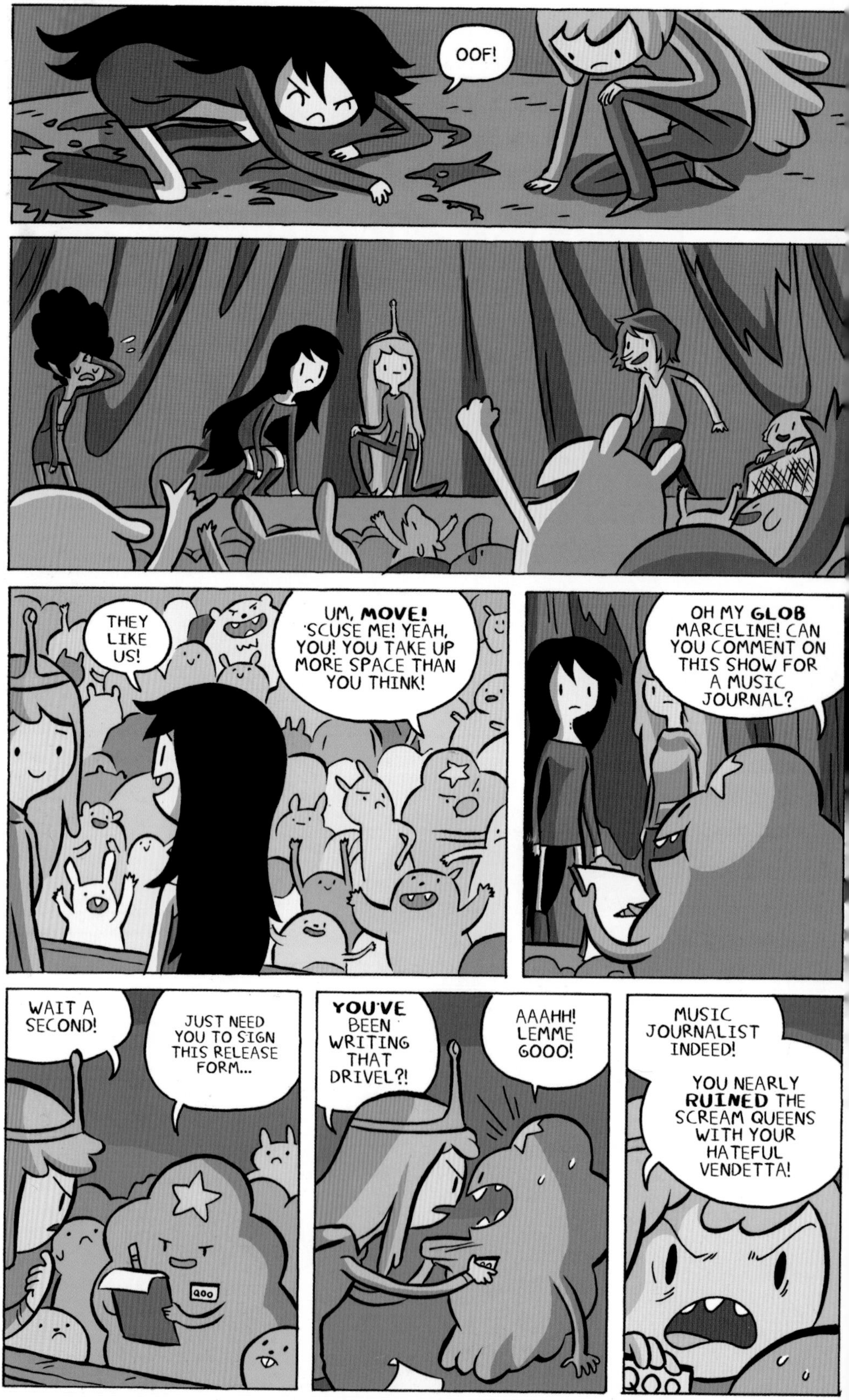

OOF!
THEY LIKE US!
UM, MOVE! 'SCUSE ME! YEAH, YOU! YOU TAKE UP MORE SPACE THAN YOU THINK!
OH MY GLOB MARCELINE! CAN YOU COMMENT ON THIS SHOW FOR A MUSIC JOURNAL?
WAIT A SECOND!
JUST NEED YOU TO SIGN THIS RELEASE FORM...
YOU'VE BEEN WRITING THAT DRIVEL?!
AAAHH! LEMME GOOO!
MUSIC JOURNALIST INDEED!
YOU NEARLY RUINED THE SCREAM QUEENS WITH YOUR HATEFUL VENDETTA!

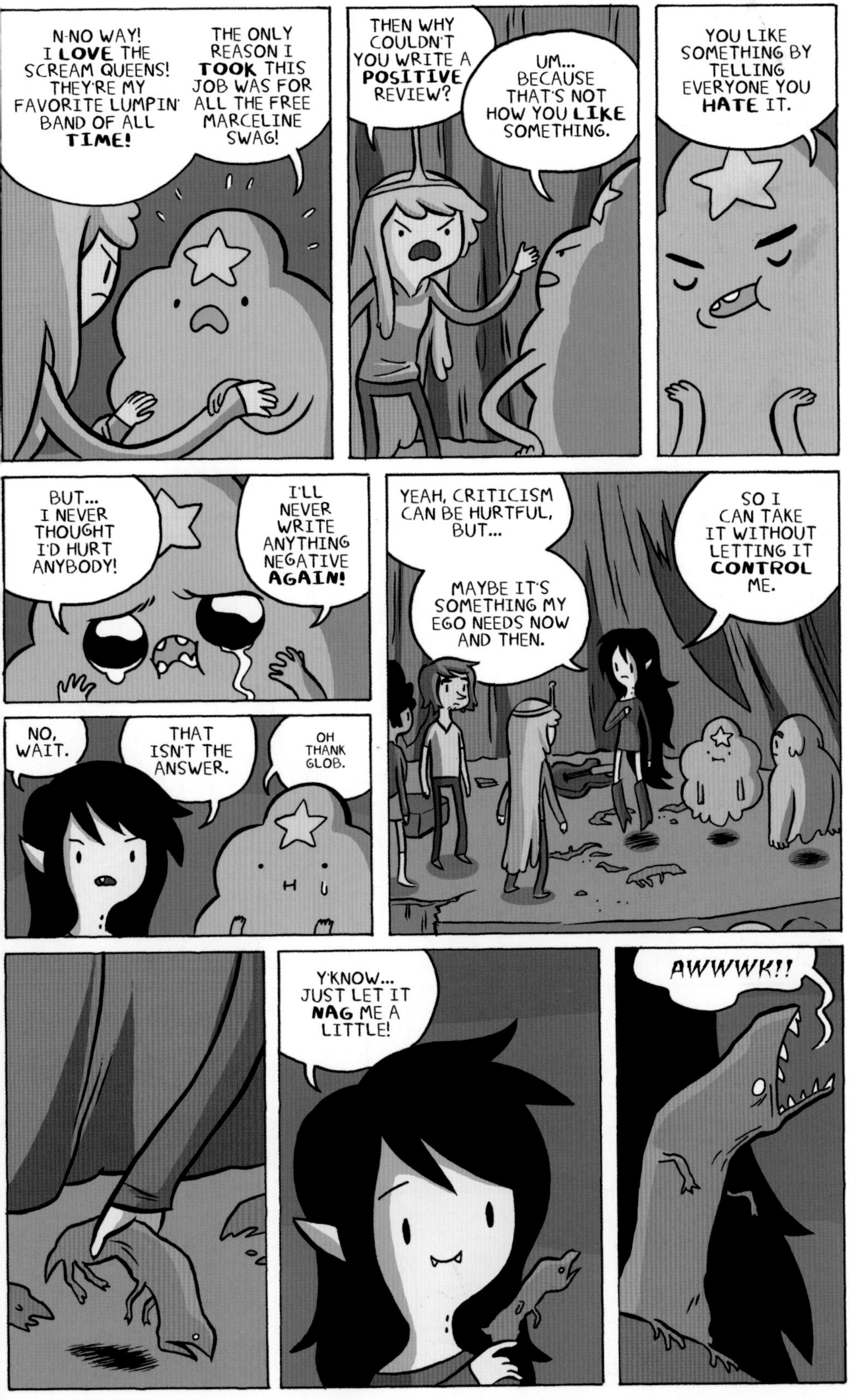
N-NO WAY! I **LOVE** THE SCREAM QUEENS! THEY'RE MY FAVORITE LUMPIN' BAND OF ALL **TIME!**
THE ONLY REASON I **TOOK** THIS JOB WAS FOR ALL THE FREE MARCELINE SWAG!
THEN WHY COULDN'T YOU WRITE A **POSITIVE** REVIEW?
UM... BECAUSE THAT'S NOT HOW YOU **LIKE** SOMETHING.
YOU LIKE SOMETHING BY TELLING EVERYONE YOU **HATE** IT.
BUT... I NEVER THOUGHT I'D HURT ANYBODY!
I'LL NEVER WRITE ANYTHING NEGATIVE **AGAIN!**
YEAH, CRITICISM CAN BE HURTFUL, BUT...
MAYBE IT'S SOMETHING MY EGO NEEDS NOW AND THEN.
SO I CAN TAKE IT WITHOUT LETTING IT **CONTROL** ME.
NO, WAIT.
THAT ISN'T THE ANSWER.
OH THANK GLOB.
Y'KNOW... JUST LET IT **NAG** ME A LITTLE!
AWWWK!!

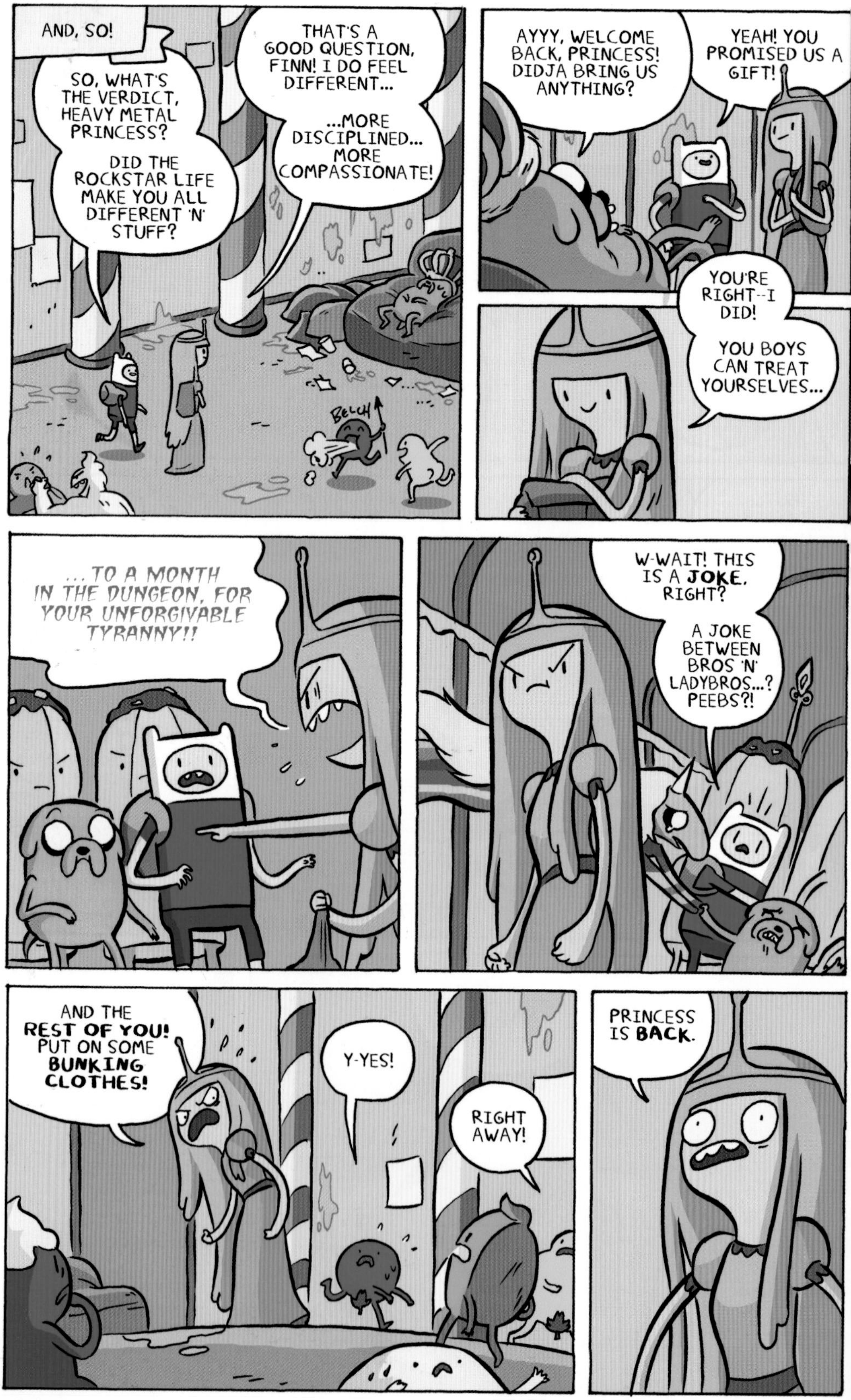
AND, SO!
SO, WHAT'S THE VERDICT, HEAVY METAL PRINCESS?
DID THE ROCKSTAR LIFE MAKE YOU ALL DIFFERENT 'N' STUFF?
THAT'S A GOOD QUESTION, FINN! I DO FEEL DIFFERENT...
...MORE DISCIPLINED... MORE COMPASSIONATE!
BELCH
AYYY, WELCOME BACK, PRINCESS! DIDJA BRING US ANYTHING?
YEAH! YOU PROMISED US A GIFT!
YOU'RE RIGHT--I DID!
YOU BOYS CAN TREAT YOURSELVES...
...TO A MONTH IN THE DUNGEON, FOR YOUR UNFORGIVABLE TYRANNY!!
W-WAIT! THIS IS A JOKE, RIGHT?
A JOKE BETWEEN BROS 'N' LADYBROS...? PEEBS?!
AND THE REST OF YOU! PUT ON SOME BUNKING CLOTHES!
Y-YES!
RIGHT AWAY!
PRINCESS IS BACK.

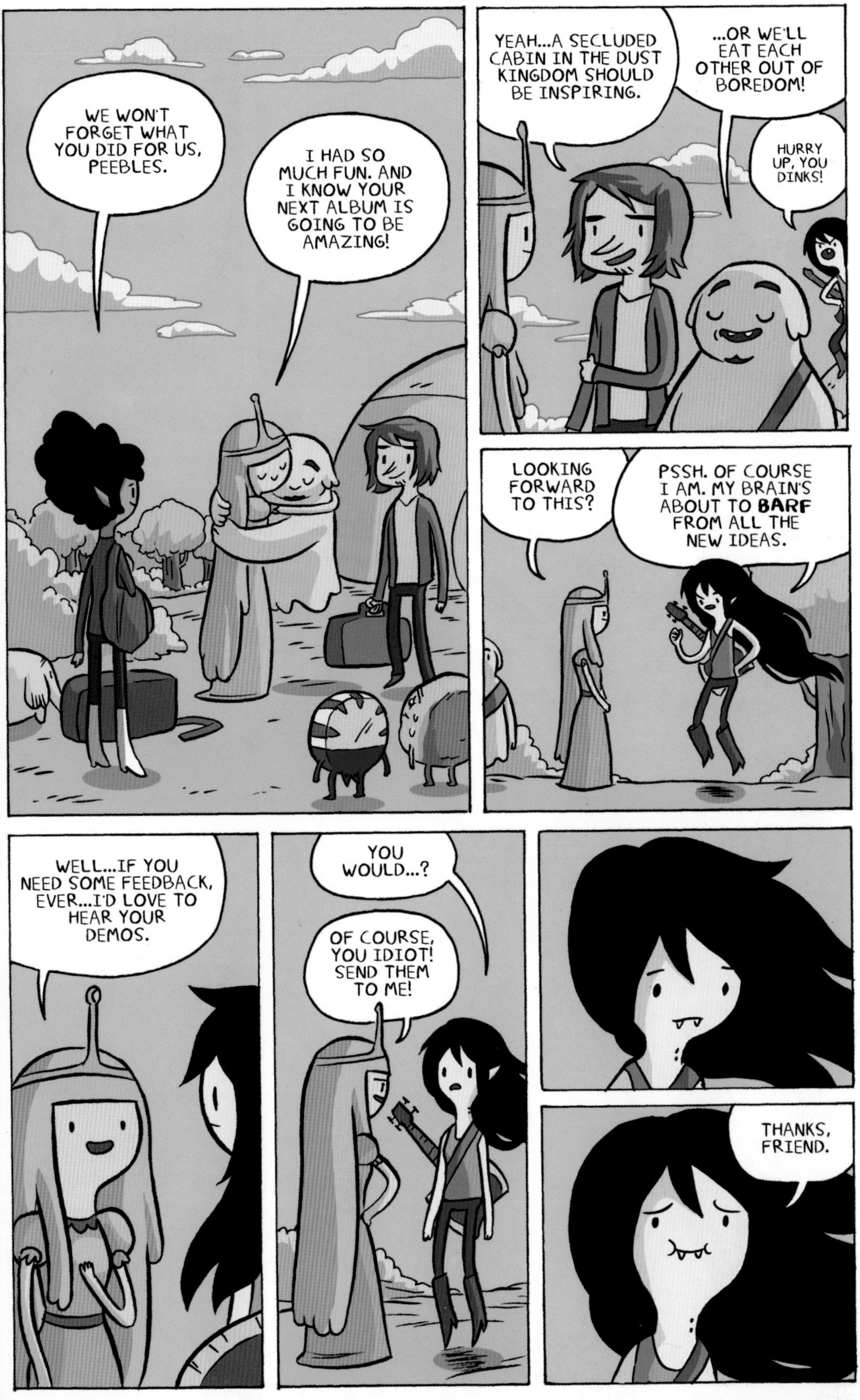

WE WON'T FORGET WHAT YOU DID FOR US, PEEBLES.
I HAD SO MUCH FUN. AND I KNOW YOUR NEXT ALBUM IS GOING TO BE AMAZING!
YEAH...A SECLUDED CABIN IN THE DUST KINGDOM SHOULD BE INSPIRING.
...OR WE'LL EAT EACH OTHER OUT OF BOREDOM!
HURRY UP, YOU DINKS!
LOOKING FORWARD TO THIS?
PSSH. OF COURSE I AM. MY BRAIN'S ABOUT TO **BARF** FROM ALL THE NEW IDEAS.
WELL...IF YOU NEED SOME FEEDBACK, EVER...I'D LOVE TO HEAR YOUR DEMOS.
YOU WOULD...?
OF COURSE, YOU IDIOT! SEND THEM TO ME!
THANKS, FRIEND.

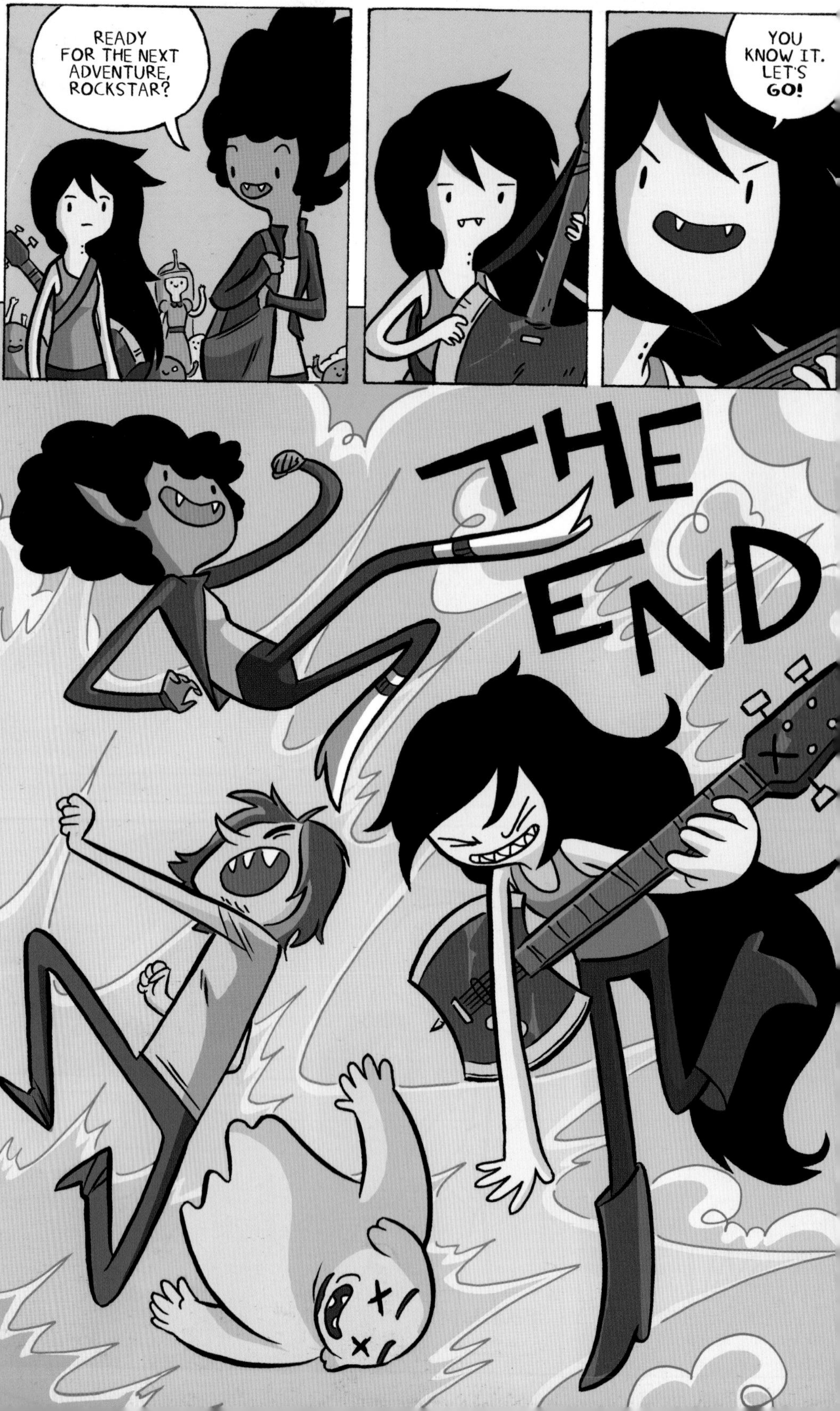
READY FOR THE NEXT ADVENTURE, ROCKSTAR?
YOU KNOW IT. LET'S GO!
THE END

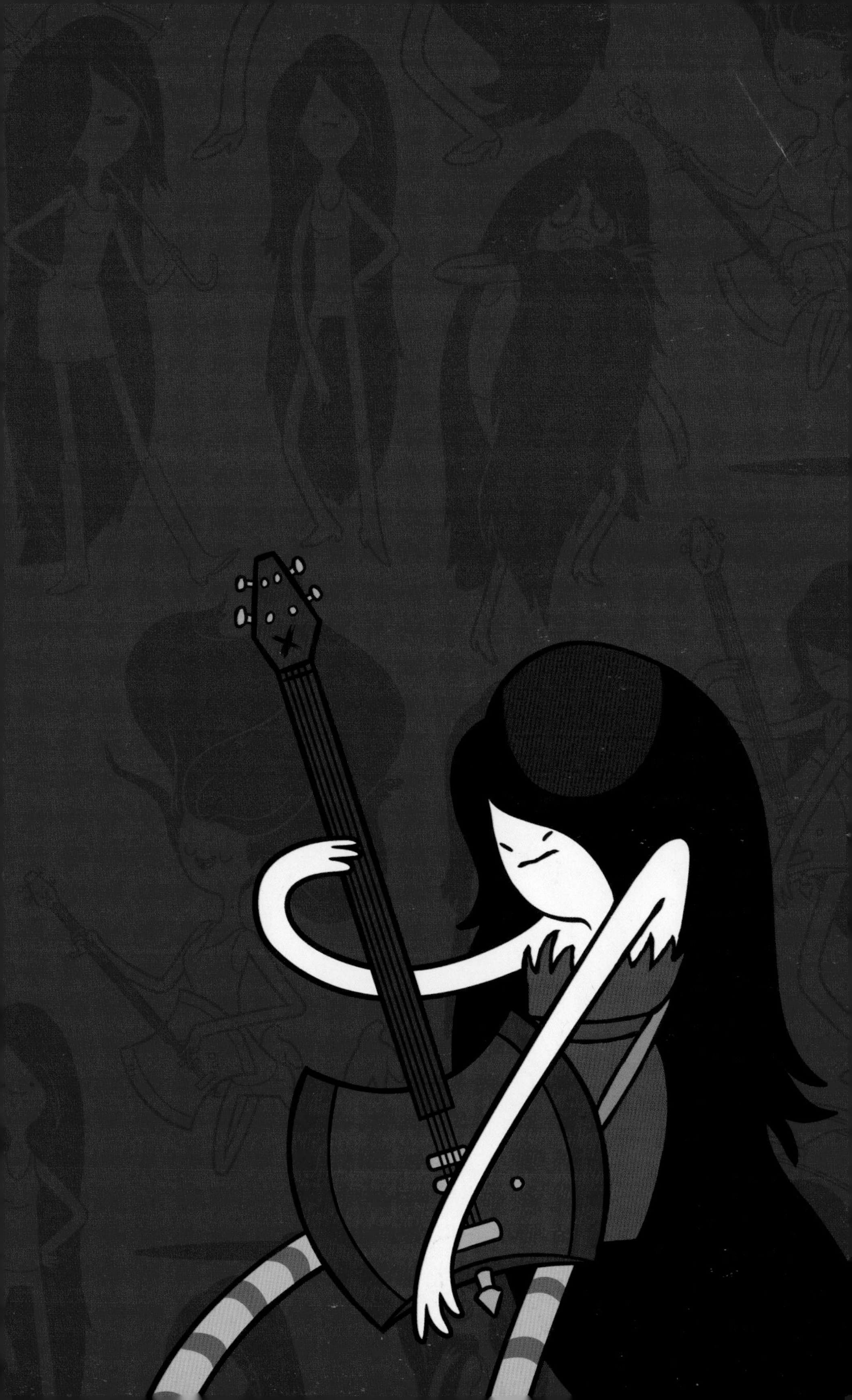

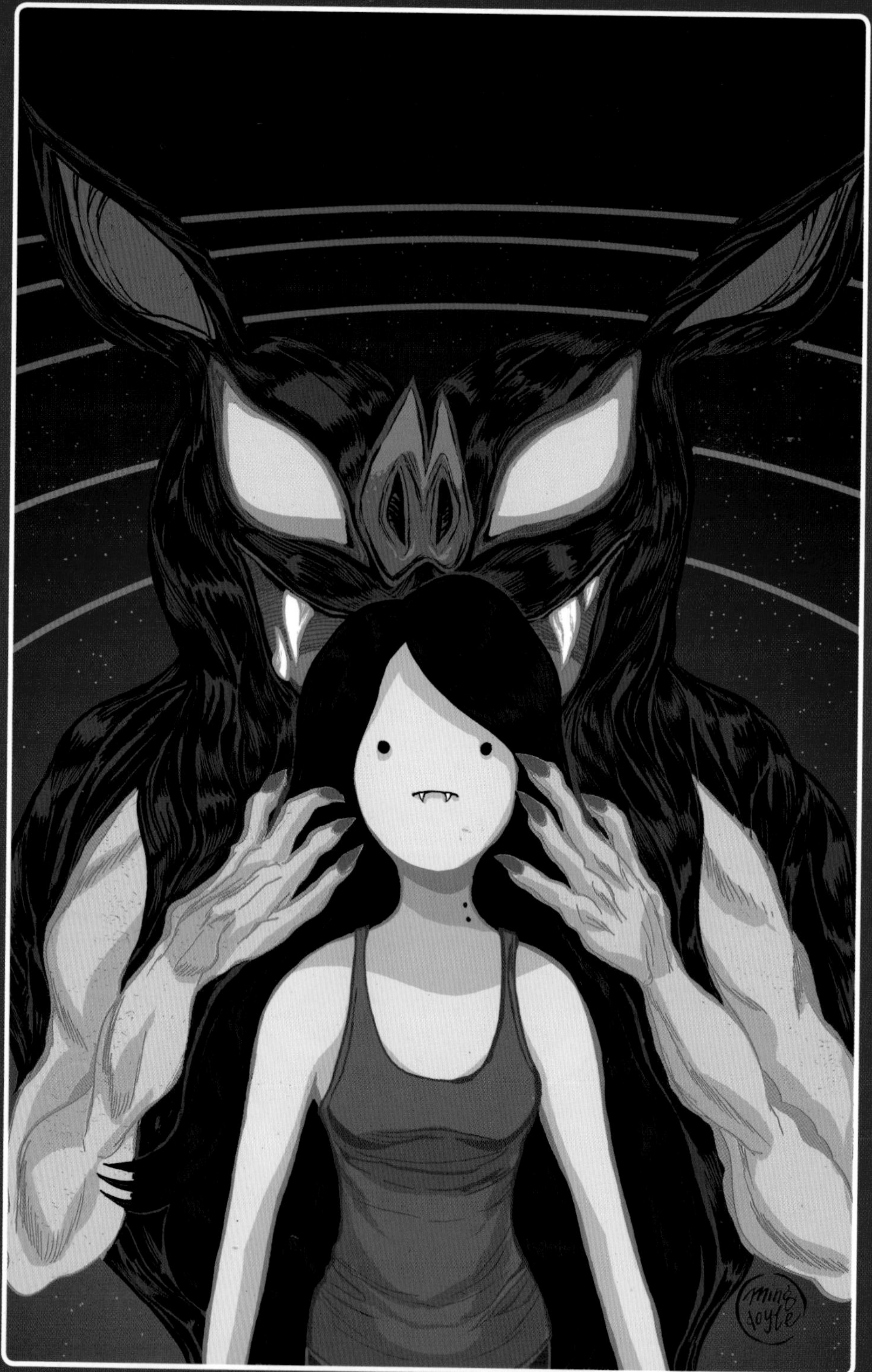
ming doyle

Adventure Time #14 Cover D by **Ming Doyle**

"Echoes"

Written and Illustrated by **S. M. Vidaurri**

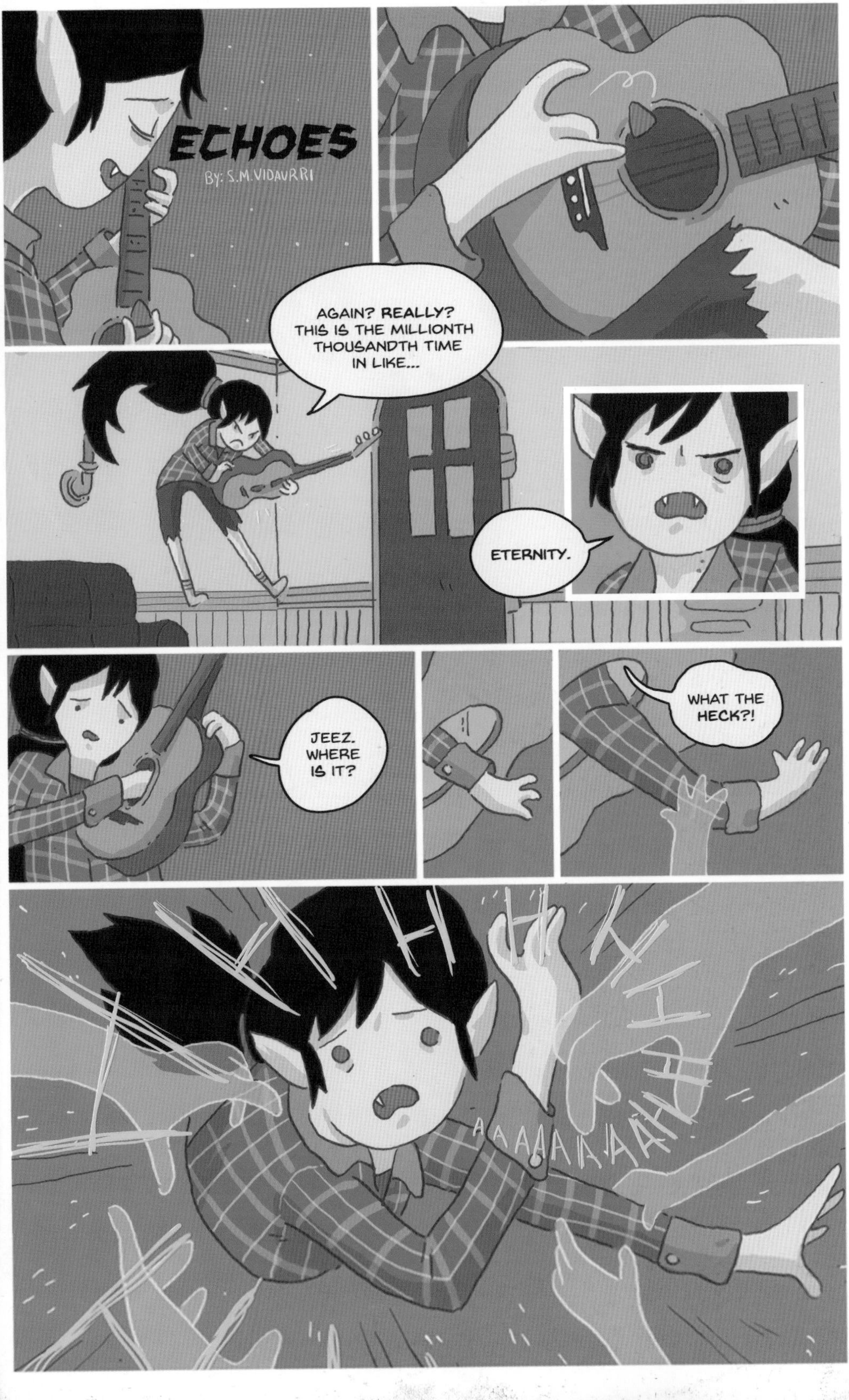
ECHOES
By: S.M. VIDAURRI
AGAIN? REALLY? THIS IS THE MILLIONTH THOUSANDTH TIME IN LIKE...
ETERNITY.
JEEZ. WHERE IS IT?
WHAT THE HECK?!

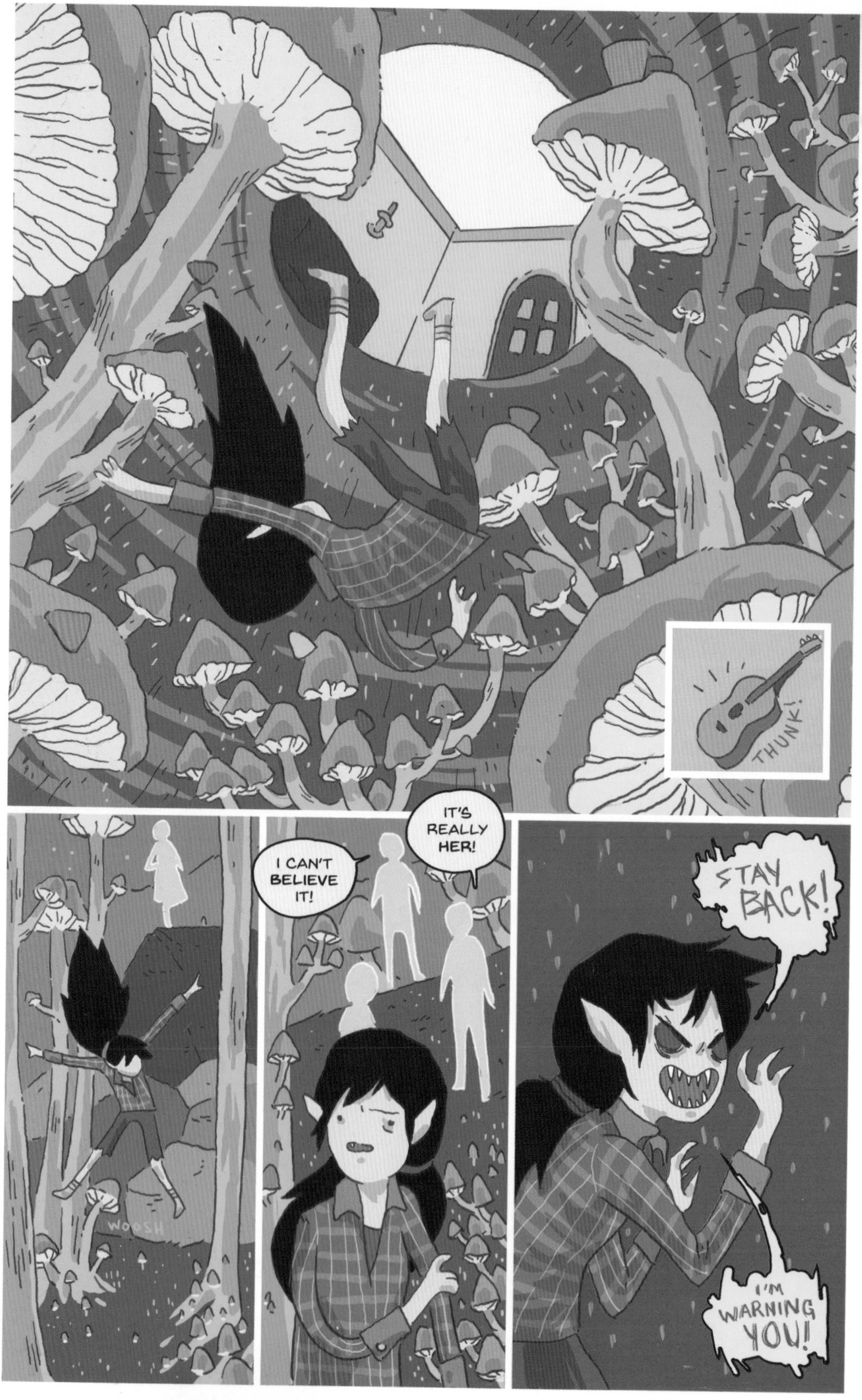
THUNK!
WOOSH
I CAN'T BELIEVE IT!
IT'S REALLY HER!
STAY BACK!
I'M WARNING YOU!

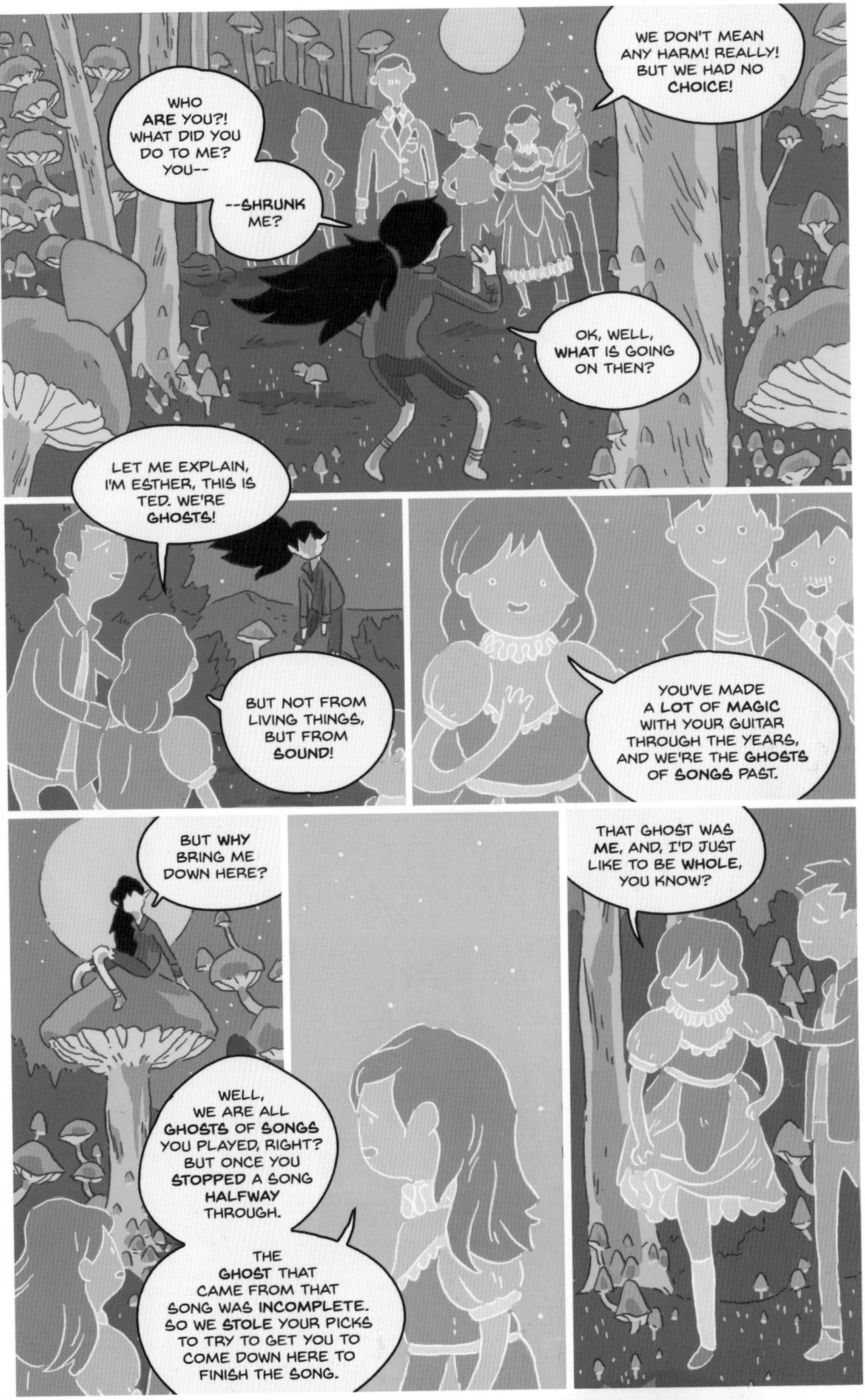
WHO ARE YOU?! WHAT DID YOU DO TO ME? YOU--
--SHRUNK ME?
WE DON'T MEAN ANY HARM! REALLY! BUT WE HAD NO CHOICE!
OK, WELL, WHAT IS GOING ON THEN?
LET ME EXPLAIN, I'M ESTHER, THIS IS TED. WE'RE GHOSTS!
BUT NOT FROM LIVING THINGS, BUT FROM SOUND!
YOU'VE MADE A LOT OF MAGIC WITH YOUR GUITAR THROUGH THE YEARS, AND WE'RE THE GHOSTS OF SONGS PAST.
BUT WHY BRING ME DOWN HERE?
WELL, WE ARE ALL GHOSTS OF SONGS YOU PLAYED, RIGHT? BUT ONCE YOU STOPPED A SONG HALFWAY THROUGH.
THE GHOST THAT CAME FROM THAT SONG WAS INCOMPLETE. SO WE STOLE YOUR PICKS TO TRY TO GET YOU TO COME DOWN HERE TO FINISH THE SONG.
THAT GHOST WAS ME, AND, I'D JUST LIKE TO BE WHOLE, YOU KNOW?

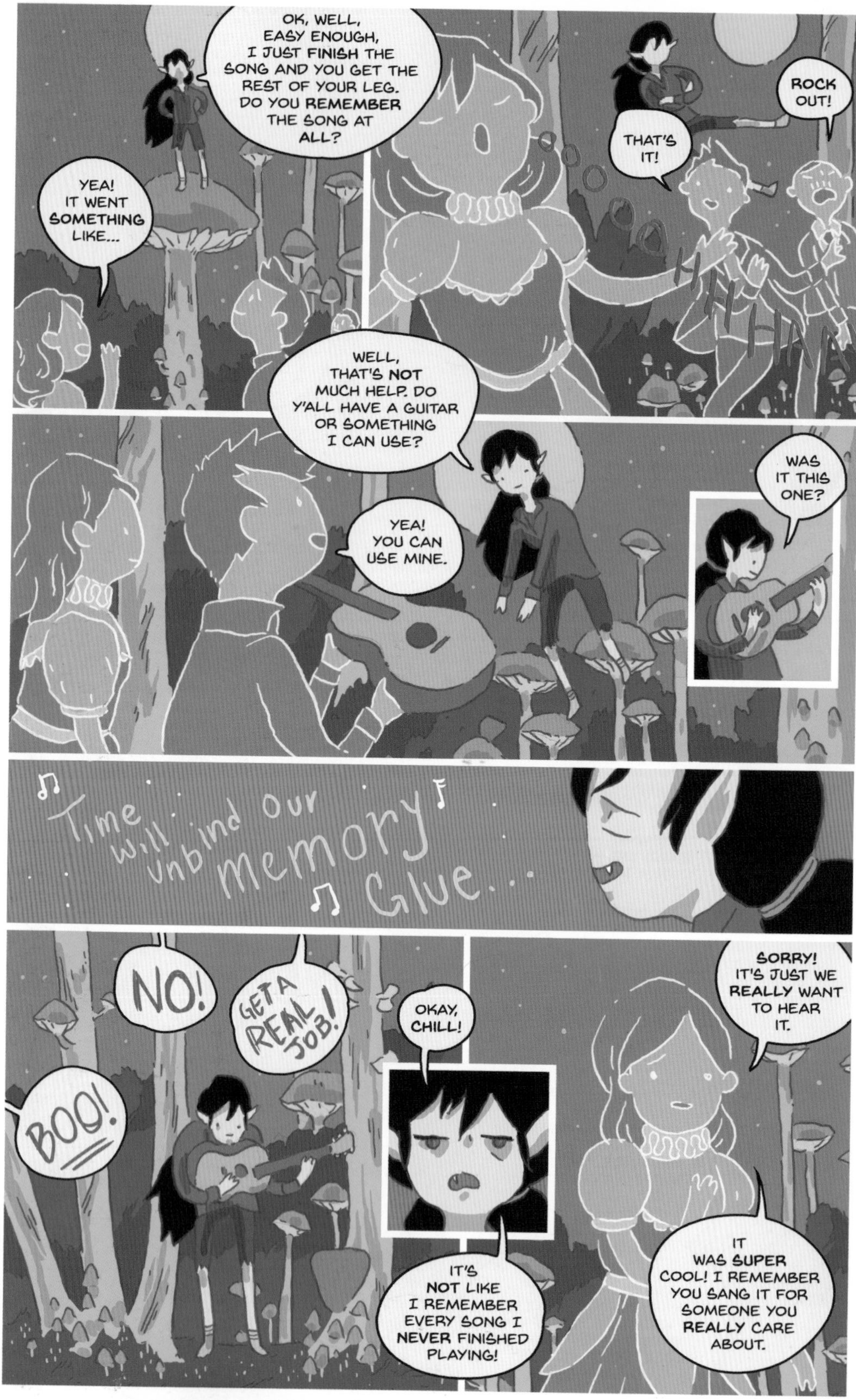
OK, WELL, EASY ENOUGH, I JUST FINISH THE SONG AND YOU GET THE REST OF YOUR LEG. DO YOU REMEMBER THE SONG AT ALL?
YEA! IT WENT SOMETHING LIKE...
OOOOOHHHHHAA
THAT'S IT!
ROCK OUT!
WELL, THAT'S NOT MUCH HELP. DO Y'ALL HAVE A GUITAR OR SOMETHING I CAN USE?
YEA! YOU CAN USE MINE.
WAS IT THIS ONE?
Time will unbind our memory Glue...
NO!
GET A REAL JOB!
BOO!
OKAY, CHILL!
IT'S NOT LIKE I REMEMBER EVERY SONG I NEVER FINISHED PLAYING!
SORRY! IT'S JUST WE REALLY WANT TO HEAR IT.
IT WAS SUPER COOL! I REMEMBER YOU SANG IT FOR SOMEONE YOU REALLY CARE ABOUT.

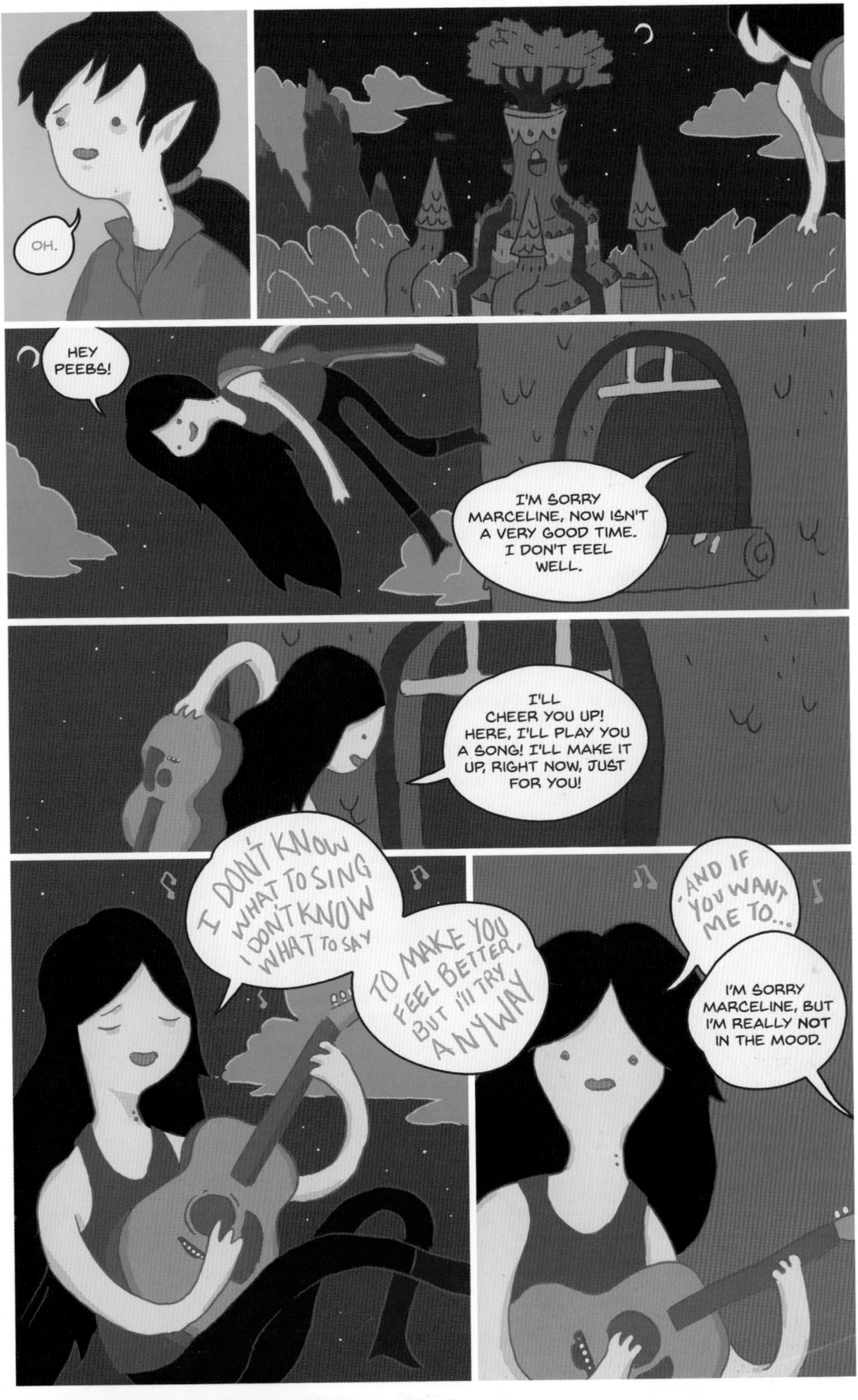
OH.
HEY PEEBS!
I'M SORRY MARCELINE, NOW ISN'T A VERY GOOD TIME. I DON'T FEEL WELL.
I'LL CHEER YOU UP! HERE, I'LL PLAY YOU A SONG! I'LL MAKE IT UP, RIGHT NOW, JUST FOR YOU!
I DON'T KNOW WHAT TO SING I DON'T KNOW WHAT TO SAY
TO MAKE YOU FEEL BETTER, BUT I'LL TRY ANYWAY
-AND IF YOU WANT ME TO...
I'M SORRY MARCELINE, BUT I'M REALLY NOT IN THE MOOD.

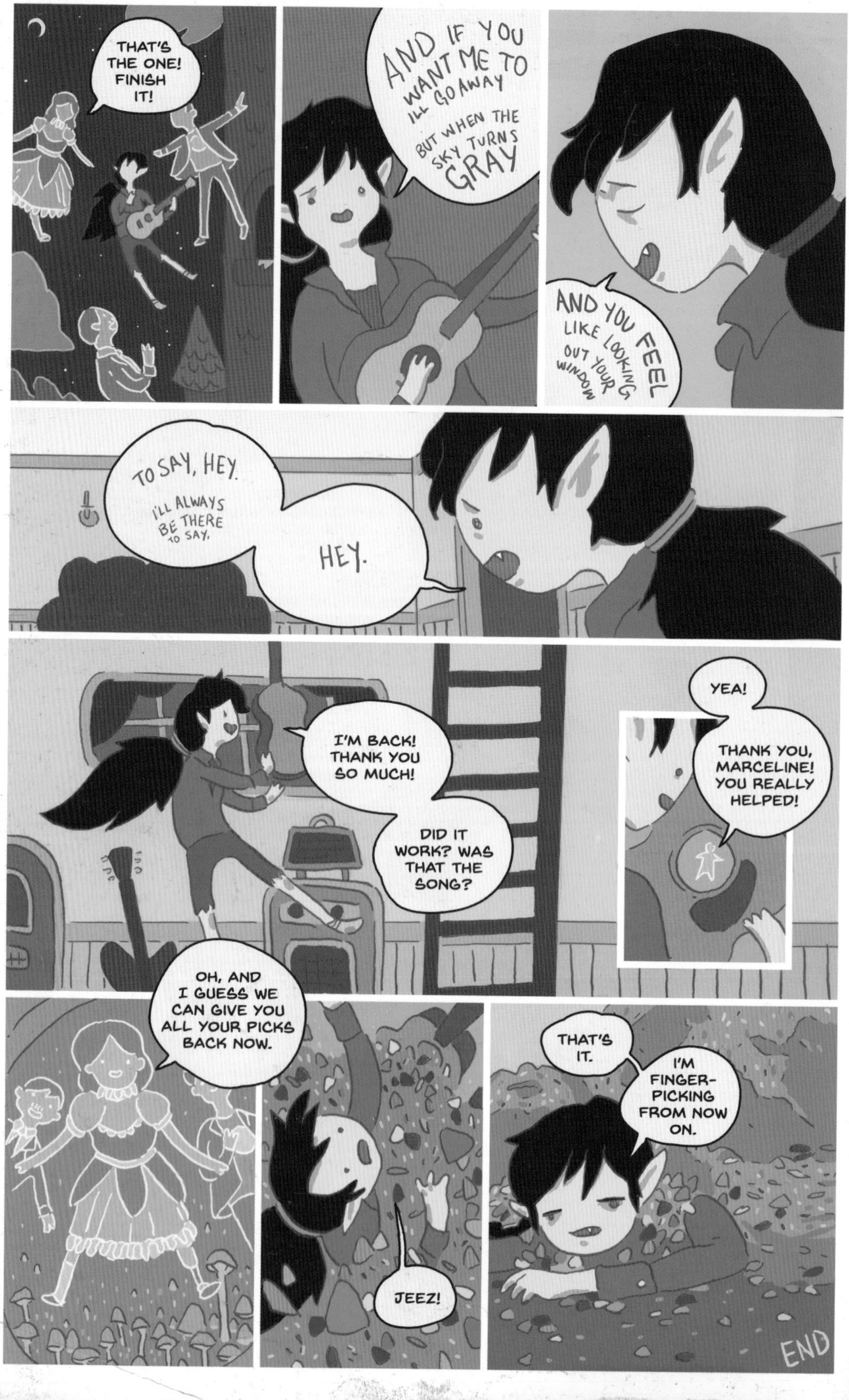
THAT'S THE ONE! FINISH IT!
AND IF YOU WANT ME TO I'LL GO AWAY
BUT WHEN THE SKY TURNS GRAY
AND YOU FEEL LIKE LOOKING OUT YOUR WINDOW
TO SAY, HEY.
I'LL ALWAYS BE THERE TO SAY,
HEY.
I'M BACK! THANK YOU SO MUCH!
DID IT WORK? WAS THAT THE SONG?
YEA!
THANK YOU, MARCELINE! YOU REALLY HELPED!
OH, AND I GUESS WE CAN GIVE YOU ALL YOUR PICKS BACK NOW.
JEEZ!
THAT'S IT.
I'M FINGER-PICKING FROM NOW ON.
END

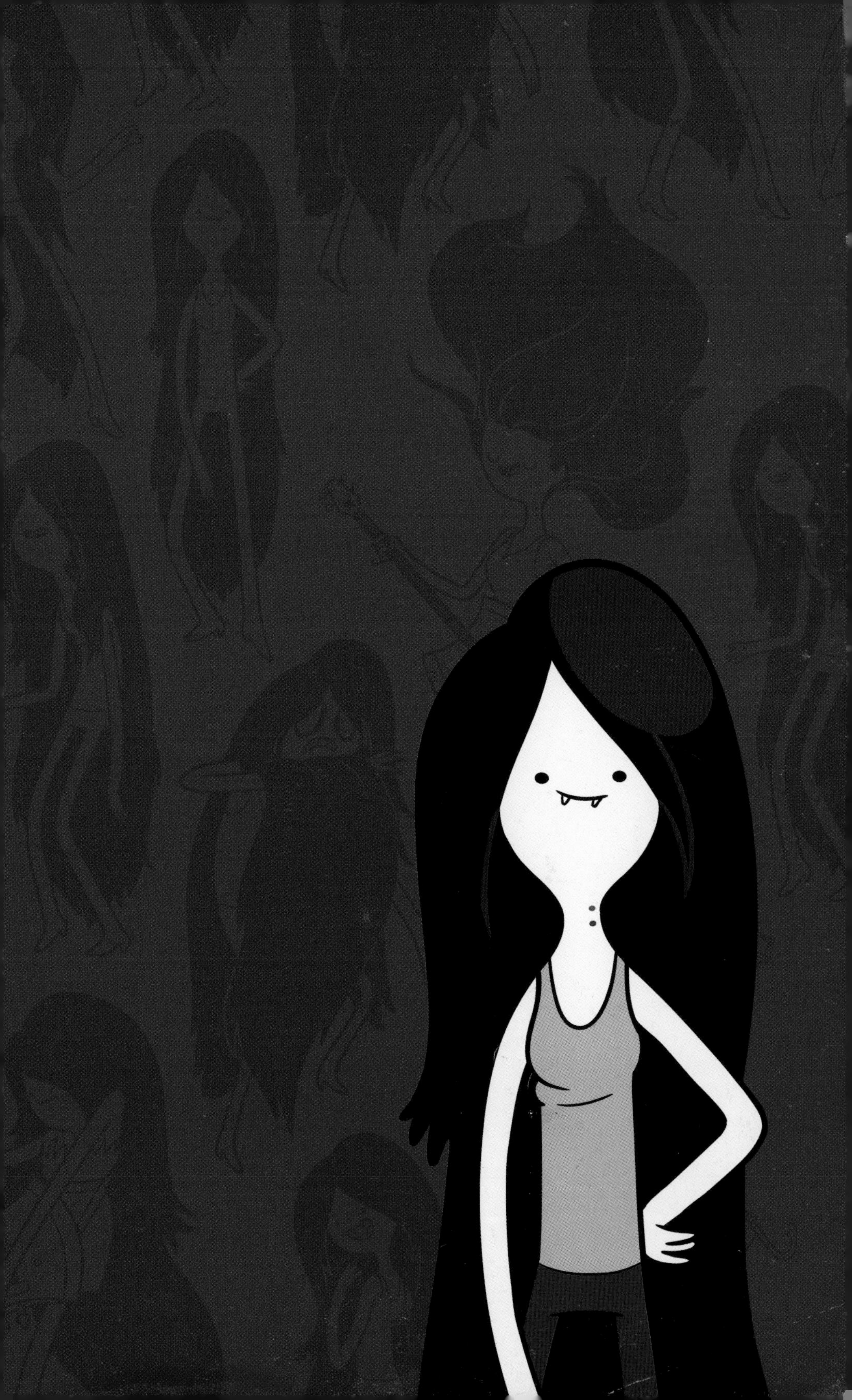

Adventure Time #19 Cover B by **Britt Sanders**
"Moon Beam"
Written and Illustrated by **Aatmaja Pandya**

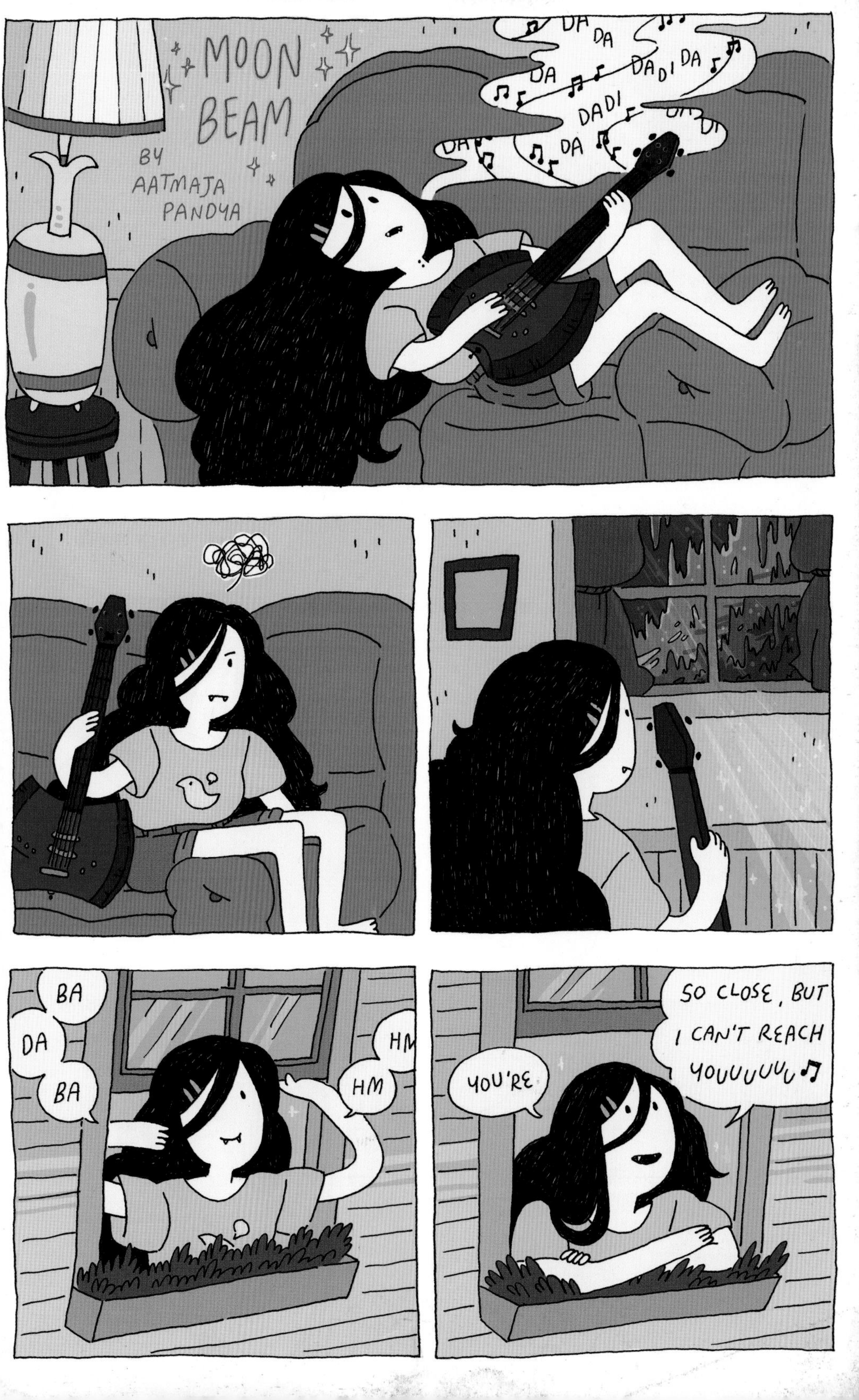
MOON BEAM
BY AATMAJA PANDYA
DA DA DA DADI DA DADI DA DA DA
BA
DA
BA
HM
HM
YOU'RE
SO CLOSE, BUT I CAN'T REACH YOUUUUUU

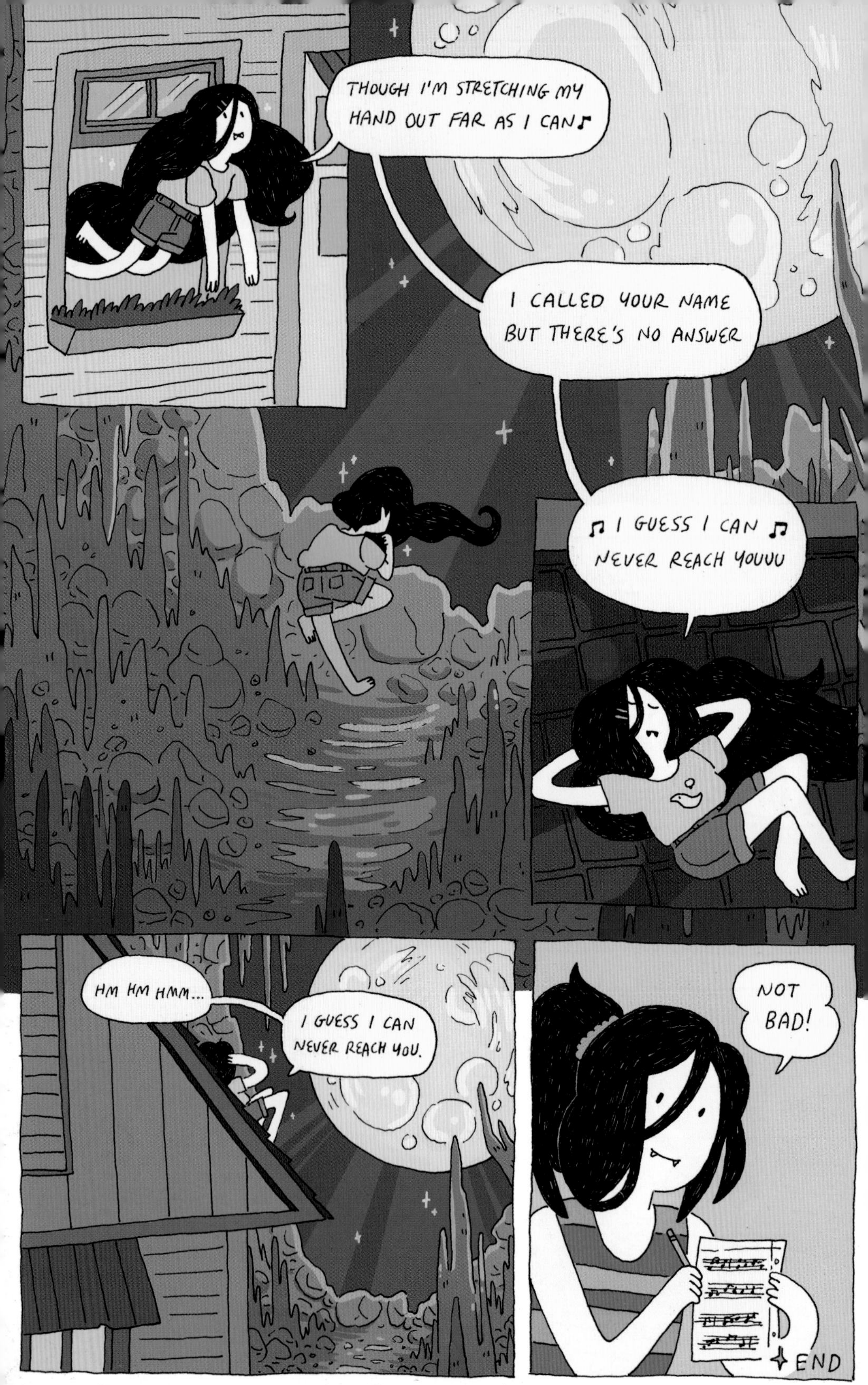
THOUGH I'M STRETCHING MY HAND OUT FAR AS I CAN♪
I CALLED YOUR NAME BUT THERE'S NO ANSWER
♫ I GUESS I CAN ♫ NEVER REACH YOUUU
HM HM HMM...
I GUESS I CAN NEVER REACH YOU.
NOT BAD!
END

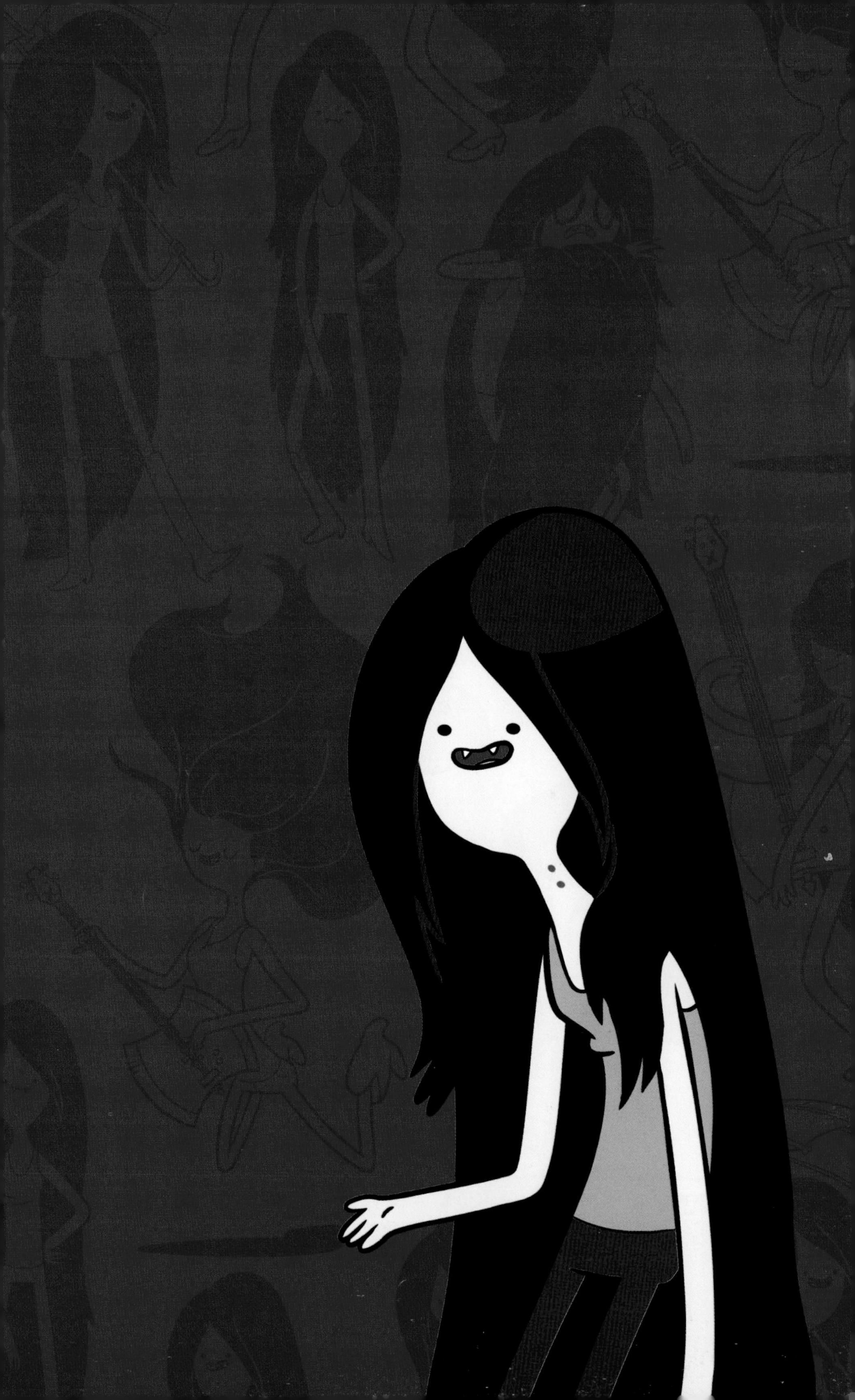

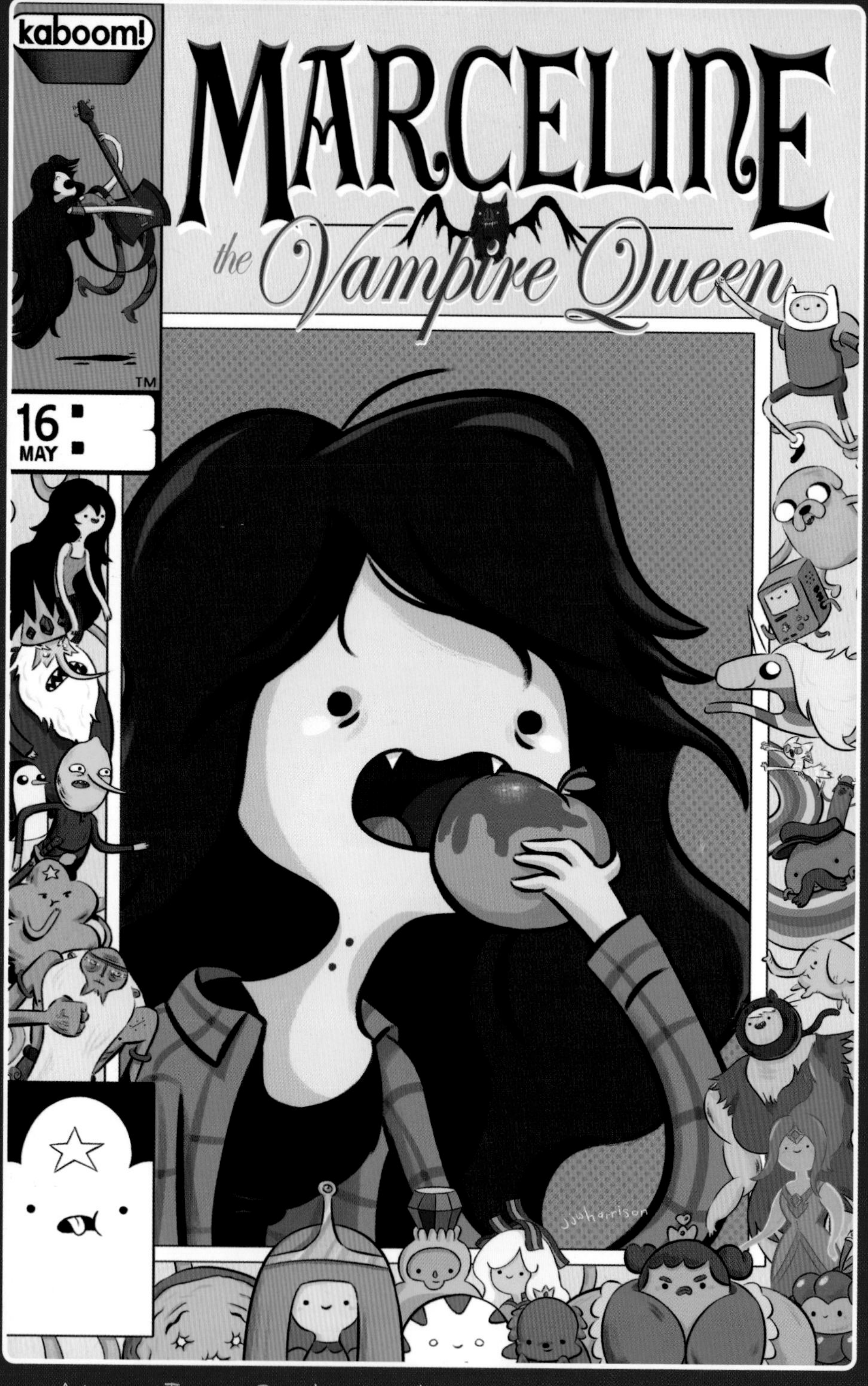
kaboom!
MARCELINE
the Vampire Queen
TM
16
MAY
jjharrison

Adventure Time #16 Brett's Collector's Exclusive Cover by **JJ Harrison**

"Broken"

Written and Illustrated by **Bethany Sellers** Colors by **Joana Lafuente**

Letters by **Jim Campbell**

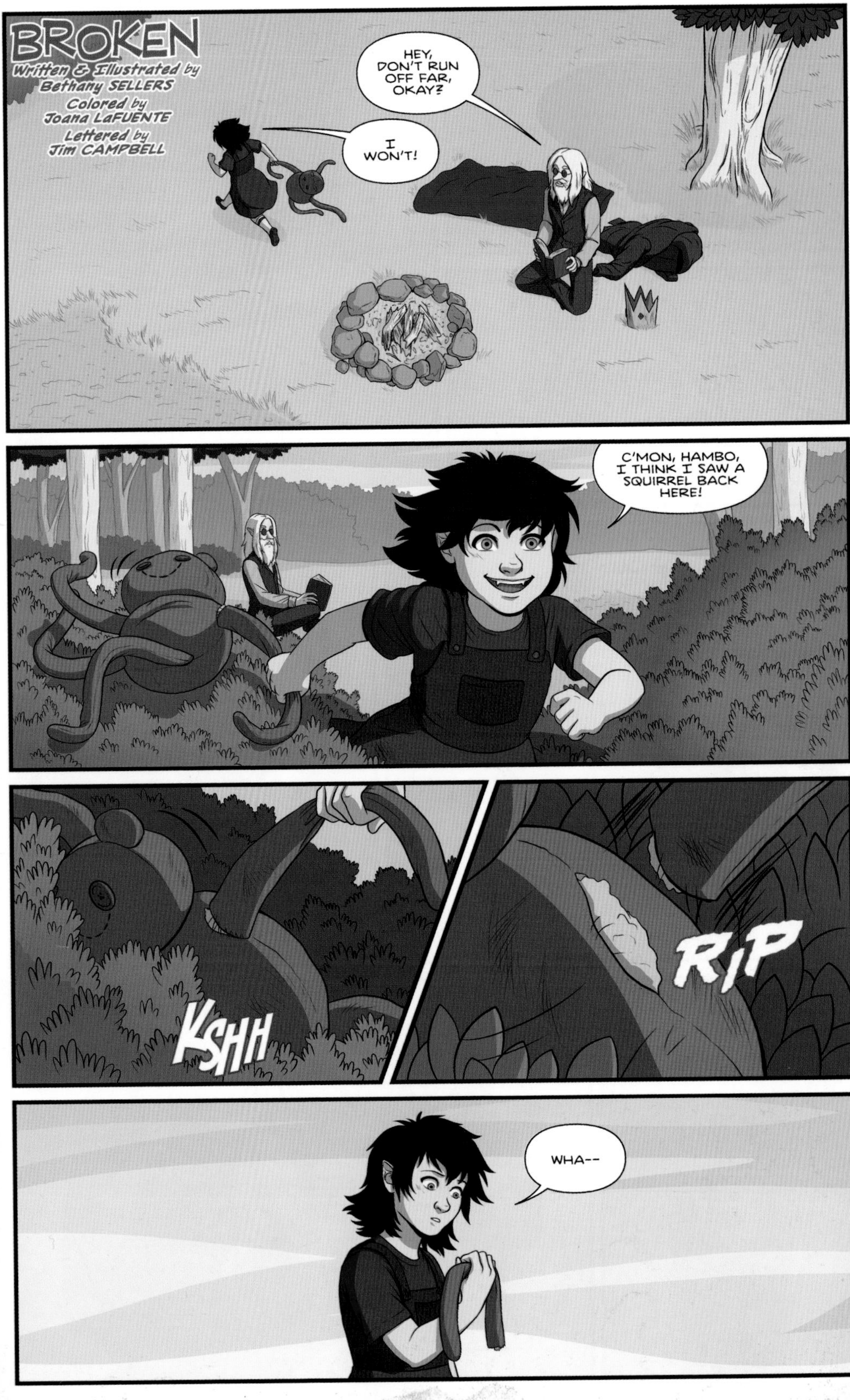
BROKEN
Written & Illustrated by Bethany SELLERS
Colored by Joana LaFUENTE
Lettered by Jim CAMPBELL
HEY, DON'T RUN OFF FAR, OKAY?
I WON'T!
C'MON, HAMBO, I THINK I SAW A SQUIRREL BACK HERE!
KSHH
RIP
WHA--

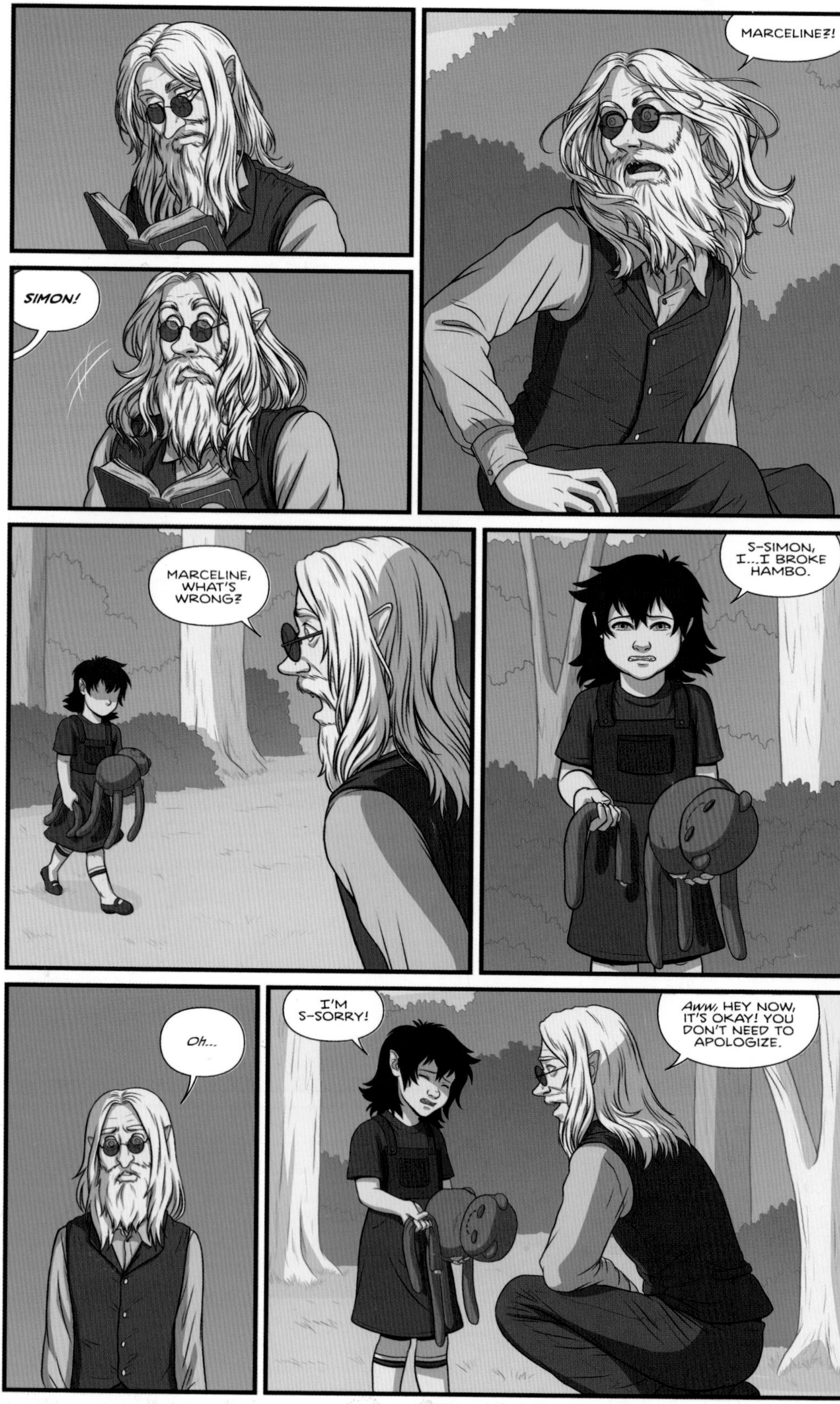
MARCELINE?!
SIMON!
MARCELINE, WHAT'S WRONG?
S-SIMON, I...I BROKE HAMBO.
Oh...
I'M S-SORRY!
Aww, HEY NOW, IT'S OKAY! YOU DON'T NEED TO APOLOGIZE.

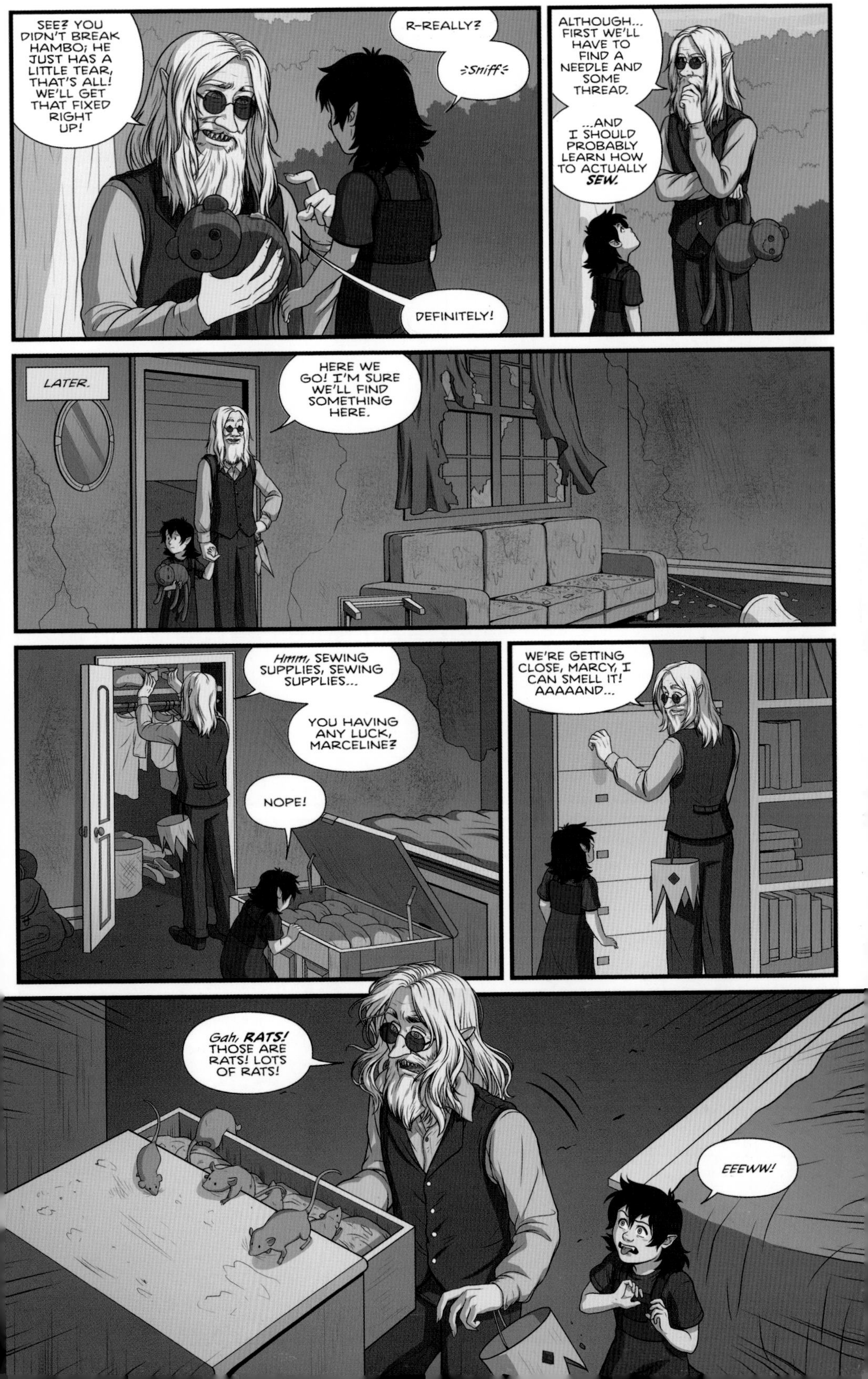
SEE? YOU DIDN'T BREAK HAMBO; HE JUST HAS A LITTLE TEAR, THAT'S ALL! WE'LL GET THAT FIXED RIGHT UP!
R-REALLY?
Sniff
DEFINITELY!
ALTHOUGH... FIRST WE'LL HAVE TO FIND A NEEDLE AND SOME THREAD.
...AND I SHOULD PROBABLY LEARN HOW TO ACTUALLY SEW.
LATER.
HERE WE GO! I'M SURE WE'LL FIND SOMETHING HERE.
Hmm, SEWING SUPPLIES, SEWING SUPPLIES...
YOU HAVING ANY LUCK, MARCELINE?
NOPE!
WE'RE GETTING CLOSE, MARCY, I CAN SMELL IT! AAAAAND...
Gah, RATS! THOSE ARE RATS! LOTS OF RATS!
EEEWW!

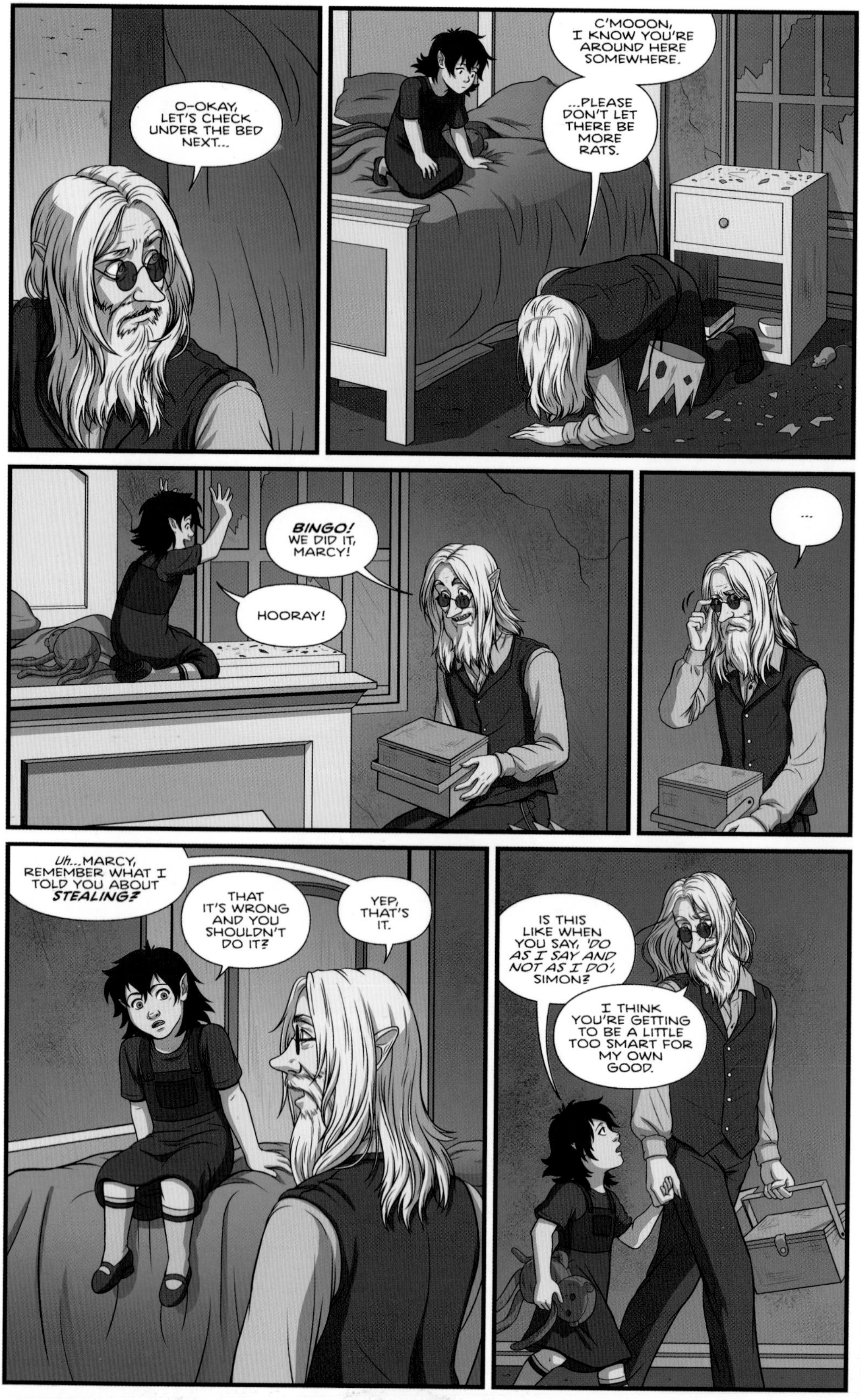
O-OKAY, LET'S CHECK UNDER THE BED NEXT...
C'MOOON, I KNOW YOU'RE AROUND HERE SOMEWHERE.
...PLEASE DON'T LET THERE BE MORE RATS.
BINGO! WE DID IT, MARCY!
HOORAY!
...
Uh... MARCY, REMEMBER WHAT I TOLD YOU ABOUT *STEALING?*
THAT IT'S WRONG AND YOU SHOULDN'T DO IT?
YEP, THAT'S IT.
IS THIS LIKE WHEN YOU SAY, *'DO AS I SAY AND NOT AS I DO'*, SIMON?
I THINK YOU'RE GETTING TO BE A LITTLE TOO SMART FOR MY OWN GOOD.

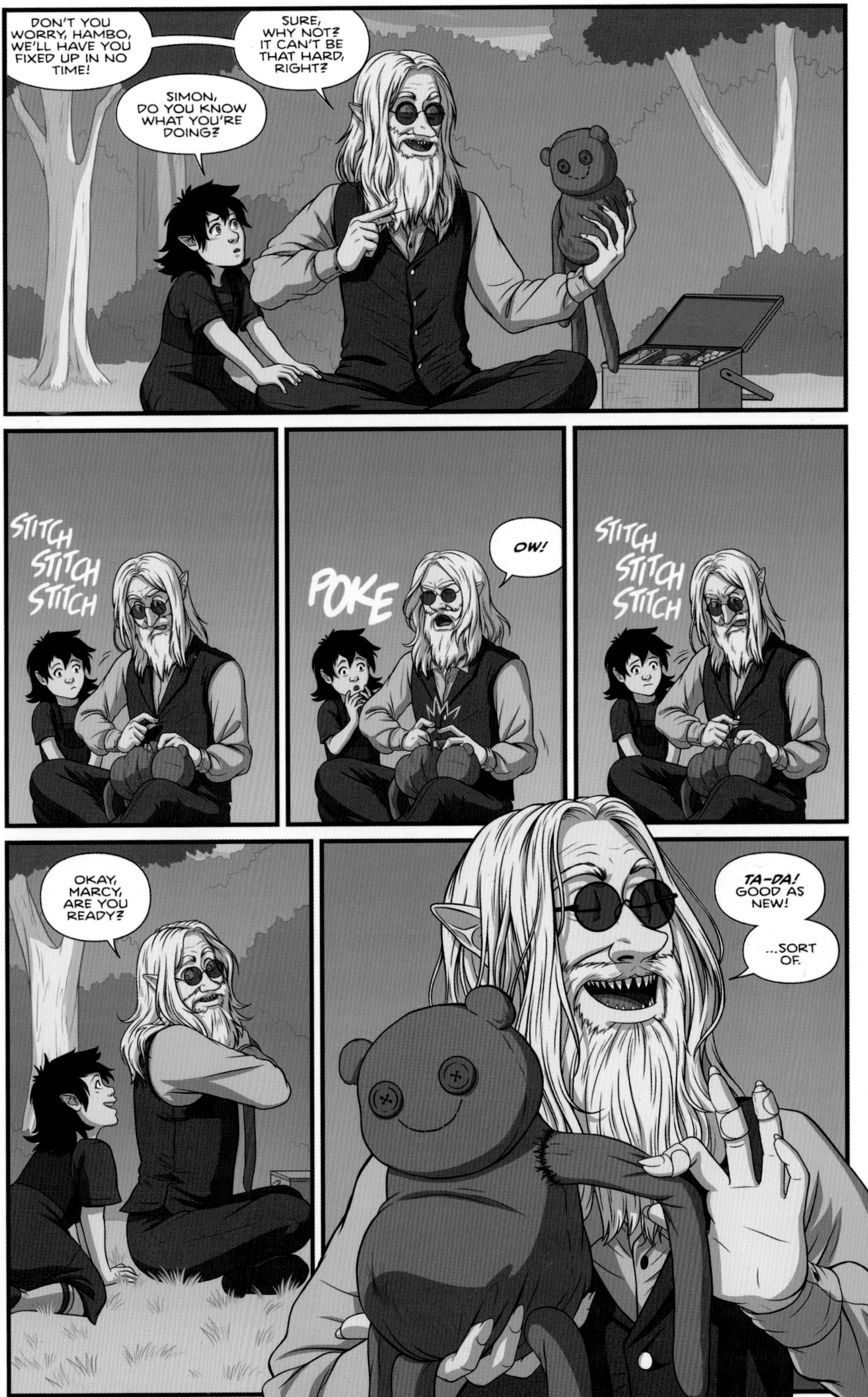
DON'T YOU WORRY, HAMBO, WE'LL HAVE YOU FIXED UP IN NO TIME!
SURE, WHY NOT? IT CAN'T BE THAT HARD, RIGHT?
SIMON, DO YOU KNOW WHAT YOU'RE DOING?
STITCH STITCH STITCH
POKE
OW!
STITCH STITCH STITCH
OKAY, MARCY, ARE YOU READY?
TA-DA! GOOD AS NEW!
...SORT OF.

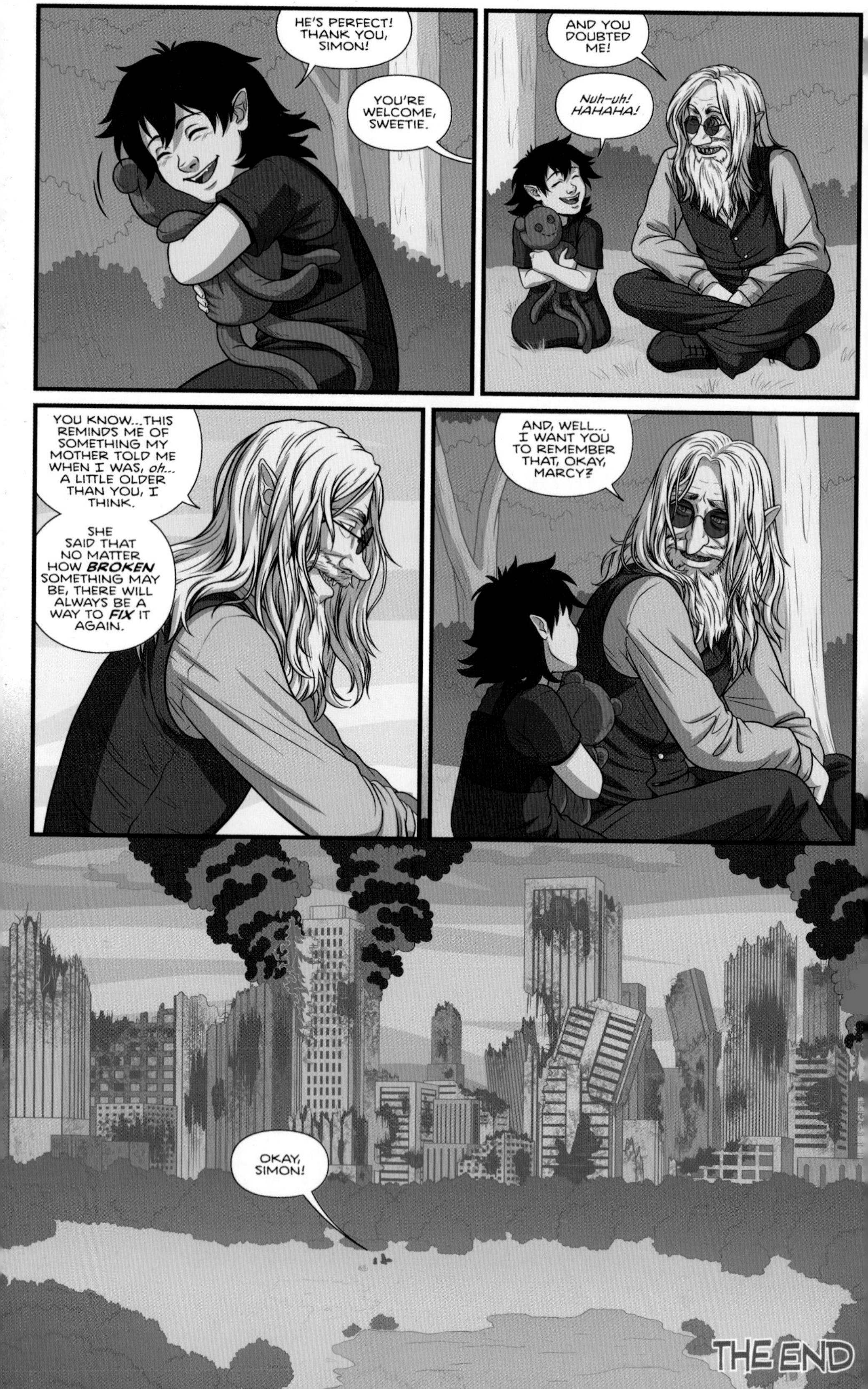
HE'S PERFECT! THANK YOU, SIMON!
YOU'RE WELCOME, SWEETIE.
AND YOU DOUBTED ME!
Nuh-uh! HAHAHA!
YOU KNOW...THIS REMINDS ME OF SOMETHING MY MOTHER TOLD ME WHEN I WAS, oh... A LITTLE OLDER THAN YOU, I THINK.
SHE SAID THAT NO MATTER HOW BROKEN SOMETHING MAY BE, THERE WILL ALWAYS BE A WAY TO FIX IT AGAIN.
AND, WELL... I WANT YOU TO REMEMBER THAT, OKAY, MARCY?
OKAY, SIMON!
THE END

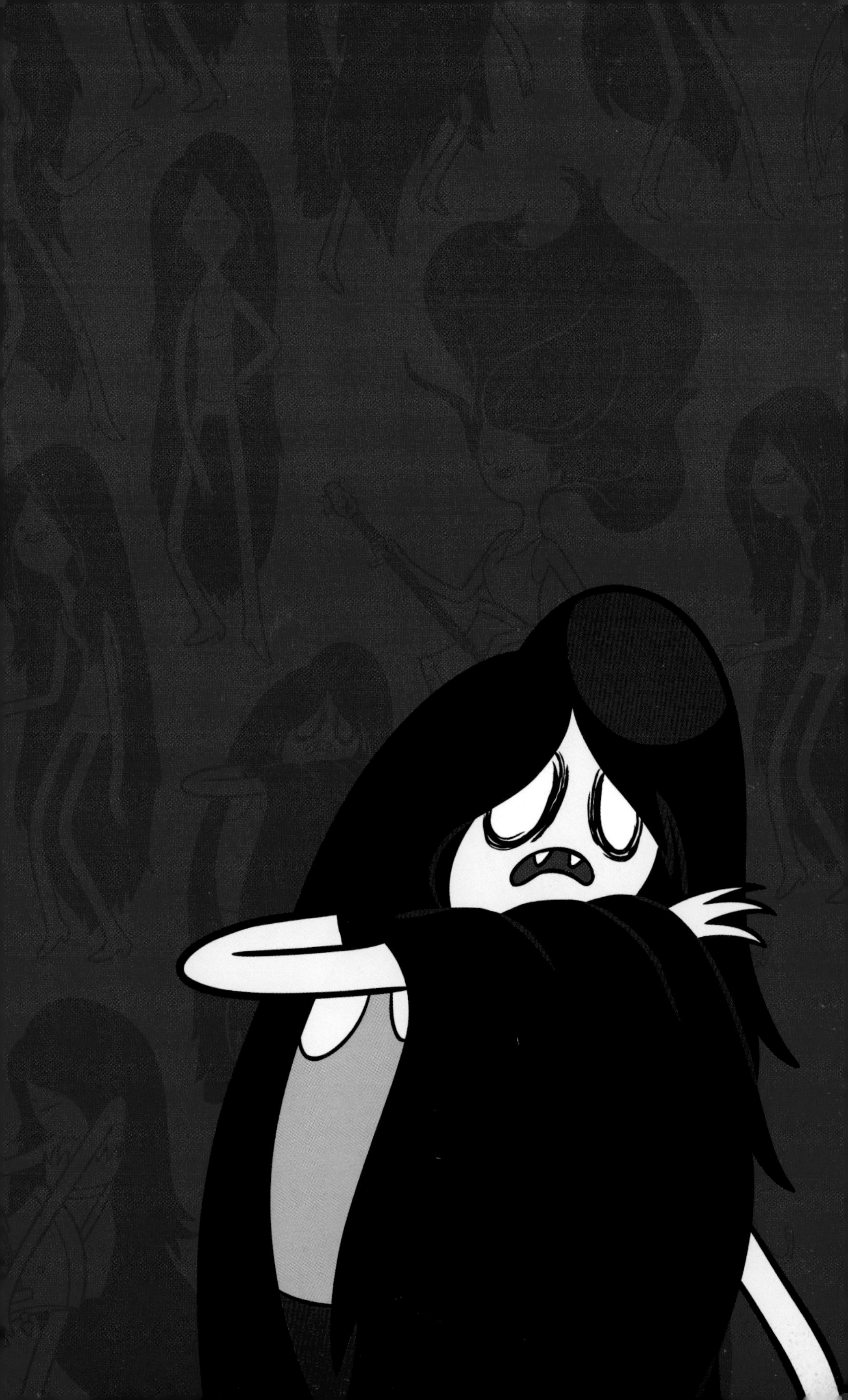

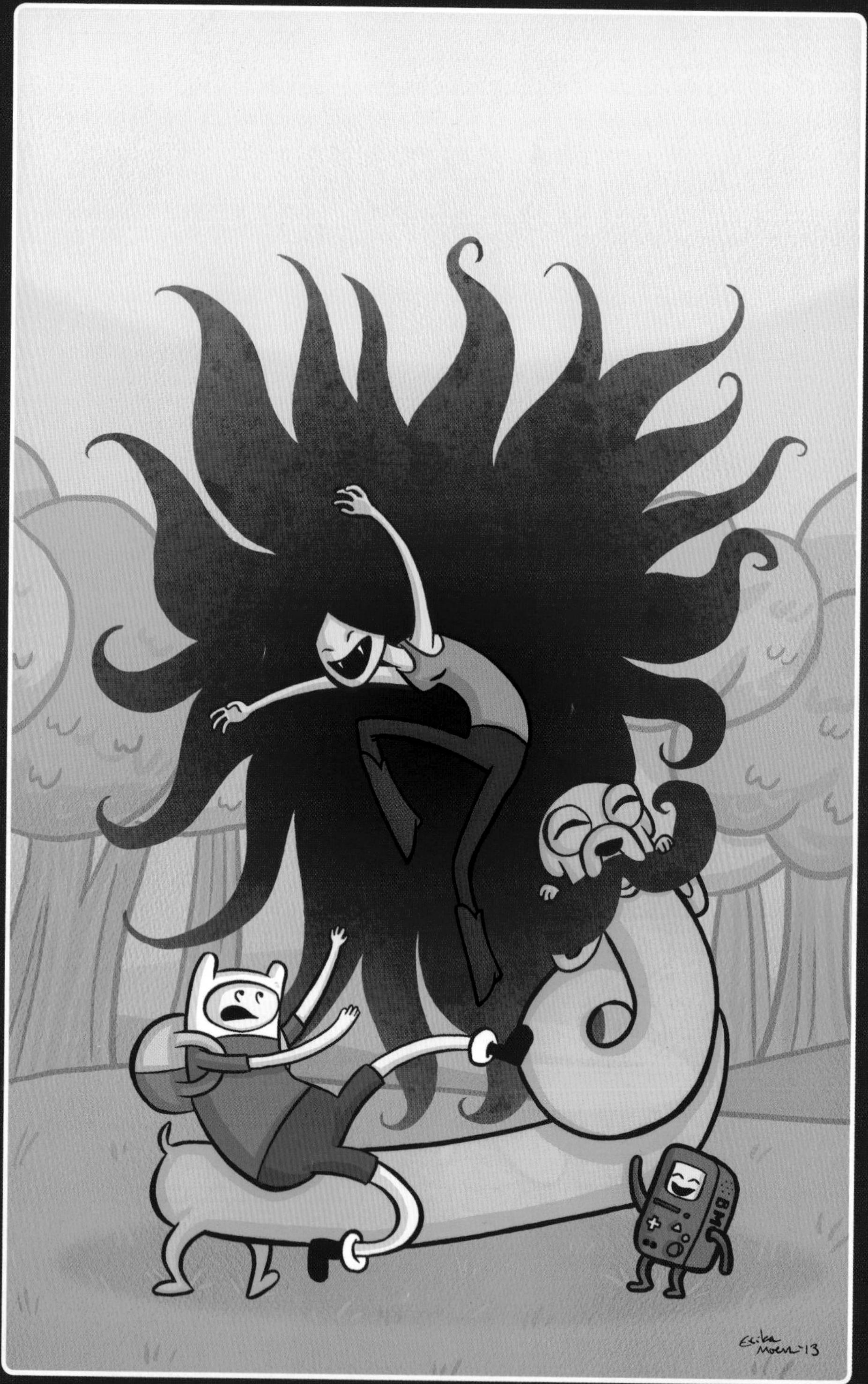
BMO
Erika Moen '13

Adventure Time #17 Cover B by **Erika Moen**

"Visions of Paternity"

Written by **Ryan Cady**

Illustrated by **Jorge Monlongo**

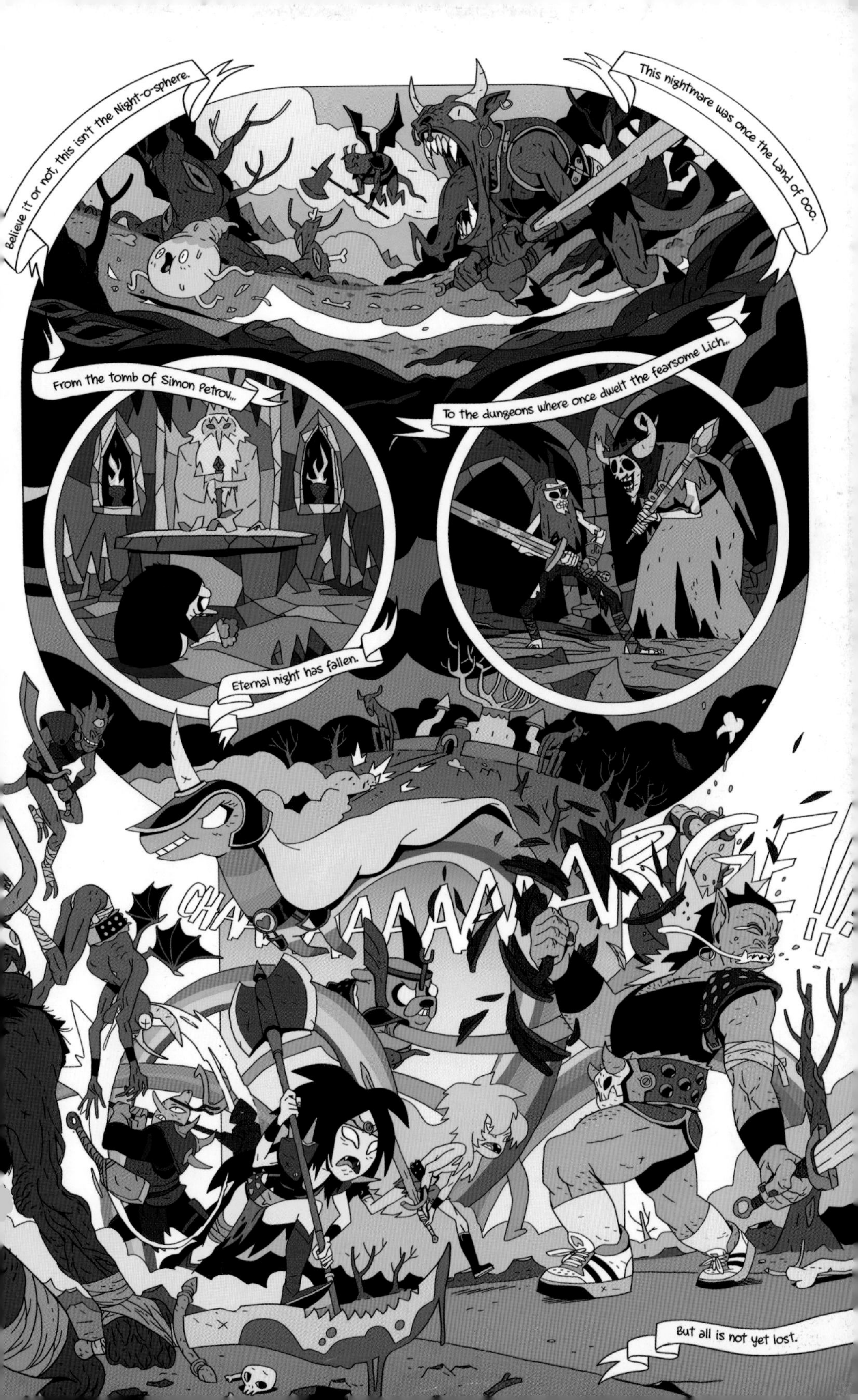
Believe it or not, this isn't the Night-o-sphere.
This nightmare was once the Land of Ooo.
From the tomb of Simon Petrov...
To the dungeons where once dwelt the fearsome Lich...
Eternal night has fallen.
CHAAAAAARGE!!!
But all is not yet lost.

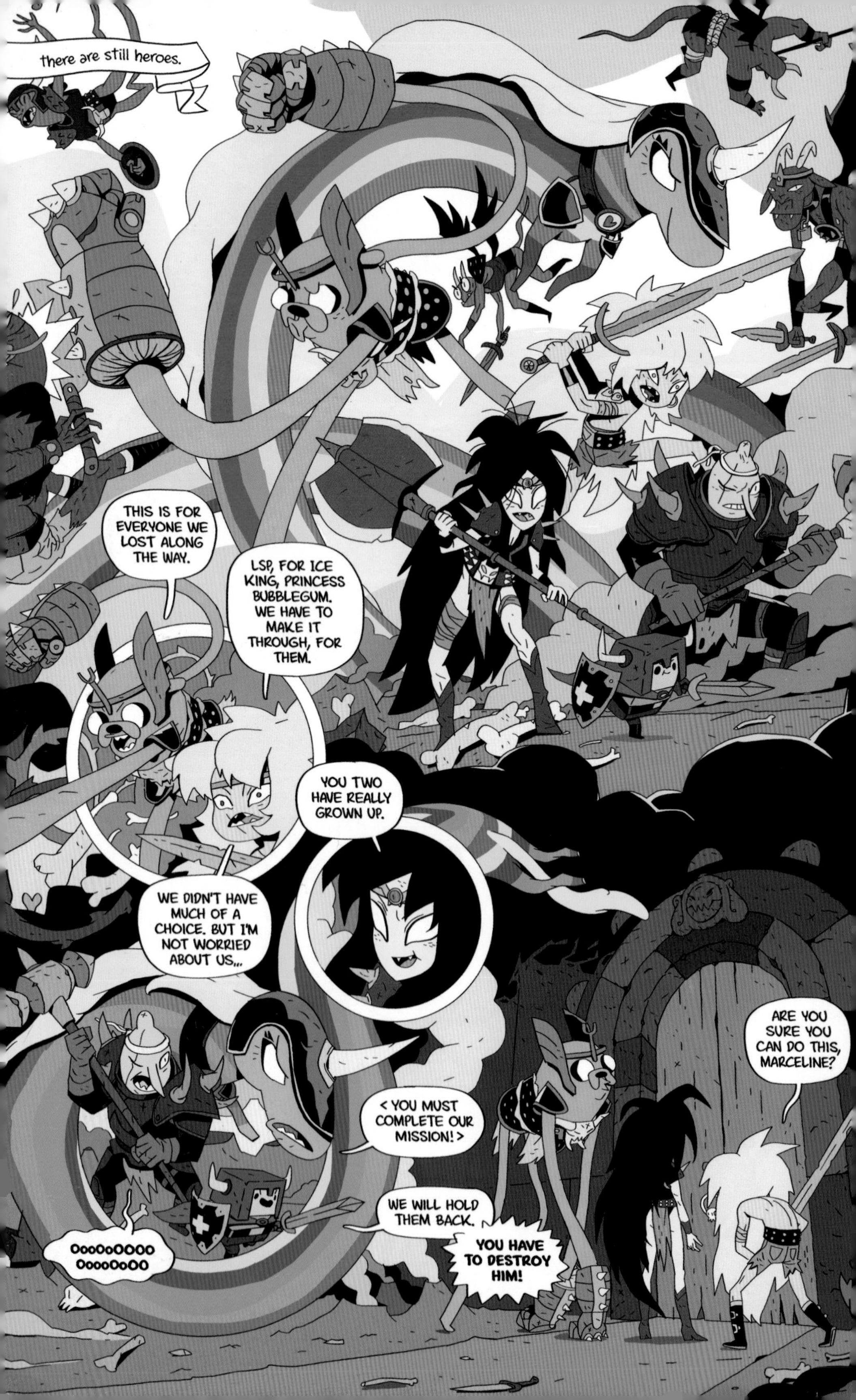
there are still heroes.
THIS IS FOR EVERYONE WE LOST ALONG THE WAY.
LSP, FOR ICE KING, PRINCESS BUBBLEGUM. WE HAVE TO MAKE IT THROUGH, FOR THEM.
YOU TWO HAVE REALLY GROWN UP.
WE DIDN'T HAVE MUCH OF A CHOICE. BUT I'M NOT WORRIED ABOUT US...
ARE YOU SURE YOU CAN DO THIS, MARCELINE?
< YOU MUST COMPLETE OUR MISSION! >
WE WILL HOLD THEM BACK.
YOU HAVE TO DESTROY HIM!
OOOOoOOOO OOOOOoOO

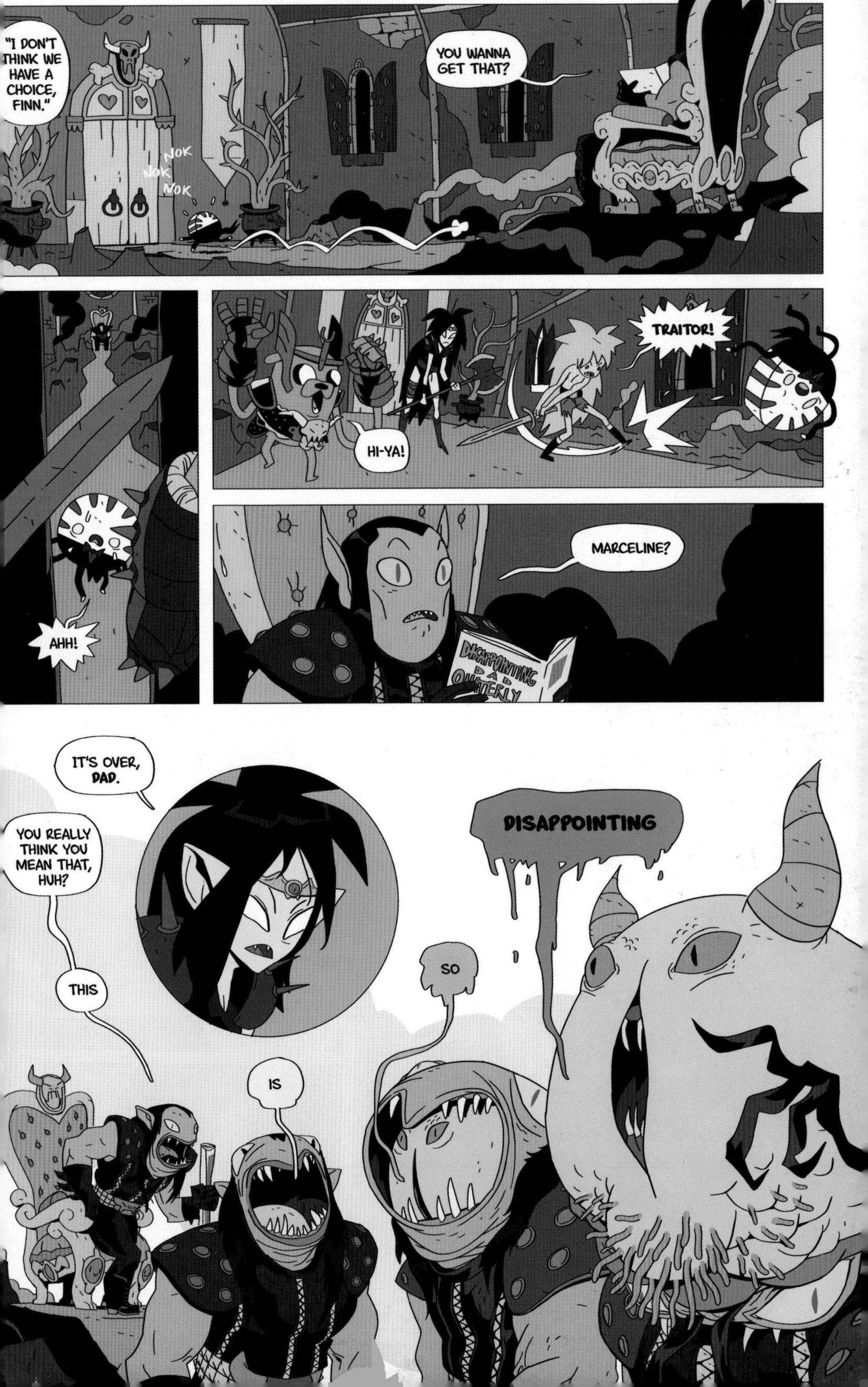
"I DON'T THINK WE HAVE A CHOICE, FINN."
NOK NOK NOK
YOU WANNA GET THAT?
TRAITOR!
HI-YA!
AHH!
MARCELINE?
DISAPPOINTING DAD QUARTERLY
IT'S OVER, DAD.
YOU REALLY THINK YOU MEAN THAT, HUH?
THIS
IS
SO
DISAPPOINTING

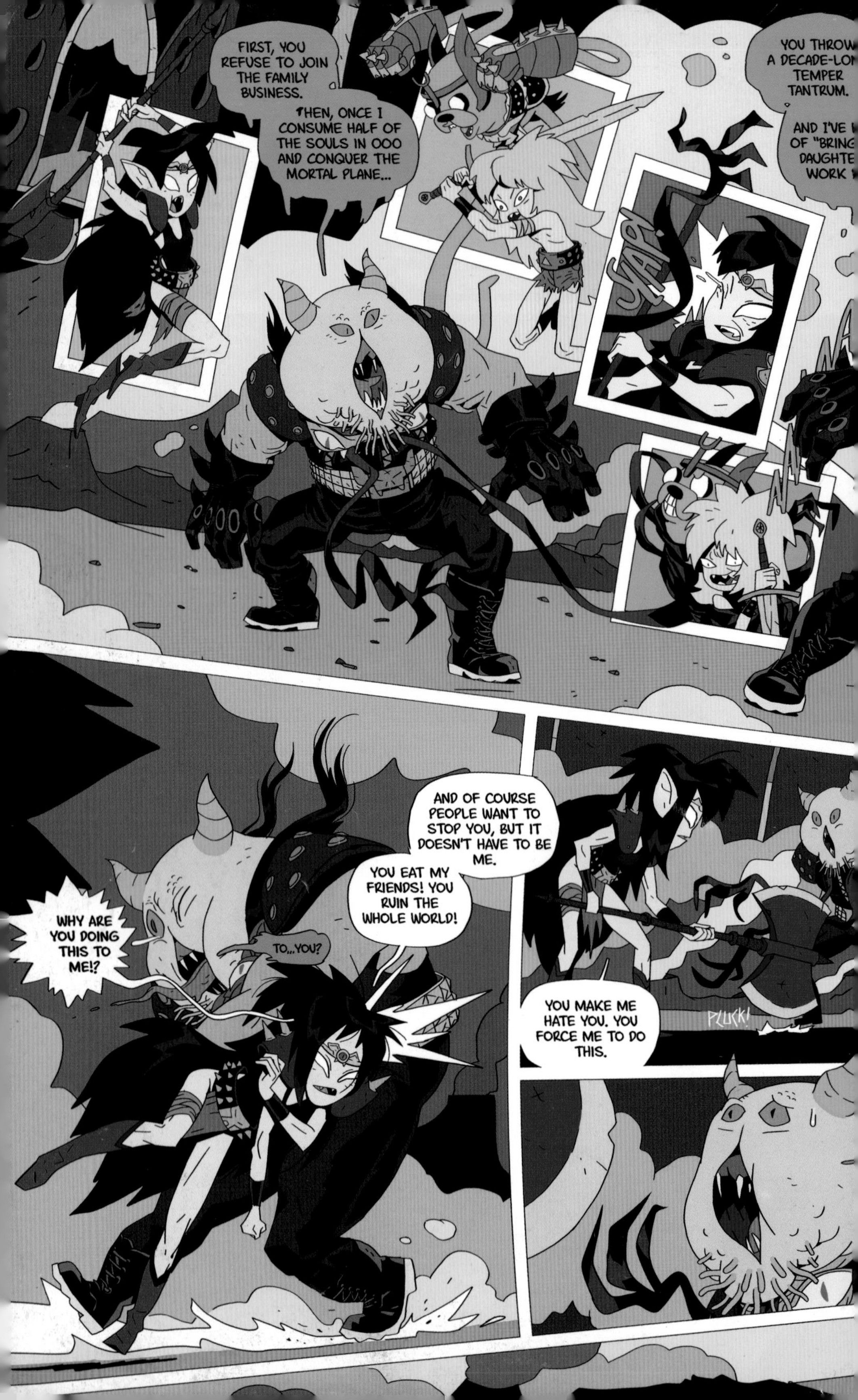
FIRST, YOU REFUSE TO JOIN THE FAMILY BUSINESS.
THEN, ONCE I CONSUME HALF OF THE SOULS IN OOO AND CONQUER THE MORTAL PLANE...
YOU THROW A DECADE-LON TEMPER TANTRUM.
AND I'VE OF "BRING DAUGHTE WORK
YAP!
WHY ARE YOU DOING THIS TO ME!?
TO...YOU?
YOU EAT MY FRIENDS! YOU RUIN THE WHOLE WORLD!
AND OF COURSE PEOPLE WANT TO STOP YOU, BUT IT DOESN'T HAVE TO BE ME.
YOU MAKE ME HATE YOU. YOU FORCE ME TO DO THIS.
PLUCK!

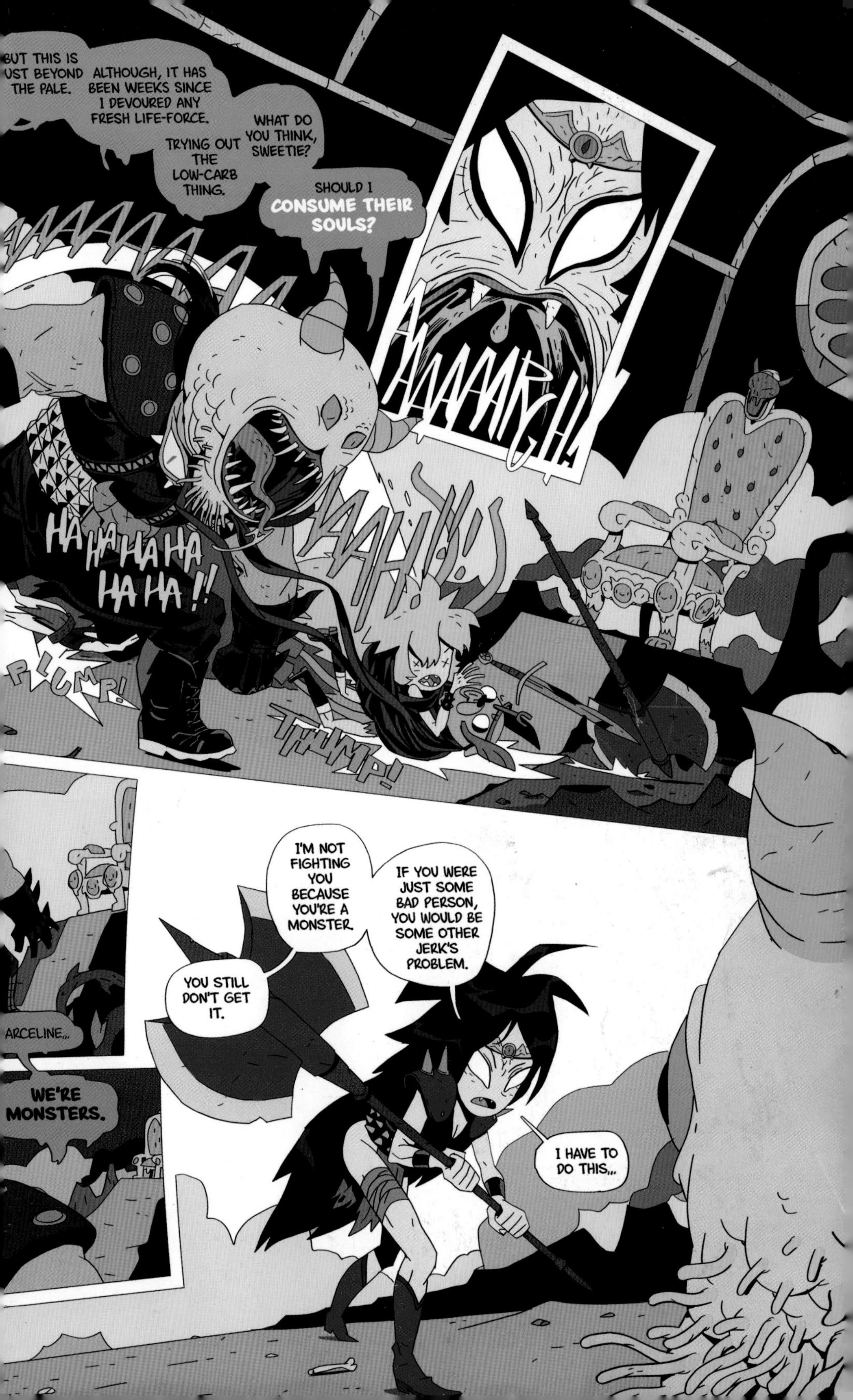
BUT THIS IS
JUST BEYOND THE PALE.
ALTHOUGH, IT HAS BEEN WEEKS SINCE I DEVOURED ANY FRESH LIFE-FORCE.
TRYING OUT THE LOW-CARB THING.
WHAT DO YOU THINK, SWEETIE?
SHOULD I CONSUME THEIR SOULS?
AAAAAAAAA
AAAAARGH!!
HA HA HA HA HA HA!!
AAAHH!!
PLUMP!
THUMP!
I'M NOT FIGHTING YOU BECAUSE YOU'RE A MONSTER.
IF YOU WERE JUST SOME BAD PERSON, YOU WOULD BE SOME OTHER JERK'S PROBLEM.
YOU STILL DON'T GET IT.
ARCELINE...
WE'RE MONSTERS.
I HAVE TO DO THIS...

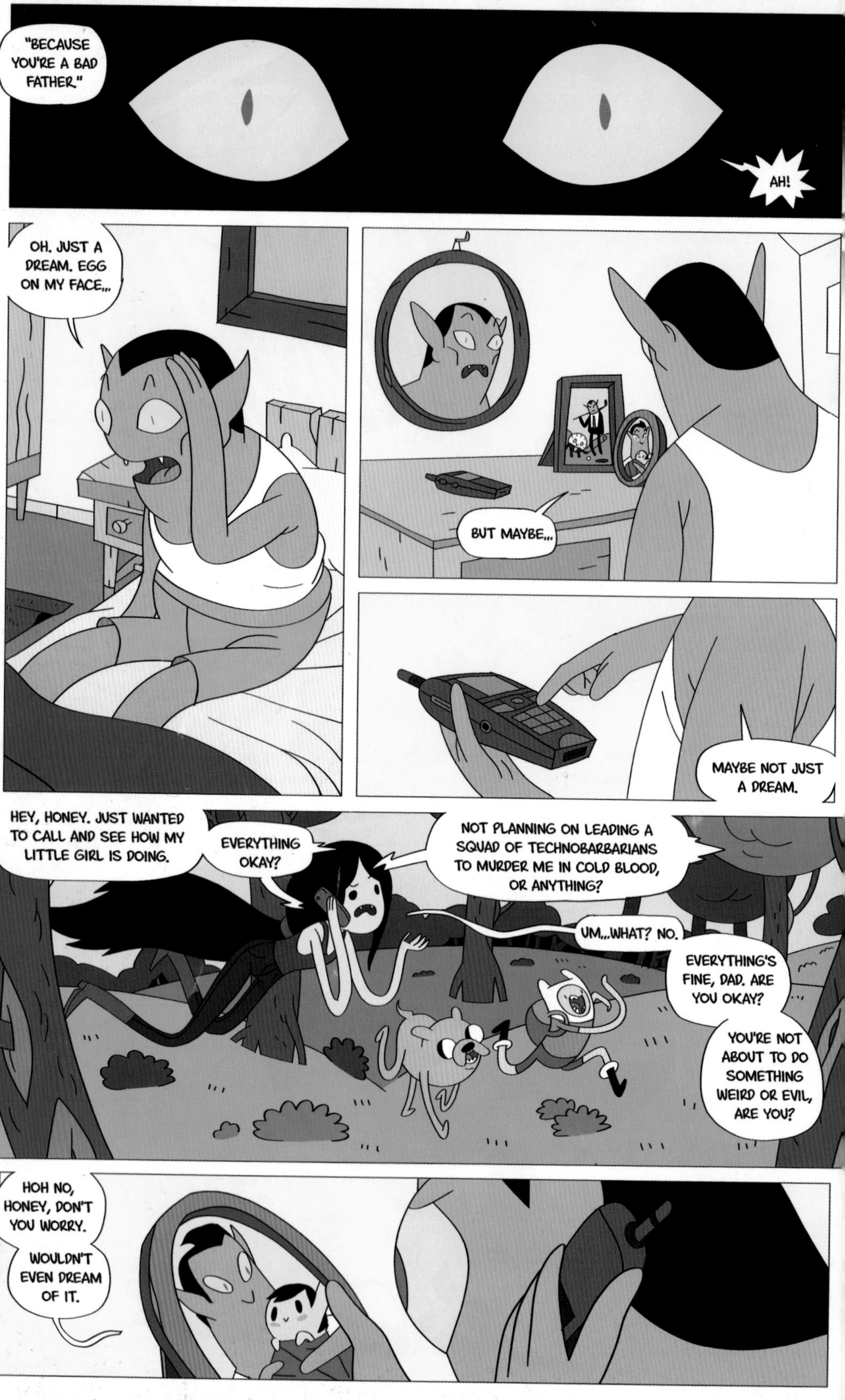
"BECAUSE YOU'RE A BAD FATHER."
AH!
OH. JUST A DREAM. EGG ON MY FACE...
BUT MAYBE...
MAYBE NOT JUST A DREAM.
HEY, HONEY. JUST WANTED TO CALL AND SEE HOW MY LITTLE GIRL IS DOING.
EVERYTHING OKAY?
NOT PLANNING ON LEADING A SQUAD OF TECHNOBARBARIANS TO MURDER ME IN COLD BLOOD, OR ANYTHING?
UM...WHAT? NO.
EVERYTHING'S FINE, DAD. ARE YOU OKAY?
YOU'RE NOT ABOUT TO DO SOMETHING WEIRD OR EVIL, ARE YOU?
HOH NO, HONEY, DON'T YOU WORRY.
WOULDN'T EVEN DREAM OF IT.

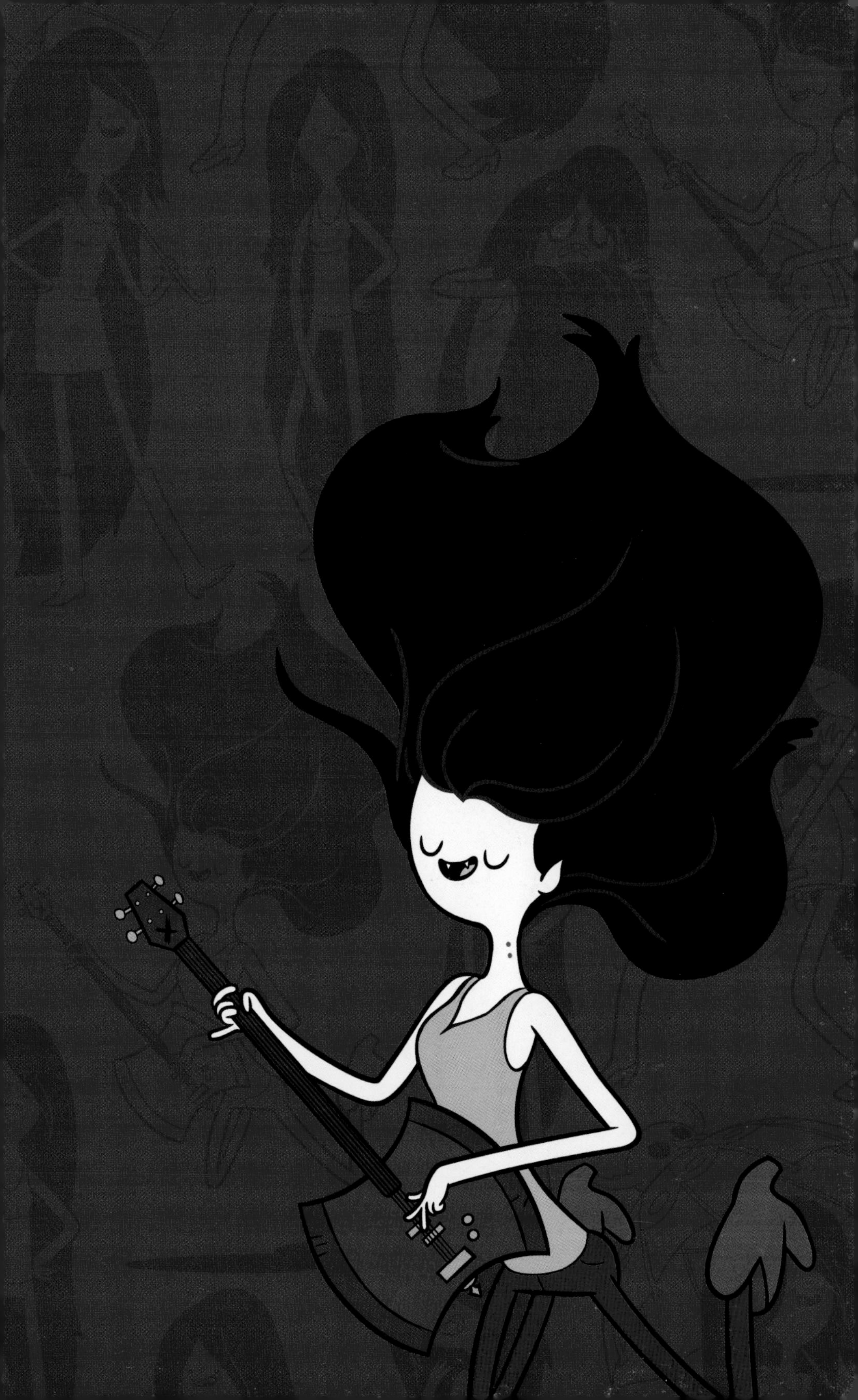

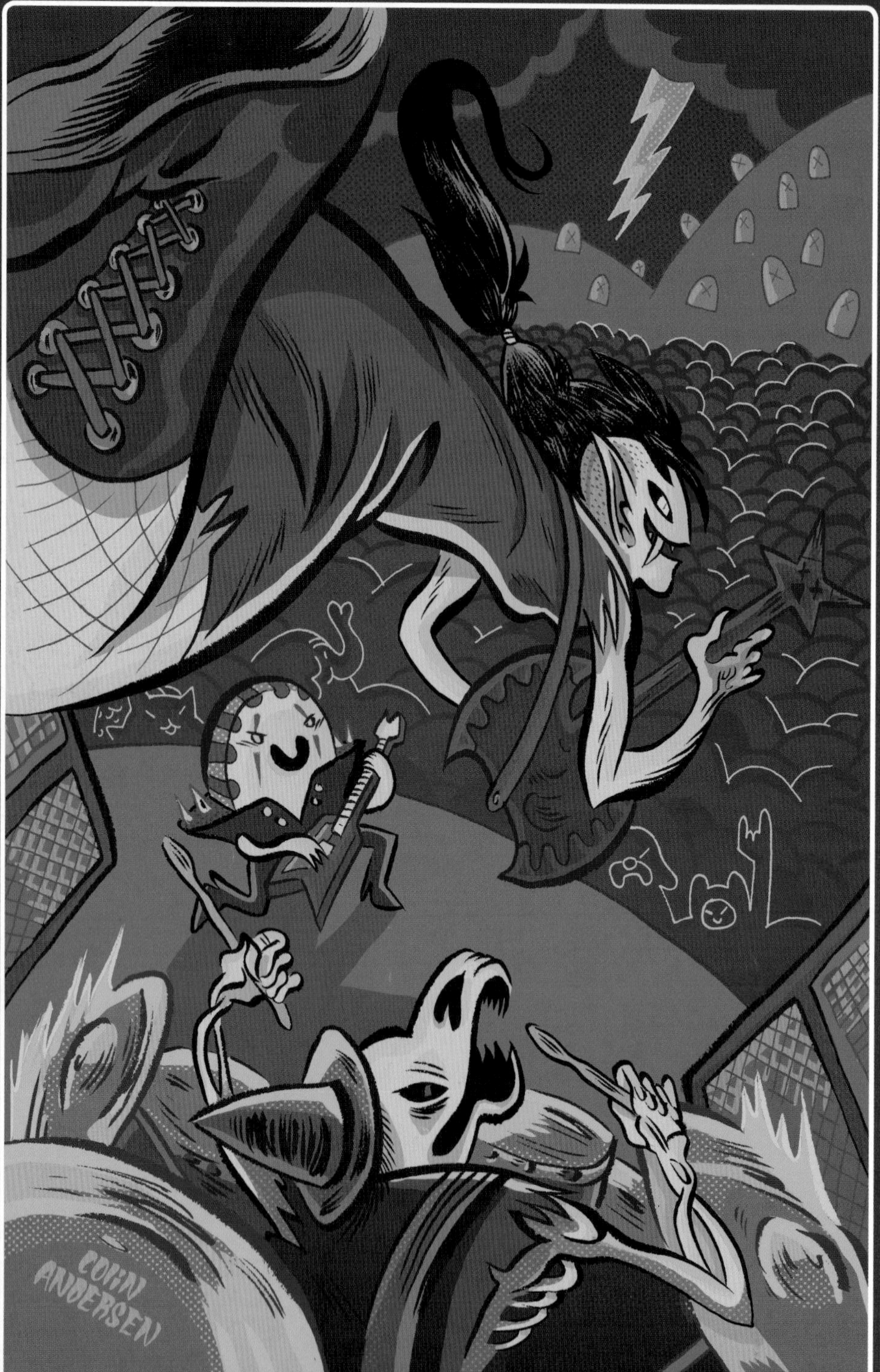
COLIN ANDERSEN

Adventure Time #30 Diamond San Diego Comic-Con Exclusive Cover by **Colin Andersen**

"Marceline the Derby Queen"

Written by **Chelsea Van Weerdhuizen**

Illustrated by **Reimena Yee**

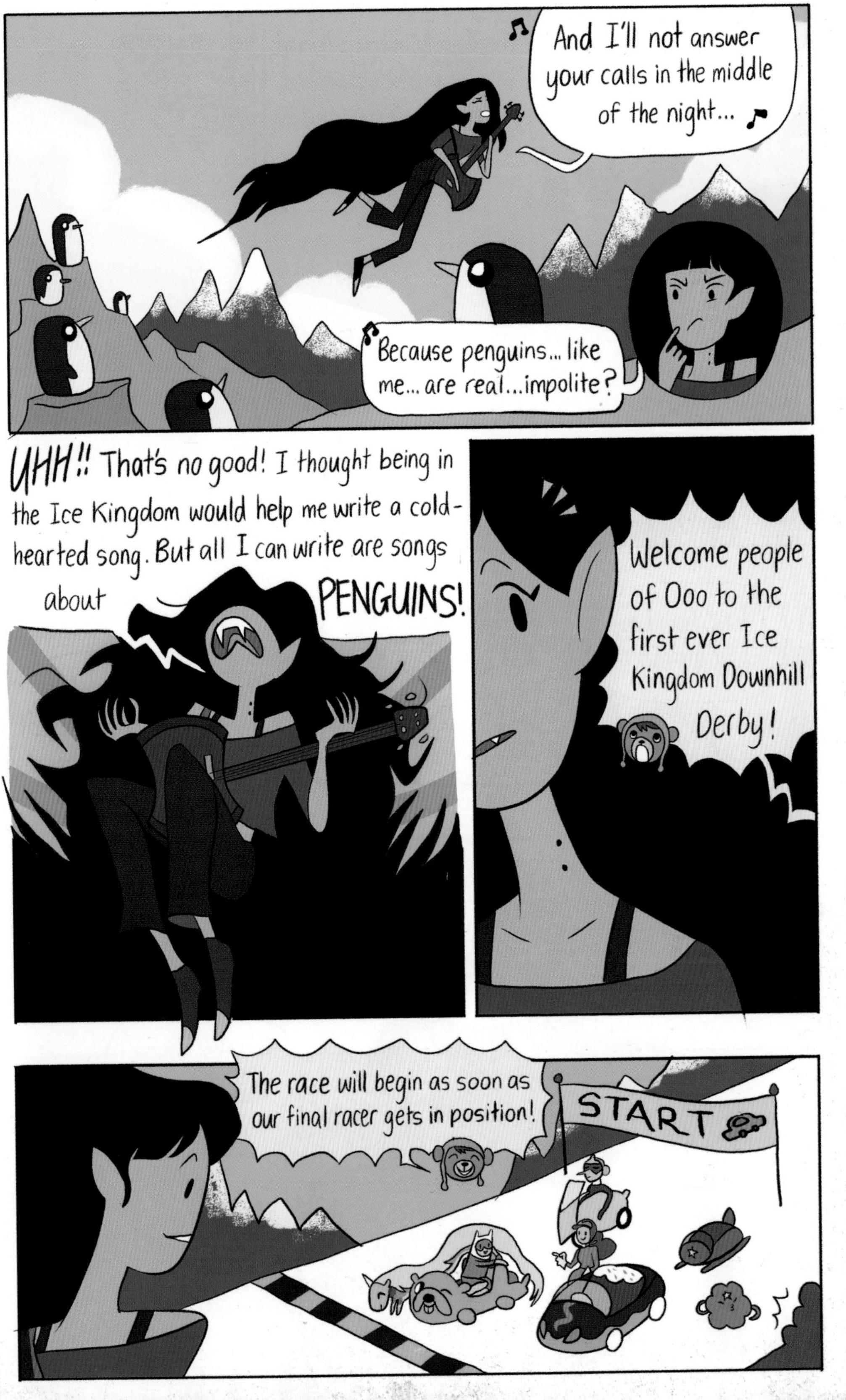
And I'll not answer your calls in the middle of the night...
Because penguins... like me... are real...impolite?
UHH!! That's no good! I thought being in the Ice Kingdom would help me write a cold-hearted song. But all I can write are songs about PENGUINS!
Welcome people of Ooo to the first ever Ice Kingdom Downhill Derby!
The race will begin as soon as our final racer gets in position!
START

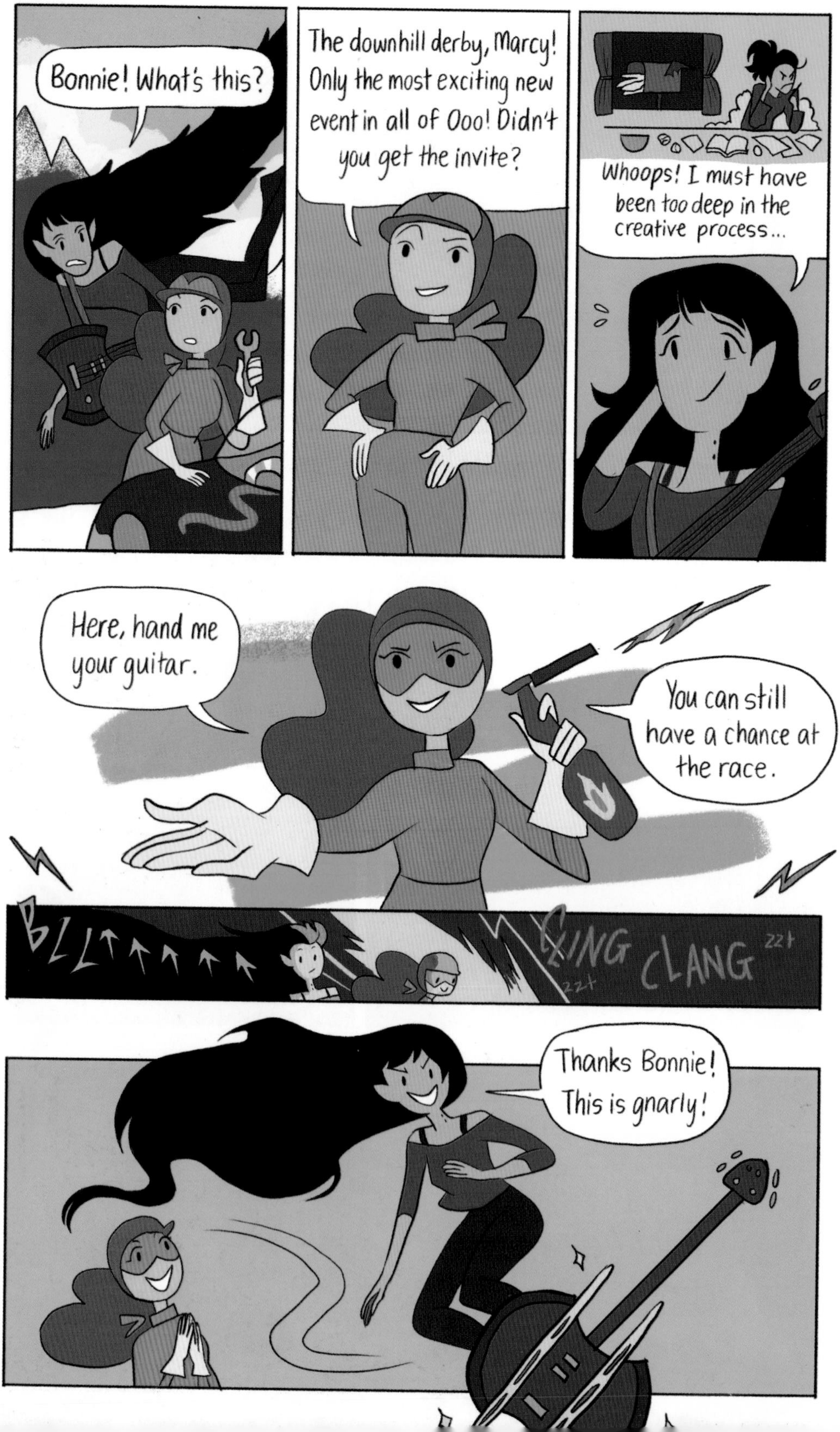
Bonnie! What's this?
The downhill derby, Marcy! Only the most exciting new event in all of Ooo! Didn't you get the invite?
Whoops! I must have been too deep in the creative process...
Here, hand me your guitar.
You can still have a chance at the race.
CLING CLANG
Thanks Bonnie! This is gnarly!

And with that, the race is on! **3**...**2**...**1**!!!

GOOOOO!!!

Hooray!

Go, Finn! Go, Marceline!

Good luck, Princess!

Look at them having fun without old Ice-y! As if this isn't my own kingdom!

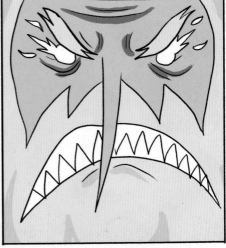

WELL, I'LL SHOW THEM!

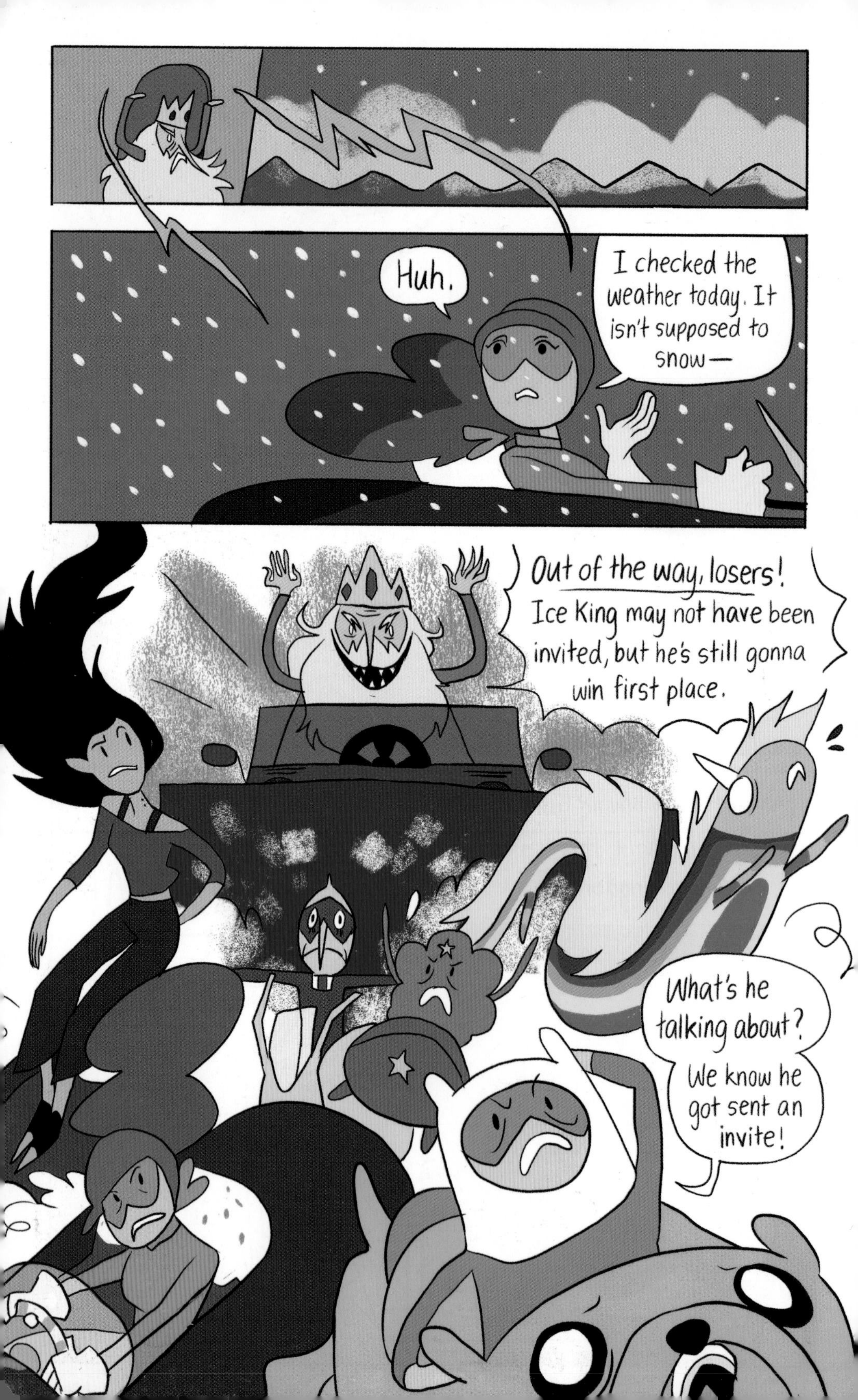
Huh.
I checked the weather today. It isn't supposed to snow—
Out of the way, losers! Ice King may not have been invited, but he's still gonna win first place.
What's he talking about?
We know he got sent an invite!

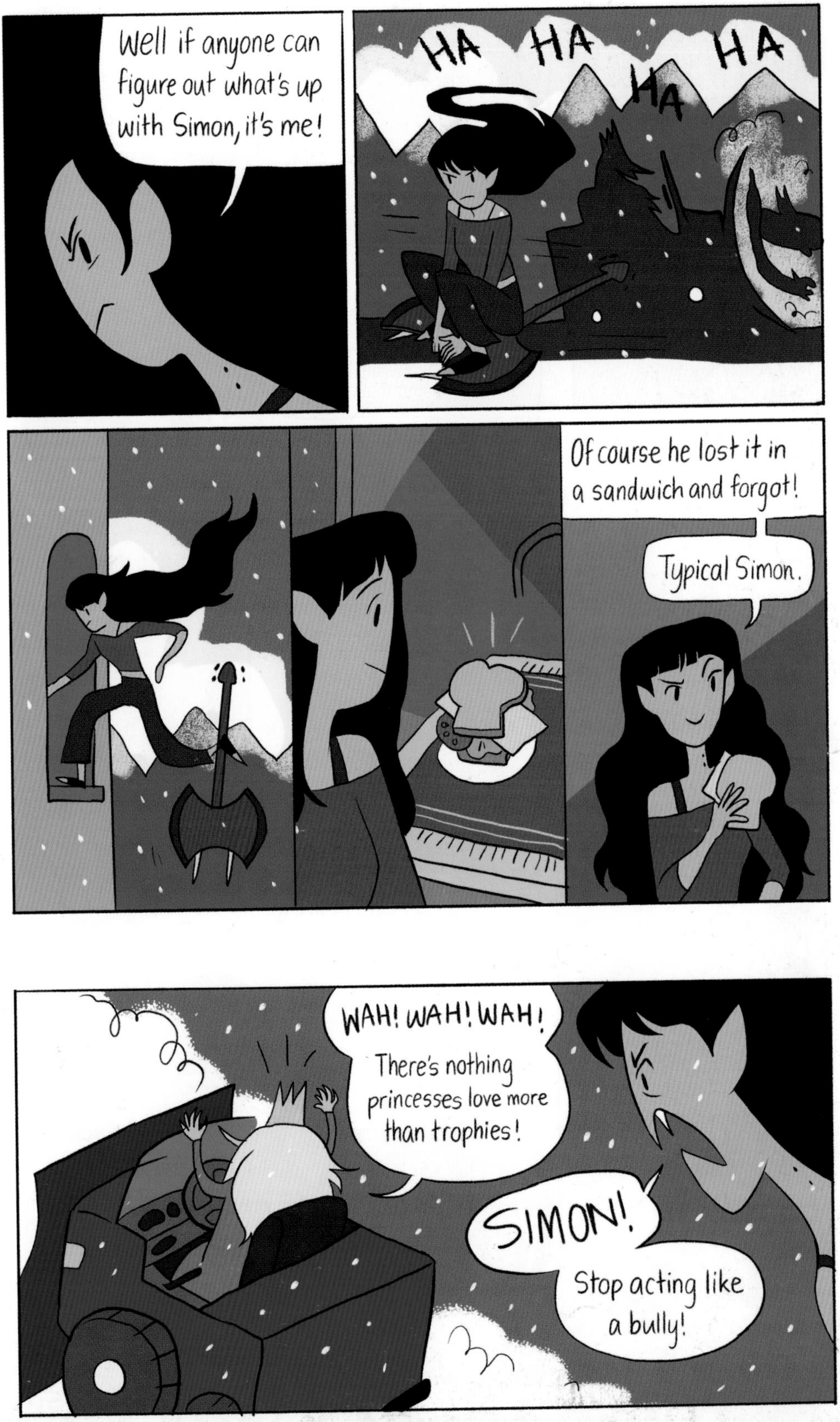
Well if anyone can figure out what's up with Simon, it's me!
HA HA HA HA
Of course he lost it in a sandwich and forgot!
Typical Simon.
WAH! WAH! WAH!
There's nothing princesses love more than trophies!
SIMON!
Stop acting like a bully!

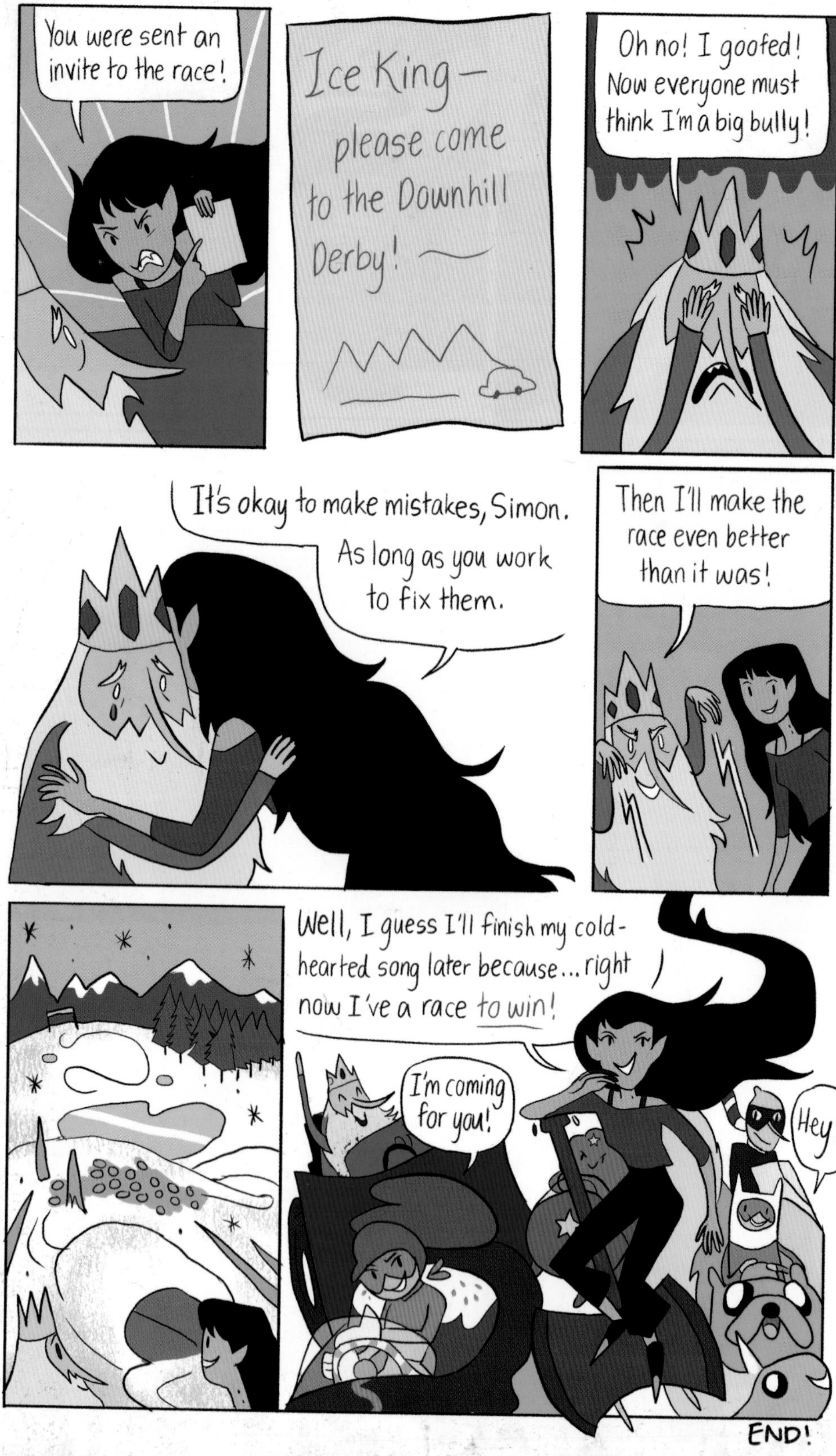
You were sent an invite to the race!
Ice King— please come to the Downhill Derby!
Oh no! I goofed! Now everyone must think I'm a big bully!
It's okay to make mistakes, Simon. As long as you work to fix them.
Then I'll make the race even better than it was!
Well, I guess I'll finish my cold-hearted song later because... right now I've a race to win!
I'm coming for you!
Hey!
END!

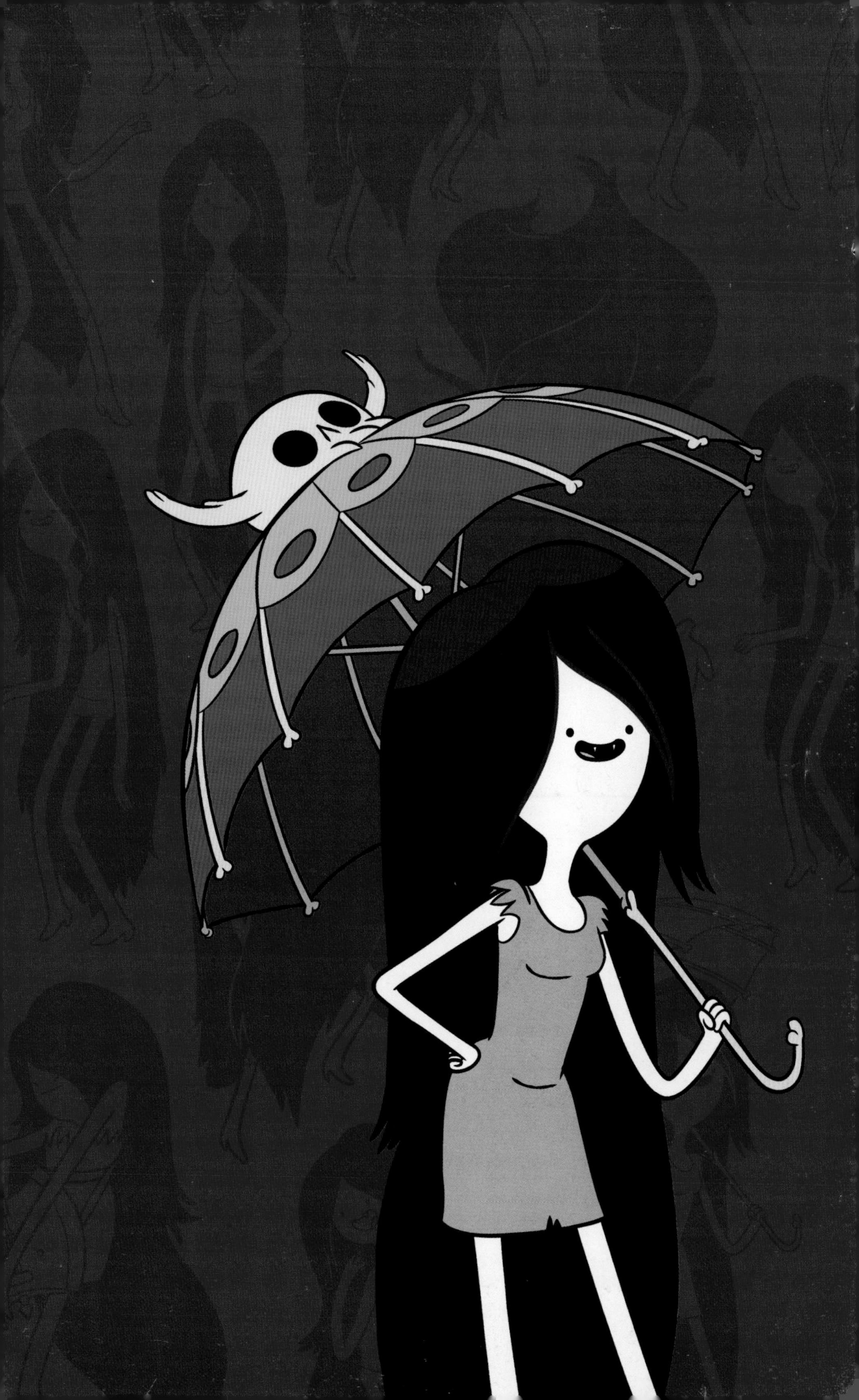

DISCOVER MORE ADVENTURE TIME

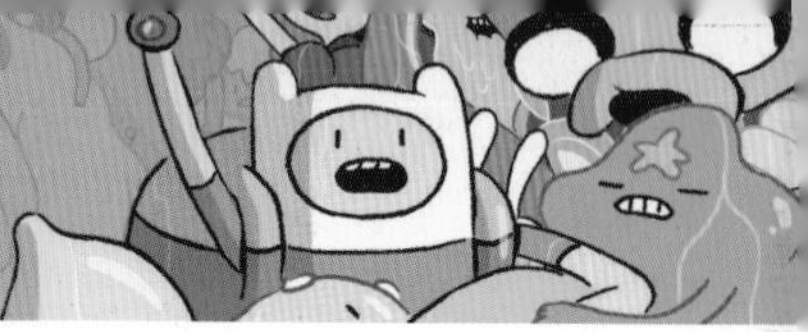

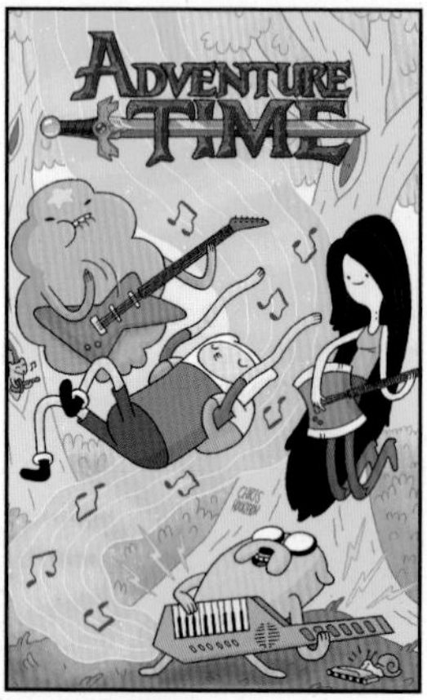
ADVENTURE TIME

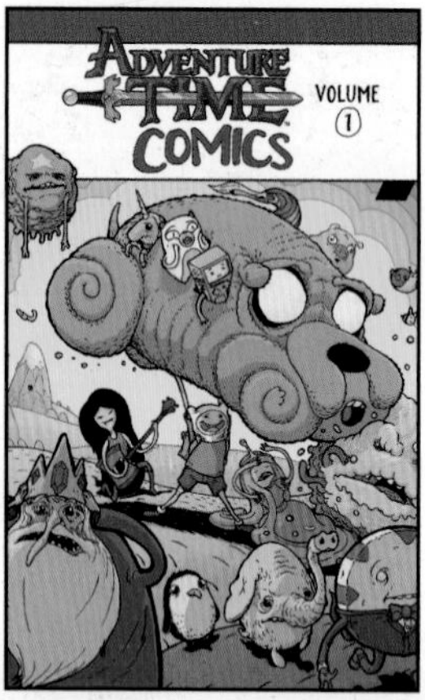
ADVENTURE TIME
VOLUME 1
COMICS

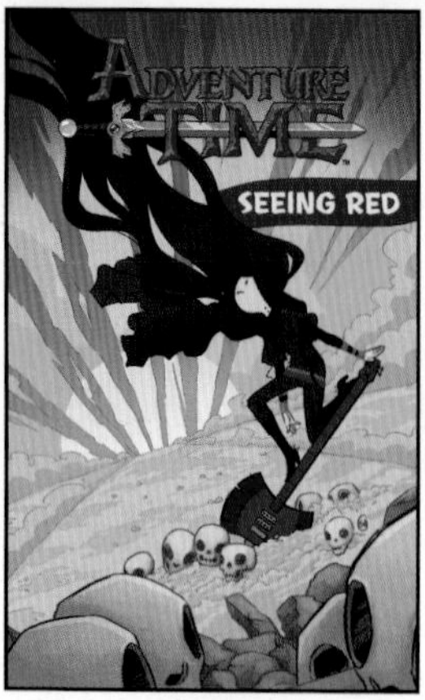
ADVENTURE TIME
SEEING RED

Adventure Time

Volume 1
ISBN: 978-1-60886-280-1 | $14.99 US

Volume 2
ISBN: 978-1-60886-323-5 | $14.99 US

Volume 3
ISBN: 978-1-60886-317-4 | $14.99

Volume 4
ISBN: 978-1-60886-351-8 | $14.99

Volume 5
ISBN: 978-1-60886-401-0 | $14.99

Volume 6
ISBN: 978-1-60886-482-9 | $14.99

Volume 7
ISBN: 978-1-60886-746-2 | $14.99

Volume 8
ISBN: 978-1-60886-795-0 | $14.99

Volume 9
ISBN: 978-1-60886-843-8 | $14.99

Volume 10
ISBN: 978-1-60886-909-1 | $14.99

Volume 11
ISBN: 978-1-60886-946-6 | $14.99

Volume 12
ISBN: 978-1-68415-005-2 | $14.99

Volume 13
ISBN: 978-1-68415-051-9 | $14.99

Volume 14
ISBN: 978-1-68415-144-8 | $14.99

Volume 15
ISBN: 978-1-68415-203-2 | $14.99

Volume 16
ISBN: 978-1-68415-272-8 | $14.99

Adventure Time Comics

Volume 1
ISBN: 978-1-60886-934-3 | $14.99

Volume 2
ISBN: 978-1-60886-984-8 | $14.99

Volume 3
ISBN: 978-1-68415-041-0 | $14.99

Volume 4
ISBN: 978-1-68415-133-2 | $14.99

Volume 5
ISBN: 978-1-68415-190-5 | $14.99

Volume 6
ISBN: 978-1-68415-258-2 | $14.99

Adventure Time Original Graphic Novels

Volume 1 Playing With Fire
ISBN: 978-1-60886-832-2 | $14.99

Volume 2 Pixel Princesses
ISBN: 978-1-60886-329-7 | $11.99

Volume 3 Seeing Red
ISBN: 978-1-60886-356-3 | $11.99

Volume 4 Bitter Sweets
ISBN: 978-1-60886-430-0 | $12.99

Volume 5 Graybles Schmaybles
ISBN: 978-1-60886-484-3 | $12.99

Volume 6 Masked Mayhem
ISBN: 978-160886-764-6 | $14.99

Volume 7 The Four Castles
ISBN: 978-160886-797-4 | $14.99

Volume 8 President Bubblegum
ISBN: 978-1-60886-846-9 | $14.99

Volume 9 The Brain Robbers
ISBN: 978-1-60886-875-9 | $14.99

Volume 10 The Orient Express
ISBN: 978-1-60886-995-4 | $14.99

Volume 11 Princess & Princess
ISBN: 978-1-68415-025-0 | $14.99

Volume 12 Thunder Road
ISBN: 978-1-68415-179-0 | $14.99

kaboom! A BOOM! Studios Imprint

AVAILABLE AT YOUR LOCAL COMICS SHOP AND BOOKSTORE

WWW.BOOM-STUDIOS.COM

CN CARTOON NETWORK.